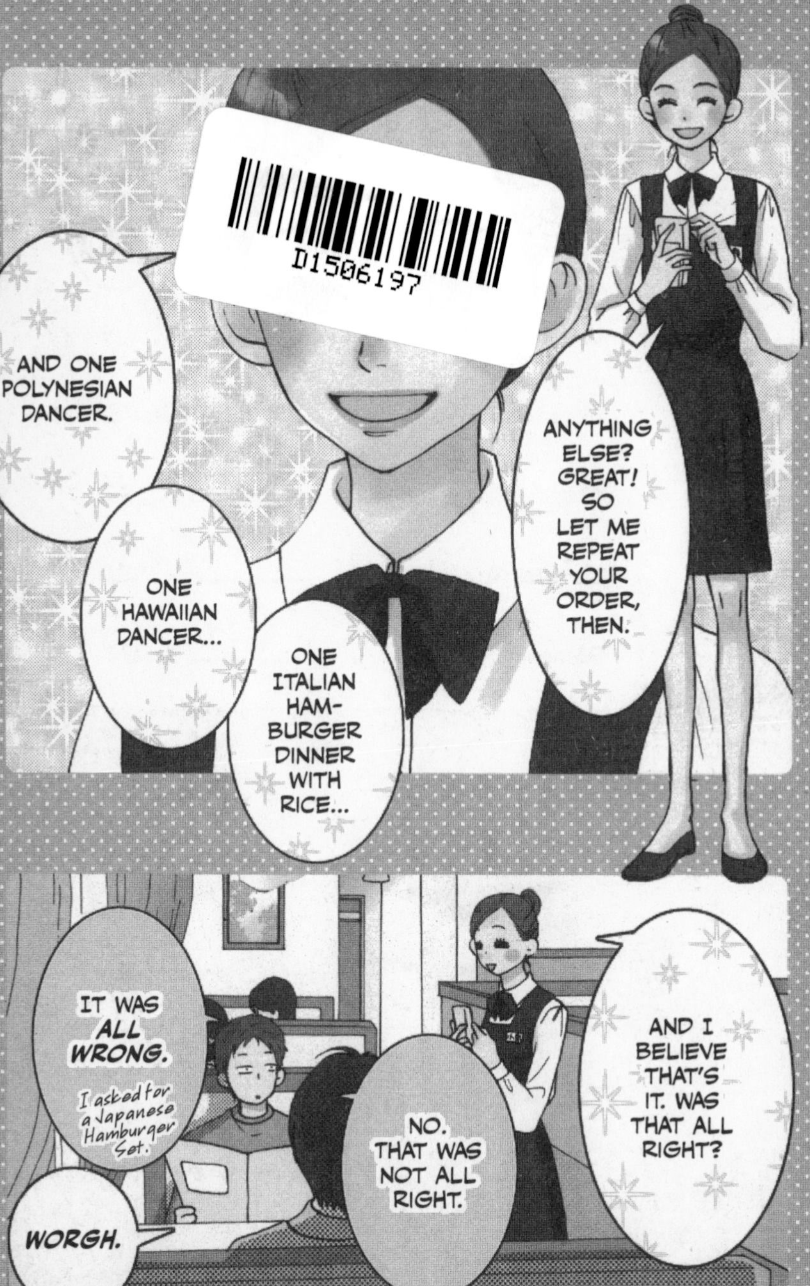
ANYTHING ELSE? GREAT! SO LET ME REPEAT YOUR ORDER, THEN.
ONE ITALIAN HAM-BURGER DINNER WITH RICE...
ONE HAWAIIAN DANCER...
AND ONE POLYNESIAN DANCER.
AND I BELIEVE THAT'S IT. WAS THAT ALL RIGHT?
NO. THAT WAS NOT ALL RIGHT.
IT WAS **ALL WRONG.**
I asked for a Japanese Hamburger Set.
WORGH.

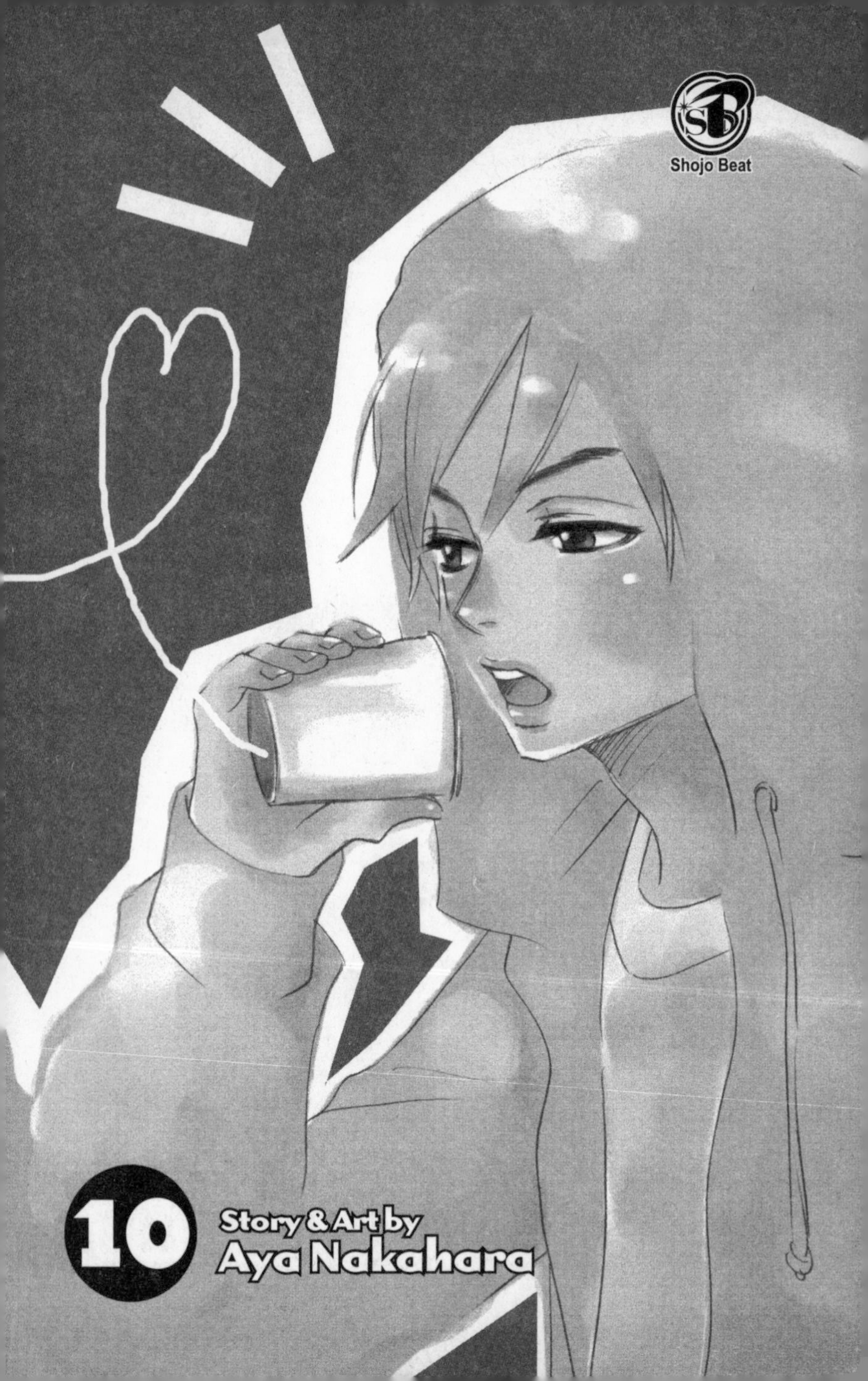
Shojo Beat
10
Story & Art by
Aya Nakahara

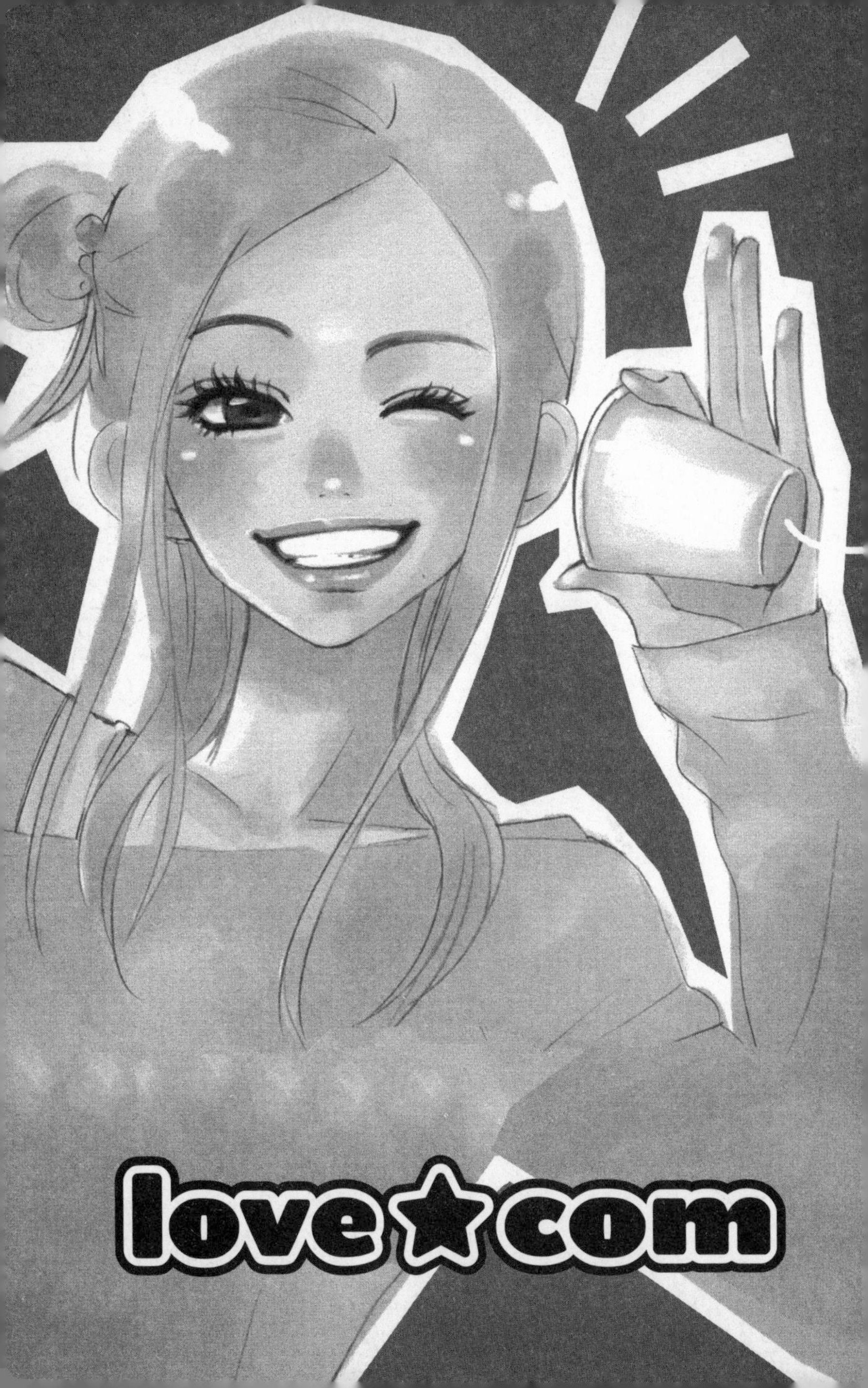
love★com

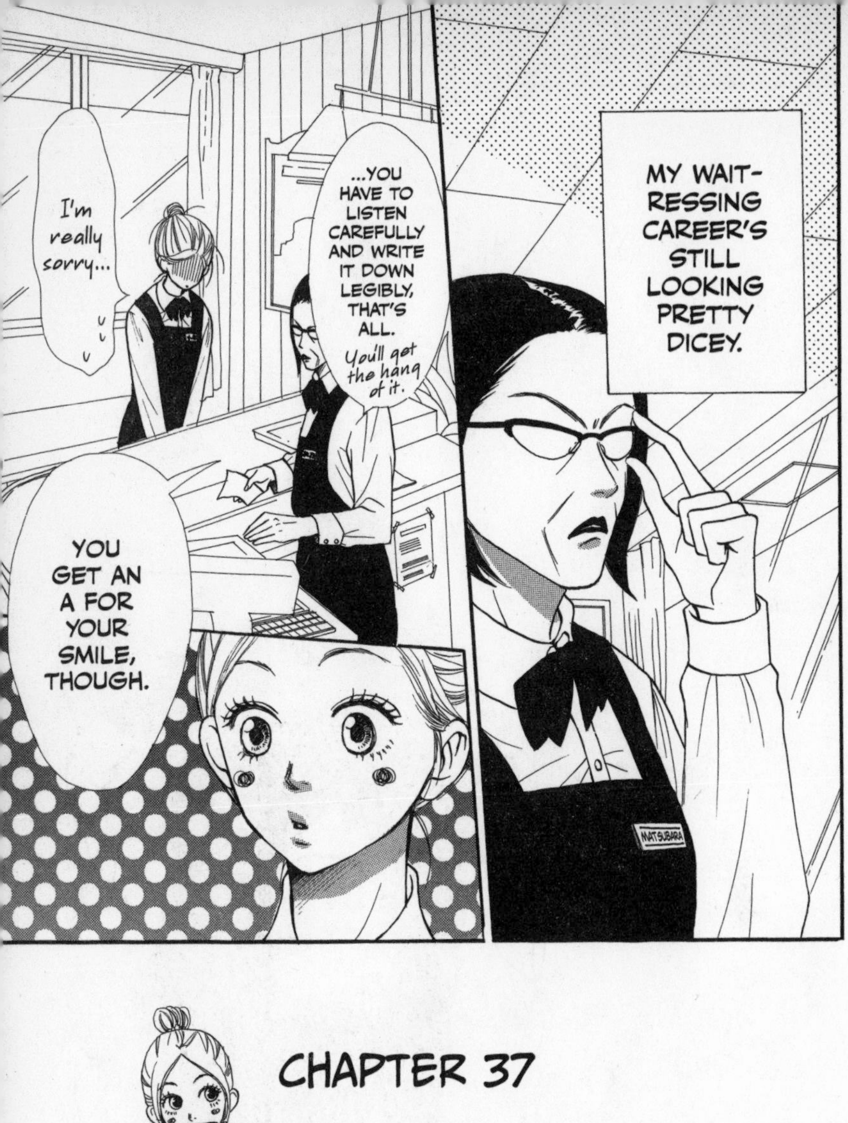
MY WAIT-RESSING CAREER'S STILL LOOKING PRETTY DICEY.
...YOU HAVE TO LISTEN CAREFULLY AND WRITE IT DOWN LEGIBLY, THAT'S ALL. You'll get the hang of it.
I'm really sorry...
YOU GET AN A FOR YOUR SMILE, THOUGH.

CHAPTER 37

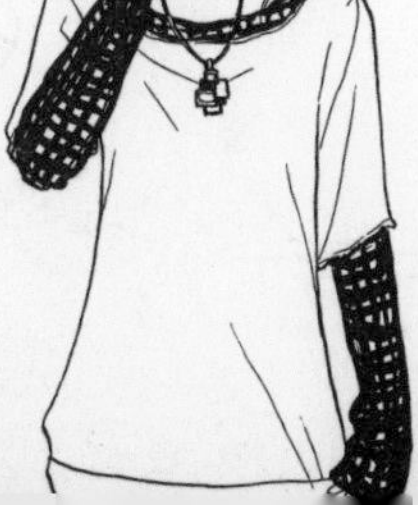

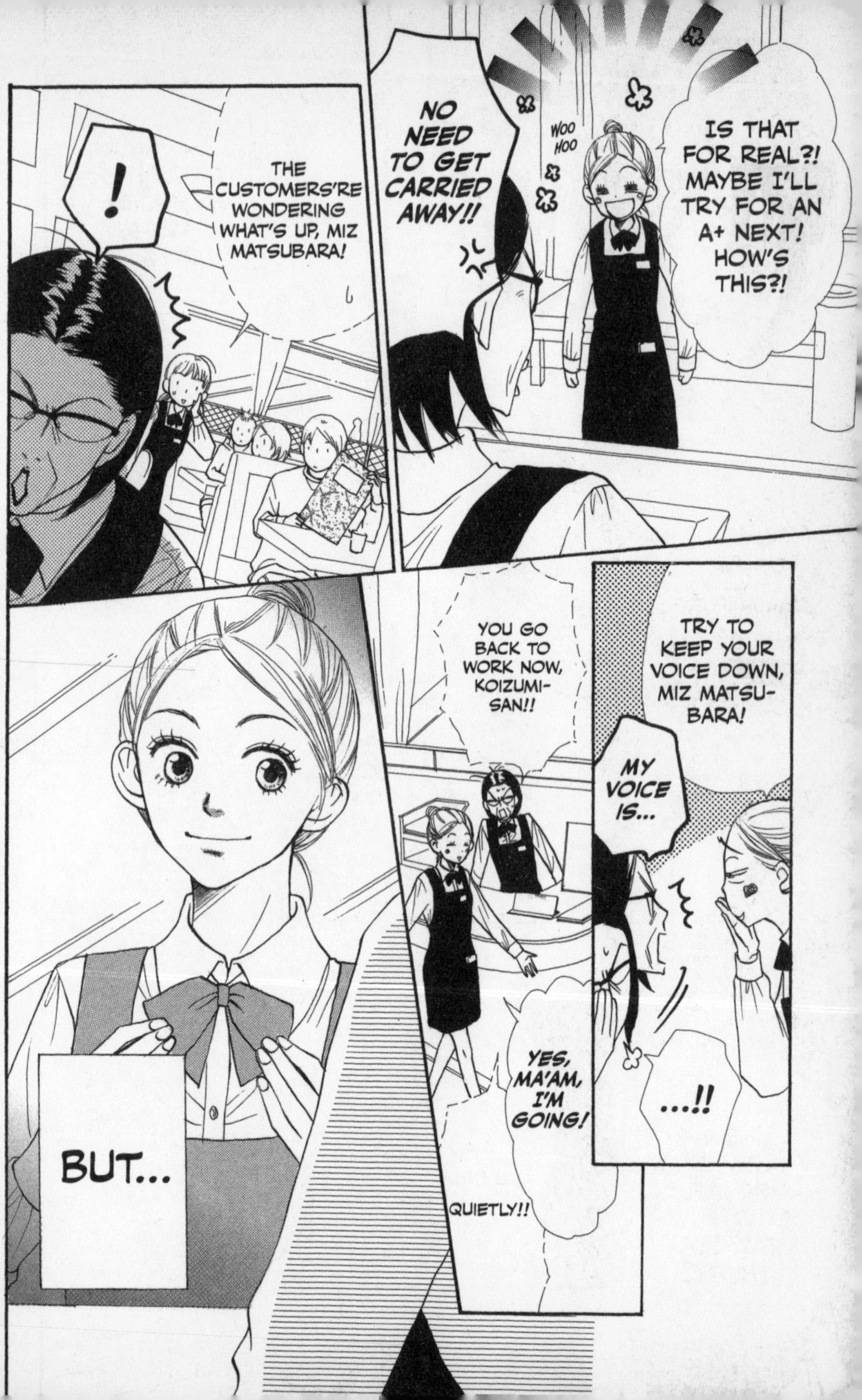
IS THAT FOR REAL?! MAYBE I'LL TRY FOR AN A+ NEXT! HOW'S THIS?!
WOO HOO
NO NEED TO GET CARRIED AWAY!!
!
THE CUSTOMERS'RE WONDERING WHAT'S UP, MIZ MATSUBARA!
TRY TO KEEP YOUR VOICE DOWN, MIZ MATSU-BARA!
MY VOICE IS...
...!!
YOU GO BACK TO WORK NOW, KOIZUMI-SAN!!
YES, MA'AM, I'M GOING!
QUIETLY!!
BUT...

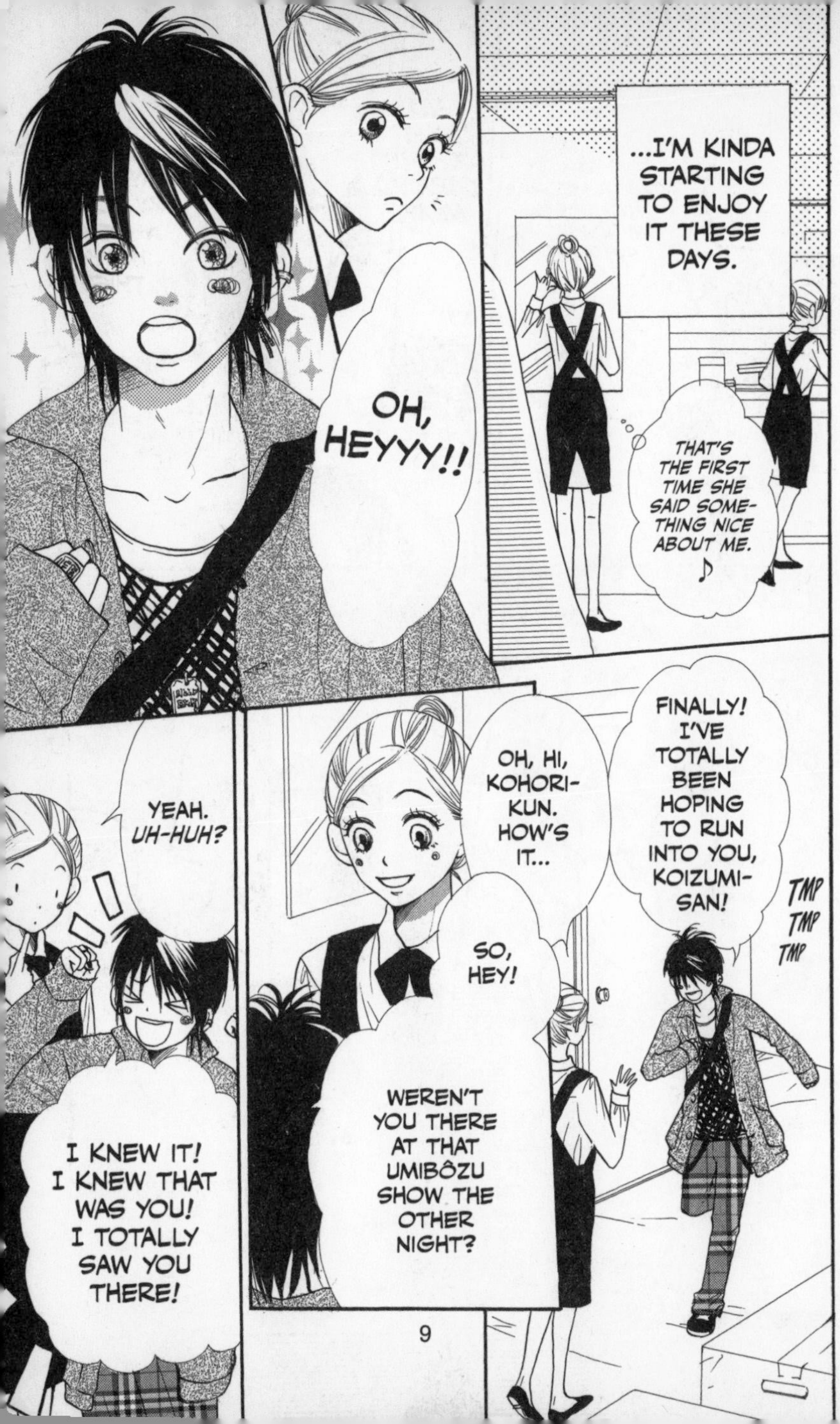
...I'M KINDA STARTING TO ENJOY IT THESE DAYS.
THAT'S THE FIRST TIME SHE SAID SOME-THING NICE ABOUT ME. ♪
OH, HEYYY!!
FINALLY! I'VE TOTALLY BEEN HOPING TO RUN INTO YOU, KOIZUMI-SAN!
TMP TMP TMP
OH, HI, KOHORI-KUN. HOW'S IT...
SO, HEY!
WEREN'T YOU THERE AT THAT UMIBÔZU SHOW THE OTHER NIGHT?
YEAH. UH-HUH?
I KNEW IT! I KNEW THAT WAS YOU! I TOTALLY SAW YOU THERE!

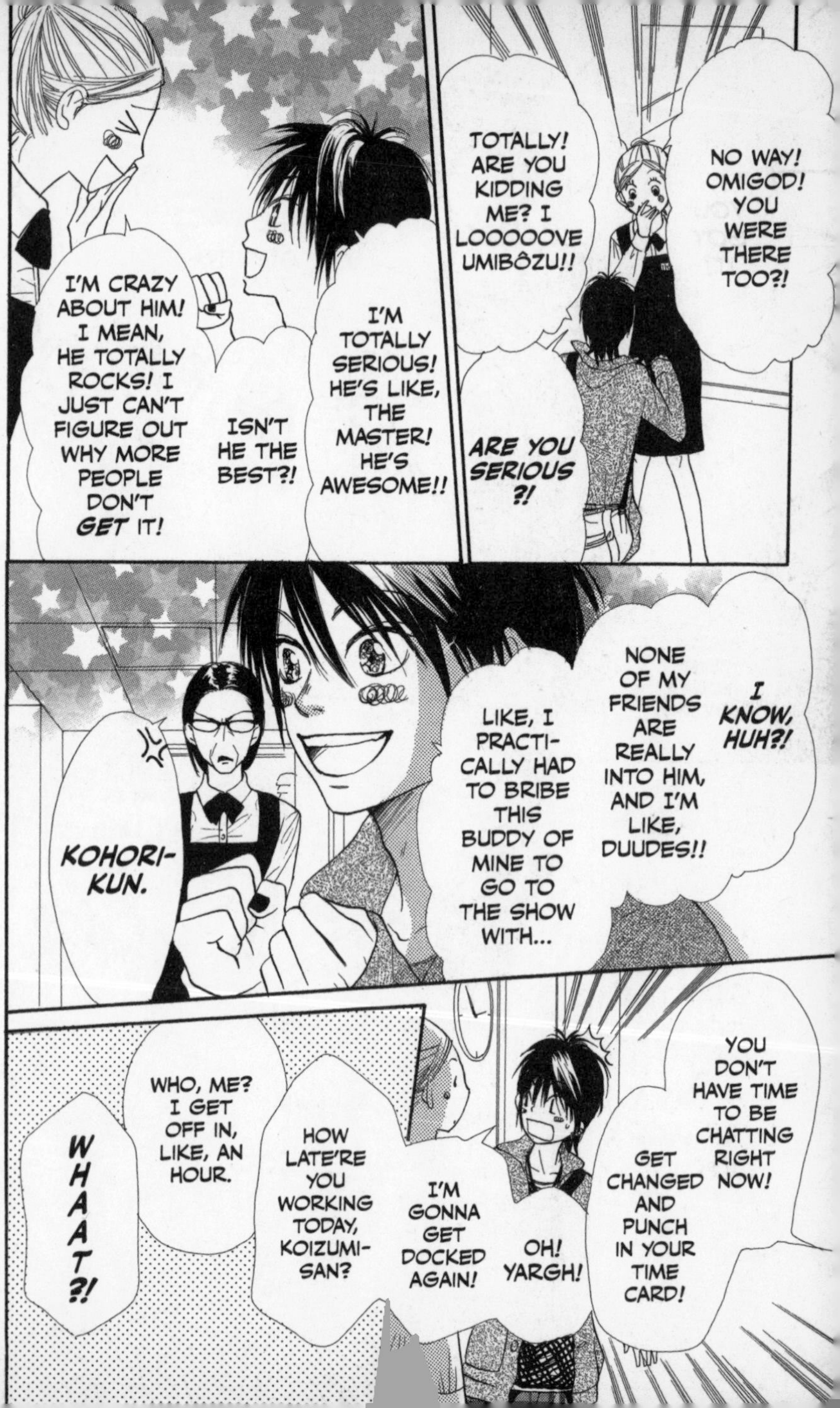
NO WAY! OMIGOD! YOU WERE THERE TOO?!
TOTALLY! ARE YOU KIDDING ME? I LOOOOOVE UMIBÔZU!!
ARE YOU SERIOUS?!
I'M TOTALLY SERIOUS! HE'S LIKE, THE MASTER! HE'S AWESOME!!
ISN'T HE THE BEST?!
I'M CRAZY ABOUT HIM! I MEAN, HE TOTALLY ROCKS! I JUST CAN'T FIGURE OUT WHY MORE PEOPLE DON'T GET IT!
I KNOW, HUH?!
NONE OF MY FRIENDS ARE REALLY INTO HIM, AND I'M LIKE, DUUDES!!
LIKE, I PRACTICALLY HAD TO BRIBE THIS BUDDY OF MINE TO GO TO THE SHOW WITH...
KOHORI-KUN.
YOU DON'T HAVE TIME TO BE CHATTING RIGHT NOW!
GET CHANGED AND PUNCH IN YOUR TIME CARD!
OH! YARGH!
I'M GONNA GET DOCKED AGAIN!
HOW LATE'RE YOU WORKING TODAY, KOIZUMI-SAN?
WHO, ME? I GET OFF IN, LIKE, AN HOUR.
WHAAAT?!

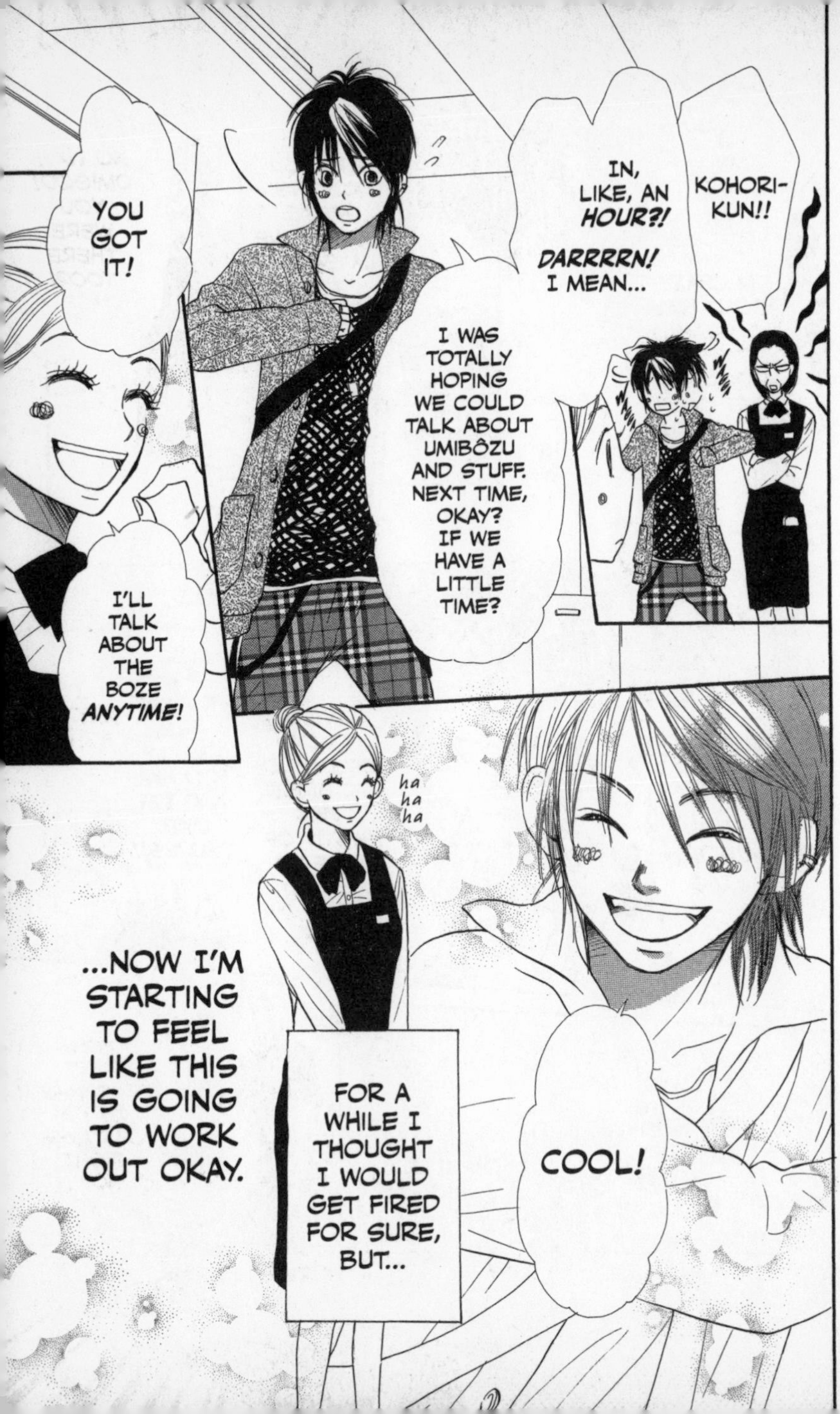
KOHORI-KUN!!
IN, LIKE, AN HOUR?!
DARRRRN! I MEAN...
I WAS TOTALLY HOPING WE COULD TALK ABOUT UMIBÔZU AND STUFF. NEXT TIME, OKAY? IF WE HAVE A LITTLE TIME?
YOU GOT IT!
I'LL TALK ABOUT THE BOZE ANYTIME!
COOL!
ha ha ha
FOR A WHILE I THOUGHT I WOULD GET FIRED FOR SURE, BUT...
...NOW I'M STARTING TO FEEL LIKE THIS IS GOING TO WORK OUT OKAY.

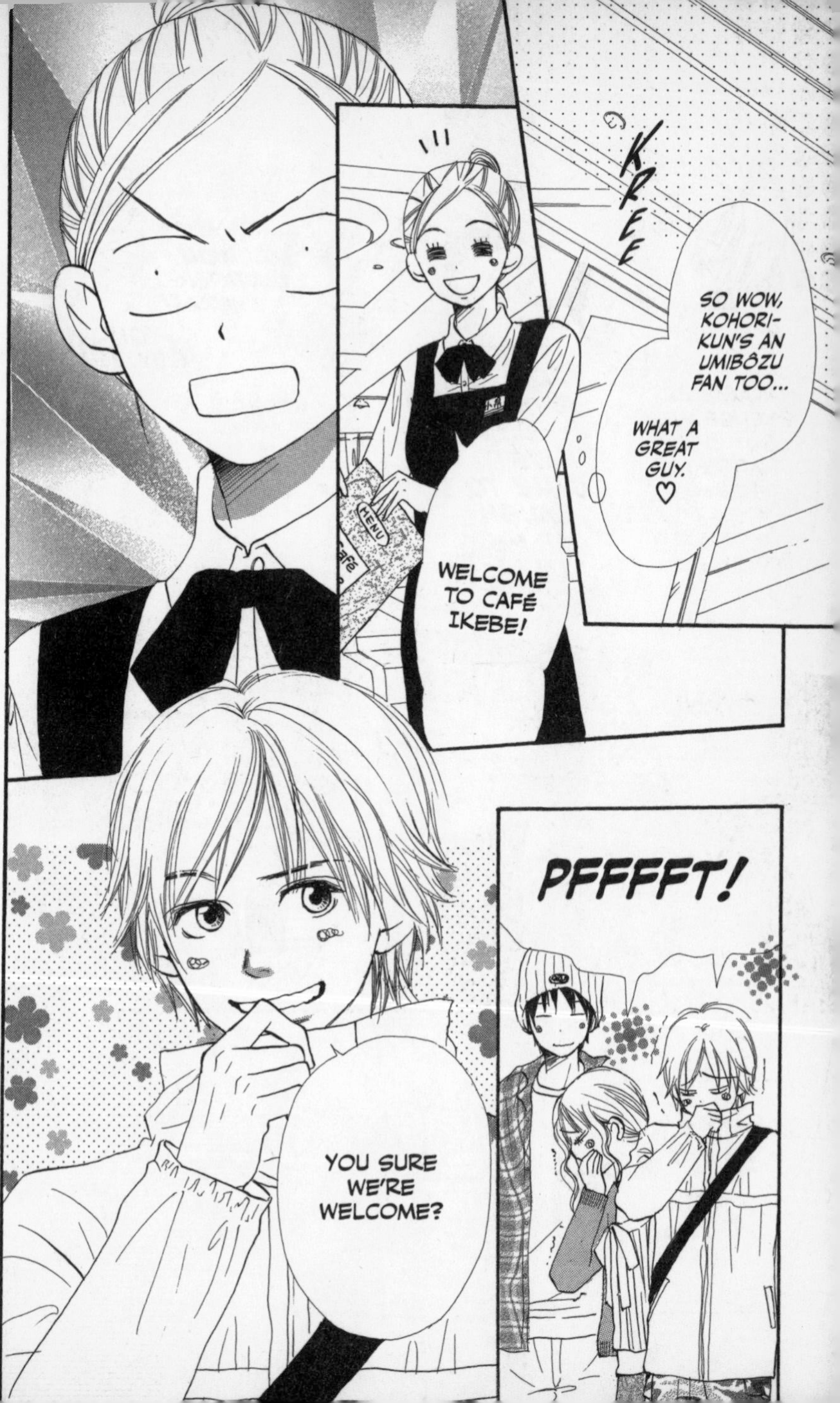
KREE
SO WOW, KOHORI-KUN'S AN UMIBÔZU FAN TOO...
WHAT A GREAT GUY. ♡
WELCOME TO CAFÉ IKEBE!
MENU
PFFFFT!
YOU SURE WE'RE WELCOME?

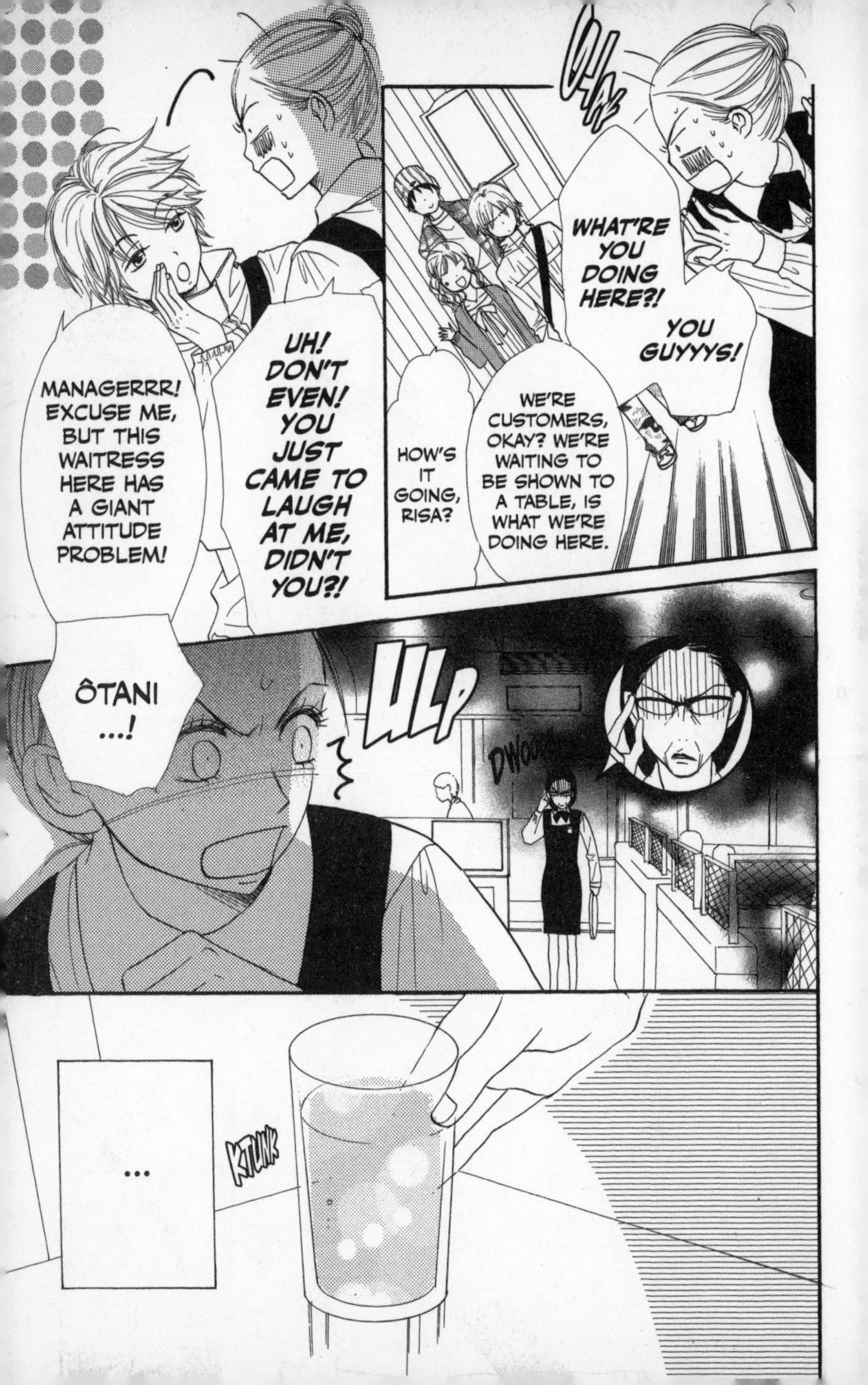
WHAT'RE YOU DOING HERE?!
YOU GUYYYS!
WE'RE CUSTOMERS, OKAY? WE'RE WAITING TO BE SHOWN TO A TABLE, IS WHAT WE'RE DOING HERE.
HOW'S IT GOING, RISA?
UH! DON'T EVEN! YOU JUST CAME TO LAUGH AT ME, DIDN'T YOU?!
MANAGERRR! EXCUSE ME, BUT THIS WAITRESS HERE HAS A GIANT ATTITUDE PROBLEM!
ULP
DWOO
ÔTANI ...!
KTUNK
...

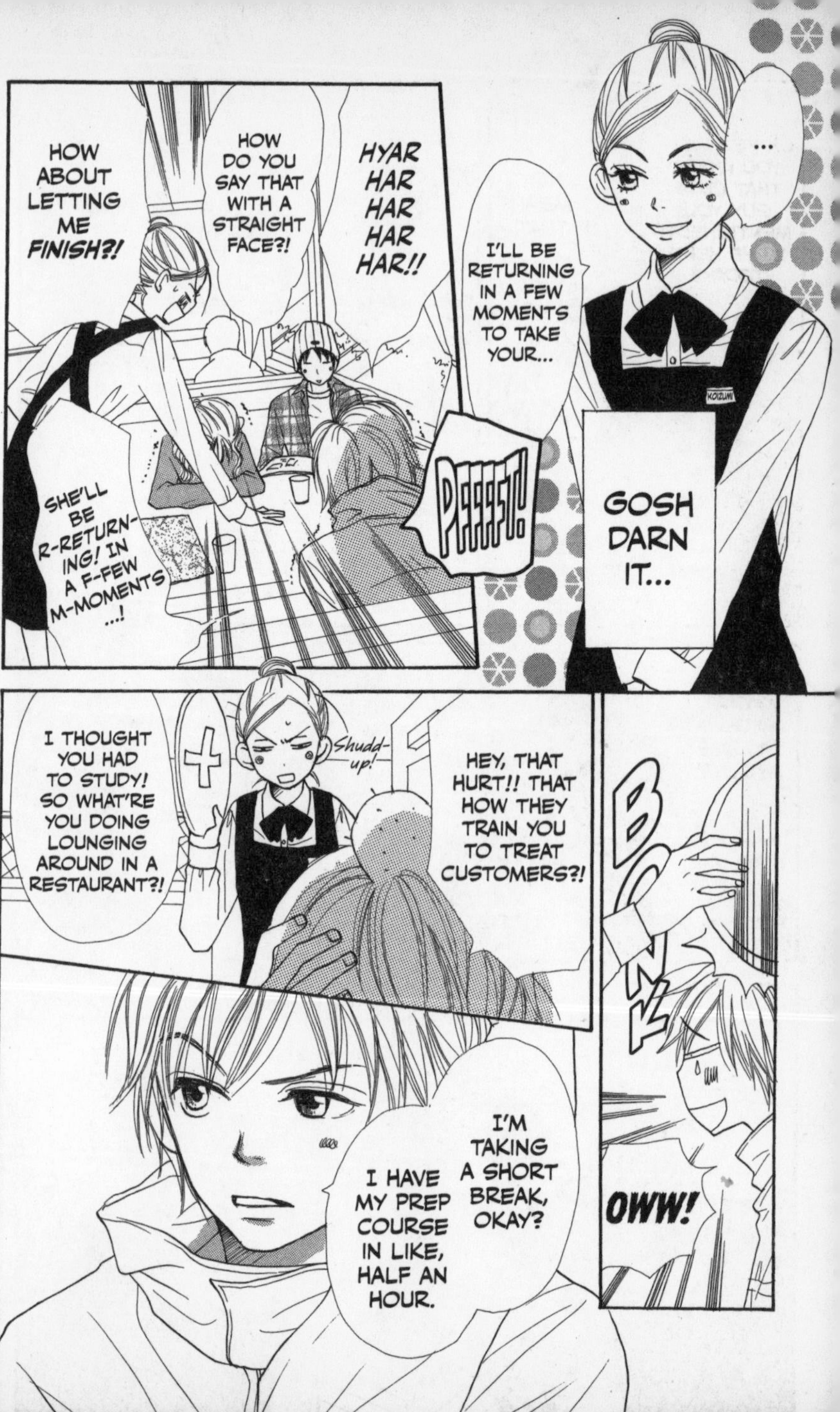
...
I'LL BE RETURNING IN A FEW MOMENTS TO TAKE YOUR...
GOSH DARN IT...
PFFFFT!
HYAR HAR HAR HAR HAR!!
HOW DO YOU SAY THAT WITH A STRAIGHT FACE?!
HOW ABOUT LETTING ME FINISH?!
SHE'LL BE R-RETURNING! IN A F-FEW M-MOMENTS ...!
BONK
OWW!
HEY, THAT HURT!! THAT HOW THEY TRAIN YOU TO TREAT CUSTOMERS?!
Shudd-up!
I THOUGHT YOU HAD TO STUDY! SO WHAT'RE YOU DOING LOUNGING AROUND IN A RESTAURANT?!
I'M TAKING A SHORT BREAK, OKAY?
I HAVE MY PREP COURSE IN LIKE, HALF AN HOUR.

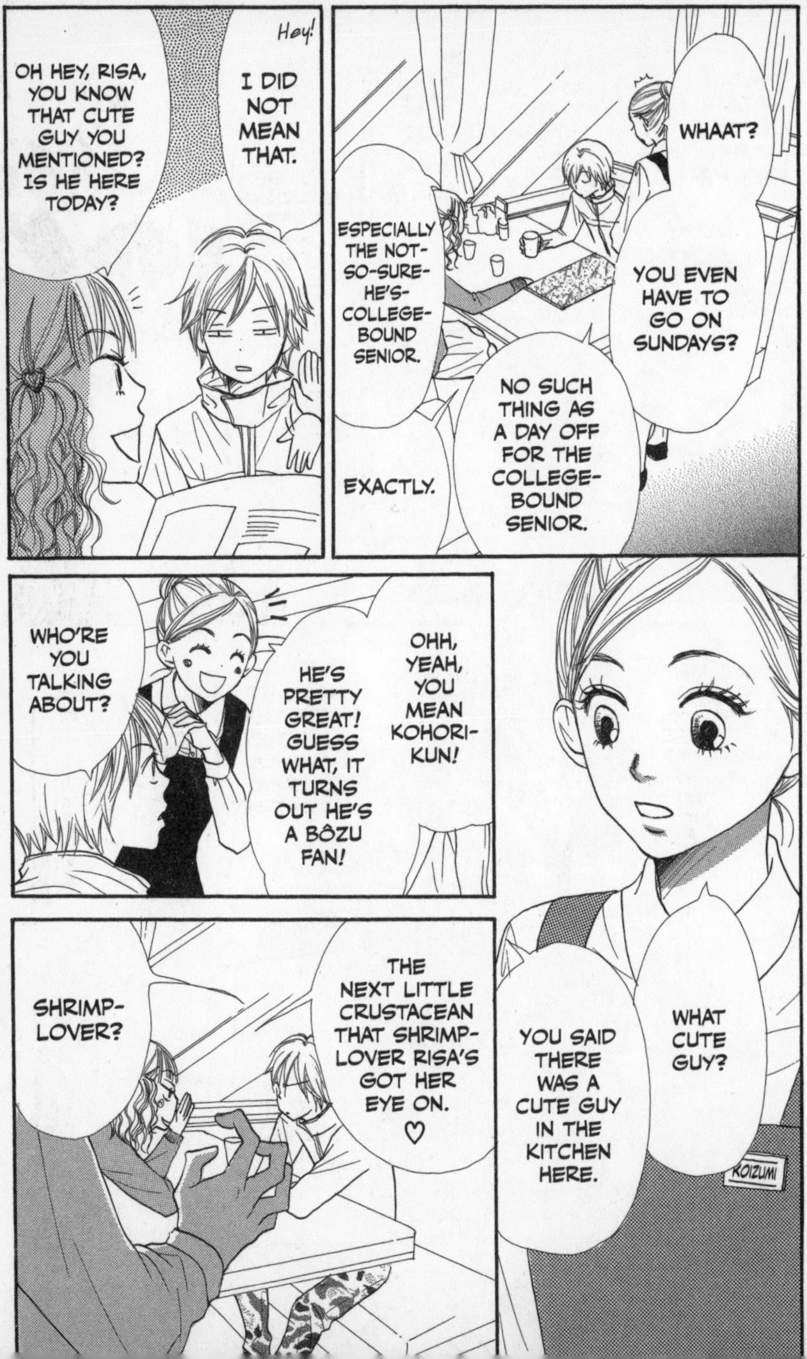
WHAAT?
YOU EVEN HAVE TO GO ON SUNDAYS?
NO SUCH THING AS A DAY OFF FOR THE COLLEGE-BOUND SENIOR.
ESPECIALLY THE NOT-SO-SURE-HE'S-COLLEGE-BOUND SENIOR.
EXACTLY.
Hey!
I DID NOT MEAN THAT.
OH HEY, RISA, YOU KNOW THAT CUTE GUY YOU MENTIONED? IS HE HERE TODAY?
WHAT CUTE GUY?
YOU SAID THERE WAS A CUTE GUY IN THE KITCHEN HERE.
KOIZUMI
OHH, YEAH, YOU MEAN KOHORI-KUN!
HE'S PRETTY GREAT! GUESS WHAT, IT TURNS OUT HE'S A BÔZU FAN!
WHO'RE YOU TALKING ABOUT?
THE NEXT LITTLE CRUSTACEAN THAT SHRIMP-LOVER RISA'S GOT HER EYE ON. ♡
SHRIMP-LOVER?

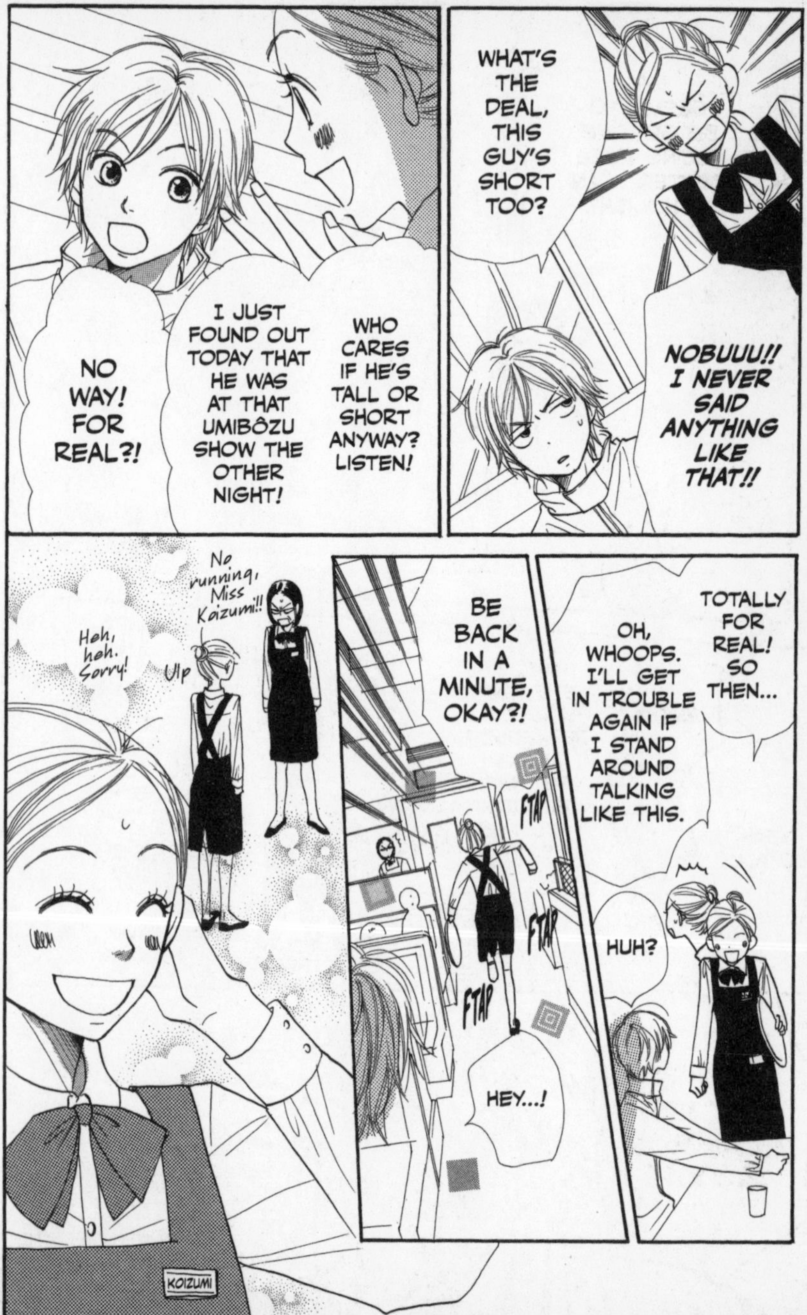
WHAT'S THE DEAL, THIS GUY'S SHORT TOO?
NOBUUU!! I NEVER SAID ANYTHING LIKE THAT!!
WHO CARES IF HE'S TALL OR SHORT ANYWAY? LISTEN!
I JUST FOUND OUT TODAY THAT HE WAS AT THAT UMIBÔZU SHOW THE OTHER NIGHT!
NO WAY! FOR REAL?!
TOTALLY FOR REAL! SO THEN...
OH, WHOOPS. I'LL GET IN TROUBLE AGAIN IF I STAND AROUND TALKING LIKE THIS.
HUH?
BE BACK IN A MINUTE, OKAY?!
FTAP
FTAP
FTAP
HEY...!
No running, Miss Koizumi!!
Ulp
Heh, heh. Sorry!
KOIZUMI

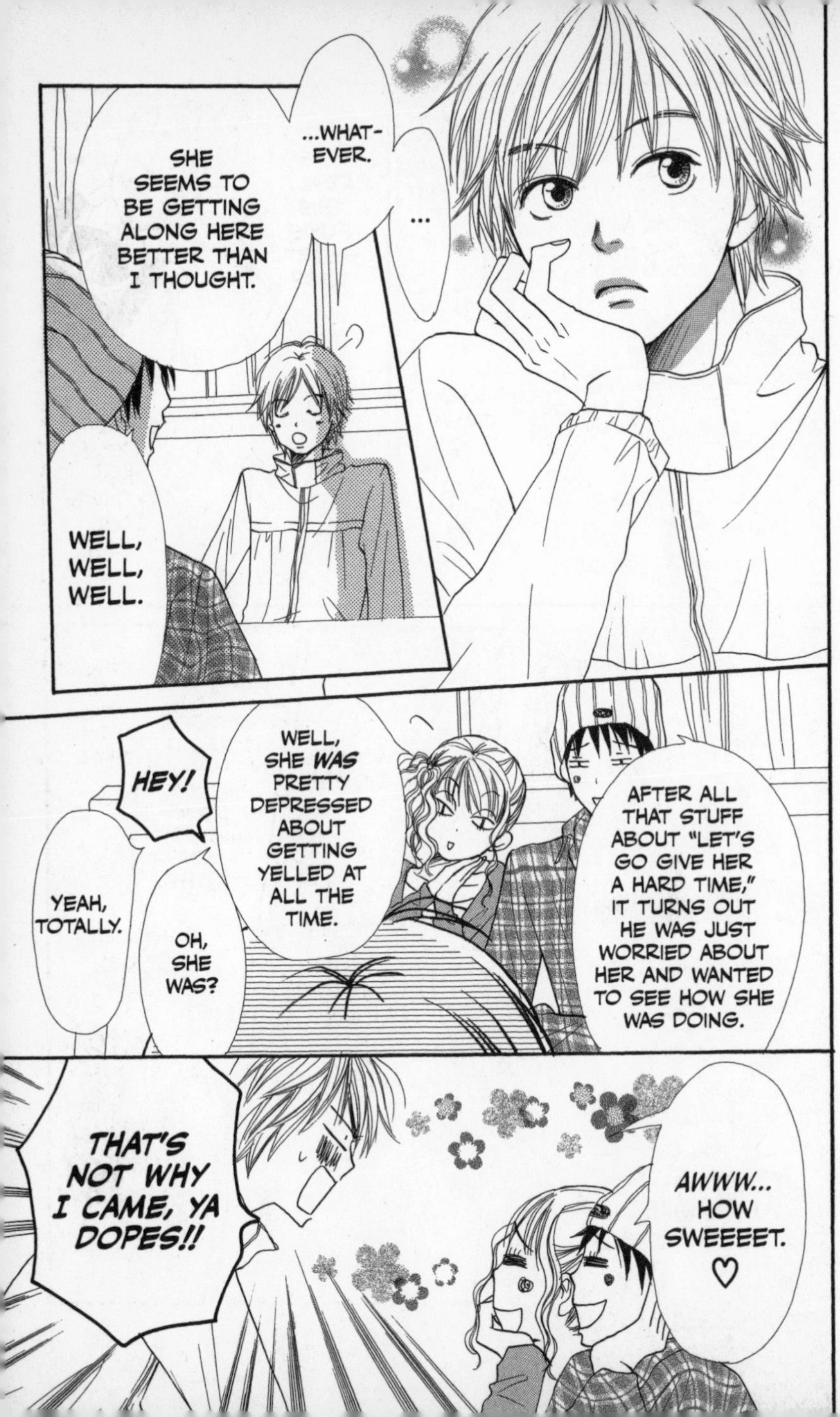
...WHAT-EVER.
...
SHE SEEMS TO BE GETTING ALONG HERE BETTER THAN I THOUGHT.
WELL, WELL, WELL.
AFTER ALL THAT STUFF ABOUT "LET'S GO GIVE HER A HARD TIME," IT TURNS OUT HE WAS JUST WORRIED ABOUT HER AND WANTED TO SEE HOW SHE WAS DOING.
WELL, SHE *WAS* PRETTY DEPRESSED ABOUT GETTING YELLED AT ALL THE TIME.
HEY!
OH, SHE WAS?
YEAH, TOTALLY.
AWWW... HOW SWEEEEET. ♥
THAT'S NOT WHY I CAME, YA DOPES!!

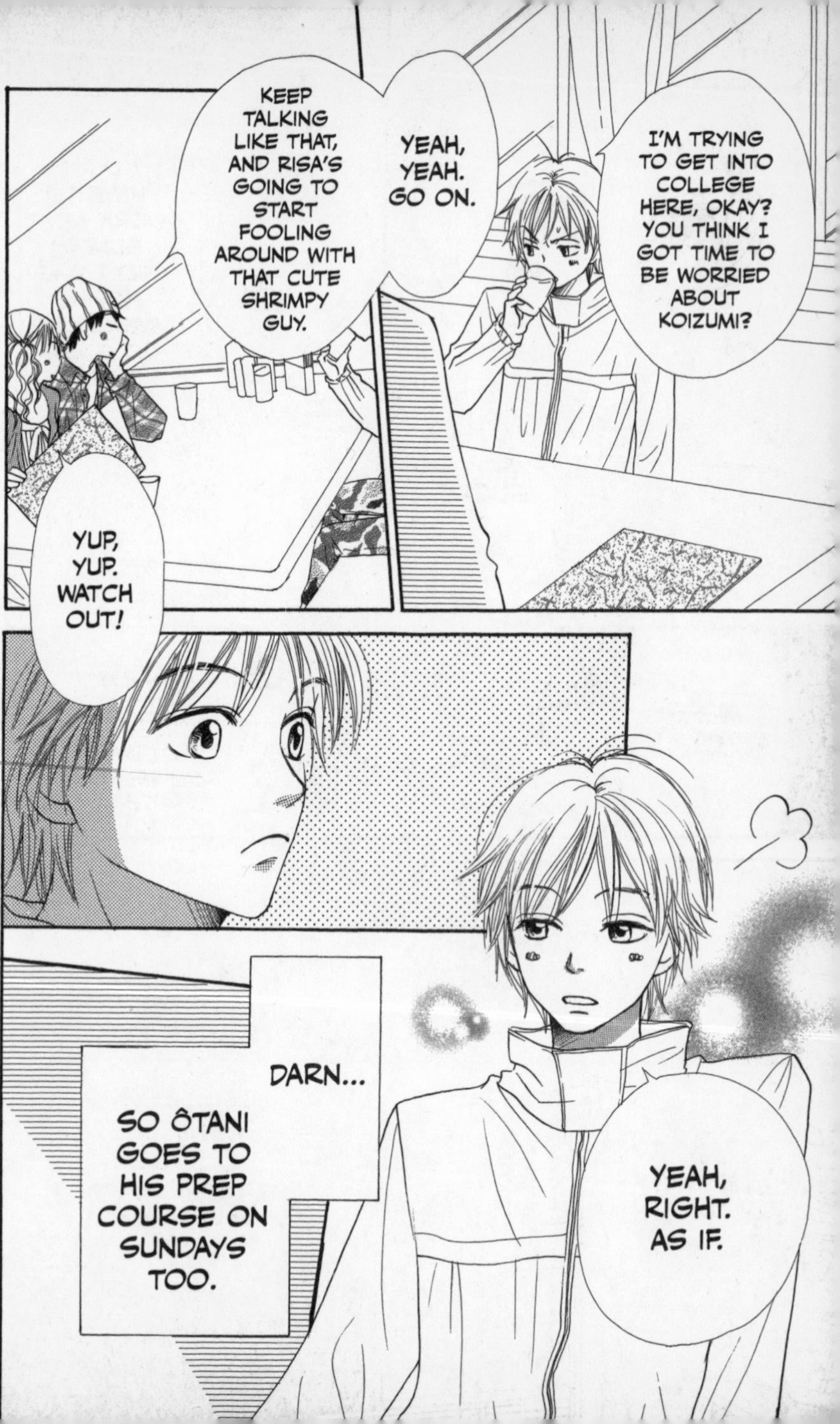
I'M TRYING TO GET INTO COLLEGE HERE, OKAY? YOU THINK I GOT TIME TO BE WORRIED ABOUT KOIZUMI?
YEAH, YEAH. GO ON.
KEEP TALKING LIKE THAT, AND RISA'S GOING TO START FOOLING AROUND WITH THAT CUTE SHRIMPY GUY.
YUP, YUP. WATCH OUT!
YEAH, RIGHT. AS IF.
DARN...
SO ÔTANI GOES TO HIS PREP COURSE ON SUNDAYS TOO.

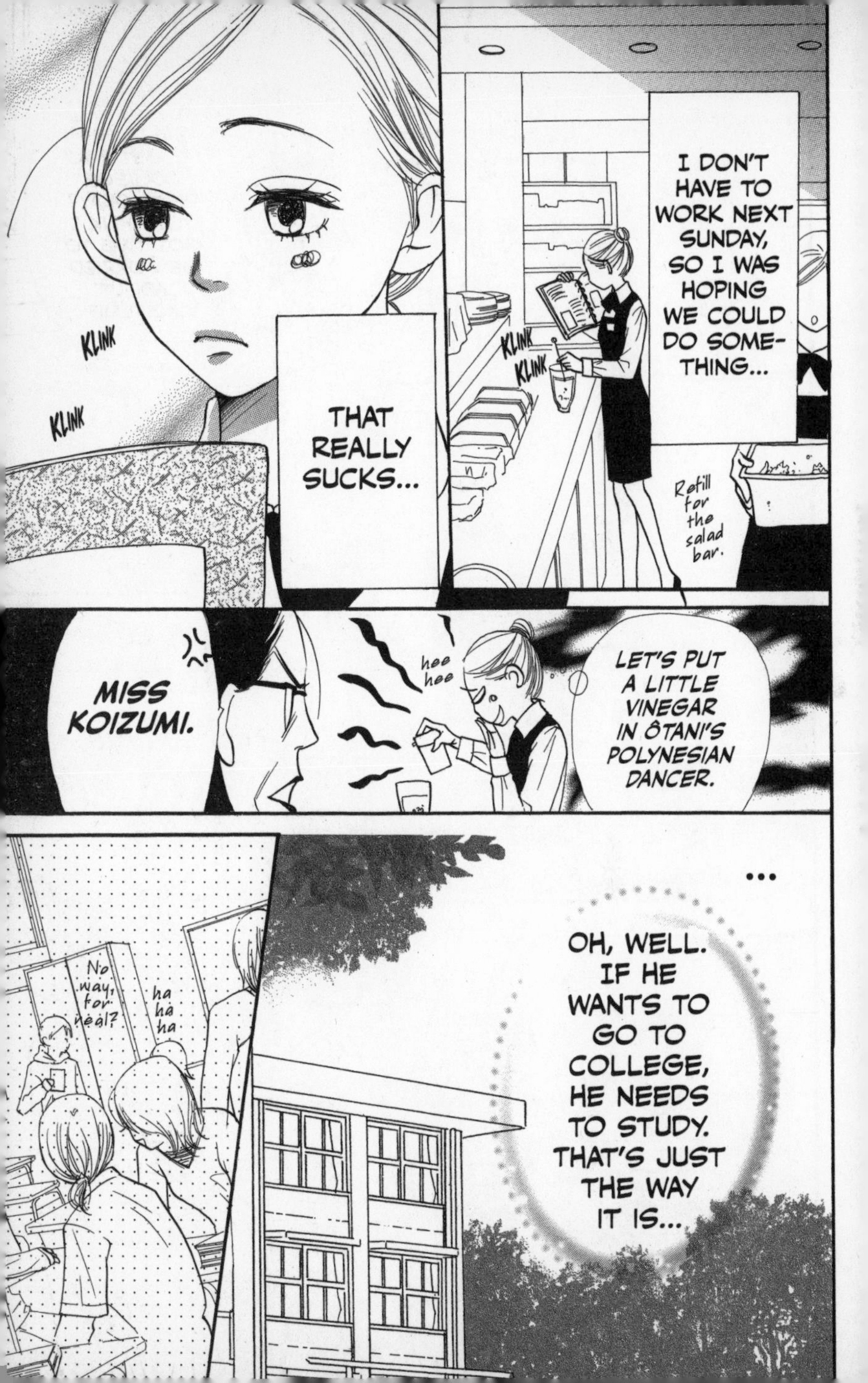
I DON'T HAVE TO WORK NEXT SUNDAY, SO I WAS HOPING WE COULD DO SOME-THING...
KLINK
KLINK
Refill for the salad bar.
THAT REALLY SUCKS...
KLINK
KLINK
LET'S PUT A LITTLE VINEGAR IN ÔTANI'S POLYNESIAN DANCER.
hee hee
MISS KOIZUMI.
...
OH, WELL. IF HE WANTS TO GO TO COLLEGE, HE NEEDS TO STUDY. THAT'S JUST THE WAY IT IS...
ha ha ha
No way, for real?

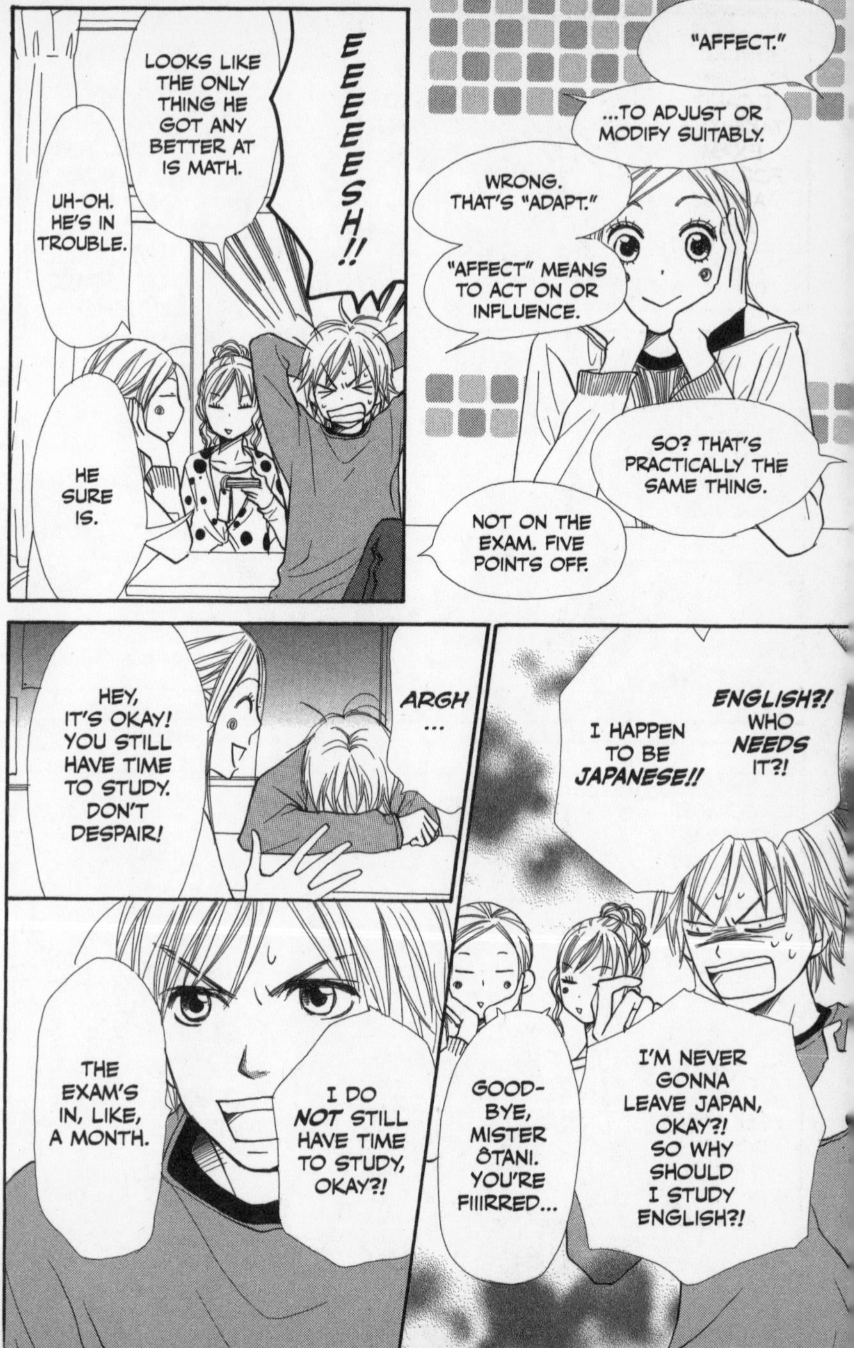
"AFFECT."
...TO ADJUST OR MODIFY SUITABLY.
WRONG. THAT'S "ADAPT."
"AFFECT" MEANS TO ACT ON OR INFLUENCE.
SO? THAT'S PRACTICALLY THE SAME THING.
NOT ON THE EXAM. FIVE POINTS OFF.
EEEEESH!!
LOOKS LIKE THE ONLY THING HE GOT ANY BETTER AT IS MATH.
UH-OH. HE'S IN TROUBLE.
HE SURE IS.
ENGLISH?! WHO *NEEDS* IT?!
I HAPPEN TO BE *JAPANESE!!*
I'M NEVER GONNA LEAVE JAPAN, OKAY?! SO WHY SHOULD I STUDY ENGLISH?!
GOOD-BYE, MISTER ÔTANI. YOU'RE FIIIRRED...
ARGH ...
HEY, IT'S OKAY! YOU STILL HAVE TIME TO STUDY. DON'T DESPAIR!
I DO *NOT* STILL HAVE TIME TO STUDY, OKAY?!
THE EXAM'S IN, LIKE, A MONTH.

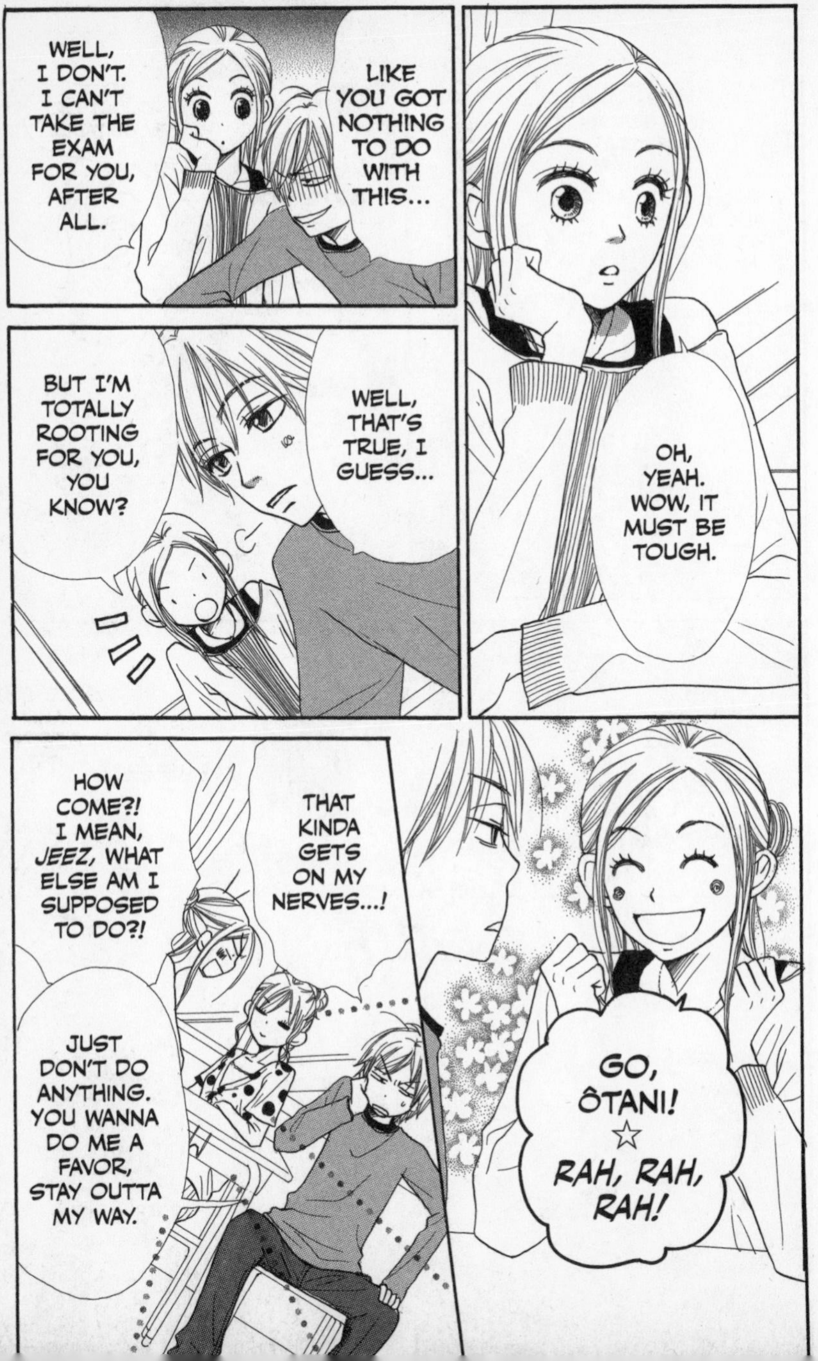
OH, YEAH. WOW, IT MUST BE TOUGH.
LIKE YOU GOT NOTHING TO DO WITH THIS...
WELL, I DON'T. I CAN'T TAKE THE EXAM FOR YOU, AFTER ALL.
WELL, THAT'S TRUE, I GUESS...
BUT I'M TOTALLY ROOTING FOR YOU, YOU KNOW?
GO, ÔTANI! ☆ RAH, RAH, RAH!
THAT KINDA GETS ON MY NERVES...!
HOW COME?! I MEAN, *JEEZ,* WHAT ELSE AM I SUPPOSED TO DO?!
JUST DON'T DO ANYTHING. YOU WANNA DO ME A FAVOR, STAY OUTTA MY WAY.

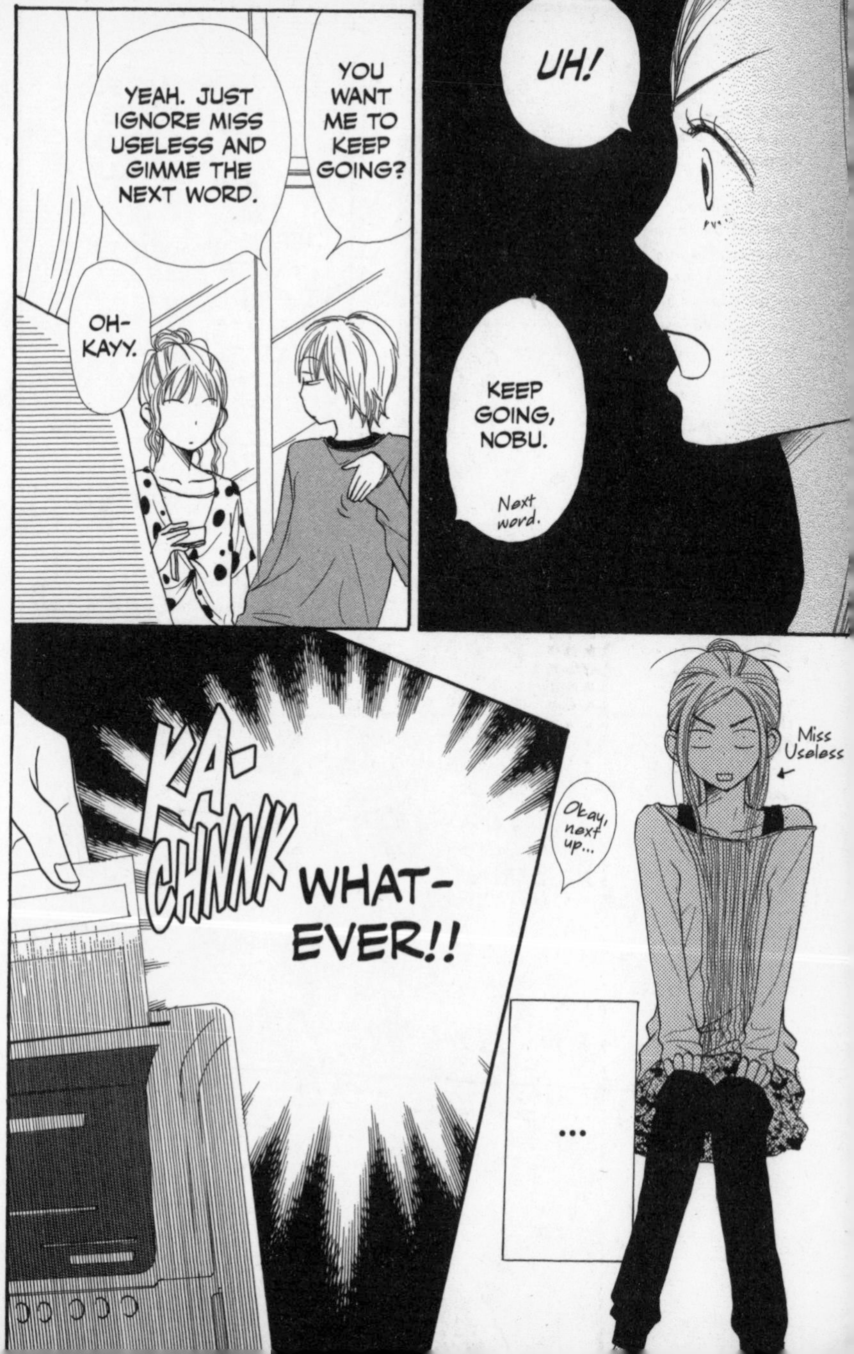
UH!
KEEP GOING, NOBU.
Next word.
YOU WANT ME TO KEEP GOING?
YEAH. JUST IGNORE MISS USELESS AND GIMME THE NEXT WORD.
OH-KAYY.
Miss Useless
Okay, next up...
...
KA-CHNNK
WHAT-EVER!!

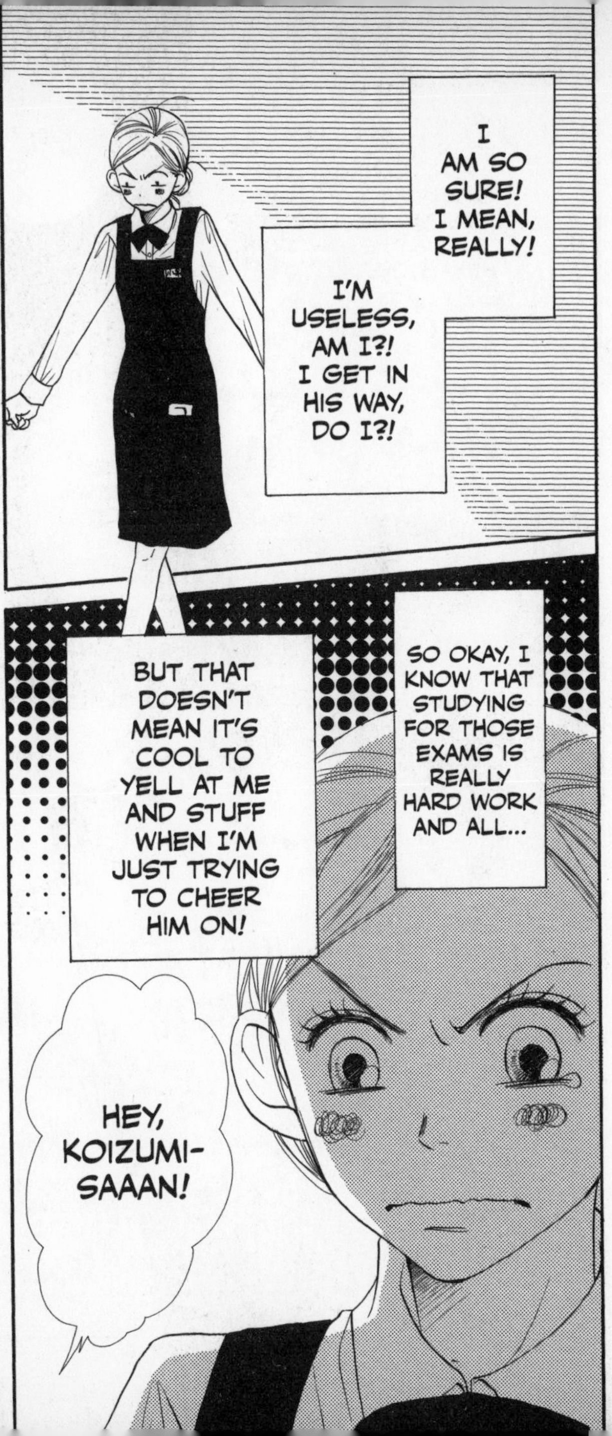
I AM SO SURE! I MEAN, REALLY!
I'M USELESS, AM I?! I GET IN HIS WAY, DO I?!
SO OKAY, I KNOW THAT STUDYING FOR THOSE EXAMS IS REALLY HARD WORK AND ALL...
BUT THAT DOESN'T MEAN IT'S COOL TO YELL AT ME AND STUFF WHEN I'M JUST TRYING TO CHEER HIM ON!
HEY, KOIZUMI-SAAAN!

Hello, Nakahara here. We're up to Volume 10.

Well, I tell ya. You get up to ten volumes of a manga, you get a little older in the process. In fact, I've aged three years since I started this one. Thanks to all of you, though, it's been a very meaningful three years...

Meanwhile, my sister had a baby girl.

She loves Aunt Aya's Dynamite Shikoku imitation. Every time I see her, I have to shout "Shikkoku, Shikkoku" and do wrestling poses, yes indeed.

In fact, I was just doing it now, so Auntie's kinda out of breath.

Shikkoku
Shikkoku

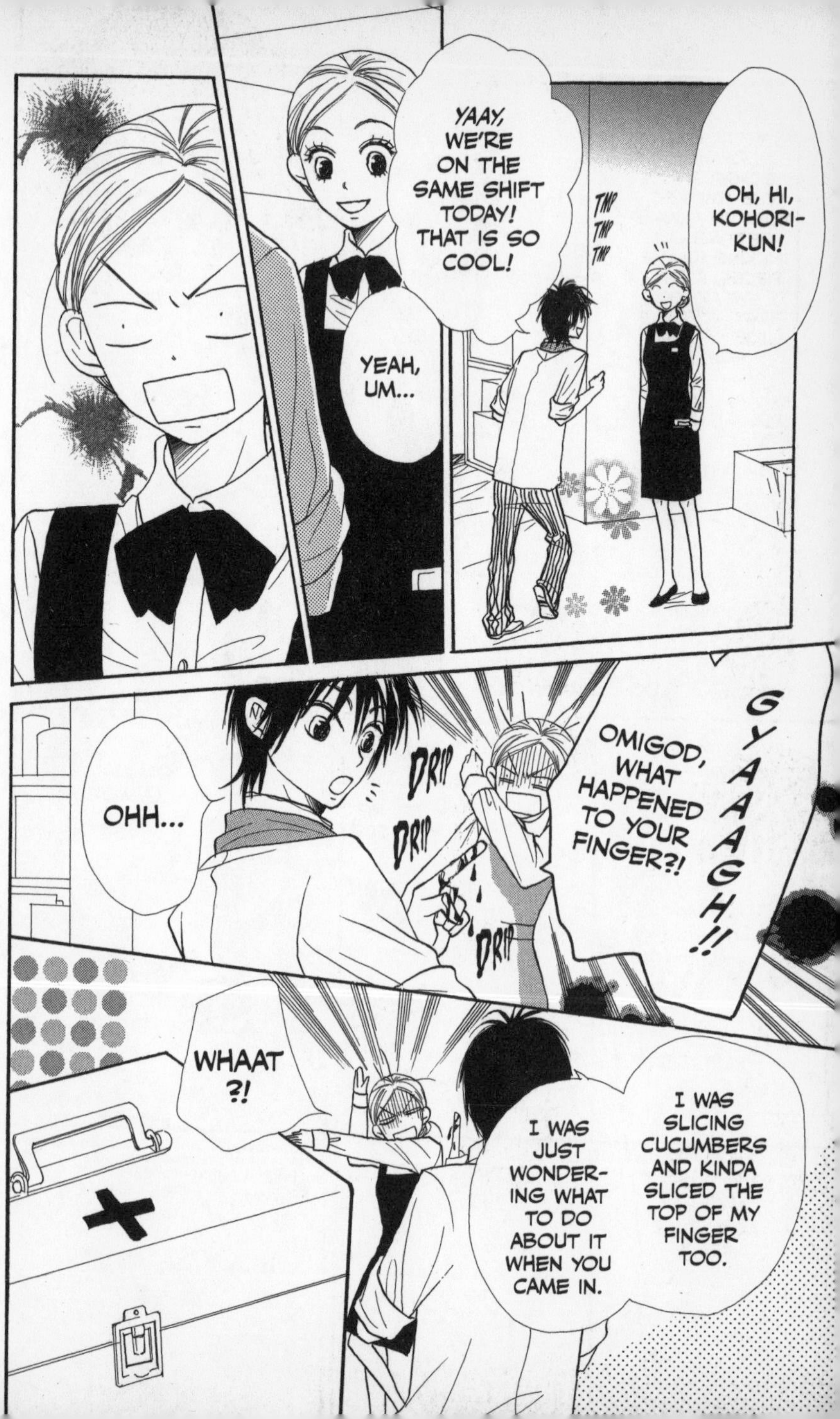
OH, HI, KOHORI-KUN!
TMP TMP TMP
YAAY, WE'RE ON THE SAME SHIFT TODAY! THAT IS SO COOL!
YEAH, UM...
GYAAAAGH!!
OMIGOD, WHAT HAPPENED TO YOUR FINGER?!
DRIP
DRIP
DRIP
OHH...
WHAAT ?!
I WAS SLICING CUCUMBERS AND KINDA SLICED THE TOP OF MY FINGER TOO.
I WAS JUST WONDER-ING WHAT TO DO ABOUT IT WHEN YOU CAME IN.

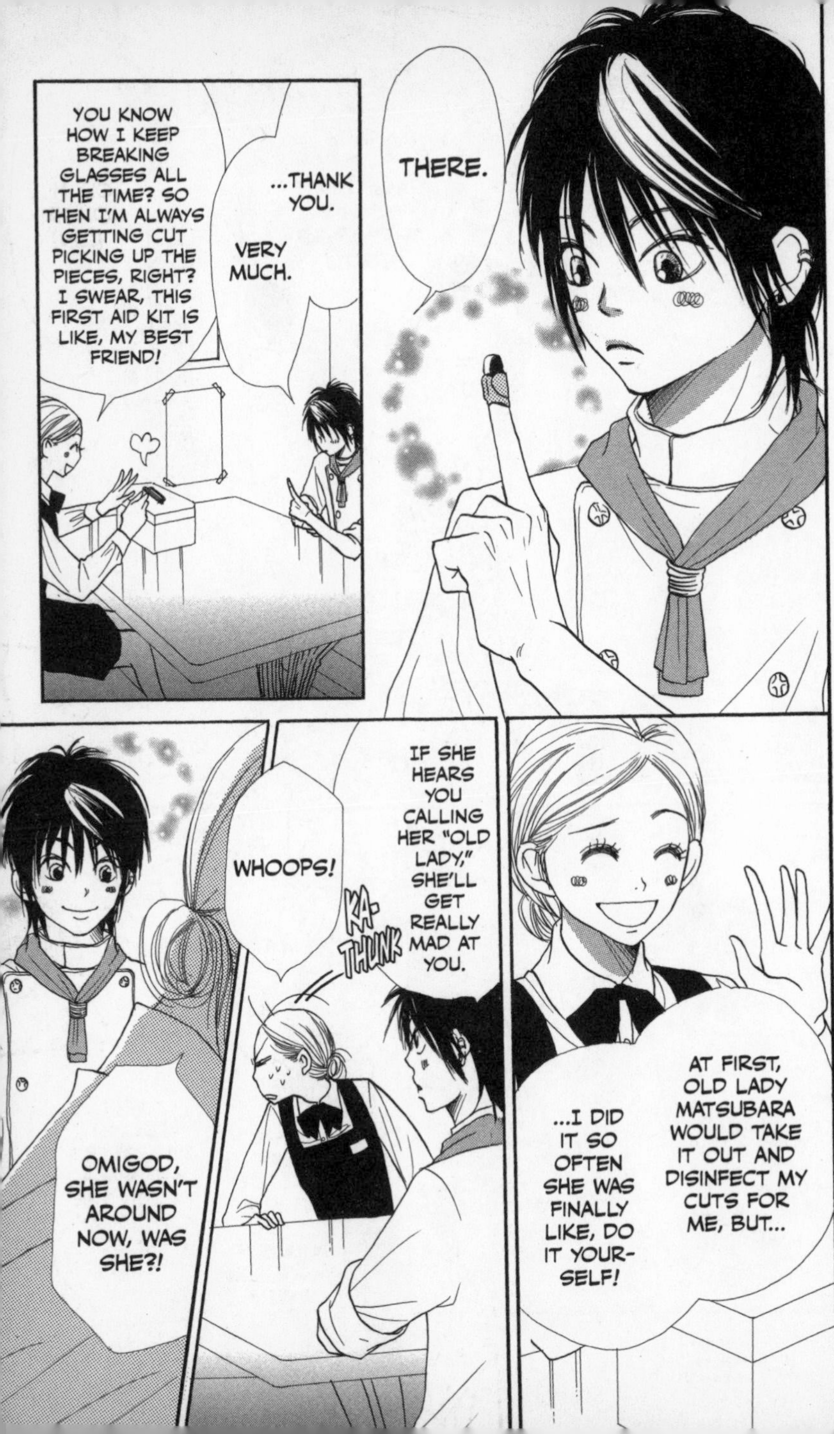
THERE.
...THANK YOU. VERY MUCH.
YOU KNOW HOW I KEEP BREAKING GLASSES ALL THE TIME? SO THEN I'M ALWAYS GETTING CUT PICKING UP THE PIECES, RIGHT? I SWEAR, THIS FIRST AID KIT IS LIKE, MY BEST FRIEND!
AT FIRST, OLD LADY MATSUBARA WOULD TAKE IT OUT AND DISINFECT MY CUTS FOR ME, BUT...
...I DID IT SO OFTEN SHE WAS FINALLY LIKE, DO IT YOUR-SELF!
IF SHE HEARS YOU CALLING HER "OLD LADY," SHE'LL GET REALLY MAD AT YOU.
WHOOPS!
KA-THUNK
OMIGOD, SHE WASN'T AROUND NOW, WAS SHE?!

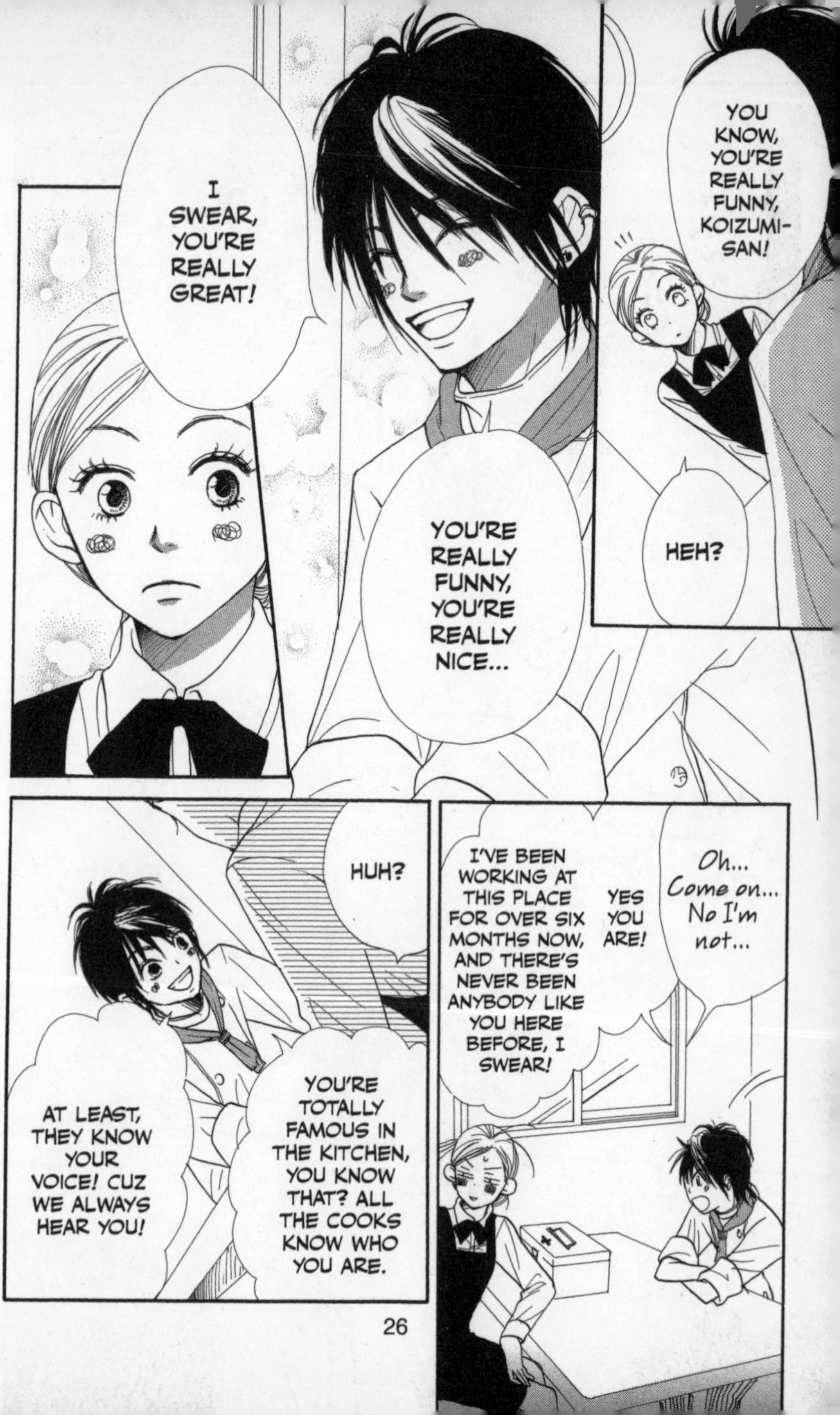

YOU KNOW, YOU'RE REALLY FUNNY, KOIZUMI-SAN!
HEH?
YOU'RE REALLY FUNNY, YOU'RE REALLY NICE...
I SWEAR, YOU'RE REALLY GREAT!
Oh... Come on... No I'm not...
YES YOU ARE!
I'VE BEEN WORKING AT THIS PLACE FOR OVER SIX MONTHS NOW, AND THERE'S NEVER BEEN ANYBODY LIKE YOU HERE BEFORE, I SWEAR!
HUH?
YOU'RE TOTALLY FAMOUS IN THE KITCHEN, YOU KNOW THAT? ALL THE COOKS KNOW WHO YOU ARE.
AT LEAST, THEY KNOW YOUR VOICE! CUZ WE ALWAYS HEAR YOU!

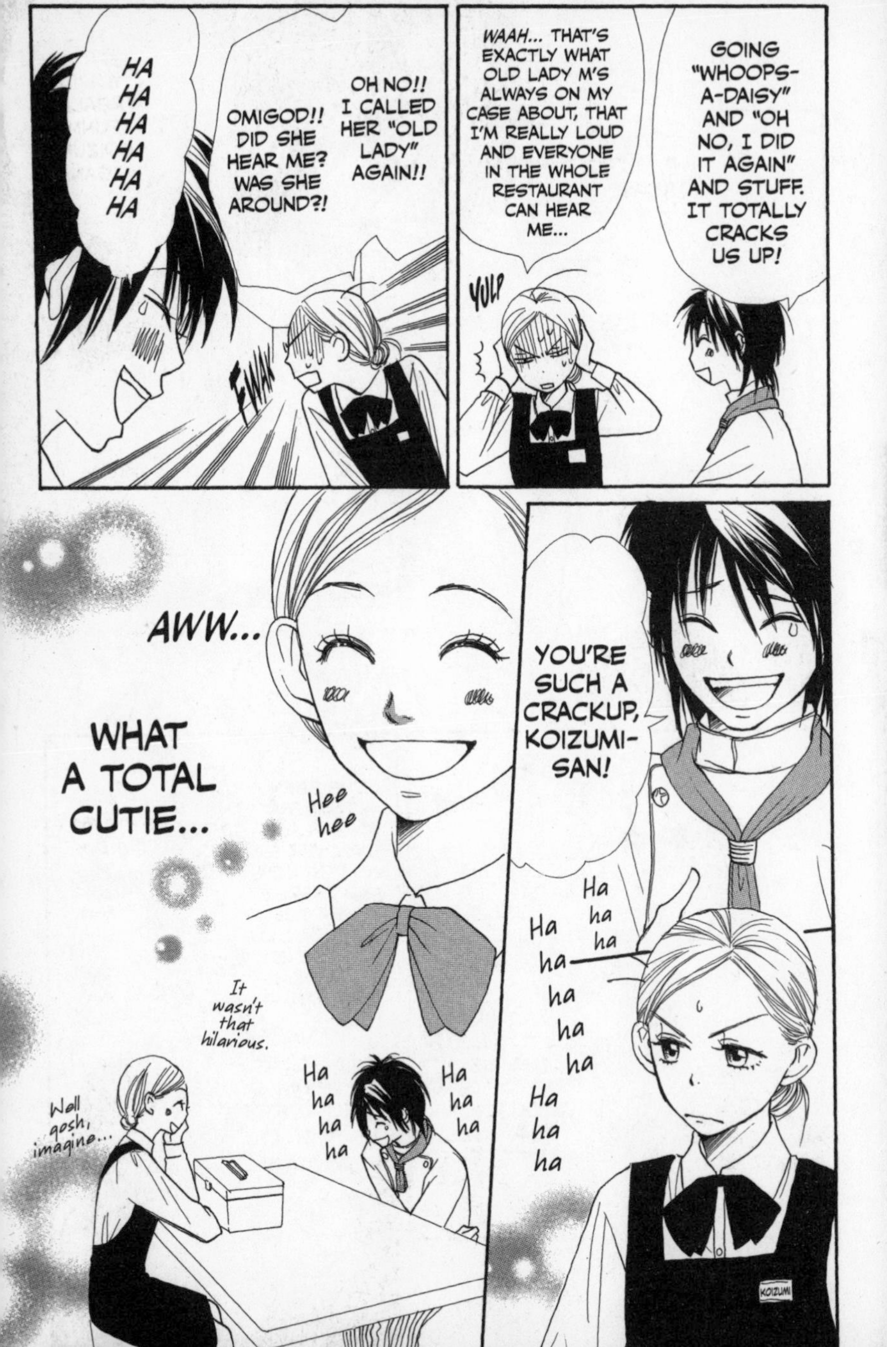
GOING "WHOOPS-A-DAISY" AND "OH NO, I DID IT AGAIN" AND STUFF. IT TOTALLY CRACKS US UP!
WAAH... THAT'S EXACTLY WHAT OLD LADY M'S ALWAYS ON MY CASE ABOUT, THAT I'M REALLY LOUD AND EVERYONE IN THE WHOLE RESTAURANT CAN HEAR ME...
YULP
OH NO!! I CALLED HER "OLD LADY" AGAIN!!
OMIGOD!! DID SHE HEAR ME? WAS SHE AROUND?!
FWAK
HA HA HA HA HA HA
YOU'RE SUCH A CRACKUP, KOIZUMI-SAN!
Ha ha ha
Ha ha ha ha ha ha
Ha ha ha
KOIZUMI
AWW...
WHAT A TOTAL CUTIE...
Hee hee
It wasn't that hilarious.
Ha ha ha ha
Ha ha ha ha
Well gosh, imagine...

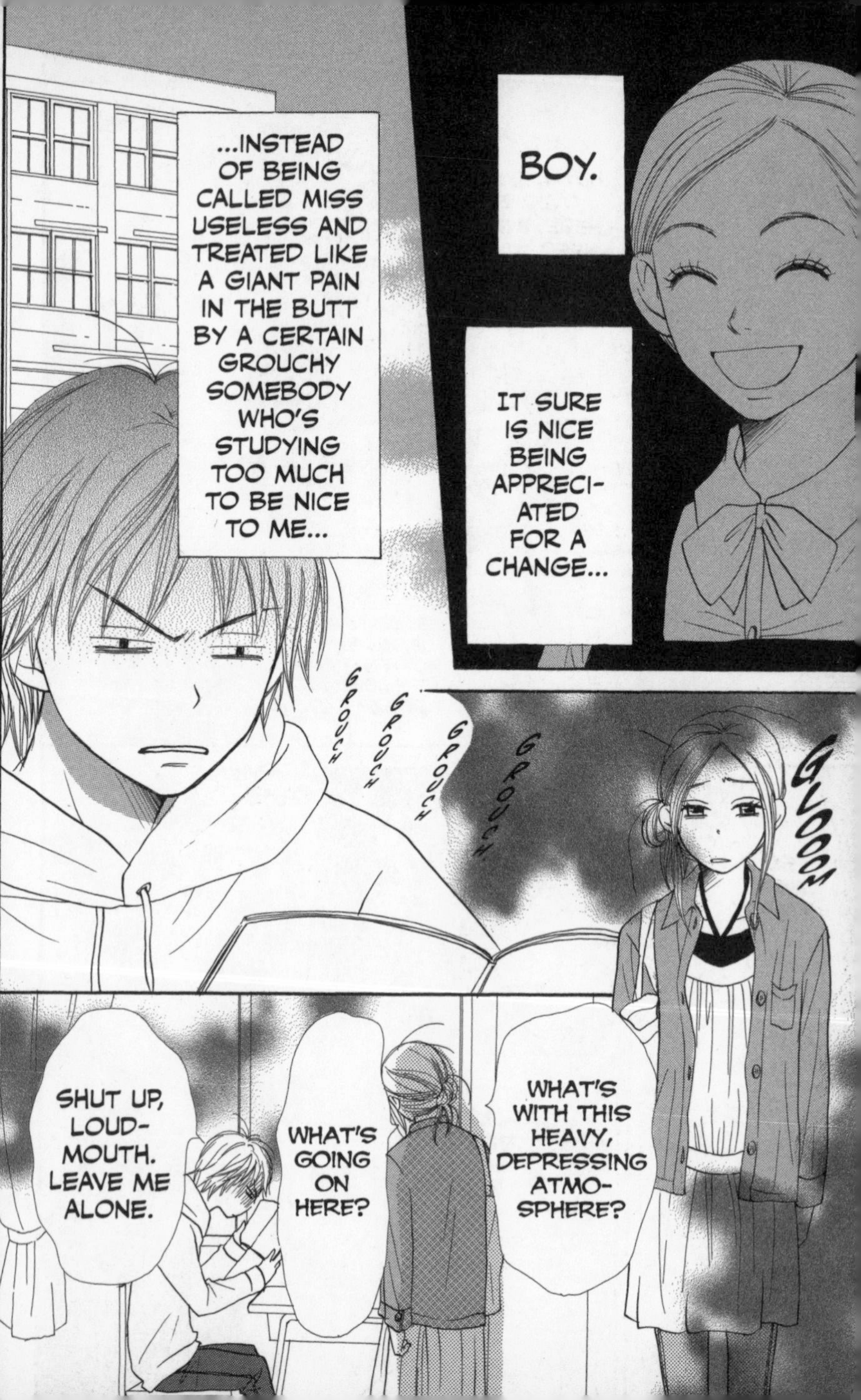
BOY.
IT SURE IS NICE BEING APPRECIATED FOR A CHANGE...
...INSTEAD OF BEING CALLED MISS USELESS AND TREATED LIKE A GIANT PAIN IN THE BUTT BY A CERTAIN GROUCHY SOMEBODY WHO'S STUDYING TOO MUCH TO BE NICE TO ME...
GROUCH GROUCH GROUCH GROUCH
GLOOOOM
WHAT'S WITH THIS HEAVY, DEPRESSING ATMOSPHERE?
WHAT'S GOING ON HERE?
SHUT UP, LOUD-MOUTH. LEAVE ME ALONE.

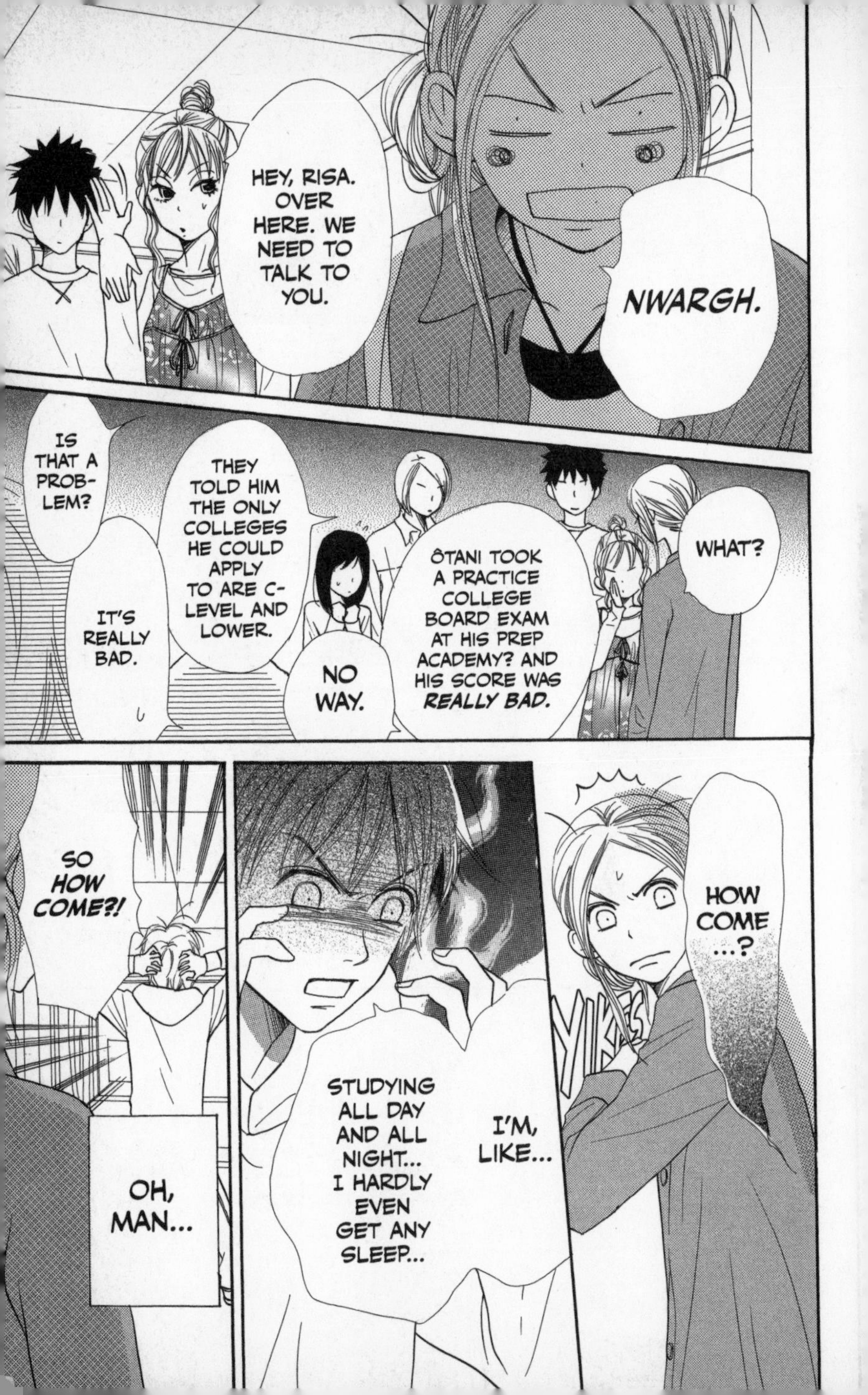
NWARGH.
HEY, RISA. OVER HERE. WE NEED TO TALK TO YOU.
WHAT?
ŌTANI TOOK A PRACTICE COLLEGE BOARD EXAM AT HIS PREP ACADEMY? AND HIS SCORE WAS REALLY BAD.
NO WAY.
THEY TOLD HIM THE ONLY COLLEGES HE COULD APPLY TO ARE C-LEVEL AND LOWER.
IS THAT A PROB-LEM?
IT'S REALLY BAD.
HOW COME ...?
I'M, LIKE...
STUDYING ALL DAY AND ALL NIGHT... I HARDLY EVEN GET ANY SLEEP...
SO HOW COME?!
OH, MAN...

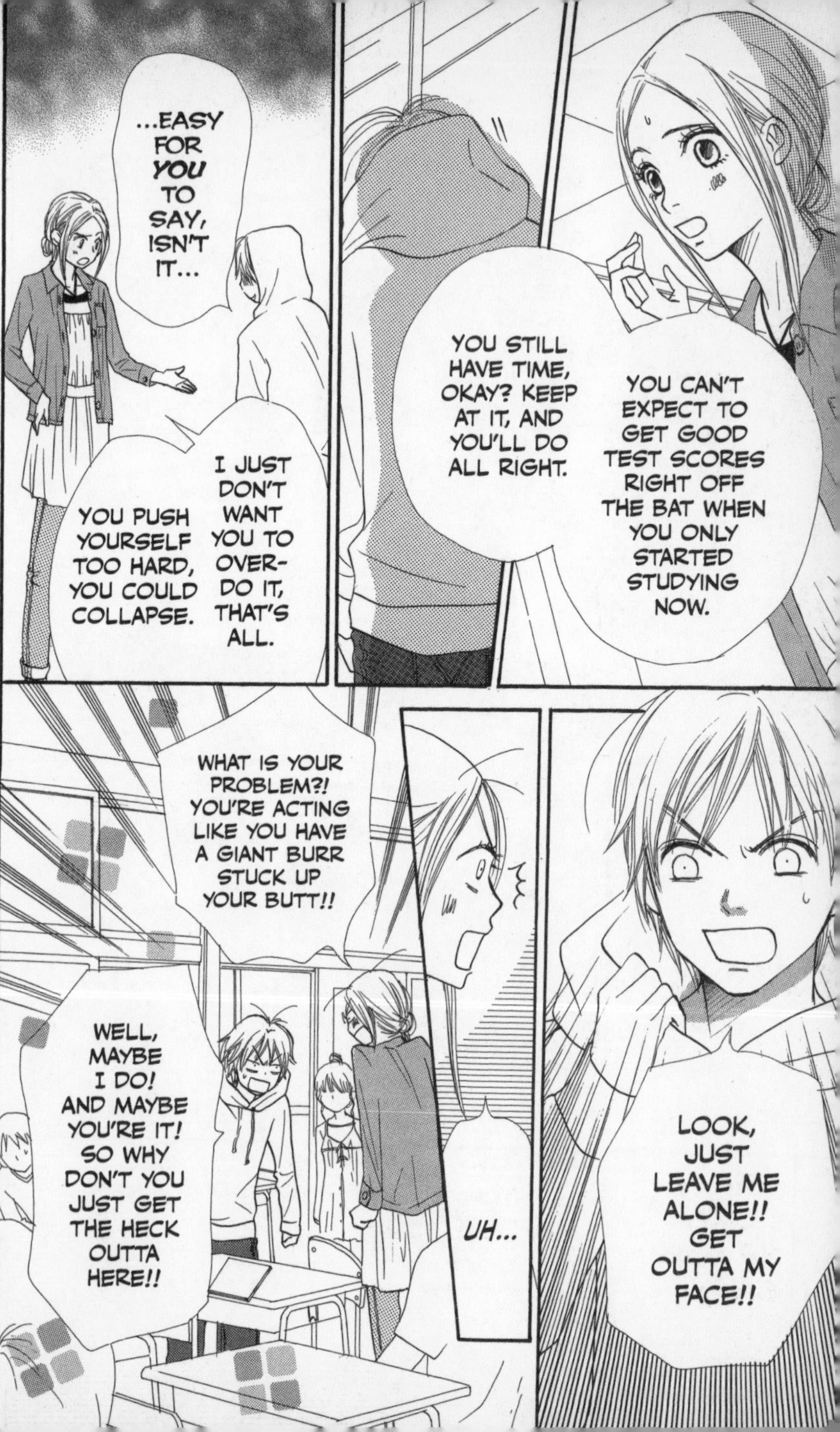
YOU CAN'T EXPECT TO GET GOOD TEST SCORES RIGHT OFF THE BAT WHEN YOU ONLY STARTED STUDYING NOW.
YOU STILL HAVE TIME, OKAY? KEEP AT IT, AND YOU'LL DO ALL RIGHT.
...EASY FOR *YOU* TO SAY, ISN'T IT...
I JUST DON'T WANT YOU TO OVER-DO IT, THAT'S ALL.
YOU PUSH YOURSELF TOO HARD, YOU COULD COLLAPSE.
LOOK, JUST LEAVE ME ALONE!! GET OUTTA MY FACE!!
UH...
WHAT IS YOUR PROBLEM?! YOU'RE ACTING LIKE YOU HAVE A GIANT BURR STUCK UP YOUR BUTT!!
WELL, MAYBE I DO! AND MAYBE YOU'RE IT! SO WHY DON'T YOU JUST GET THE HECK OUTTA HERE!!

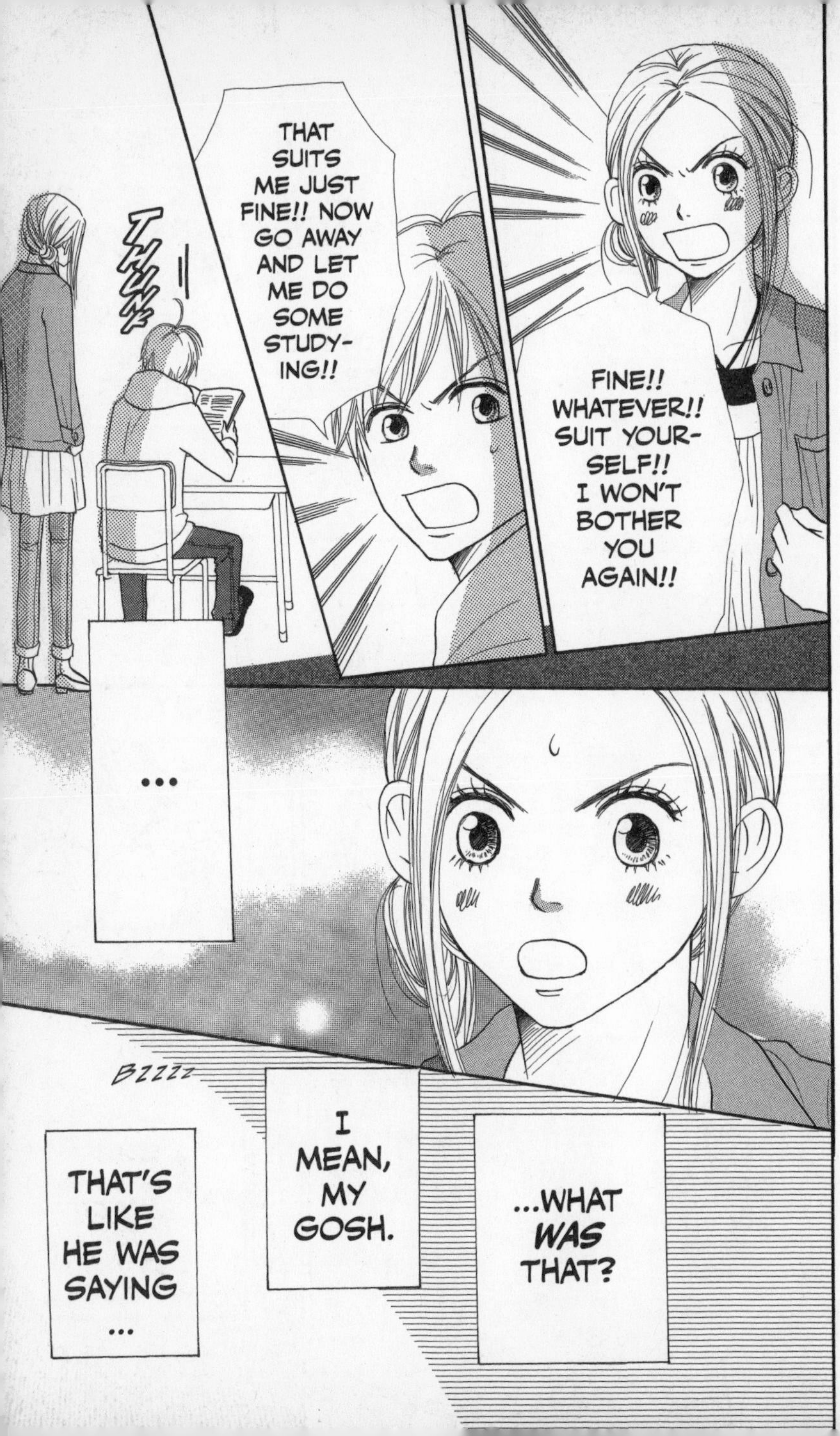
FINE!! WHATEVER!! SUIT YOURSELF!! I WON'T BOTHER YOU AGAIN!!
THAT SUITS ME JUST FINE!! NOW GO AWAY AND LET ME DO SOME STUDYING!!
THUNK
...
...WHAT WAS THAT?
I MEAN, MY GOSH.
BZZZZ
THAT'S LIKE HE WAS SAYING ...

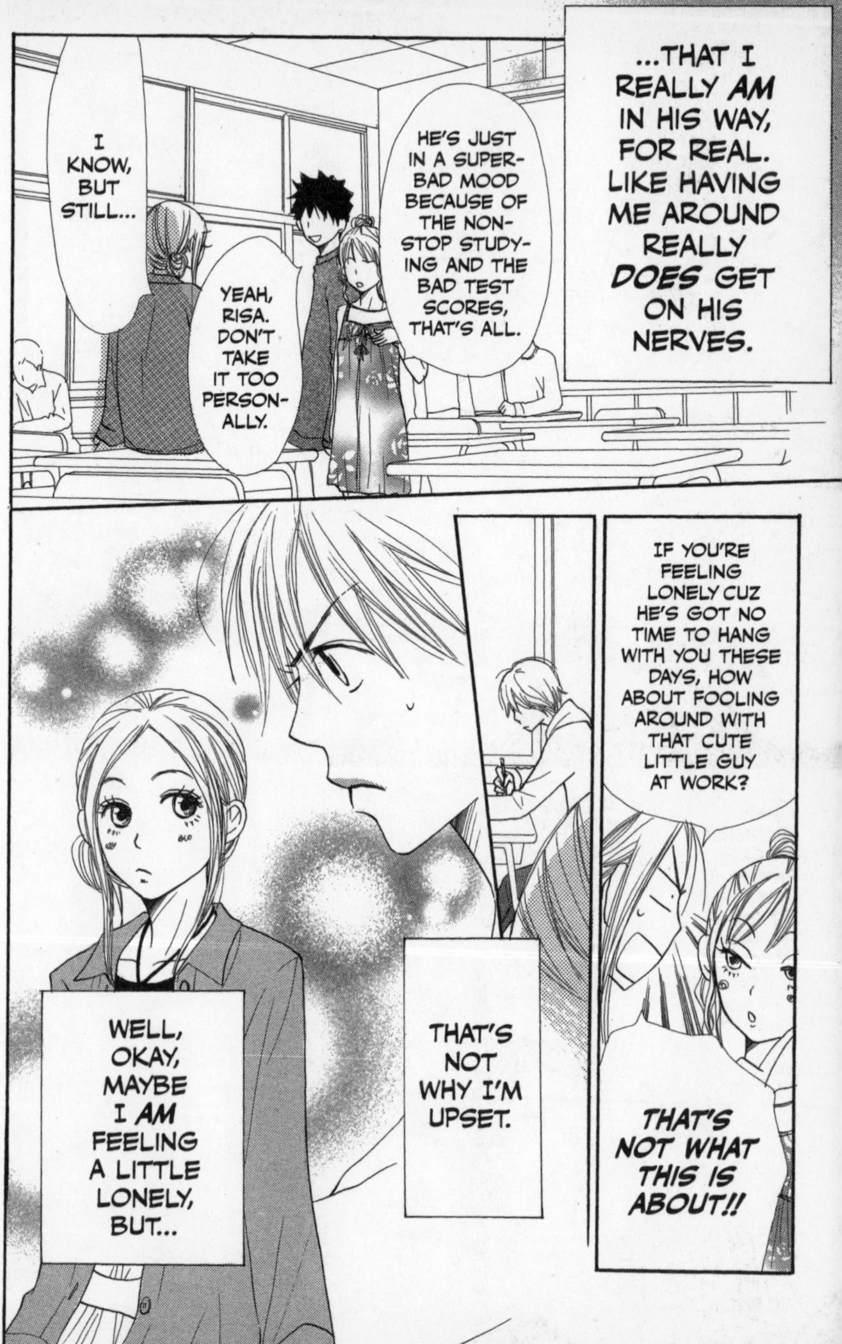
...THAT I REALLY *AM* IN HIS WAY, FOR REAL. LIKE HAVING ME AROUND REALLY *DOES* GET ON HIS NERVES.
HE'S JUST IN A SUPER-BAD MOOD BECAUSE OF THE NON-STOP STUDYING AND THE BAD TEST SCORES, THAT'S ALL.
YEAH, RISA. DON'T TAKE IT TOO PERSONALLY.
I KNOW, BUT STILL...
IF YOU'RE FEELING LONELY CUZ HE'S GOT NO TIME TO HANG WITH YOU THESE DAYS, HOW ABOUT FOOLING AROUND WITH THAT CUTE LITTLE GUY AT WORK?
WELL, OKAY, MAYBE I *AM* FEELING A LITTLE LONELY, BUT...
THAT'S NOT WHY I'M UPSET.
THAT'S NOT WHAT THIS IS ABOUT!!

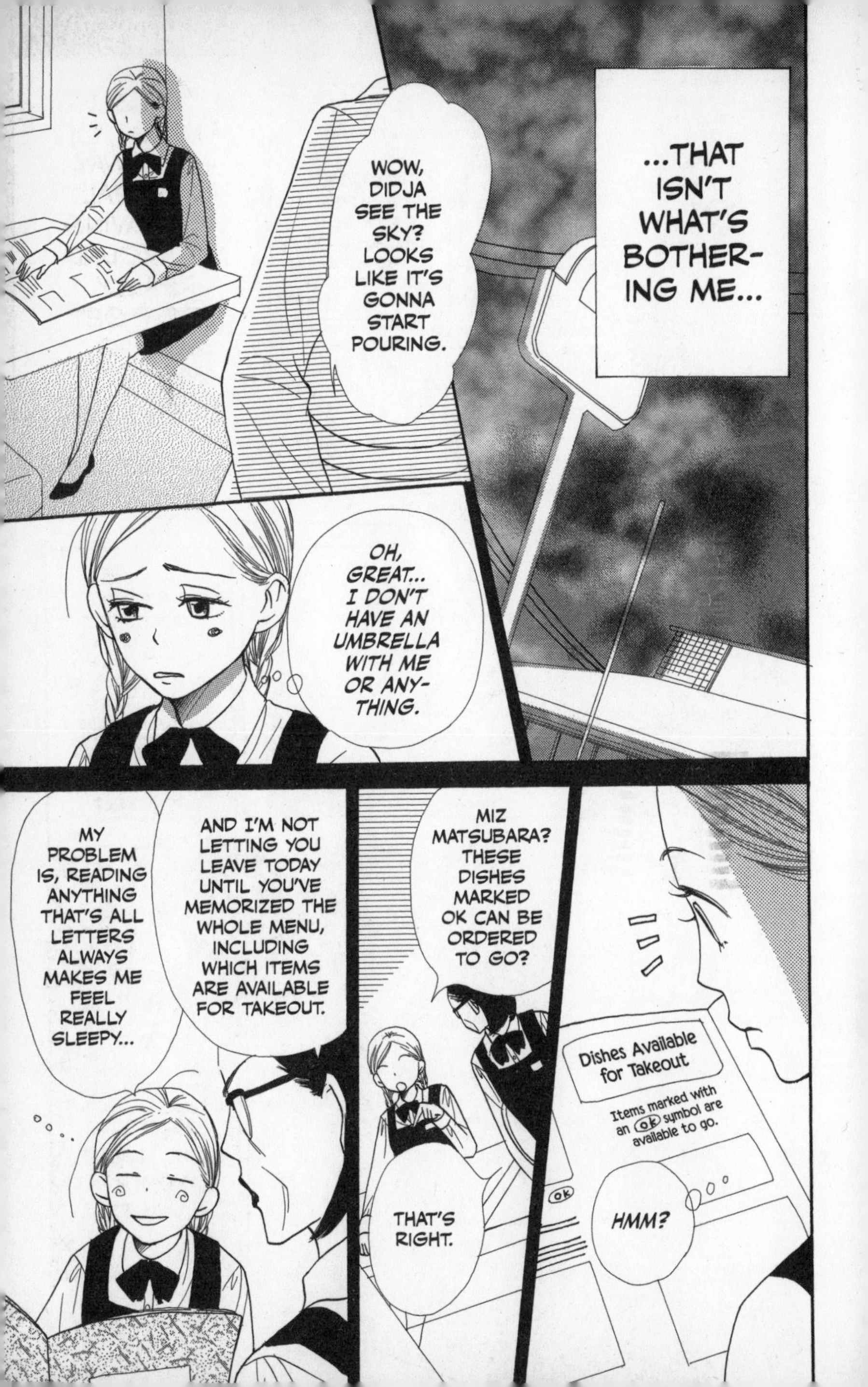
...THAT ISN'T WHAT'S BOTHERING ME...
WOW, DIDJA SEE THE SKY? LOOKS LIKE IT'S GONNA START POURING.
OH, GREAT... I DON'T HAVE AN UMBRELLA WITH ME OR ANYTHING.
Dishes Available for Takeout
Items marked with an ok symbol are available to go.
ok
HMM?
MIZ MATSUBARA? THESE DISHES MARKED OK CAN BE ORDERED TO GO?
THAT'S RIGHT.
AND I'M NOT LETTING YOU LEAVE TODAY UNTIL YOU'VE MEMORIZED THE WHOLE MENU, INCLUDING WHICH ITEMS ARE AVAILABLE FOR TAKEOUT.
MY PROBLEM IS, READING ANYTHING THAT'S ALL LETTERS ALWAYS MAKES ME FEEL REALLY SLEEPY...

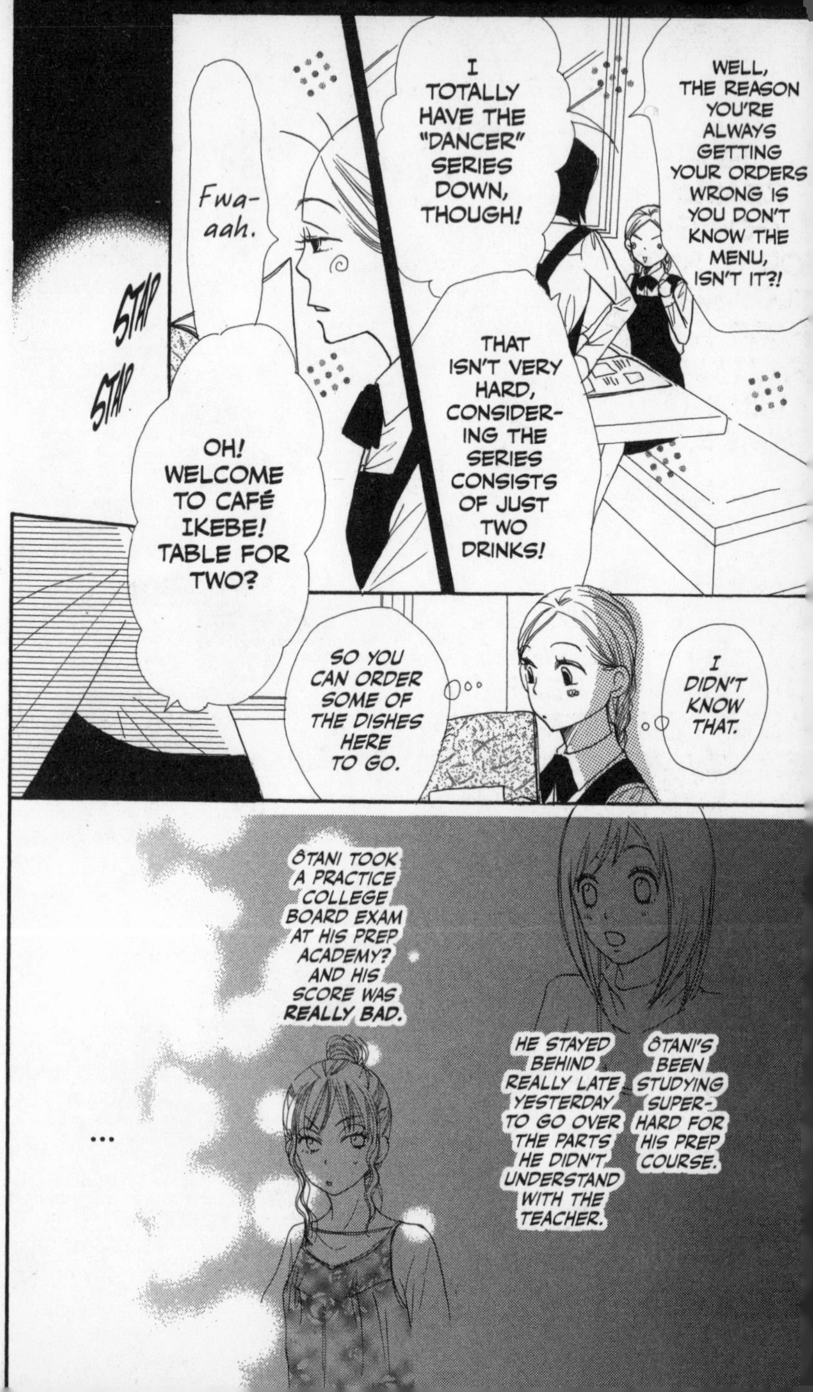
WELL, THE REASON YOU'RE ALWAYS GETTING YOUR ORDERS WRONG IS YOU DON'T KNOW THE MENU, ISN'T IT?!
I TOTALLY HAVE THE "DANCER" SERIES DOWN, THOUGH!
THAT ISN'T VERY HARD, CONSIDER-ING THE SERIES CONSISTS OF JUST TWO DRINKS!
Fwa-aah.
STAP
STAP
OH! WELCOME TO CAFÉ IKEBE! TABLE FOR TWO?
I DIDN'T KNOW THAT.
SO YOU CAN ORDER SOME OF THE DISHES HERE TO GO.
ŌTANI'S BEEN STUDYING SUPER-HARD FOR HIS PREP COURSE.
HE STAYED BEHIND REALLY LATE YESTERDAY TO GO OVER THE PARTS HE DIDN'T UNDERSTAND WITH THE TEACHER.
ŌTANI TOOK A PRACTICE COLLEGE BOARD EXAM AT HIS PREP ACADEMY? AND HIS SCORE WAS REALLY BAD.
...

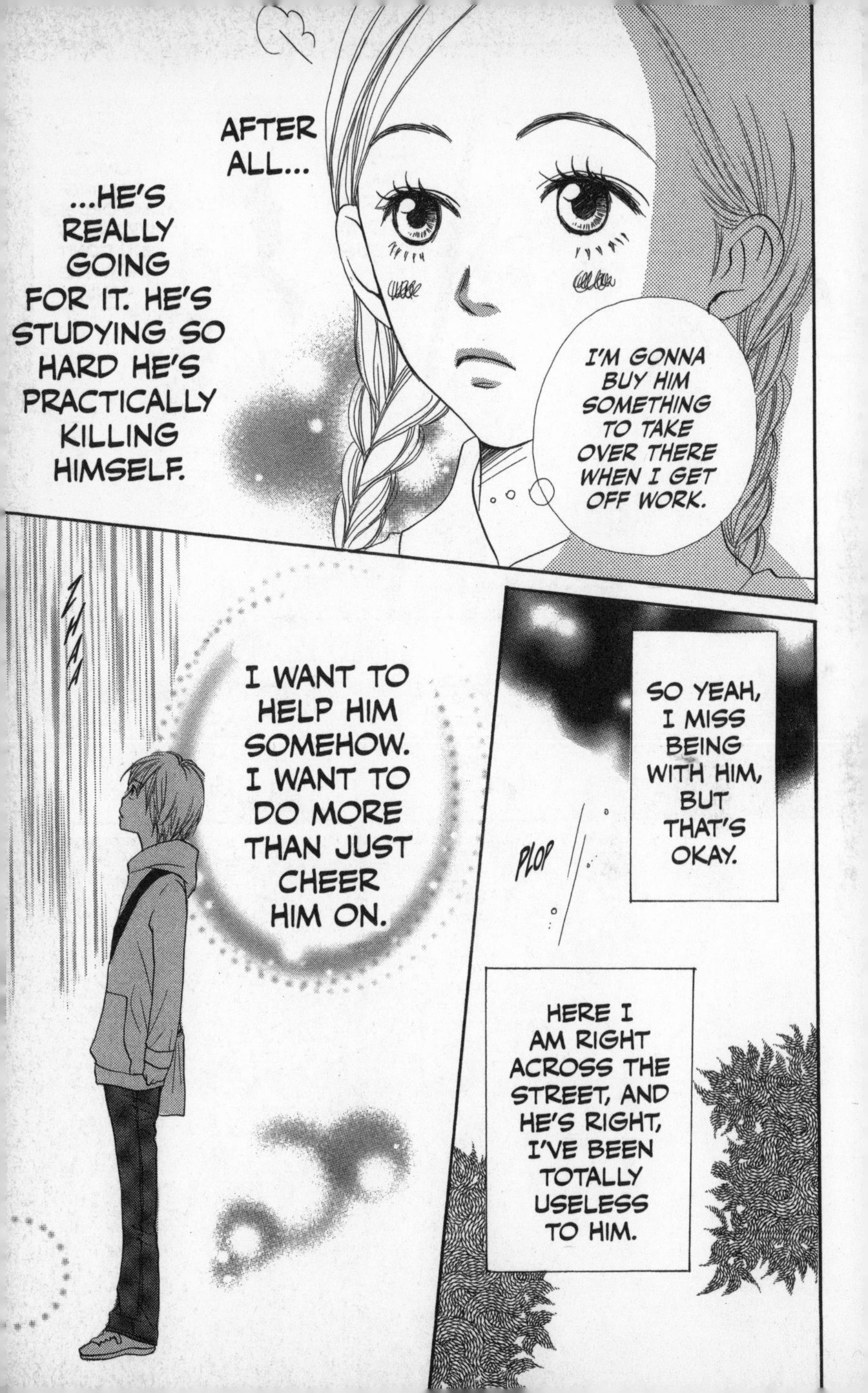
I'M GONNA BUY HIM SOMETHING TO TAKE OVER THERE WHEN I GET OFF WORK.
AFTER ALL...
...HE'S REALLY GOING FOR IT. HE'S STUDYING SO HARD HE'S PRACTICALLY KILLING HIMSELF.
SO YEAH, I MISS BEING WITH HIM, BUT THAT'S OKAY.
PLOP
HERE I AM RIGHT ACROSS THE STREET, AND HE'S RIGHT, I'VE BEEN TOTALLY USELESS TO HIM.
I WANT TO HELP HIM SOMEHOW. I WANT TO DO MORE THAN JUST CHEER HIM ON.

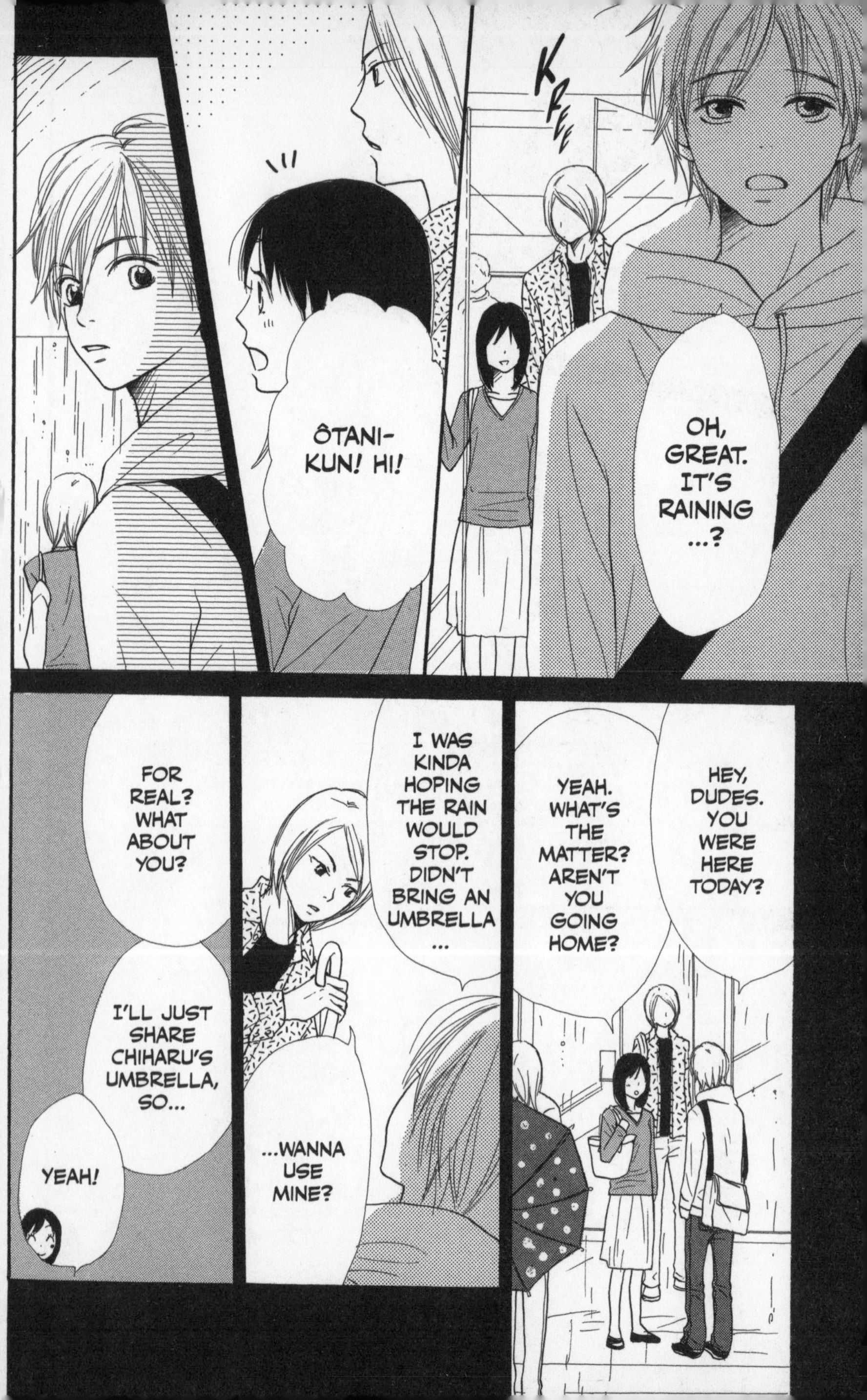
KREEE
OH, GREAT. IT'S RAINING ...?
ÔTANI-KUN! HI!
HEY, DUDES. YOU WERE HERE TODAY?
YEAH. WHAT'S THE MATTER? AREN'T YOU GOING HOME?
I WAS KINDA HOPING THE RAIN WOULD STOP. DIDN'T BRING AN UMBRELLA ...
...WANNA USE MINE?
FOR REAL? WHAT ABOUT YOU?
I'LL JUST SHARE CHIHARU'S UMBRELLA, SO...
YEAH!

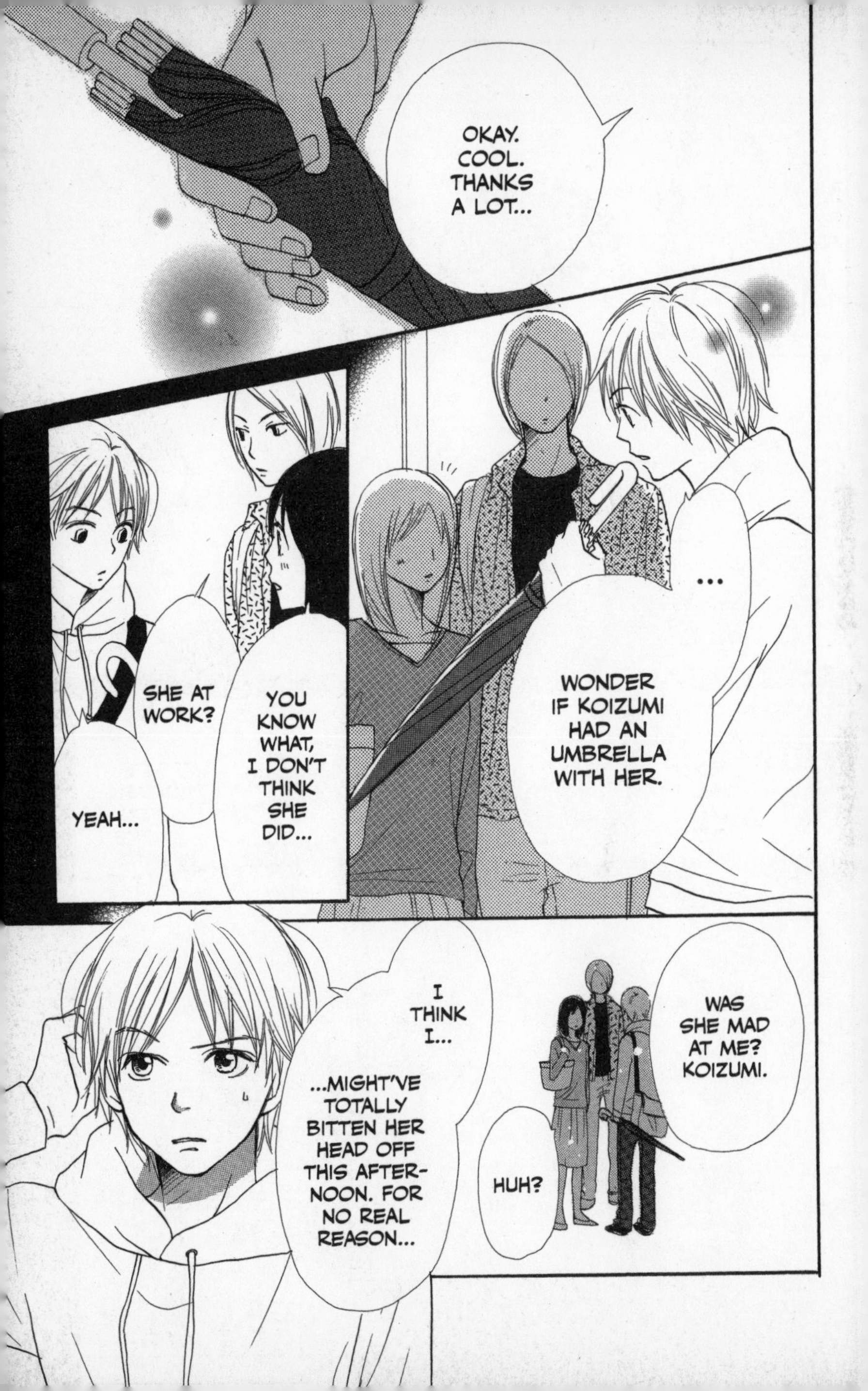
OKAY. COOL. THANKS A LOT...
...
WONDER IF KOIZUMI HAD AN UMBRELLA WITH HER.
YOU KNOW WHAT, I DON'T THINK SHE DID...
SHE AT WORK?
YEAH...
WAS SHE MAD AT ME? KOIZUMI.
HUH?
I THINK I...
...MIGHT'VE TOTALLY BITTEN HER HEAD OFF THIS AFTERNOON. FOR NO REAL REASON...

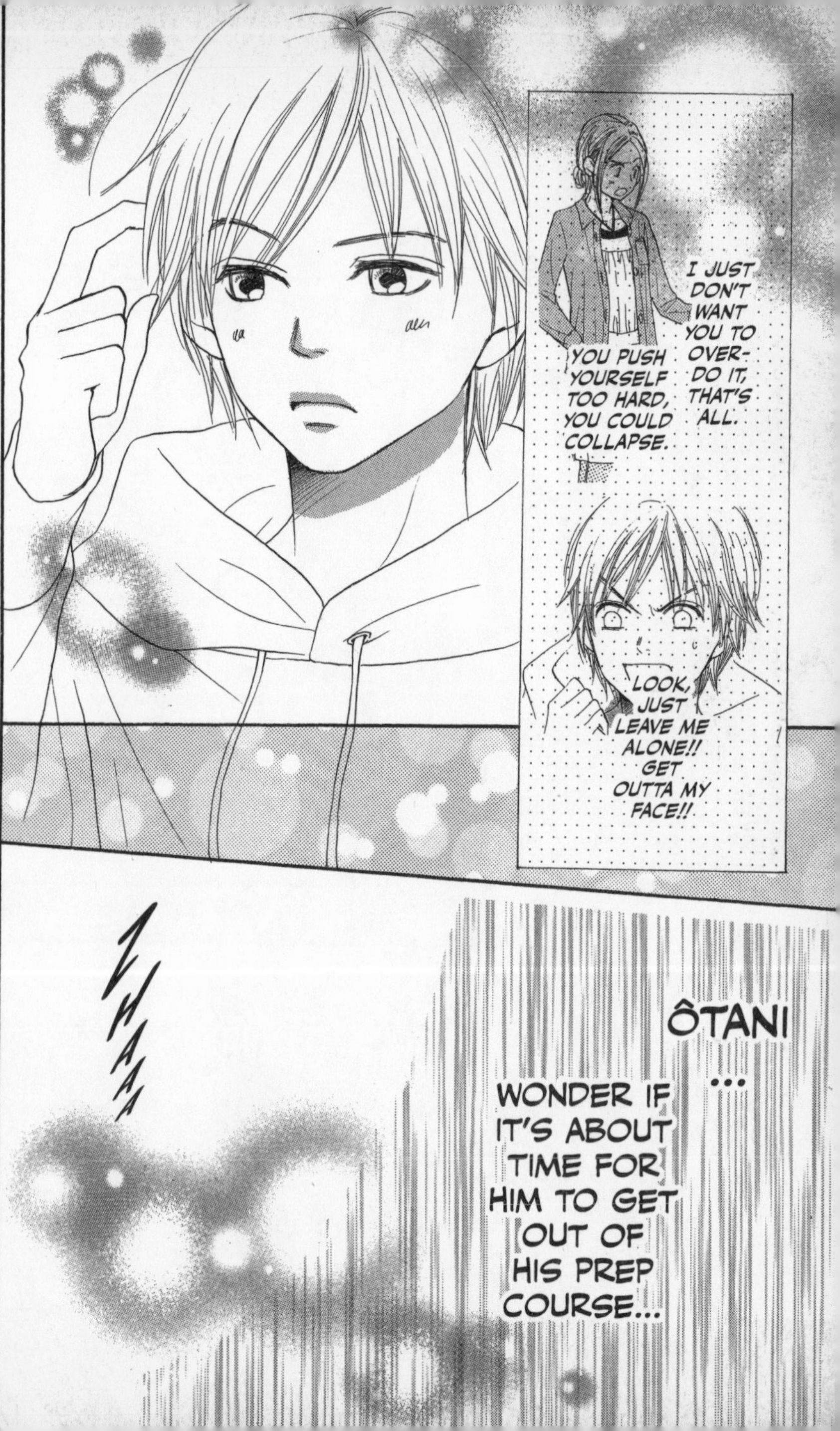
I JUST DON'T WANT YOU TO OVER-DO IT, THAT'S ALL.
YOU PUSH YOURSELF TOO HARD, YOU COULD COLLAPSE.
LOOK, JUST LEAVE ME ALONE!! GET OUTTA MY FACE!!
ÔTANI...
WONDER IF IT'S ABOUT TIME FOR HIM TO GET OUT OF HIS PREP COURSE...
VVHAAA

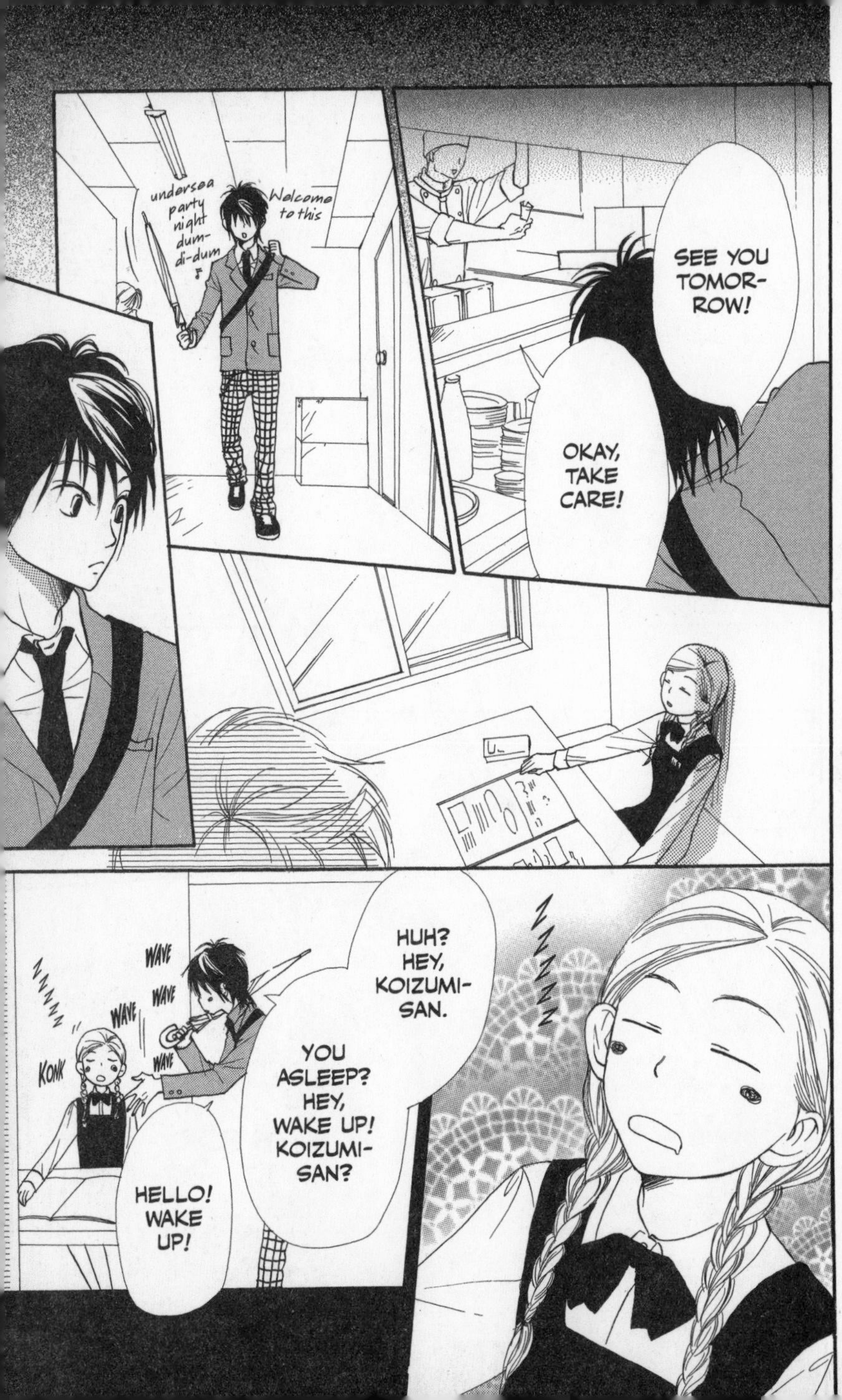
SEE YOU TOMORROW!
OKAY, TAKE CARE!
Welcome to this
undersea party night dum-di-dum
ZZZZZ
HUH? HEY, KOIZUMI-SAN.
YOU ASLEEP? HEY, WAKE UP! KOIZUMI-SAN?
WAVE
WAVE
WAVE
WAVE
ZZZZZ
KONK
HELLO! WAKE UP!

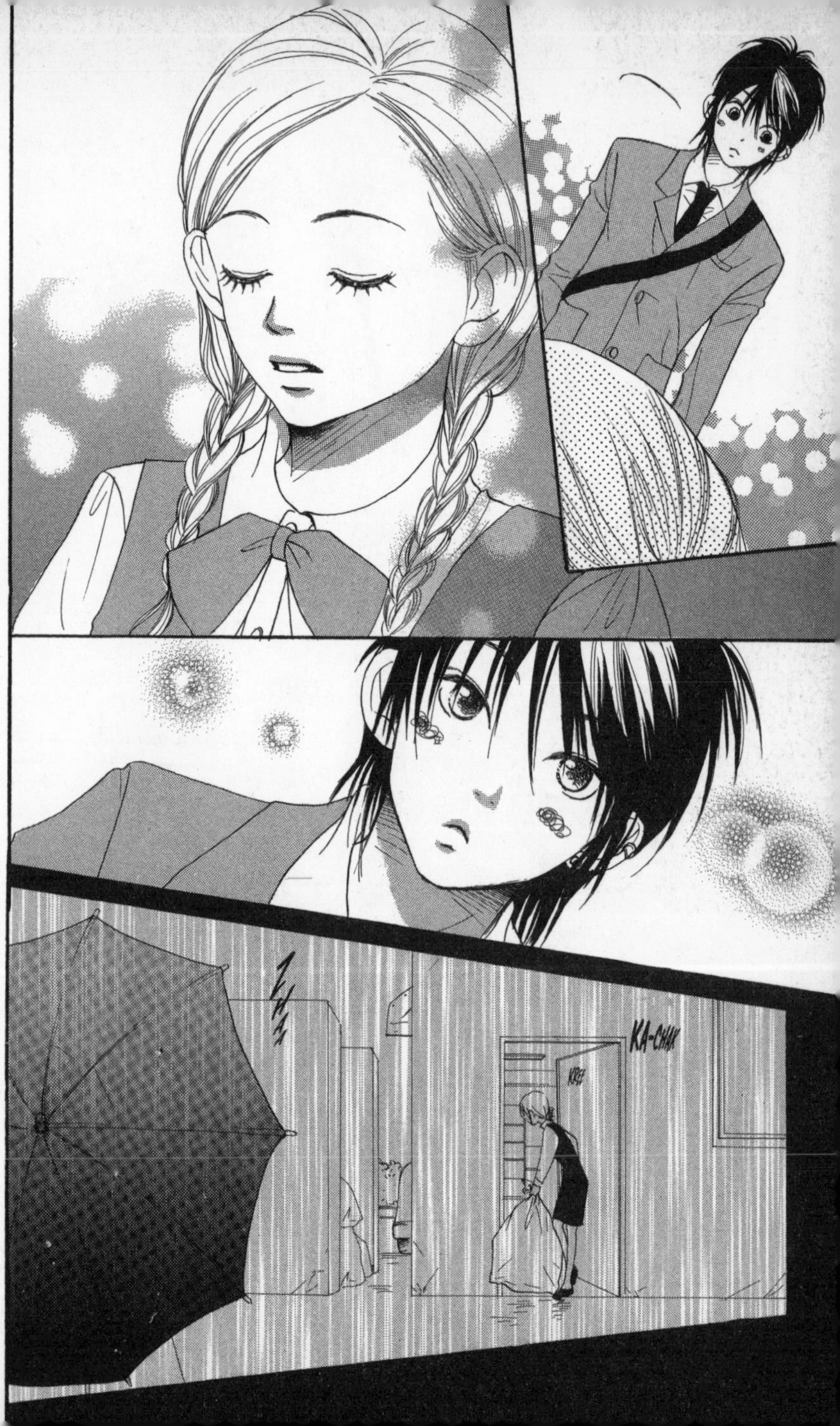
KA-CHAK

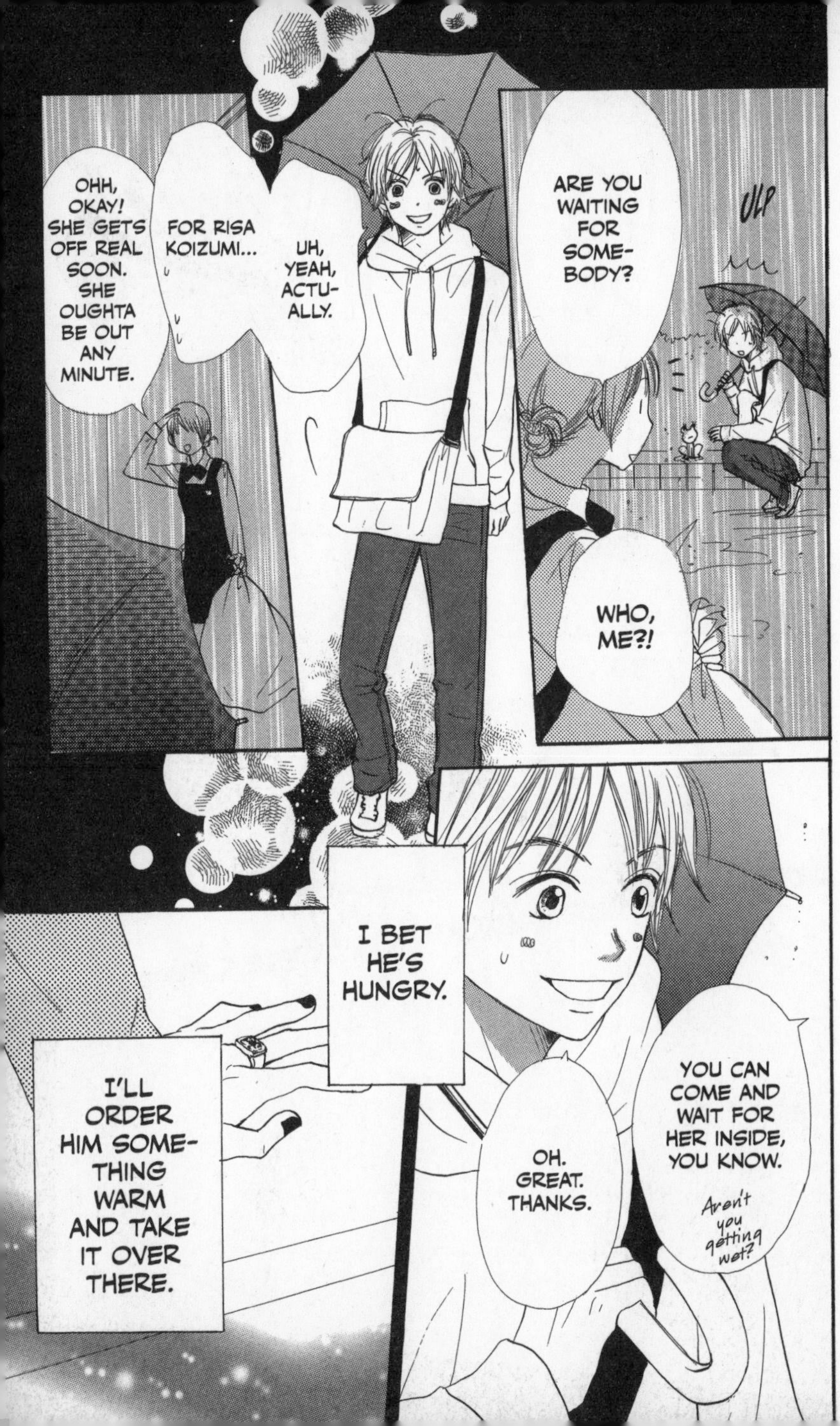
ULP
ARE YOU WAITING FOR SOME-BODY?
WHO, ME?!
UH, YEAH, ACTU-ALLY.
FOR RISA KOIZUMI...
OHH, OKAY! SHE GETS OFF REAL SOON. SHE OUGHTA BE OUT ANY MINUTE.
YOU CAN COME AND WAIT FOR HER INSIDE, YOU KNOW.
Aren't you getting wet?
OH. GREAT. THANKS.
I BET HE'S HUNGRY.
I'LL ORDER HIM SOME-THING WARM AND TAKE IT OVER THERE.

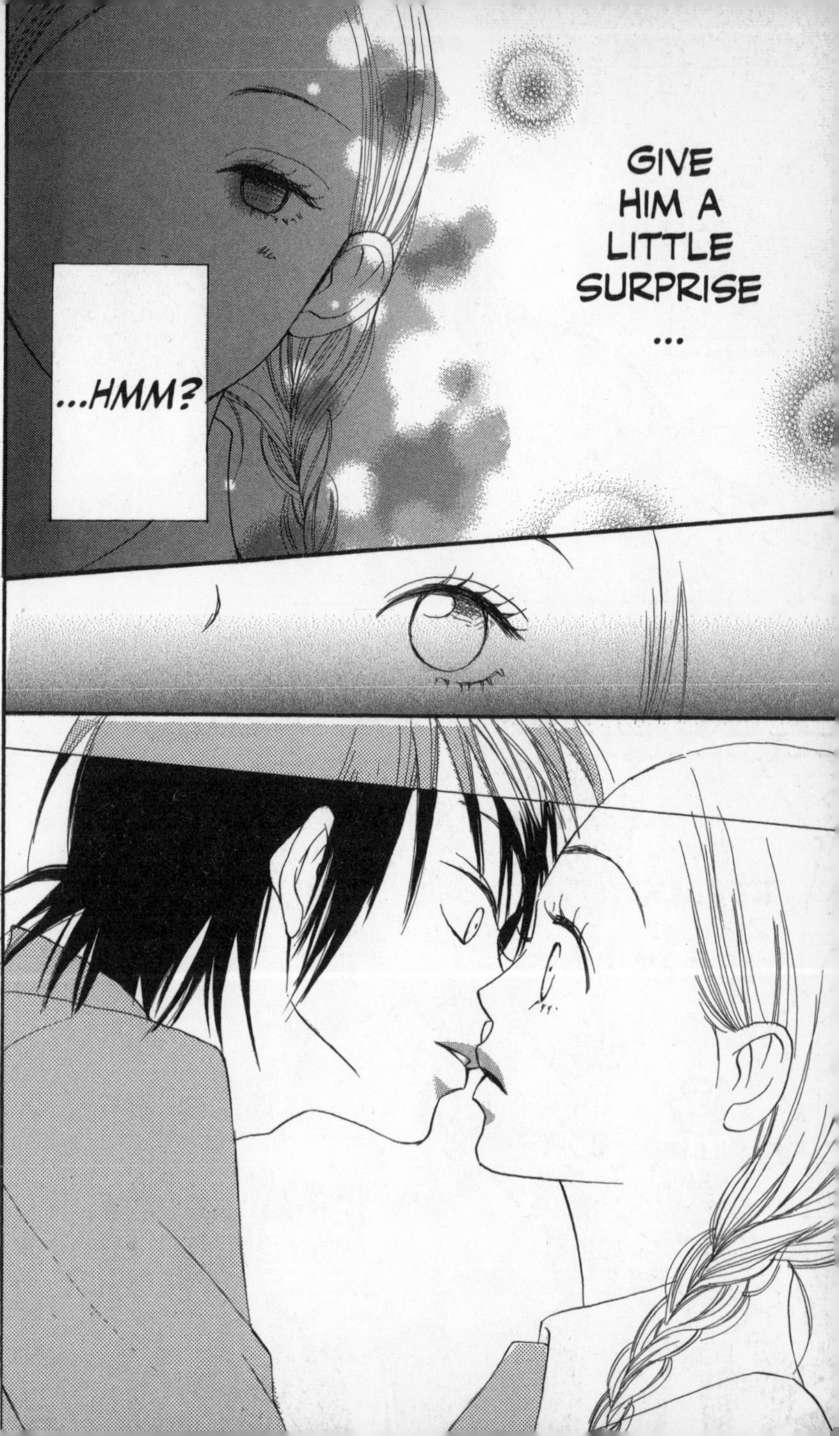
GIVE HIM A LITTLE SURPRISE ...
...HMM?

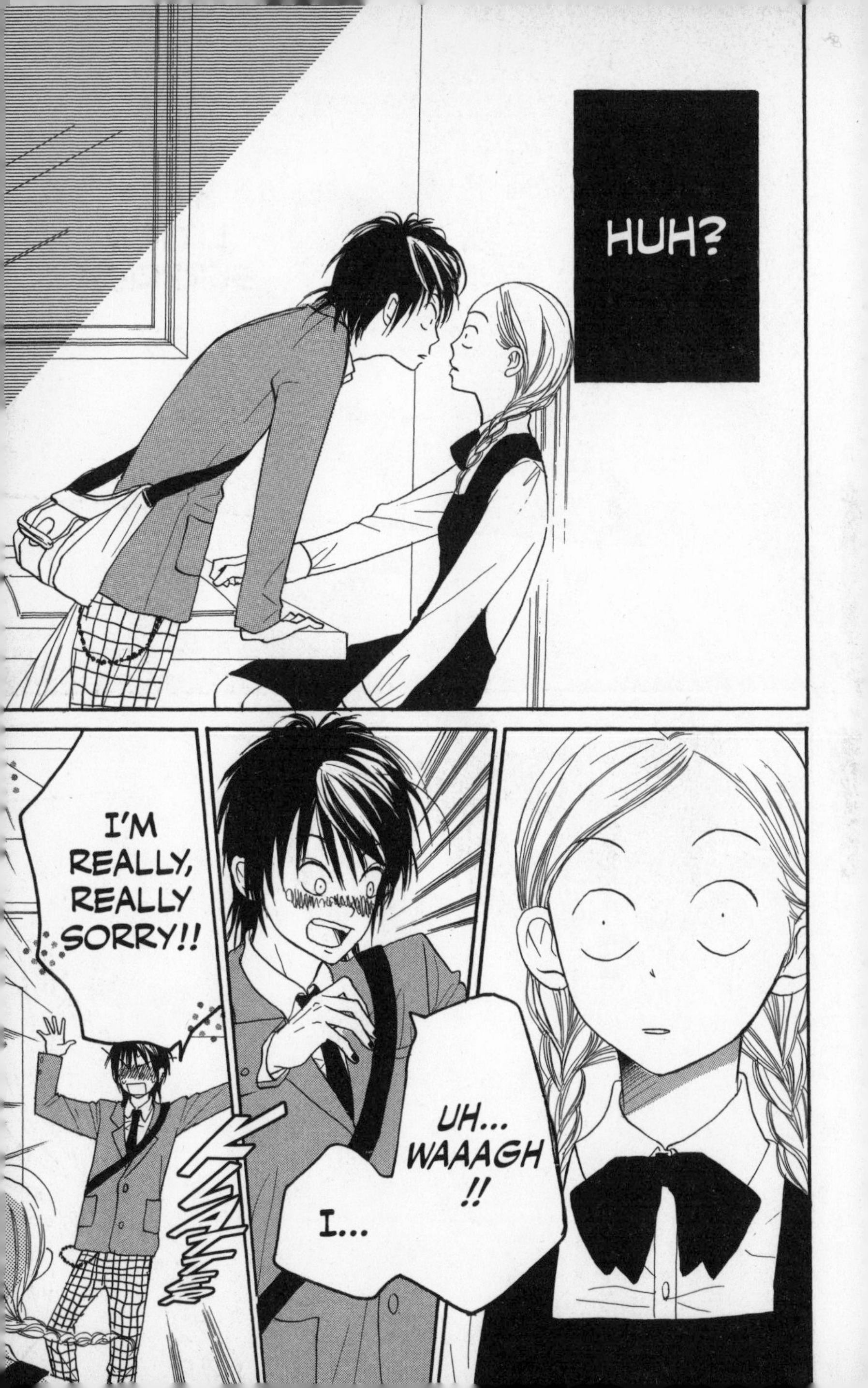
HUH?
UH... WAAAGH!!
I...
I'M REALLY, REALLY SORRY!!

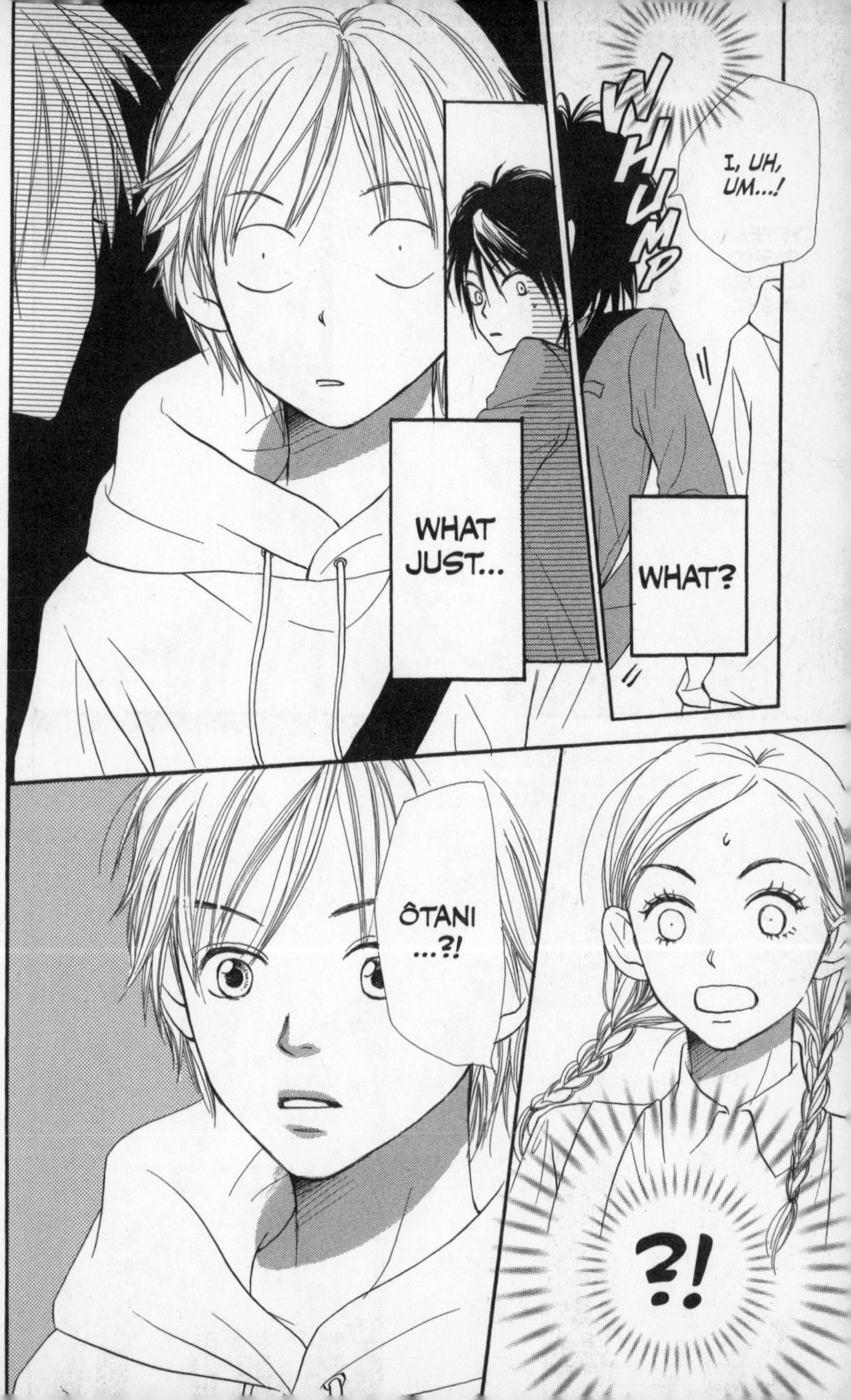
I, UH, UM...!
WHUMP
WHAT?
WHAT JUST...
?!
ÔTANI ...?!

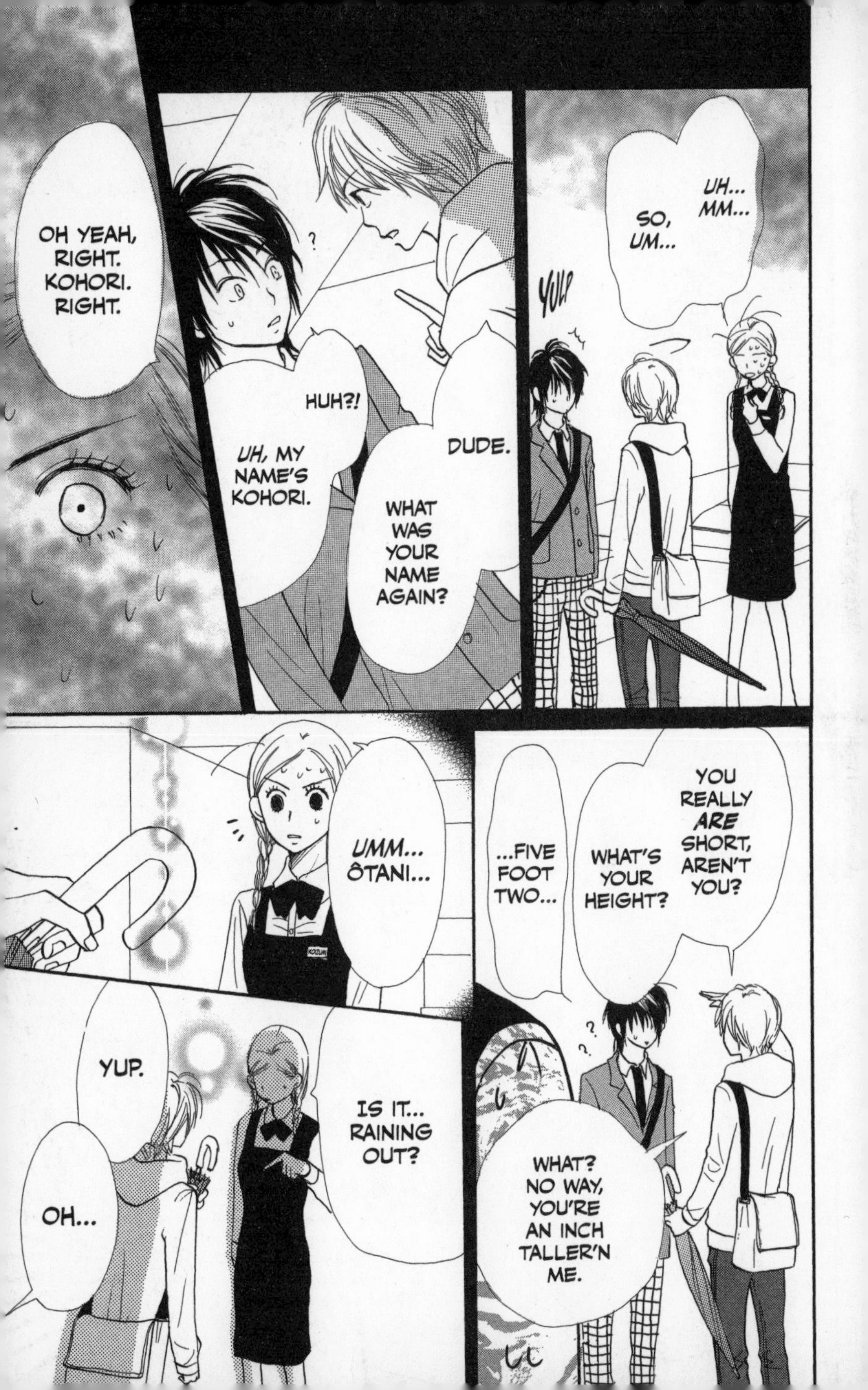
UH... MM...
SO, UM...
YULP
DUDE.
WHAT WAS YOUR NAME AGAIN?
HUH?!
UH, MY NAME'S KOHORI.
OH YEAH, RIGHT. KOHORI. RIGHT.
YOU REALLY ARE SHORT, AREN'T YOU?
WHAT'S YOUR HEIGHT?
...FIVE FOOT TWO...
WHAT? NO WAY, YOU'RE AN INCH TALLER'N ME.
UMM... ÔTANI...
IS IT... RAINING OUT?
YUP.
OH...

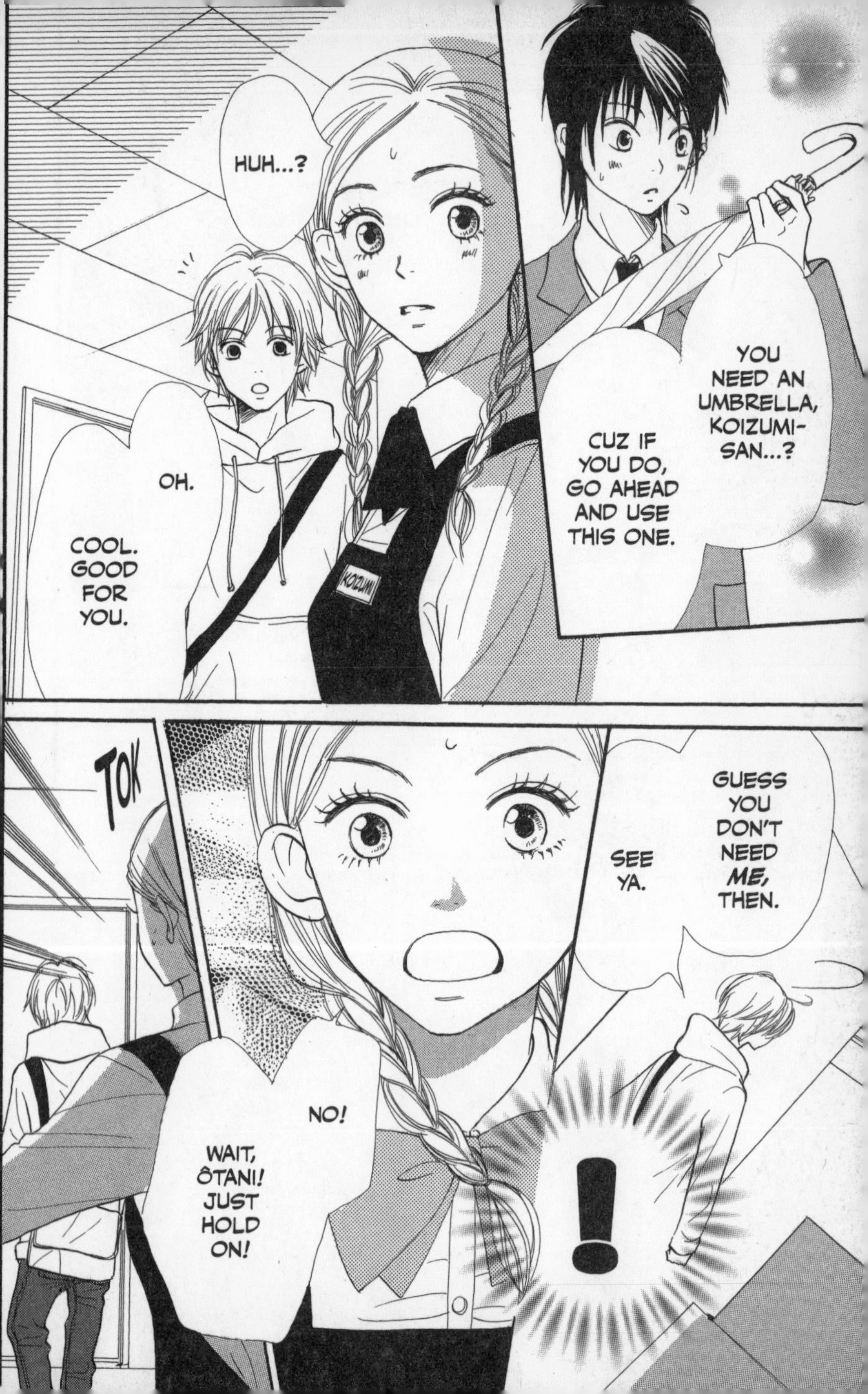
YOU NEED AN UMBRELLA, KOIZUMI-SAN...?
CUZ IF YOU DO, GO AHEAD AND USE THIS ONE.
HUH...?
OH.
COOL. GOOD FOR YOU.
KOIZUMI
GUESS YOU DON'T NEED *ME,* THEN.
SEE YA.
!
NO!
WAIT, ŌTANI! JUST HOLD ON!
TOK

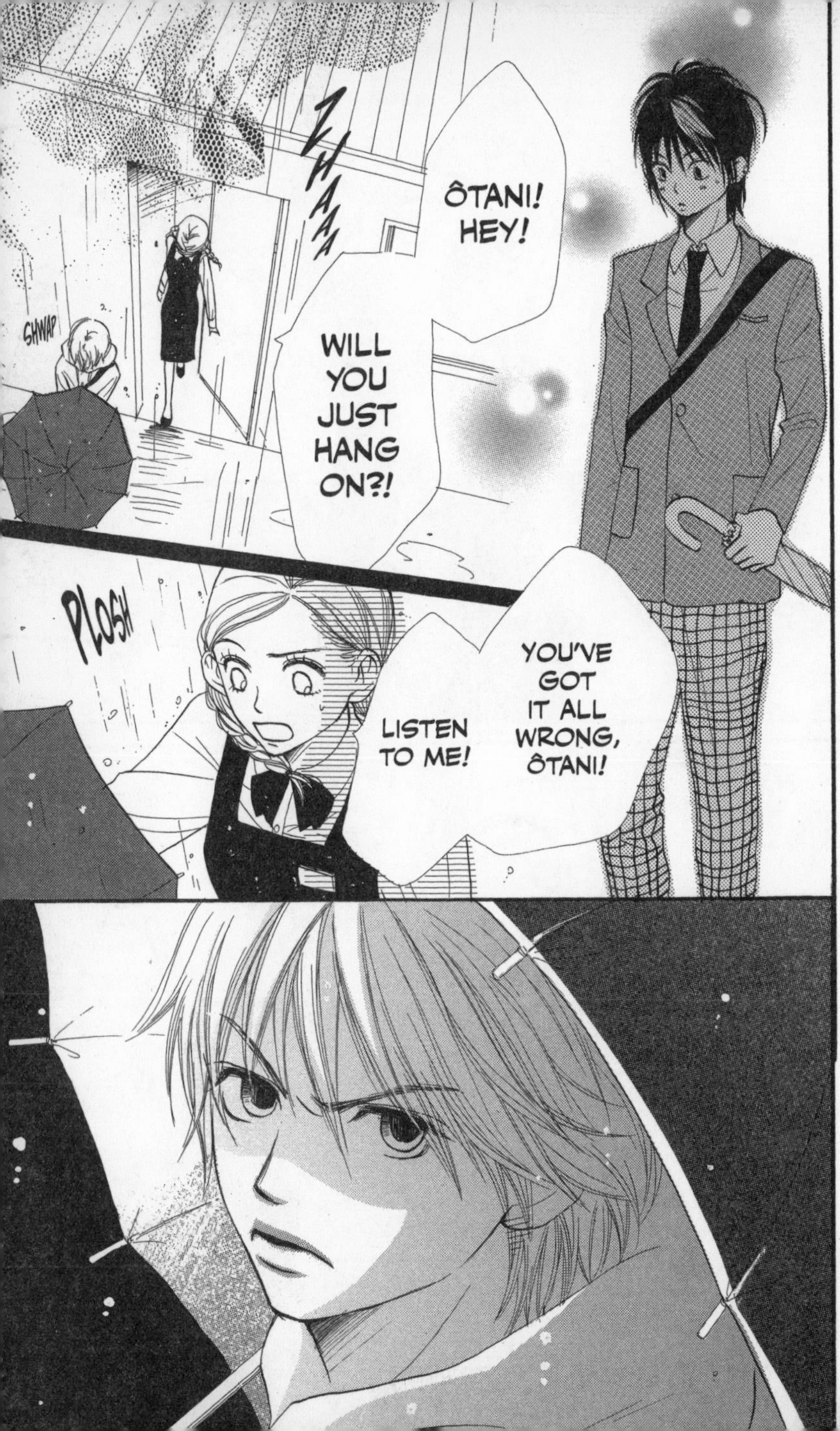
ZHAAAA
ÔTANI! HEY!
WILL YOU JUST HANG ON?!
SHWAP
PLOSH
YOU'VE GOT IT ALL WRONG, ÔTANI!
LISTEN TO ME!

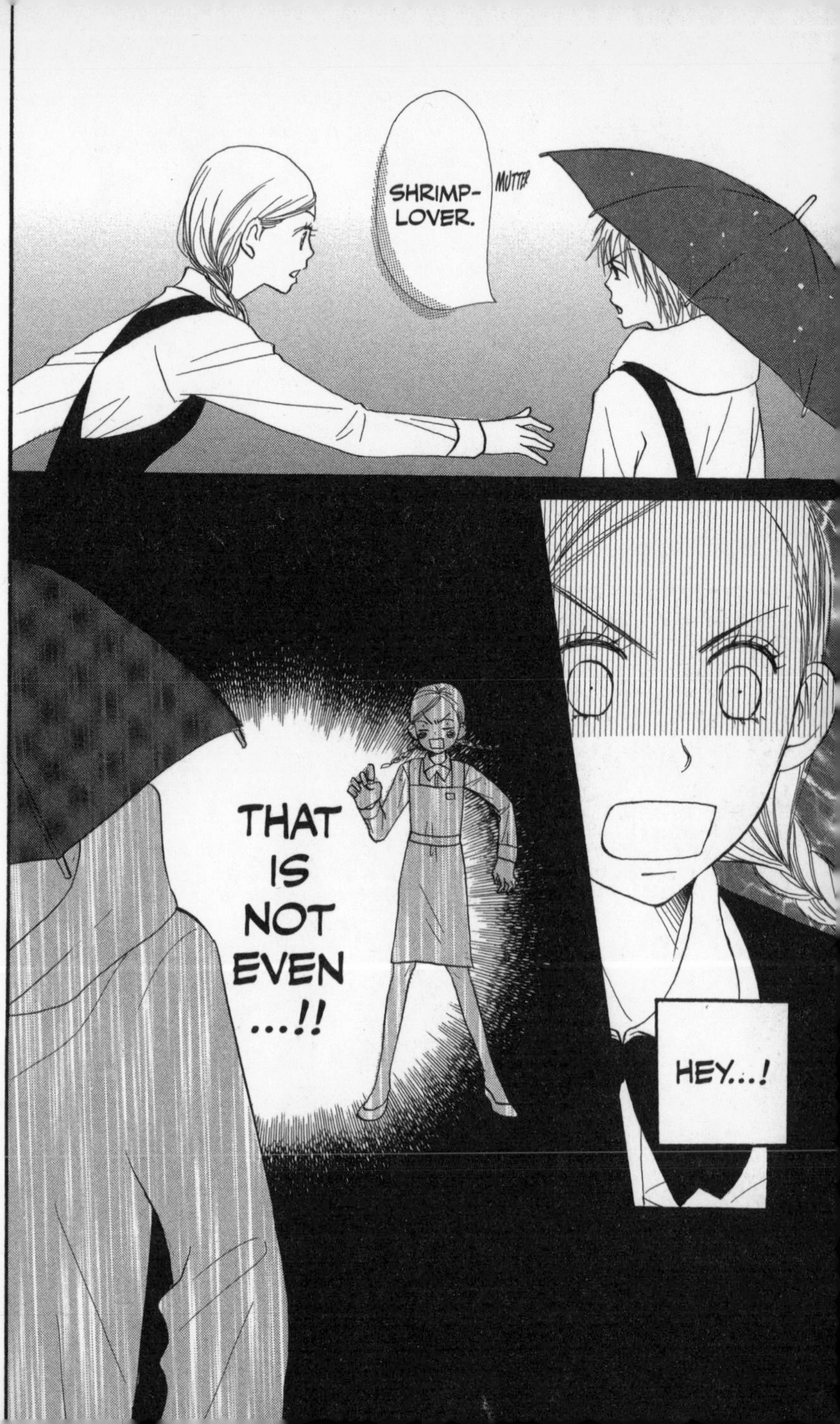
SHRIMP-LOVER.
MUTTER
HEY...!
THAT IS NOT EVEN ...!!

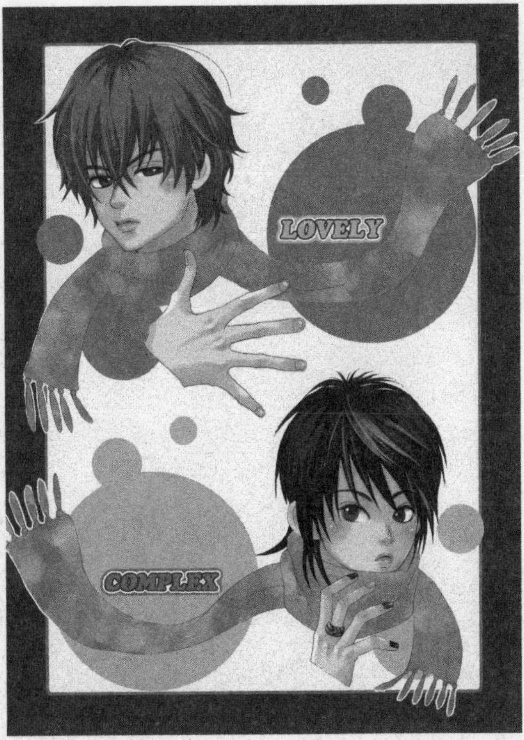
LOVELY
COMPLEX

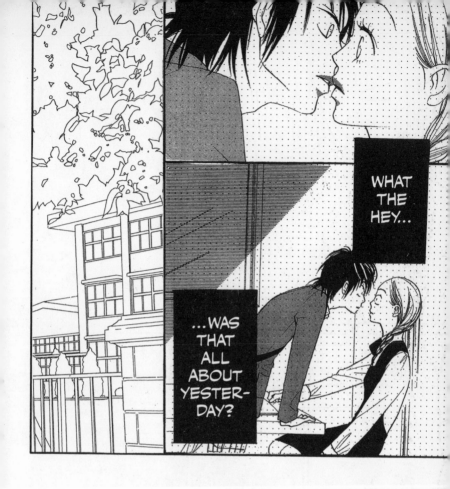

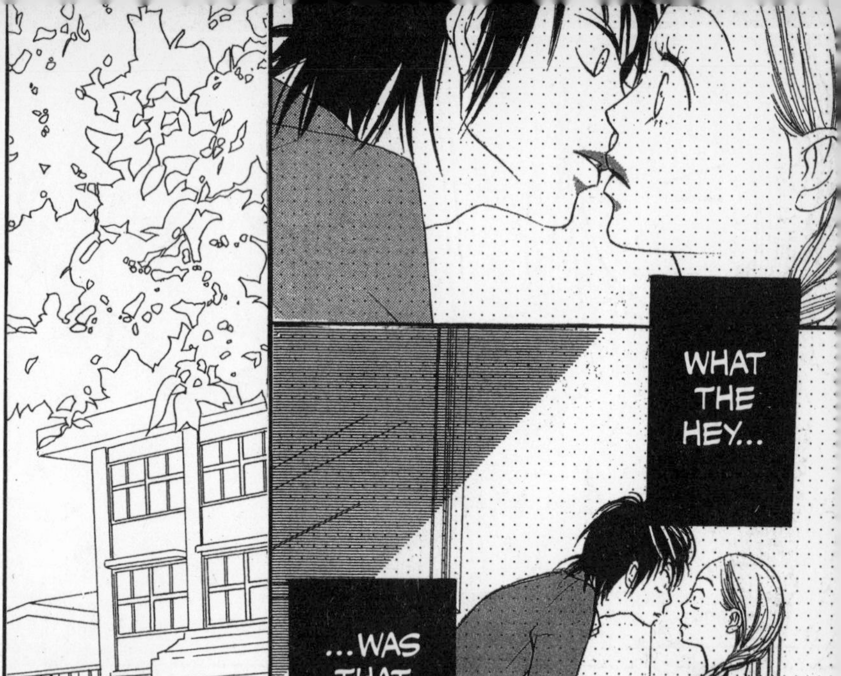
WHAT THE HEY...
...WAS THAT ALL ABOUT YESTER-DAY?

CHAPTER 38

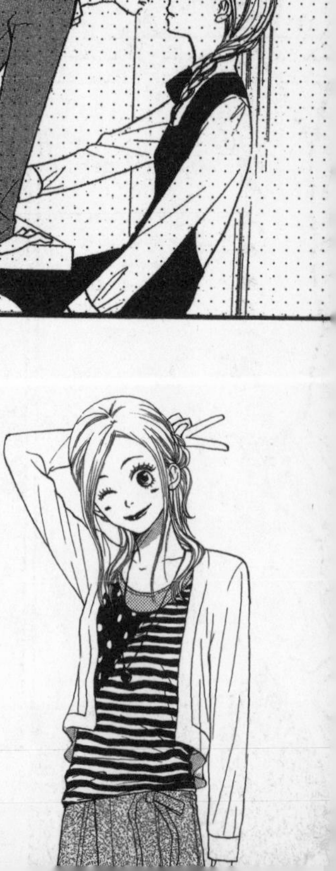

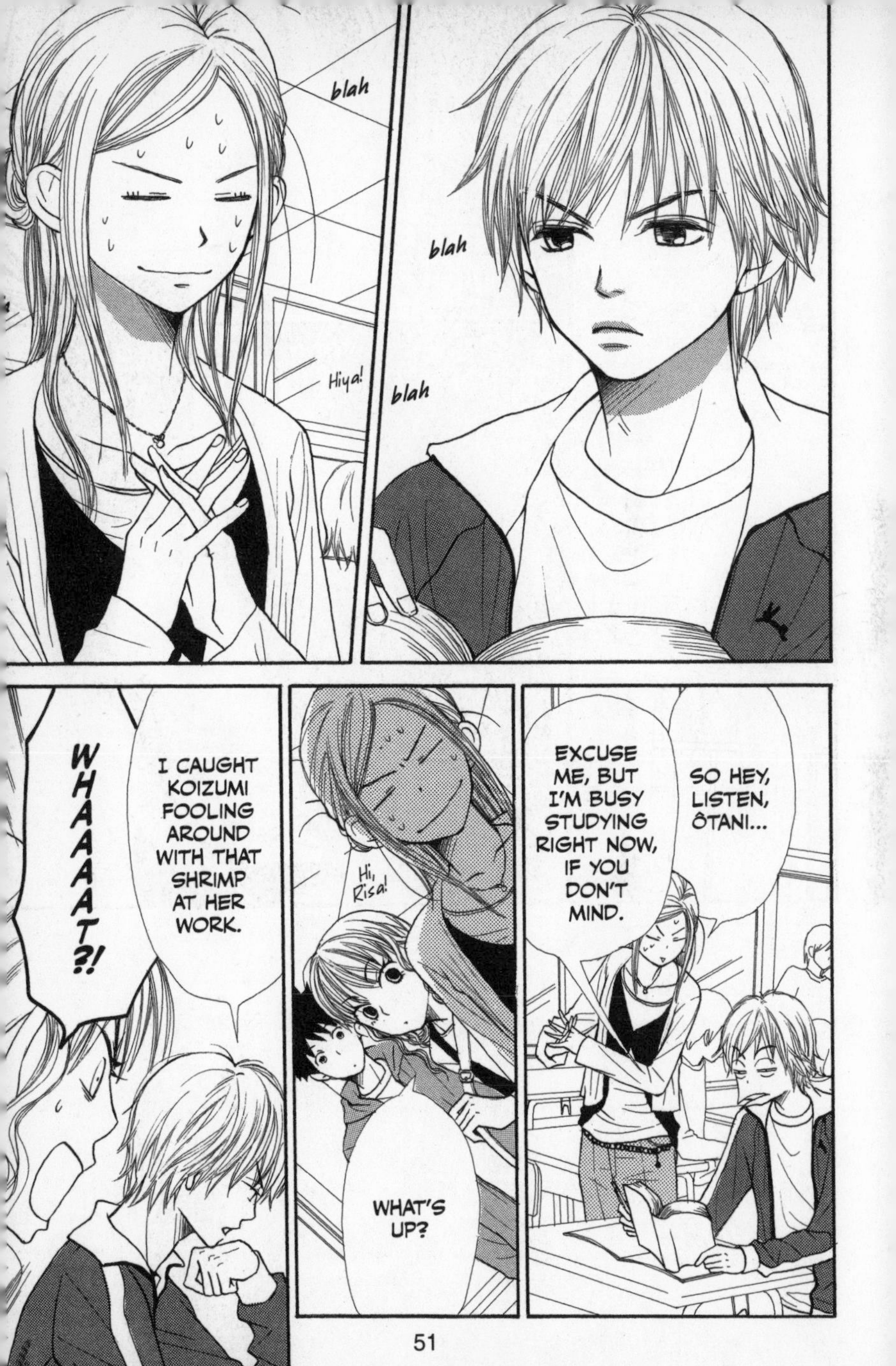
blah
blah
blah
Hiya!
SO HEY, LISTEN, ŌTANI...
EXCUSE ME, BUT I'M BUSY STUDYING RIGHT NOW, IF YOU DON'T MIND.
Hi, Risa!
WHAT'S UP?
I CAUGHT KOIZUMI FOOLING AROUND WITH THAT SHRIMP AT HER WORK.
WHAAAAAT?!

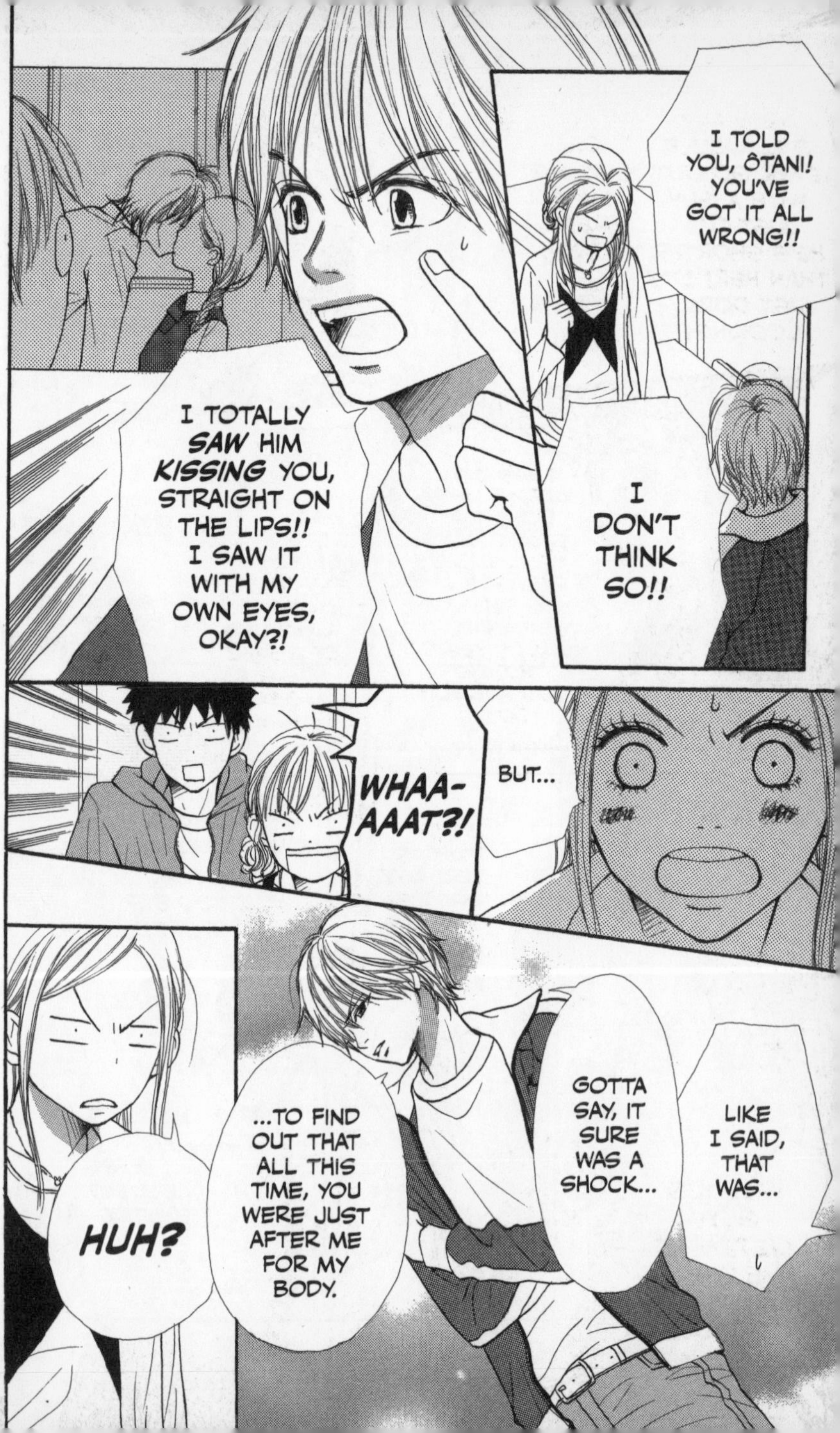
I TOLD YOU, ÔTANI! YOU'VE GOT IT ALL WRONG!!
I DON'T THINK SO!!
I TOTALLY SAW HIM KISSING YOU, STRAIGHT ON THE LIPS!! I SAW IT WITH MY OWN EYES, OKAY?!
BUT...
WHAAA-AAAT?!
LIKE I SAID, THAT WAS...
GOTTA SAY, IT SURE WAS A SHOCK...
...TO FIND OUT THAT ALL THIS TIME, YOU WERE JUST AFTER ME FOR MY BODY.
HUH?

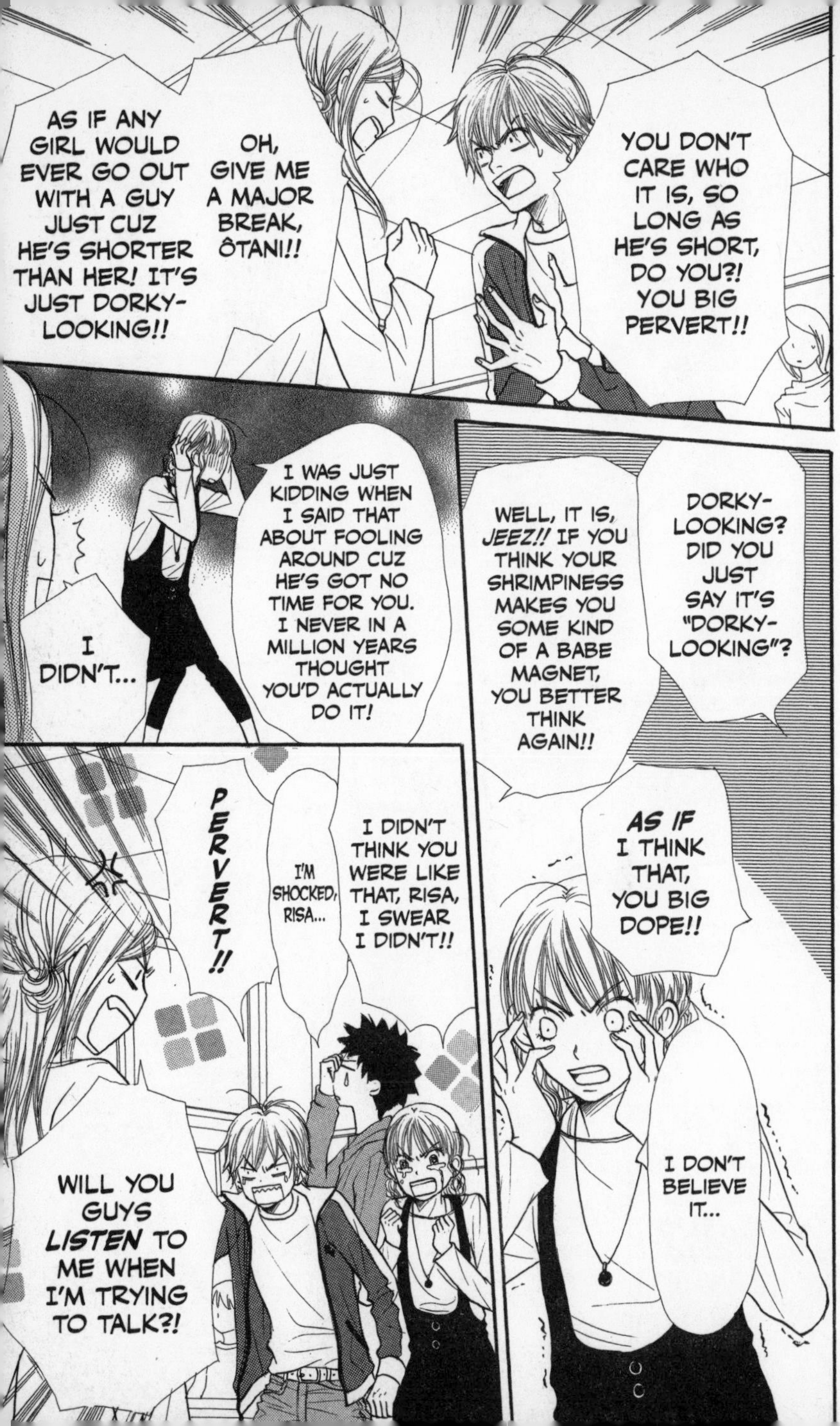
YOU DON'T CARE WHO IT IS, SO LONG AS HE'S SHORT, DO YOU?! YOU BIG PERVERT!!
OH, GIVE ME A MAJOR BREAK, ÔTANI!!
AS IF ANY GIRL WOULD EVER GO OUT WITH A GUY JUST CUZ HE'S SHORTER THAN HER! IT'S JUST DORKY-LOOKING!!
DORKY-LOOKING? DID YOU JUST SAY IT'S "DORKY-LOOKING"?
WELL, IT IS, JEEZ!! IF YOU THINK YOUR SHRIMPINESS MAKES YOU SOME KIND OF A BABE MAGNET, YOU BETTER THINK AGAIN!!
I WAS JUST KIDDING WHEN I SAID THAT ABOUT FOOLING AROUND CUZ HE'S GOT NO TIME FOR YOU. I NEVER IN A MILLION YEARS THOUGHT YOU'D ACTUALLY DO IT!
I DIDN'T...
AS IF I THINK THAT, YOU BIG DOPE!!
I DON'T BELIEVE IT...
I DIDN'T THINK YOU WERE LIKE THAT, RISA, I SWEAR I DIDN'T!!
I'M SHOCKED, RISA...
PERVERT!!
WILL YOU GUYS LISTEN TO ME WHEN I'M TRYING TO TALK?!

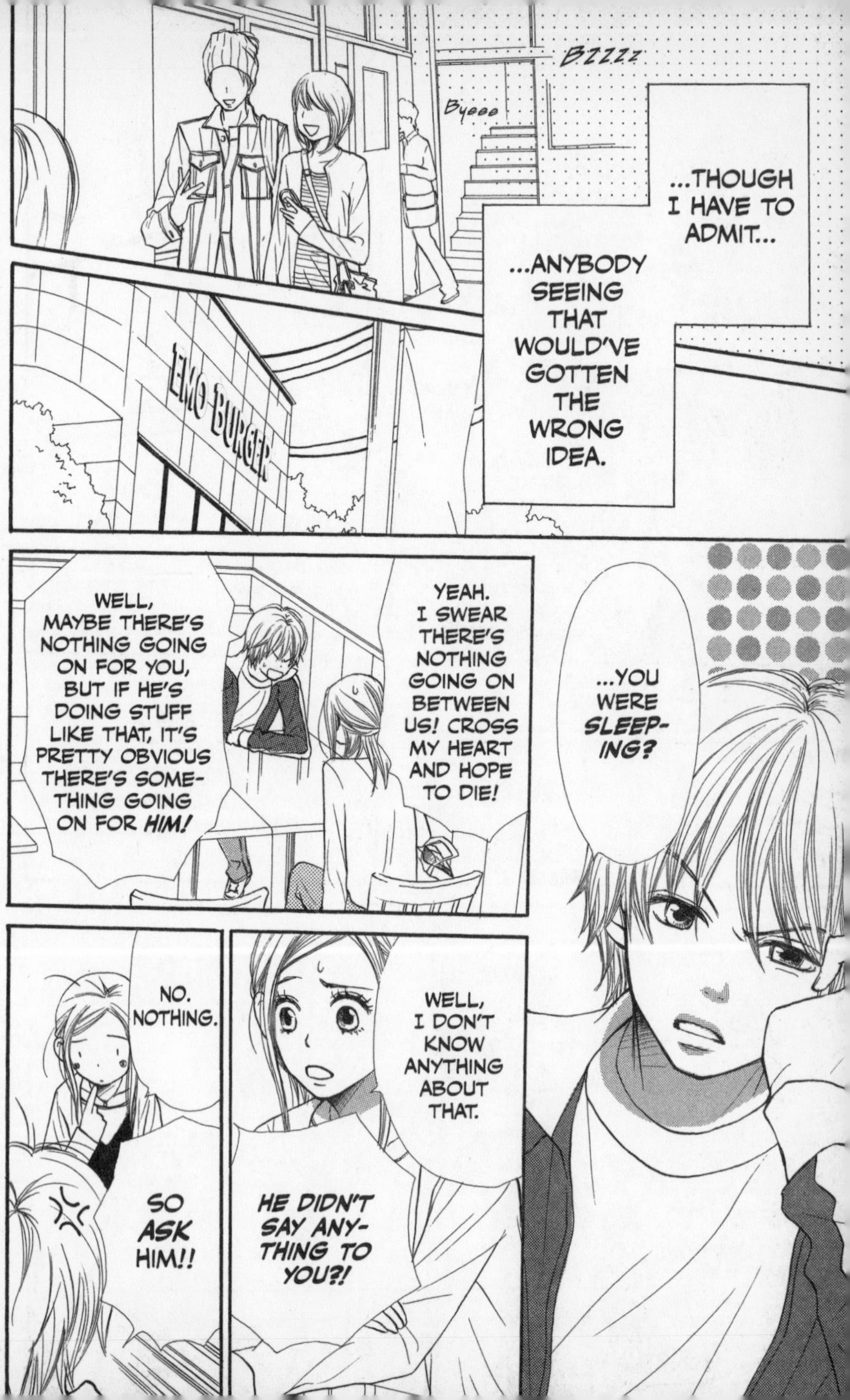
BZZZZ
Byeee
...THOUGH I HAVE TO ADMIT...
...ANYBODY SEEING THAT WOULD'VE GOTTEN THE WRONG IDEA.
EMO BURGER
...YOU WERE *SLEEPING?*
YEAH. I SWEAR THERE'S NOTHING GOING ON BETWEEN US! CROSS MY HEART AND HOPE TO DIE!
WELL, MAYBE THERE'S NOTHING GOING ON FOR YOU, BUT IF HE'S DOING STUFF LIKE THAT, IT'S PRETTY OBVIOUS THERE'S SOMETHING GOING ON FOR *HIM!*
WELL, I DON'T KNOW ANYTHING ABOUT THAT.
HE DIDN'T SAY ANYTHING TO YOU?!
NO. NOTHING.
SO *ASK* HIM!!

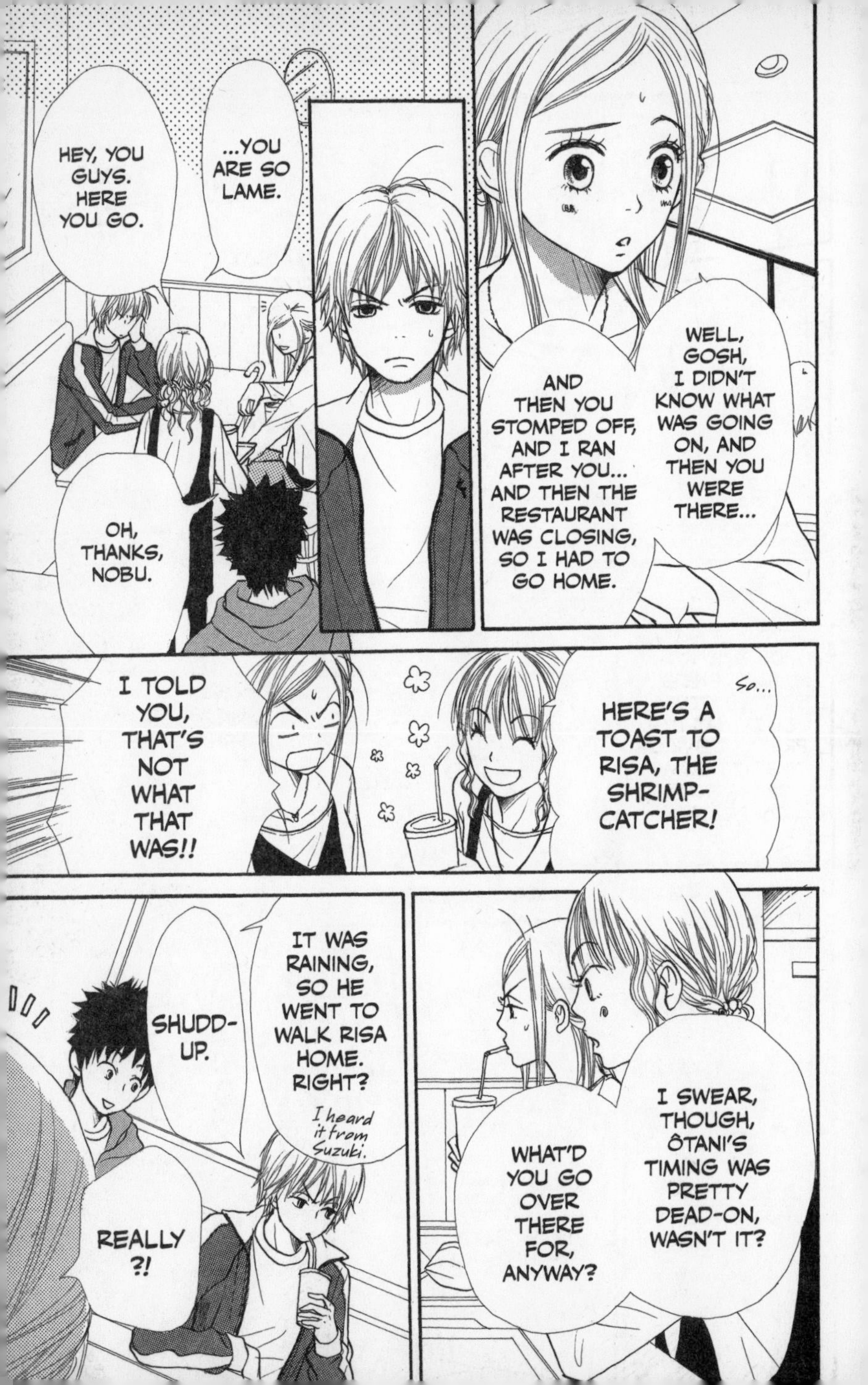
WELL, GOSH, I DIDN'T KNOW WHAT WAS GOING ON, AND THEN YOU WERE THERE...
AND THEN YOU STOMPED OFF, AND I RAN AFTER YOU... AND THEN THE RESTAURANT WAS CLOSING, SO I HAD TO GO HOME.
...YOU ARE SO LAME.
HEY, YOU GUYS. HERE YOU GO.
OH, THANKS, NOBU.
So...
HERE'S A TOAST TO RISA, THE SHRIMP-CATCHER!
I TOLD YOU, THAT'S NOT WHAT THAT WAS!!
I SWEAR, THOUGH, ŌTANI'S TIMING WAS PRETTY DEAD-ON, WASN'T IT?
WHAT'D YOU GO OVER THERE FOR, ANYWAY?
IT WAS RAINING, SO HE WENT TO WALK RISA HOME. RIGHT?
I heard it from Suzuki.
SHUDD-UP.
REALLY ?!

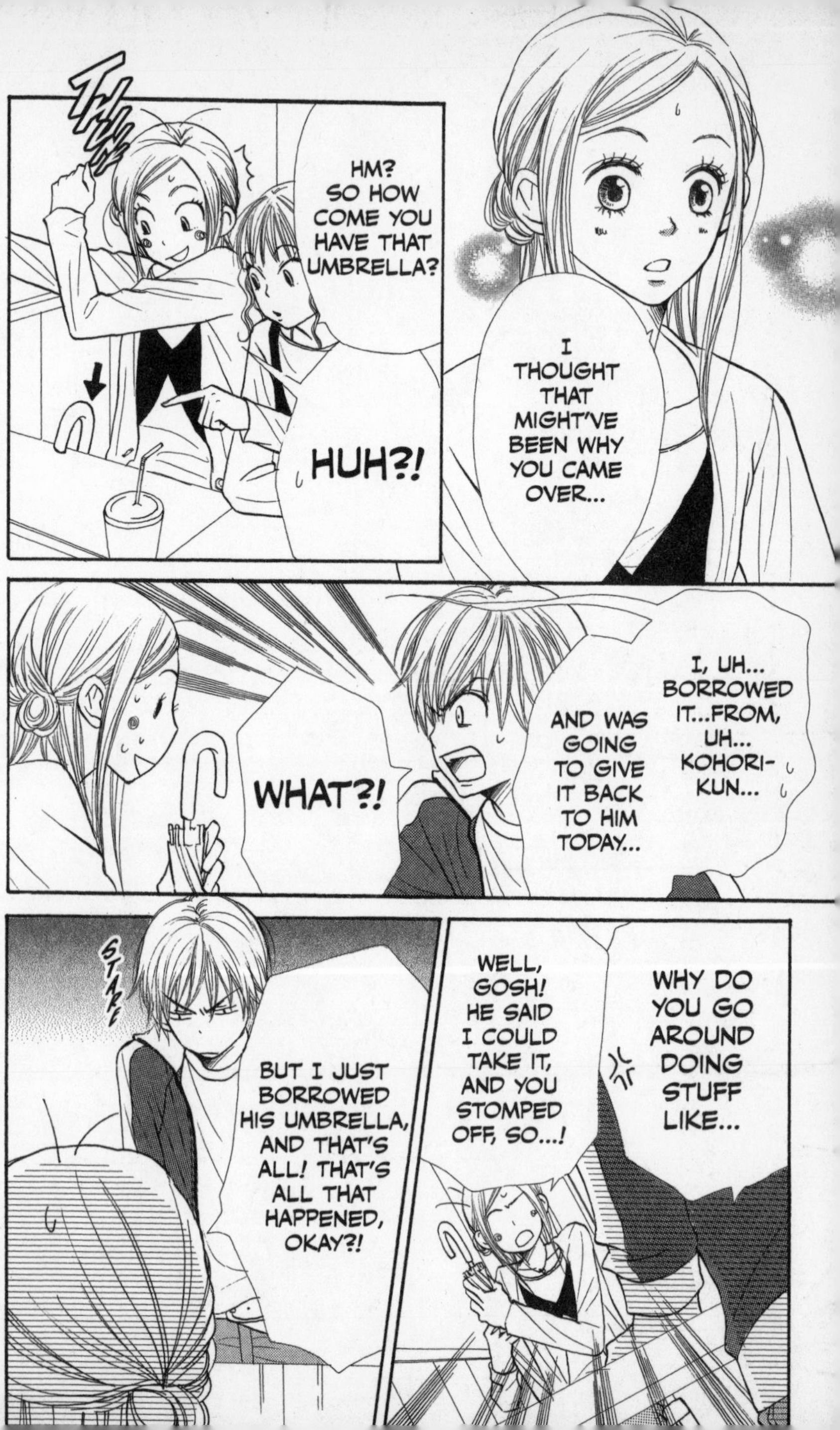
I THOUGHT THAT MIGHT'VE BEEN WHY YOU CAME OVER...
HM? SO HOW COME YOU HAVE THAT UMBRELLA?
HUH?!
I, UH... BORROWED IT...FROM, UH... KOHORI-KUN...
AND WAS GOING TO GIVE IT BACK TO HIM TODAY...
WHAT?!
WHY DO YOU GO AROUND DOING STUFF LIKE...
WELL, GOSH! HE SAID I COULD TAKE IT, AND YOU STOMPED OFF, SO...!
STARE
BUT I JUST BORROWED HIS UMBRELLA, AND THAT'S ALL! THAT'S ALL THAT HAPPENED, OKAY?!

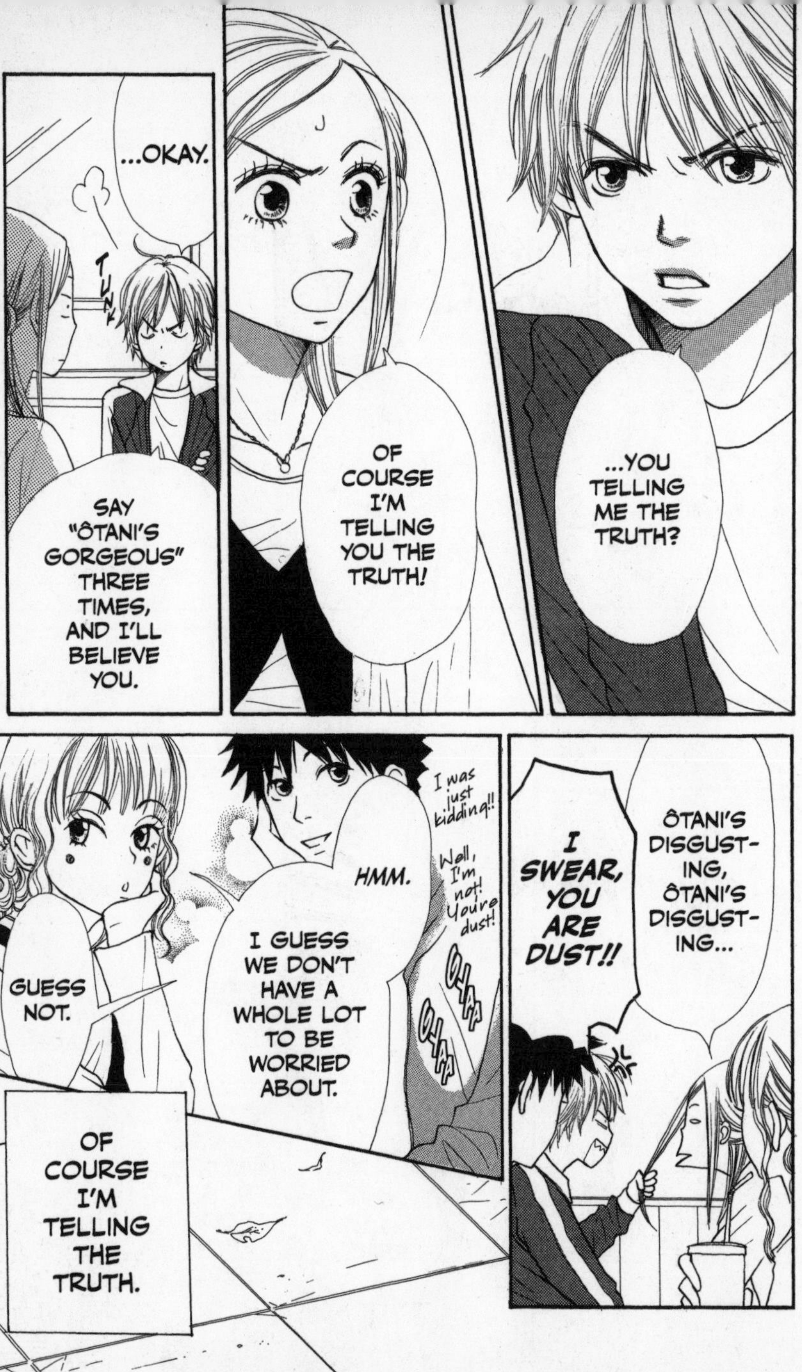
...YOU TELLING ME THE TRUTH?
OF COURSE I'M TELLING YOU THE TRUTH!
...OKAY.
TUNK
SAY "ÔTANI'S GORGEOUS" THREE TIMES, AND I'LL BELIEVE YOU.
ÔTANI'S DISGUST-ING, ÔTANI'S DISGUST-ING...
I SWEAR, YOU ARE DUST!!
I was just kidding!!
Well, I'm not! You're dust!
HMM.
I GUESS WE DON'T HAVE A WHOLE LOT TO BE WORRIED ABOUT.
GUESS NOT.
OF COURSE I'M TELLING THE TRUTH.

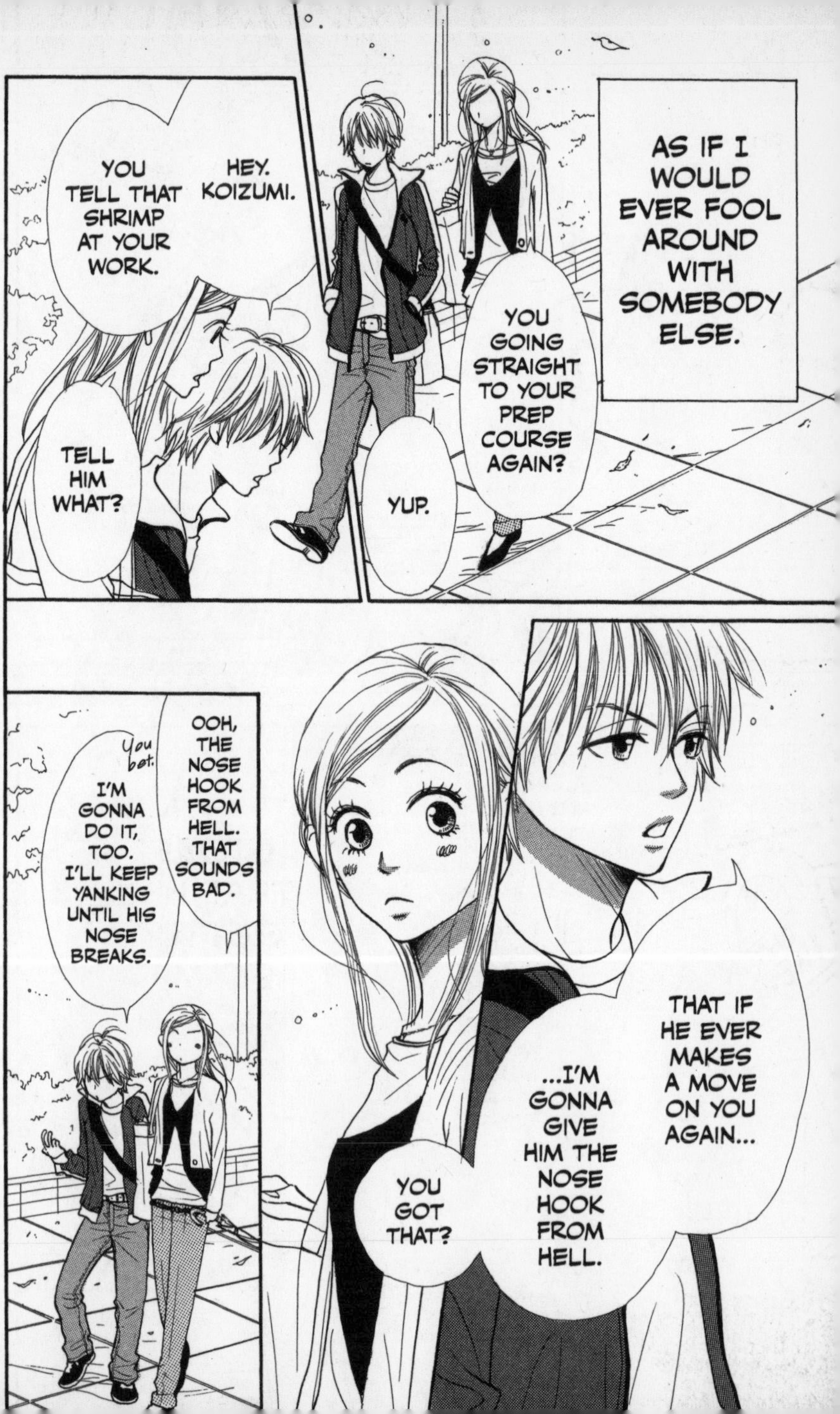
AS IF I WOULD EVER FOOL AROUND WITH SOMEBODY ELSE.
YOU GOING STRAIGHT TO YOUR PREP COURSE AGAIN?
YUP.
HEY. KOIZUMI.
YOU TELL THAT SHRIMP AT YOUR WORK.
TELL HIM WHAT?
THAT IF HE EVER MAKES A MOVE ON YOU AGAIN...
...I'M GONNA GIVE HIM THE NOSE HOOK FROM HELL.
YOU GOT THAT?
OOH, THE NOSE HOOK FROM HELL. THAT SOUNDS BAD.
You bet.
I'M GONNA DO IT, TOO. I'LL KEEP YANKING UNTIL HIS NOSE BREAKS.

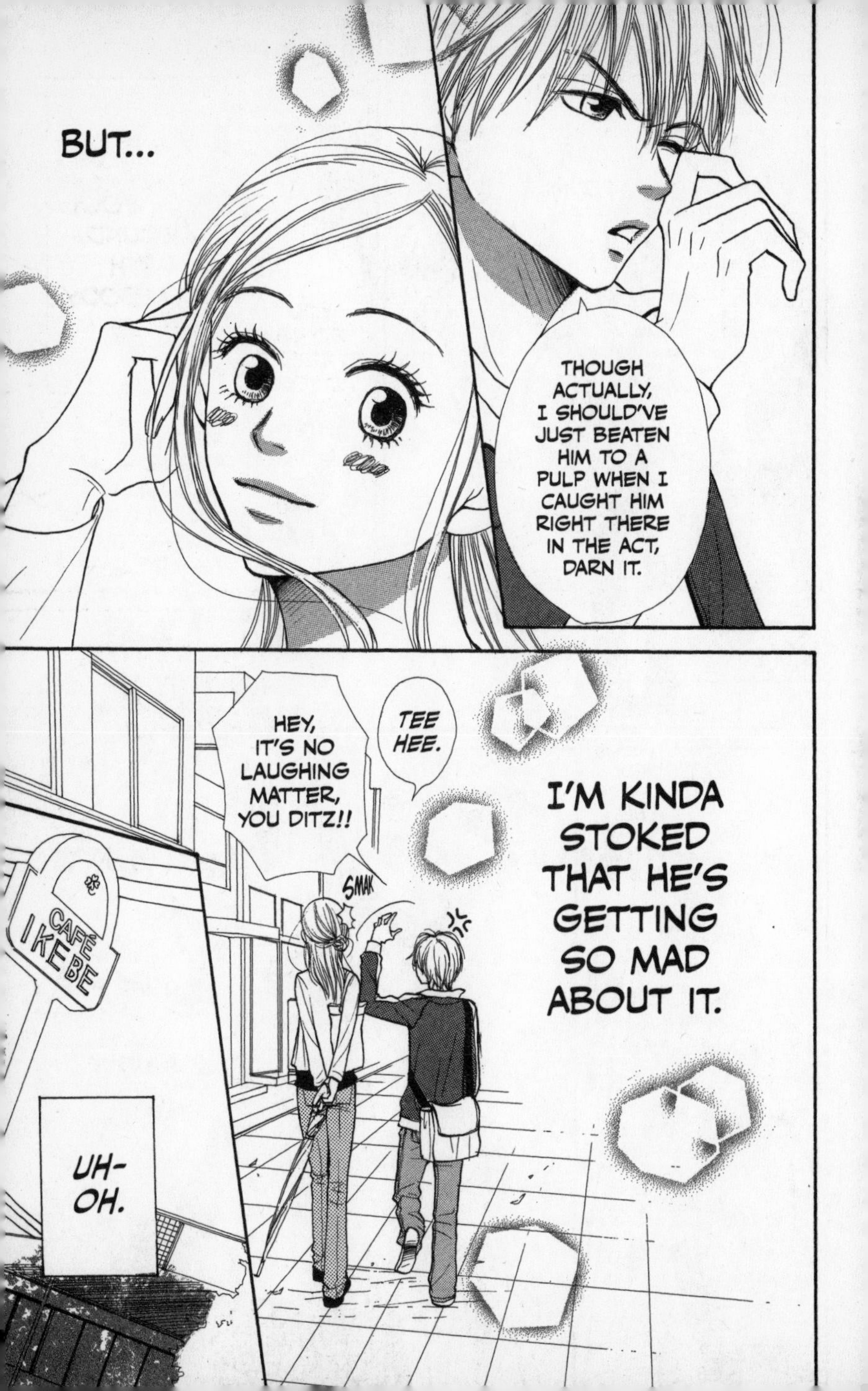
THOUGH ACTUALLY, I SHOULD'VE JUST BEATEN HIM TO A PULP WHEN I CAUGHT HIM RIGHT THERE IN THE ACT, DARN IT.
BUT...
I'M KINDA STOKED THAT HE'S GETTING SO MAD ABOUT IT.
TEE HEE.
HEY, IT'S NO LAUGHING MATTER, YOU DITZ!!
SMAK
CAFÉ IKEBE
UH-OH.

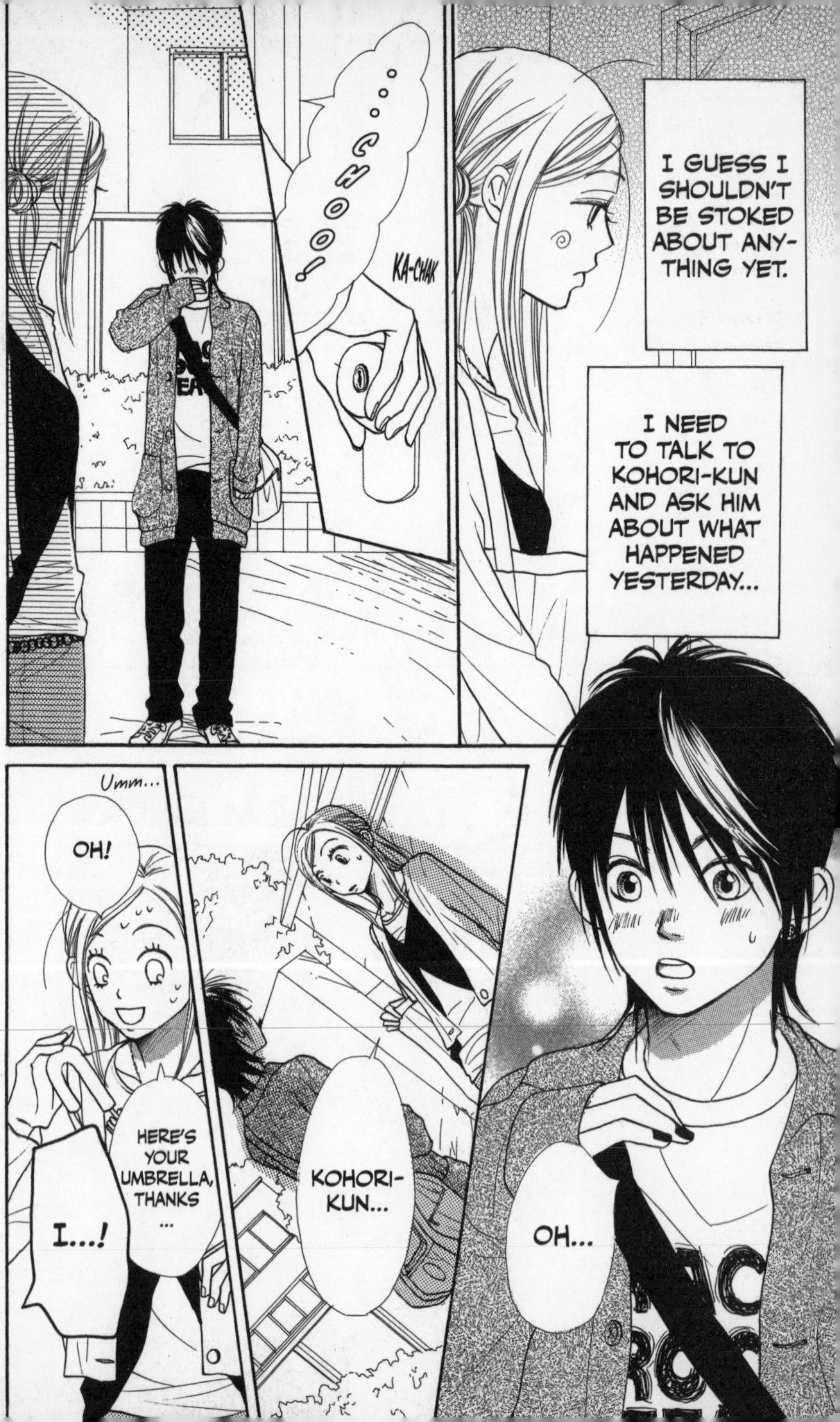
I GUESS I SHOULDN'T BE STOKED ABOUT ANYTHING YET.
I NEED TO TALK TO KOHORI-KUN AND ASK HIM ABOUT WHAT HAPPENED YESTERDAY...
...CHOO!
KA-CHAK
OH...
KOHORI-KUN...
Umm...
OH!
HERE'S YOUR UMBRELLA, THANKS ...
I...!

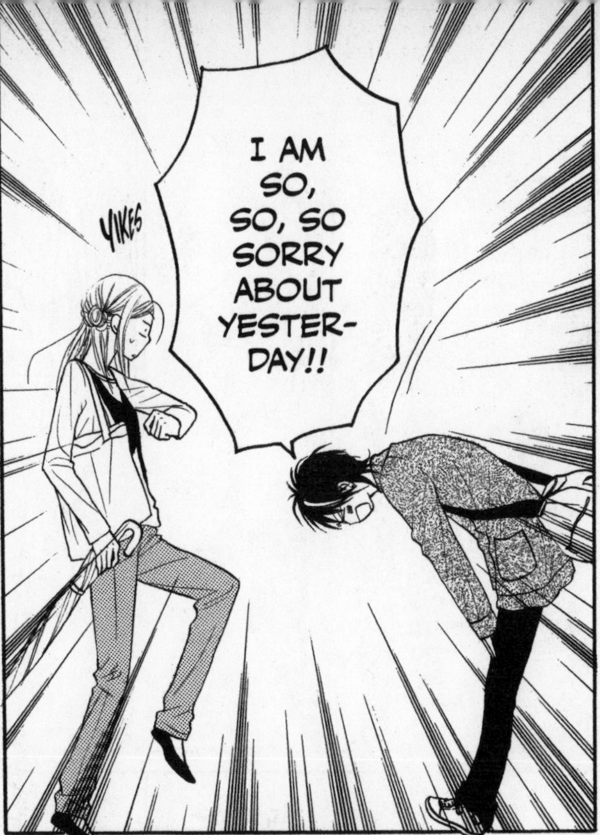
I AM SO, SO, SO SORRY ABOUT YESTER-DAY!!
YIKES

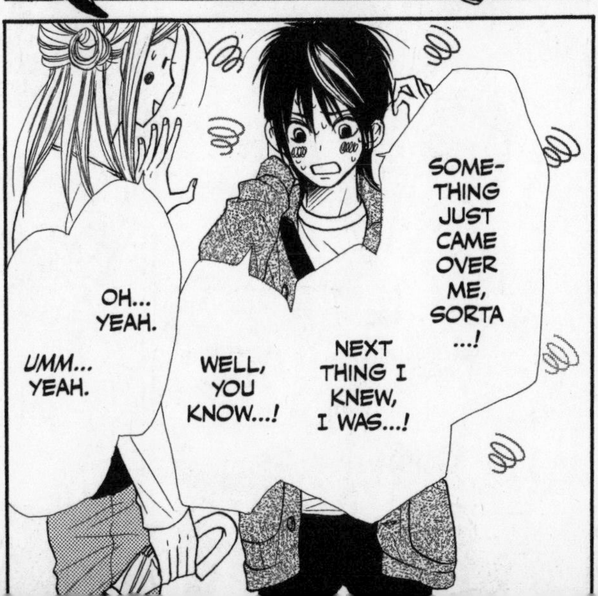
SOME-THING JUST CAME OVER ME, SORTA ...!
NEXT THING I KNEW, I WAS...!
WELL, YOU KNOW...!
OH... YEAH.
UMM... YEAH.

☆2

A second Love☆Com drama CD's been released! Wow... boom boom boom pa-twoo pa-twoo!

In terms of the story, it packs in episodes from Vol. 4 to the first part of Vol. 5. And I mean, really packs them in!

The same voice actors who appeared in the first CD gave great performances again in this one. There sure is a lot of talking in this manga... I felt kinda bad...

The new CD has Umibozu, Mrs. Boze, and Mighty appearing for the first time. The voice actors who play them are really great.

If you haven't heard it yet, give it a listen! You'll love it!
pa-twoon pa-twoon

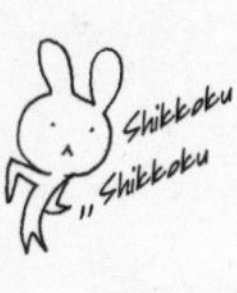
Shikkoku
Shikkoku

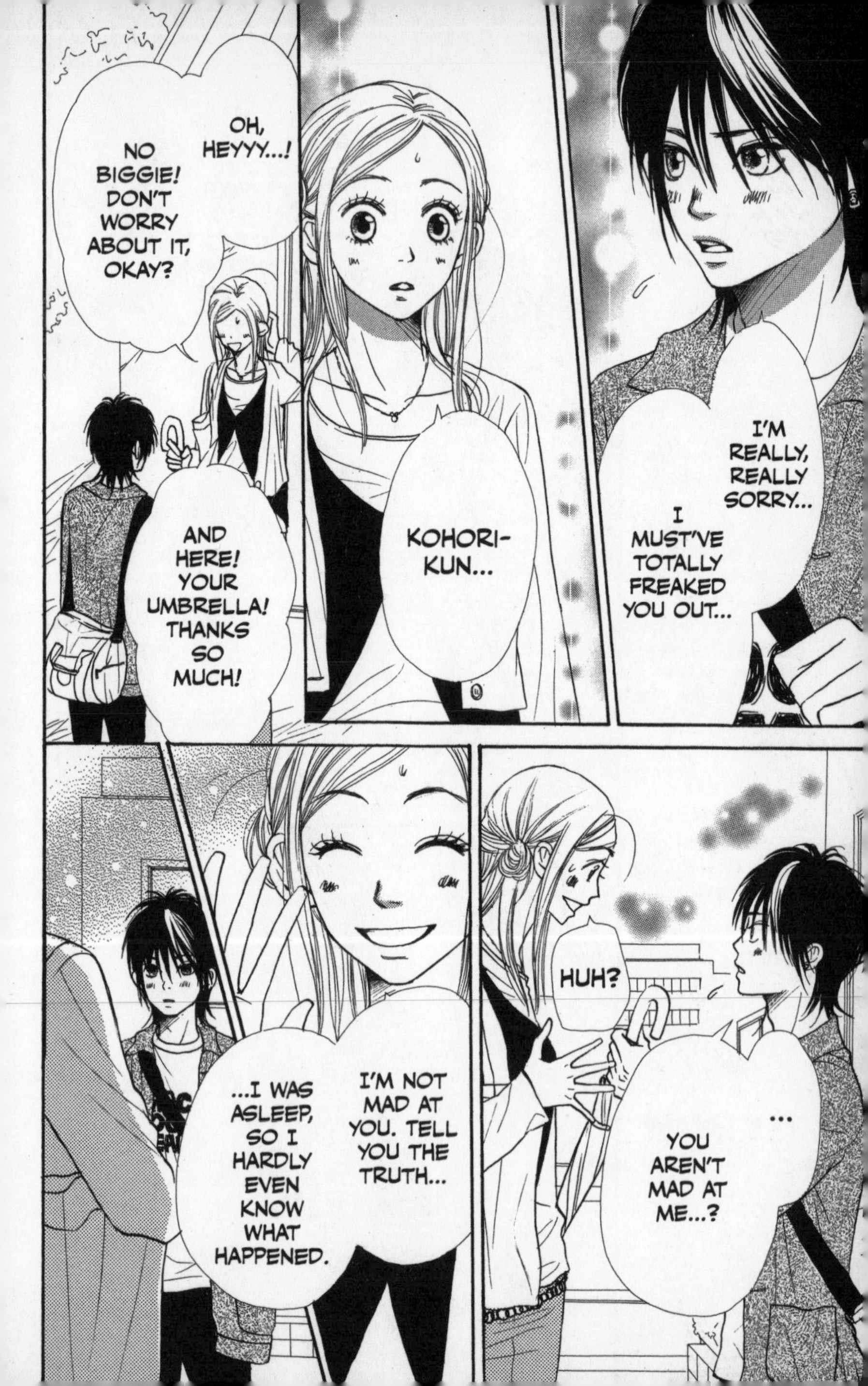
I'M REALLY, REALLY SORRY...
I MUST'VE TOTALLY FREAKED YOU OUT...
KOHORI-KUN...
OH, HEYYY...!
NO BIGGIE! DON'T WORRY ABOUT IT, OKAY?
AND HERE! YOUR UMBRELLA! THANKS SO MUCH!
HUH?
...
YOU AREN'T MAD AT ME...?
I'M NOT MAD AT YOU. TELL YOU THE TRUTH...
...I WAS ASLEEP, SO I HARDLY EVEN KNOW WHAT HAPPENED.

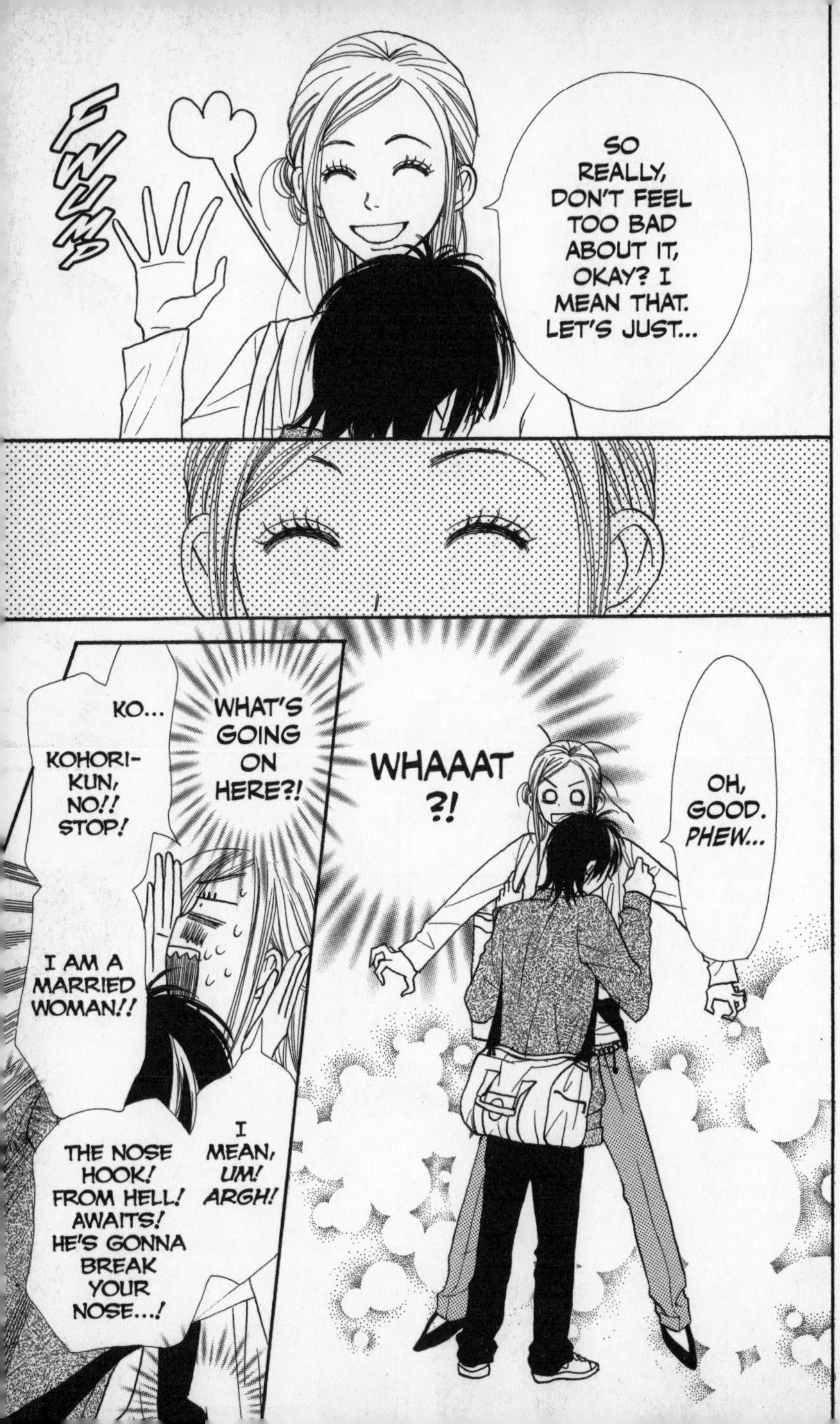
SO REALLY, DON'T FEEL TOO BAD ABOUT IT, OKAY? I MEAN THAT. LET'S JUST...
FWUMP
OH, GOOD. PHEW...
WHAAAT?!
WHAT'S GOING ON HERE?!
KO...
KOHORI-KUN, NO!! STOP!
I AM A MARRIED WOMAN!!
I MEAN, UM! ARGH!
THE NOSE HOOK! FROM HELL! AWAITS! HE'S GONNA BREAK YOUR NOSE...!

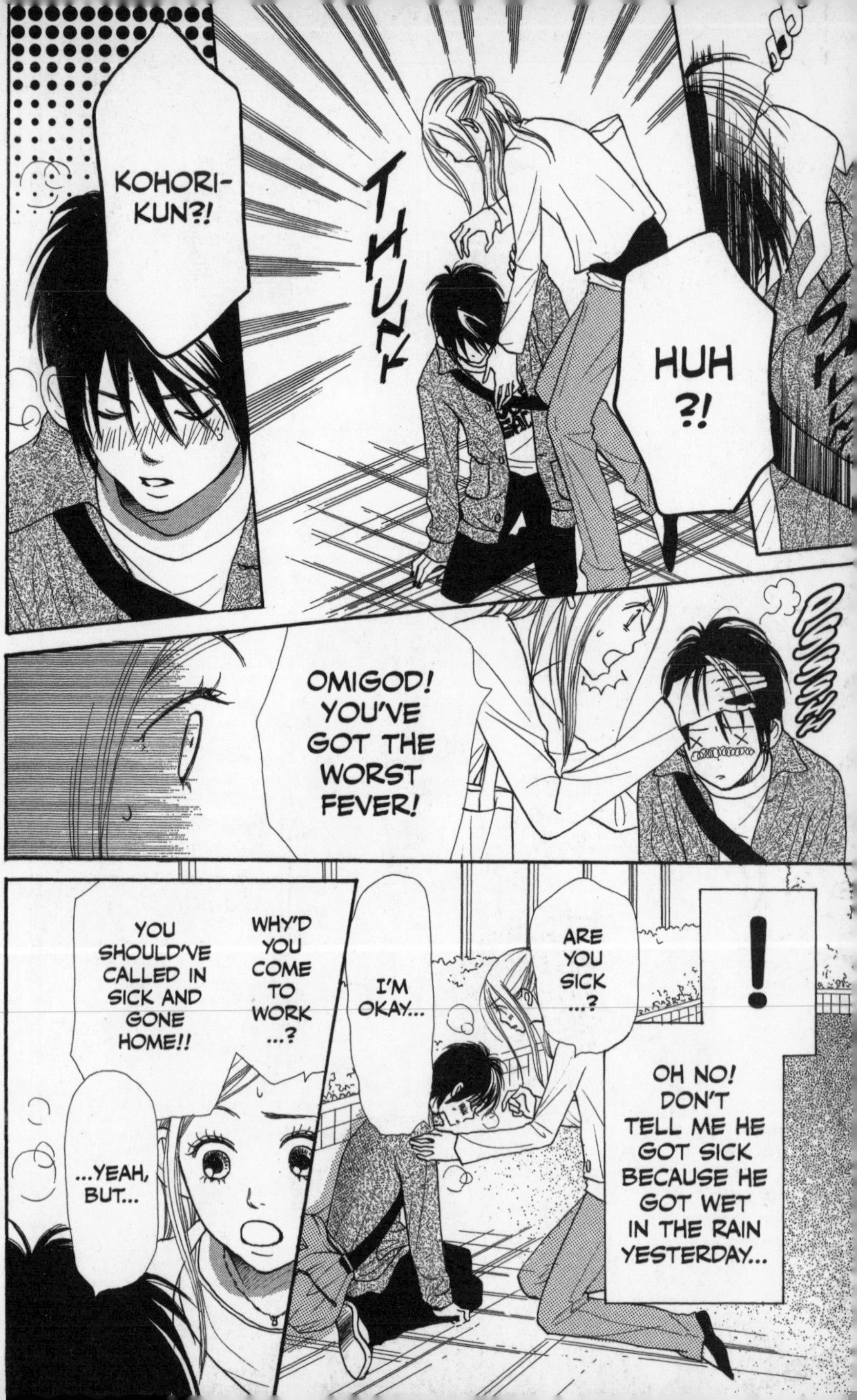
HUH ?!
THUNK
KOHORI-KUN?!
OMIGOD! YOU'VE GOT THE WORST FEVER!
!
OH NO! DON'T TELL ME HE GOT SICK BECAUSE HE GOT WET IN THE RAIN YESTERDAY...
ARE YOU SICK ...?
I'M OKAY...
WHY'D YOU COME TO WORK ...?
YOU SHOULD'VE CALLED IN SICK AND GONE HOME!!
...YEAH, BUT...

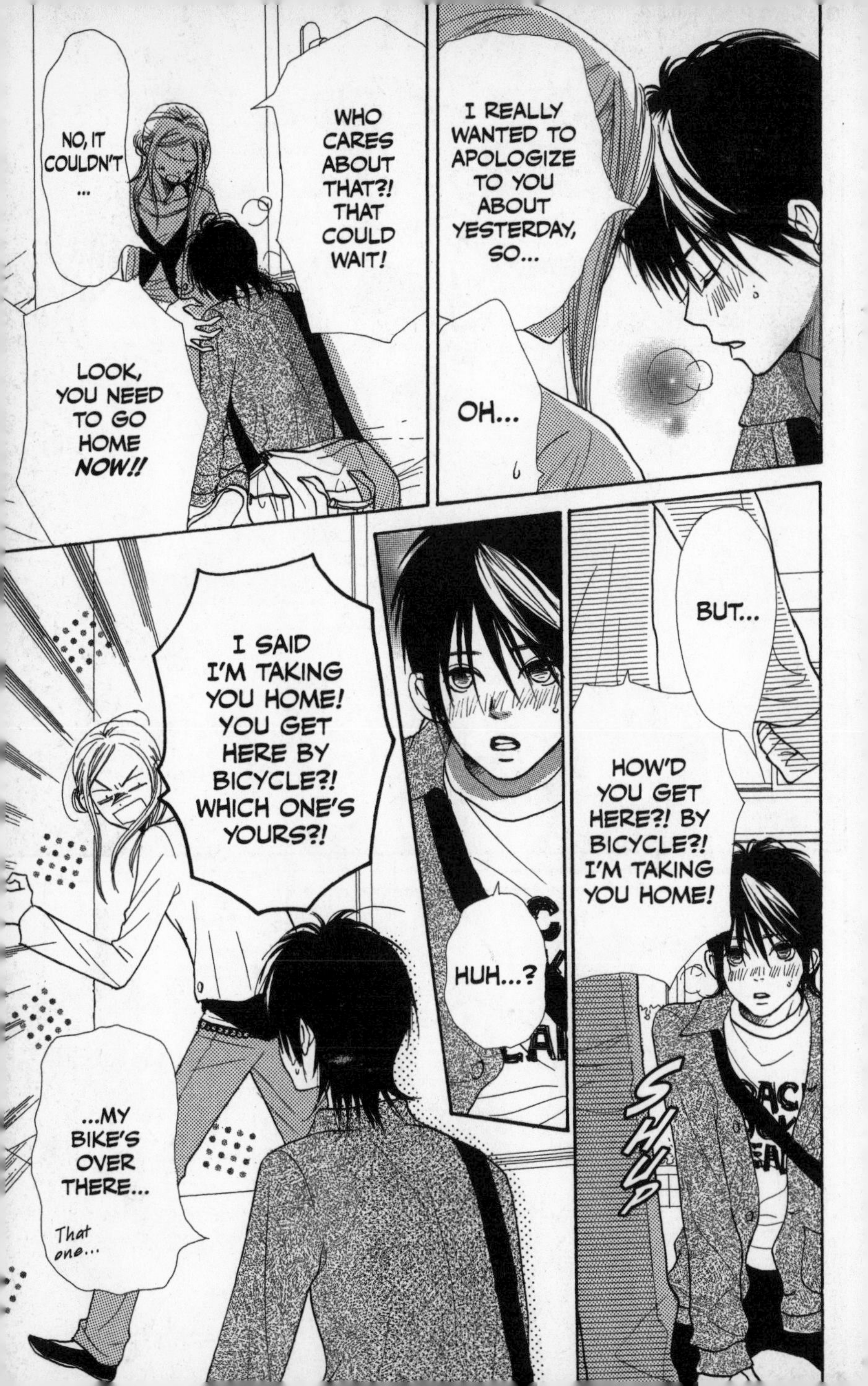

I REALLY WANTED TO APOLOGIZE TO YOU ABOUT YESTERDAY, SO...
OH...
WHO CARES ABOUT THAT?! THAT COULD WAIT!
NO, IT COULDN'T ...
LOOK, YOU NEED TO GO HOME *NOW!!*
BUT...
HOW'D YOU GET HERE?! BY BICYCLE?! I'M TAKING YOU HOME!
SHUP
HUH...?
I SAID I'M TAKING YOU HOME! YOU GET HERE BY BICYCLE?! WHICH ONE'S YOURS?!
...MY BIKE'S OVER THERE...
That one...

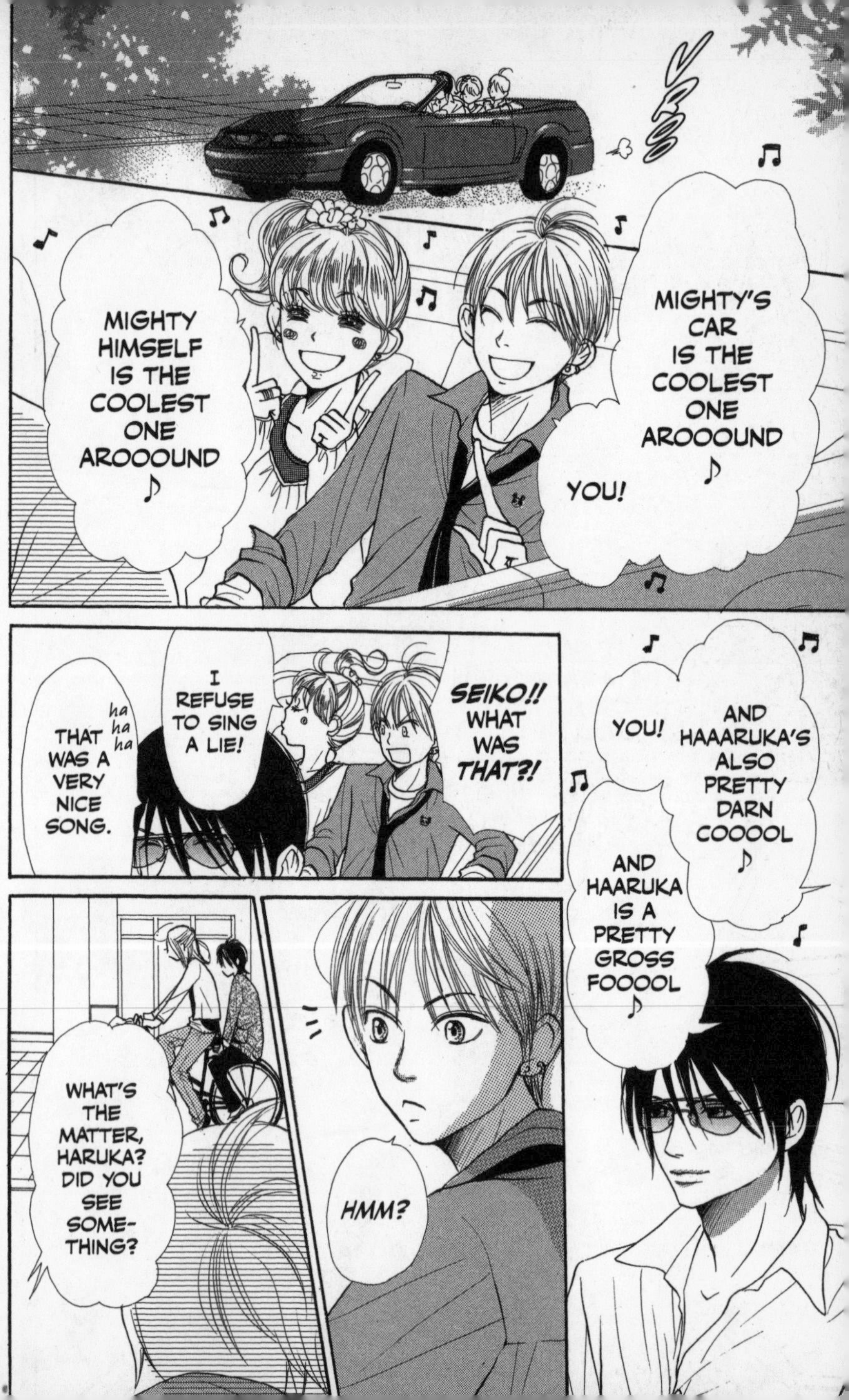
VROOO
MIGHTY'S CAR IS THE COOLEST ONE AROOOUND ♪
YOU!
MIGHTY HIMSELF IS THE COOLEST ONE AROOOUND ♪
AND HAARUKA'S ALSO PRETTY DARN COOOOL ♪
YOU!
AND HAARUKA IS A PRETTY GROSS FOOOOL ♪
SEIKO!! WHAT WAS THAT?!
I REFUSE TO SING A LIE!
ha ha ha
THAT WAS A VERY NICE SONG.
HMM?
WHAT'S THE MATTER, HARUKA? DID YOU SEE SOME-THING?

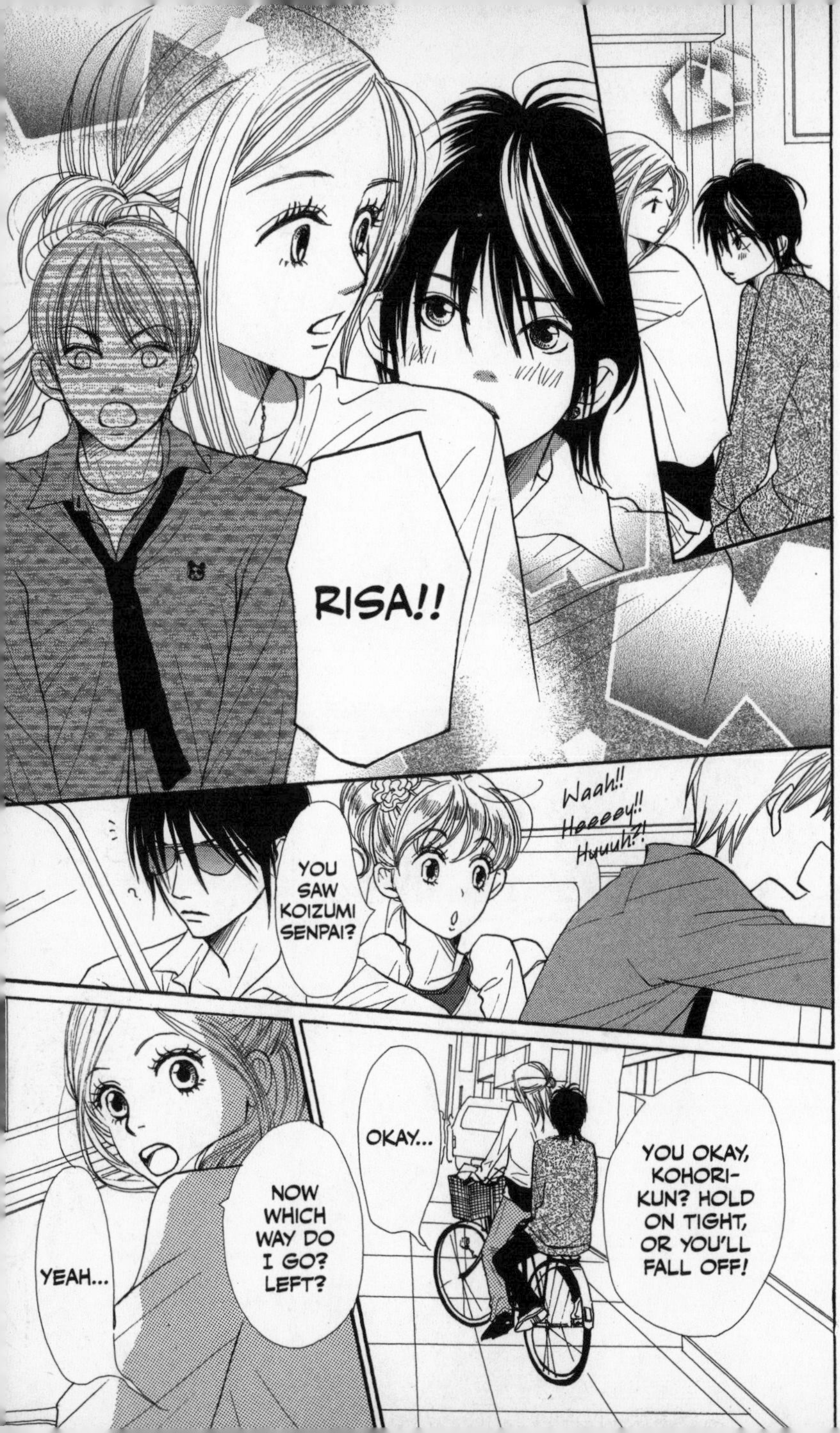
RISA!!
Waah!! Heeeey!! Huuuh?!
YOU SAW KOIZUMI SENPAI?
YOU OKAY, KOHORI-KUN? HOLD ON TIGHT, OR YOU'LL FALL OFF!
OKAY...
NOW WHICH WAY DO I GO? LEFT?
YEAH...

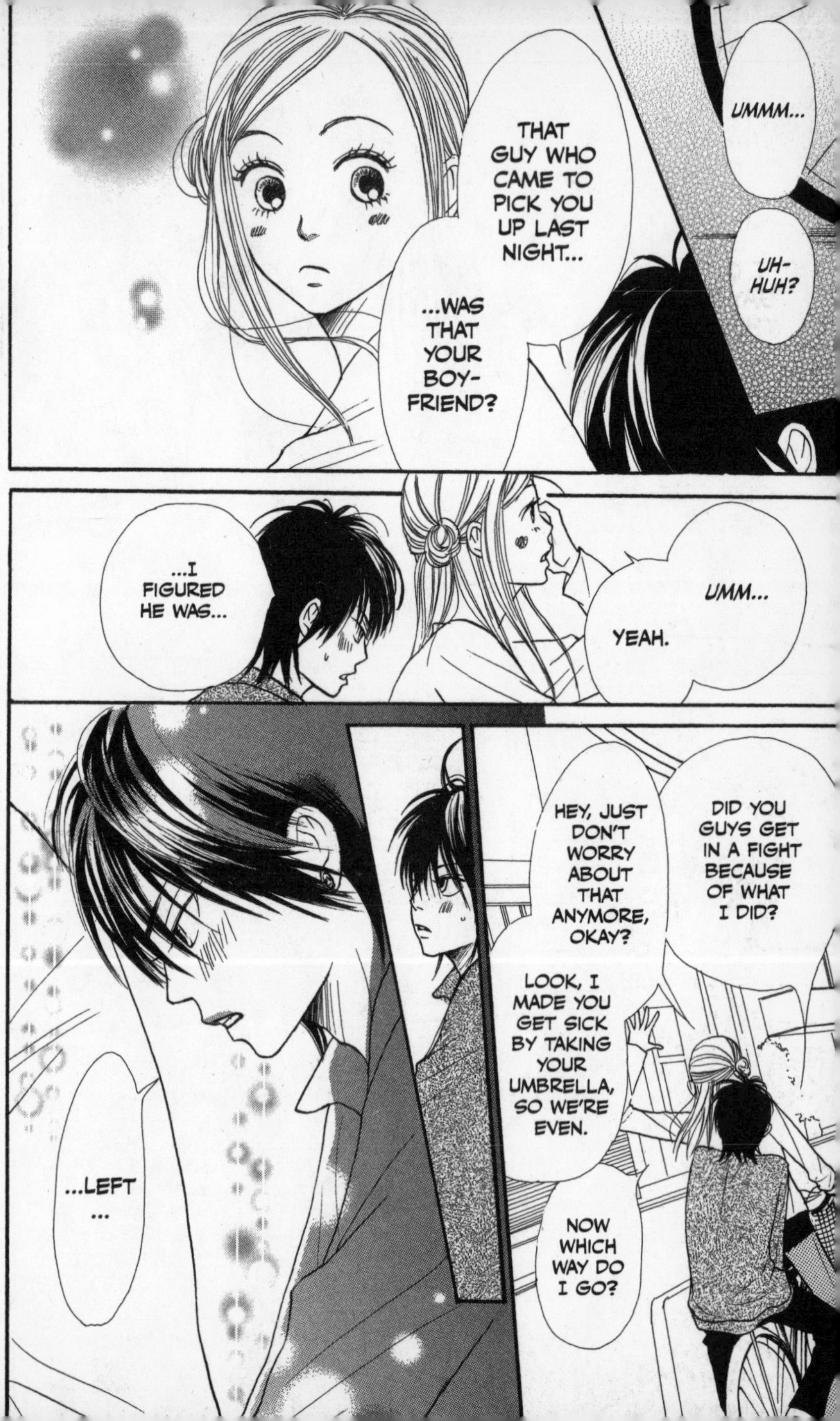
UMMM...
UH-HUH?
THAT GUY WHO CAME TO PICK YOU UP LAST NIGHT...
...WAS THAT YOUR BOY-FRIEND?
UMM...
YEAH.
...I FIGURED HE WAS...
DID YOU GUYS GET IN A FIGHT BECAUSE OF WHAT I DID?
HEY, JUST DON'T WORRY ABOUT THAT ANYMORE, OKAY?
LOOK, I MADE YOU GET SICK BY TAKING YOUR UMBRELLA, SO WE'RE EVEN.
NOW WHICH WAY DO I GO?
...LEFT ...

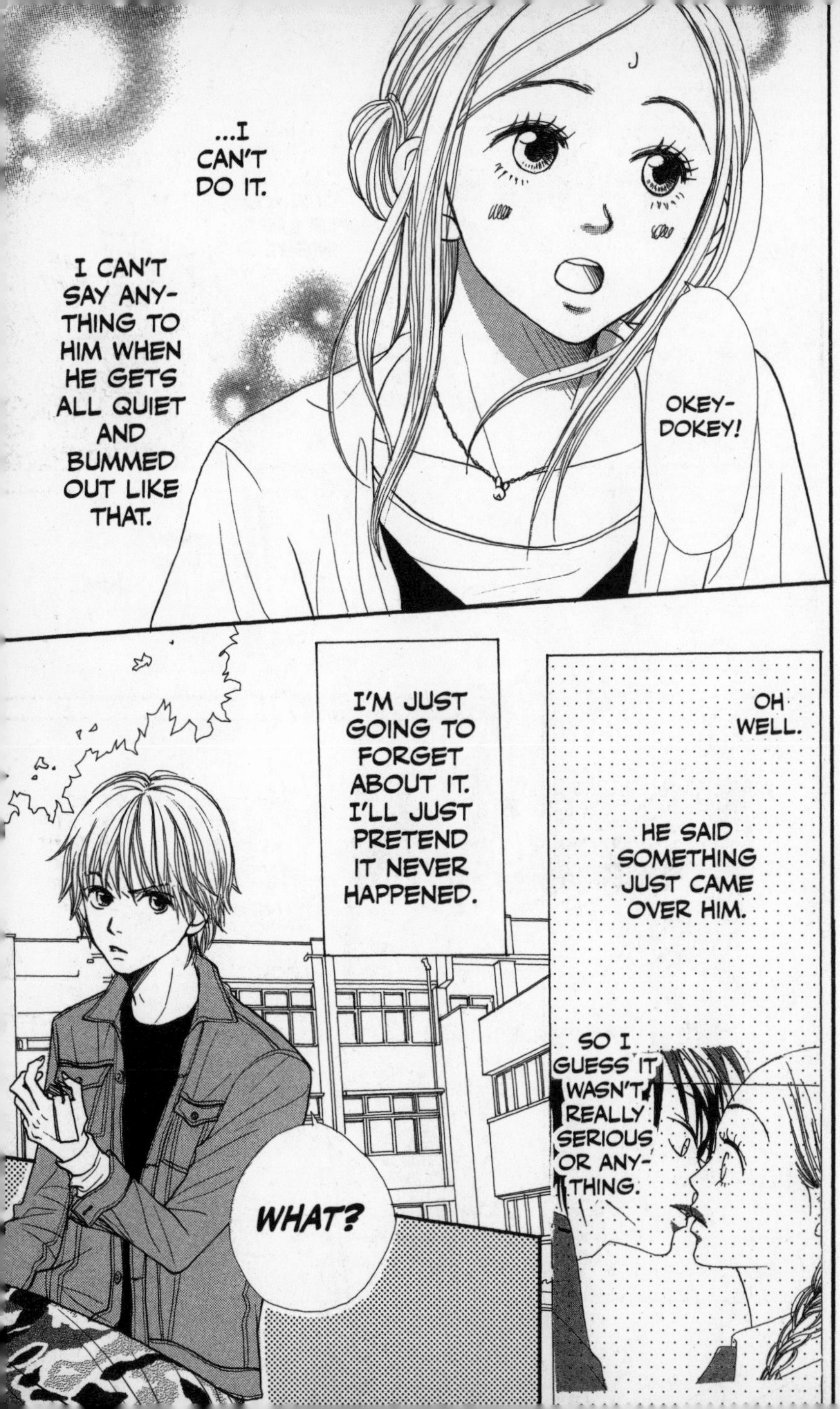
OKEY-DOKEY!
...I CAN'T DO IT.
I CAN'T SAY ANY-THING TO HIM WHEN HE GETS ALL QUIET AND BUMMED OUT LIKE THAT.
OH WELL.
HE SAID SOMETHING JUST CAME OVER HIM.
SO I GUESS IT WASN'T REALLY SERIOUS OR ANY-THING.
I'M JUST GOING TO FORGET ABOUT IT. I'LL JUST PRETEND IT NEVER HAPPENED.
WHAT?

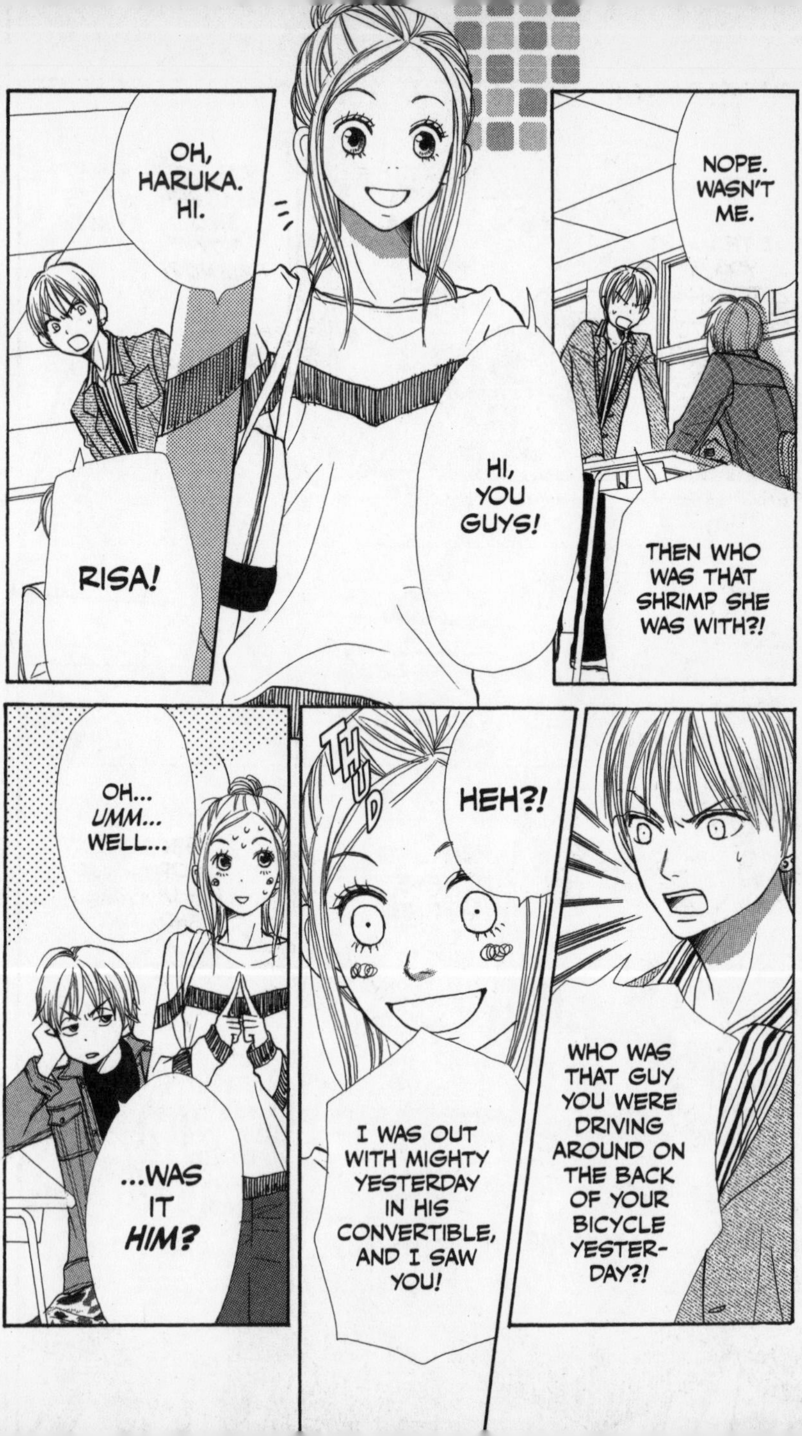
NOPE. WASN'T ME.
THEN WHO WAS THAT SHRIMP SHE WAS WITH?!
HI, YOU GUYS!
OH, HARUKA. HI.
RISA!
WHO WAS THAT GUY YOU WERE DRIVING AROUND ON THE BACK OF YOUR BICYCLE YESTER-DAY?!
HEH?!
THUD
I WAS OUT WITH MIGHTY YESTERDAY IN HIS CONVERTIBLE, AND I SAW YOU!
OH... *UMM...* WELL...
...WAS IT *HIM?*

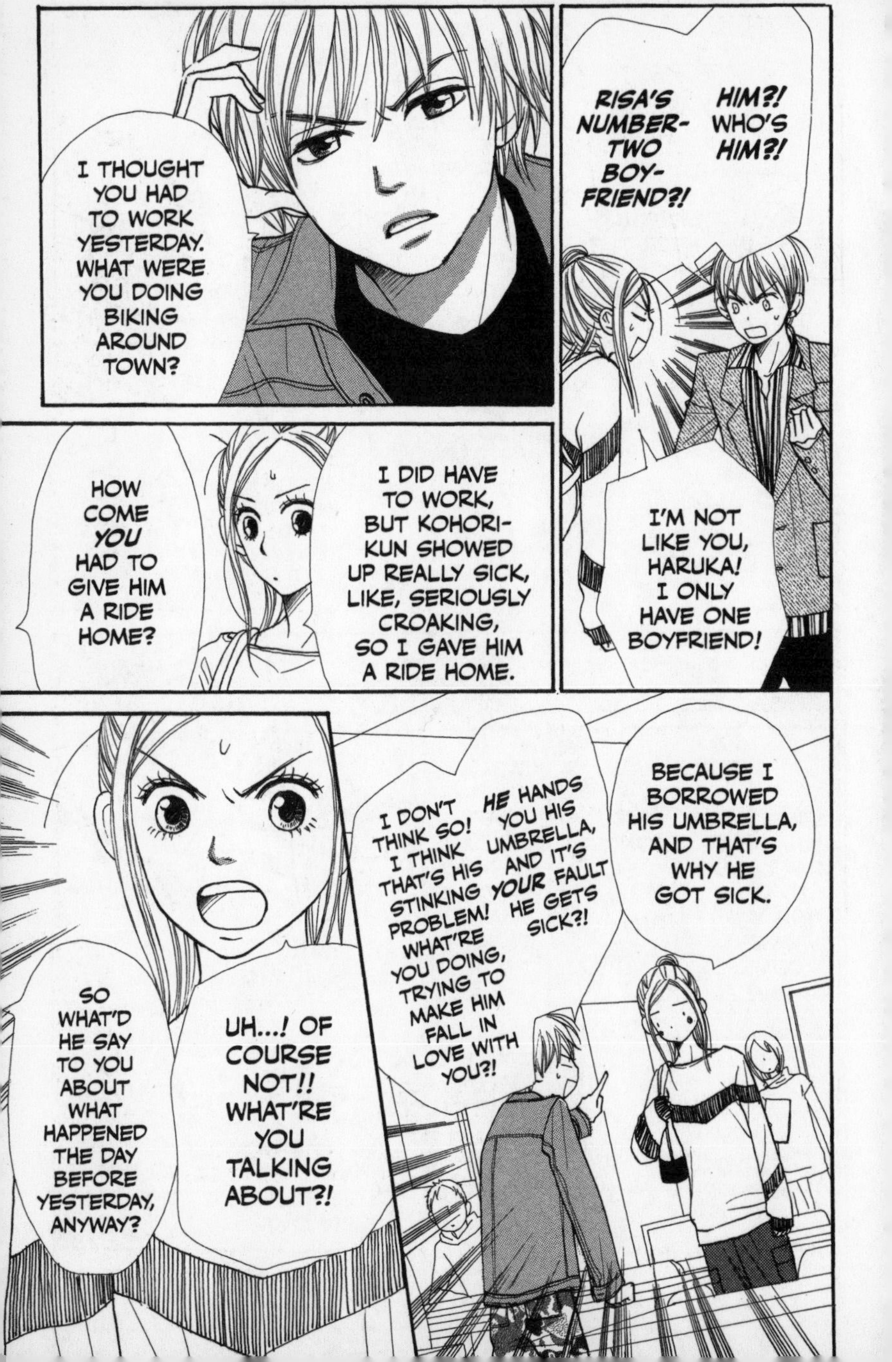
HIM?! WHO'S HIM?!
RISA'S NUMBER-TWO BOYFRIEND?!
I'M NOT LIKE YOU, HARUKA! I ONLY HAVE ONE BOYFRIEND!
I THOUGHT YOU HAD TO WORK YESTERDAY. WHAT WERE YOU DOING BIKING AROUND TOWN?
I DID HAVE TO WORK, BUT KOHORI-KUN SHOWED UP REALLY SICK, LIKE, SERIOUSLY CROAKING, SO I GAVE HIM A RIDE HOME.
HOW COME *YOU* HAD TO GIVE HIM A RIDE HOME?
BECAUSE I BORROWED HIS UMBRELLA, AND THAT'S WHY HE GOT SICK.
HE HANDS YOU HIS UMBRELLA, AND IT'S *YOUR* FAULT HE GETS SICK?!
I DON'T THINK SO! I THINK THAT'S HIS STINKING PROBLEM! WHAT'RE YOU DOING, TRYING TO MAKE HIM FALL IN LOVE WITH YOU?!
UH...! OF COURSE NOT!! WHAT'RE YOU TALKING ABOUT?!
SO WHAT'D HE SAY TO YOU ABOUT WHAT HAPPENED THE DAY BEFORE YESTERDAY, ANYWAY?

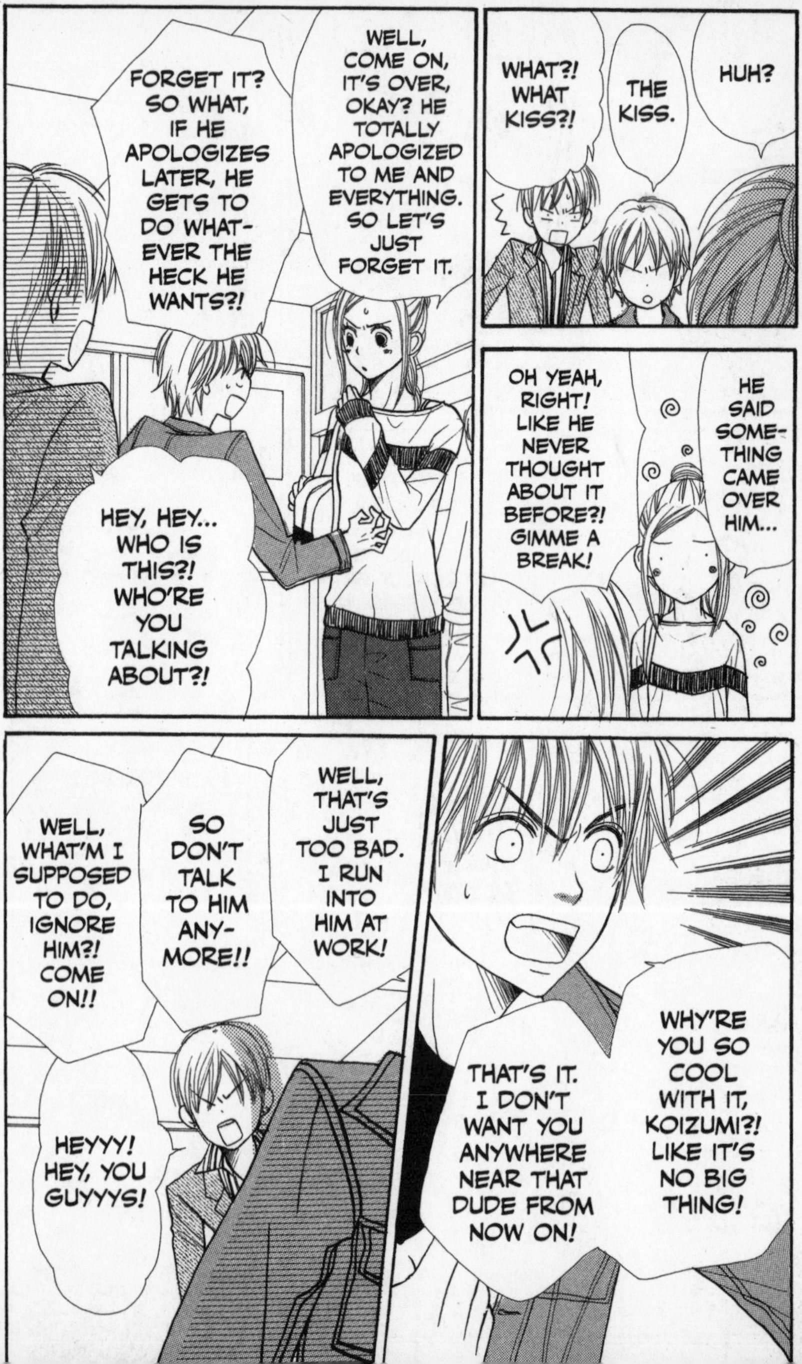
HUH?
THE KISS.
WHAT?! WHAT KISS?!
HE SAID SOMETHING CAME OVER HIM...
OH YEAH, RIGHT! LIKE HE NEVER THOUGHT ABOUT IT BEFORE?! GIMME A BREAK!
WELL, COME ON, IT'S OVER, OKAY? HE TOTALLY APOLOGIZED TO ME AND EVERYTHING. SO LET'S JUST FORGET IT.
FORGET IT? SO WHAT, IF HE APOLOGIZES LATER, HE GETS TO DO WHATEVER THE HECK HE WANTS?!
HEY, HEY... WHO IS THIS?! WHO'RE YOU TALKING ABOUT?!
WHY'RE YOU SO COOL WITH IT, KOIZUMI?! LIKE IT'S NO BIG THING!
THAT'S IT. I DON'T WANT YOU ANYWHERE NEAR THAT DUDE FROM NOW ON!
WELL, THAT'S JUST TOO BAD. I RUN INTO HIM AT WORK!
SO DON'T TALK TO HIM ANYMORE!!
WELL, WHAT'M I SUPPOSED TO DO, IGNORE HIM?! COME ON!!
HEYYY! HEY, YOU GUYYYS!

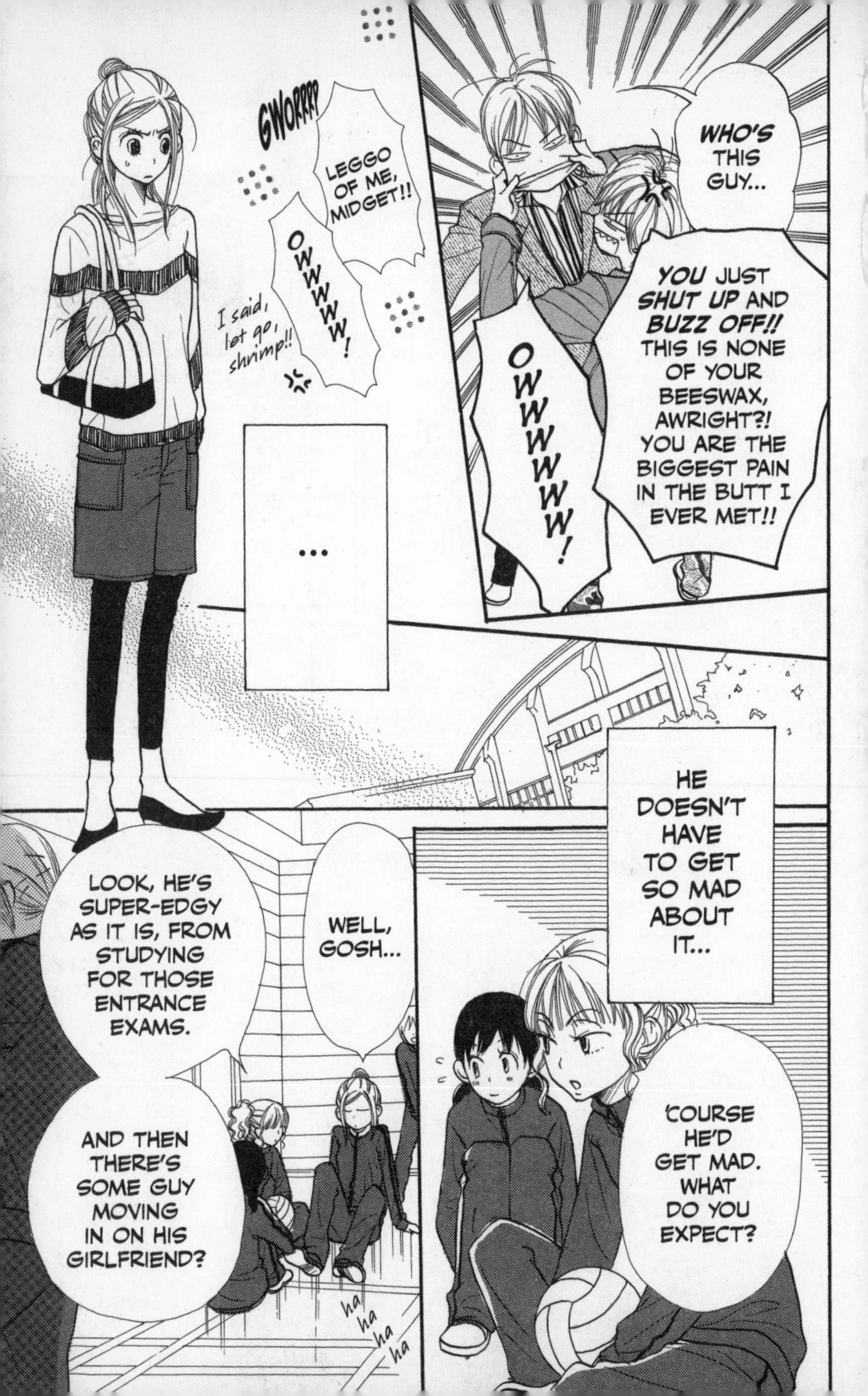
WHO'S THIS GUY...
YOU JUST SHUT UP AND BUZZ OFF!! THIS IS NONE OF YOUR BEESWAX, AWRIGHT?! YOU ARE THE BIGGEST PAIN IN THE BUTT I EVER MET!!
OWWWWWW!
HE DOESN'T HAVE TO GET SO MAD ABOUT IT...
GWORRRR
LEGGO OF ME, MIDGET!!
OWWWWW!
I said, let go, shrimp!!
...
'COURSE HE'D GET MAD. WHAT DO YOU EXPECT?
WELL, GOSH...
LOOK, HE'S SUPER-EDGY AS IT IS, FROM STUDYING FOR THOSE ENTRANCE EXAMS.
AND THEN THERE'S SOME GUY MOVING IN ON HIS GIRLFRIEND?
ha ha ha ha

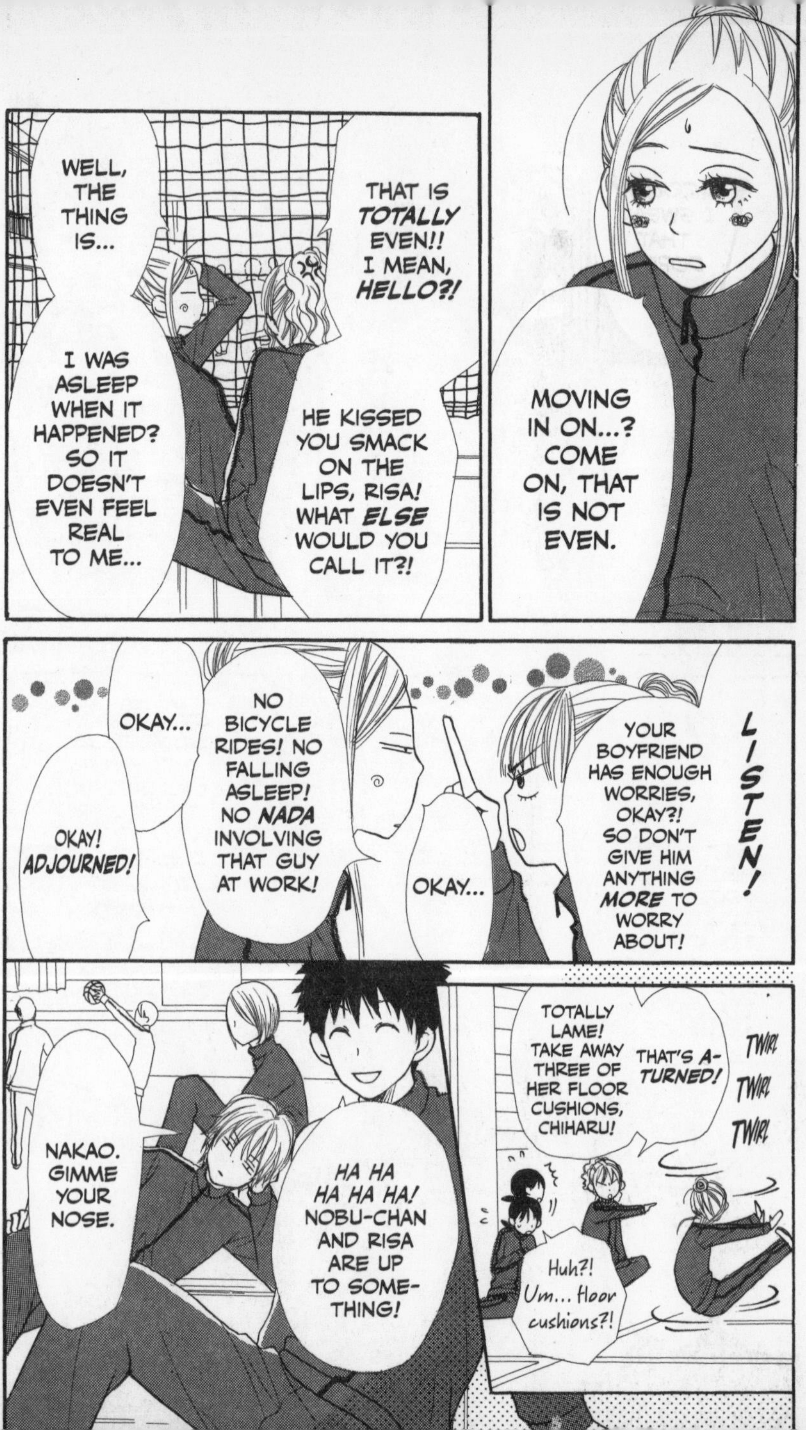
MOVING IN ON...? COME ON, THAT IS NOT EVEN.
THAT IS *TOTALLY* EVEN!! I MEAN, *HELLO?!*
WELL, THE THING IS...
HE KISSED YOU SMACK ON THE LIPS, RISA! WHAT *ELSE* WOULD YOU CALL IT?!
I WAS ASLEEP WHEN IT HAPPENED? SO IT DOESN'T EVEN FEEL REAL TO ME...
LISTEN!
YOUR BOYFRIEND HAS ENOUGH WORRIES, OKAY?! SO DON'T GIVE HIM ANYTHING *MORE* TO WORRY ABOUT!
OKAY...
NO BICYCLE RIDES! NO FALLING ASLEEP! NO *NADA* INVOLVING THAT GUY AT WORK!
OKAY...
OKAY! *ADJOURNED!*
TWIRL
TWIRL
TWIRL
THAT'S A-*TURNED!*
TOTALLY LAME! TAKE AWAY THREE OF HER FLOOR CUSHIONS, CHIHARU!
Huh?! Um... floor cushions?!
HA HA HA HA HA! NOBU-CHAN AND RISA ARE UP TO SOME-THING!
NAKAO. GIMME YOUR NOSE.

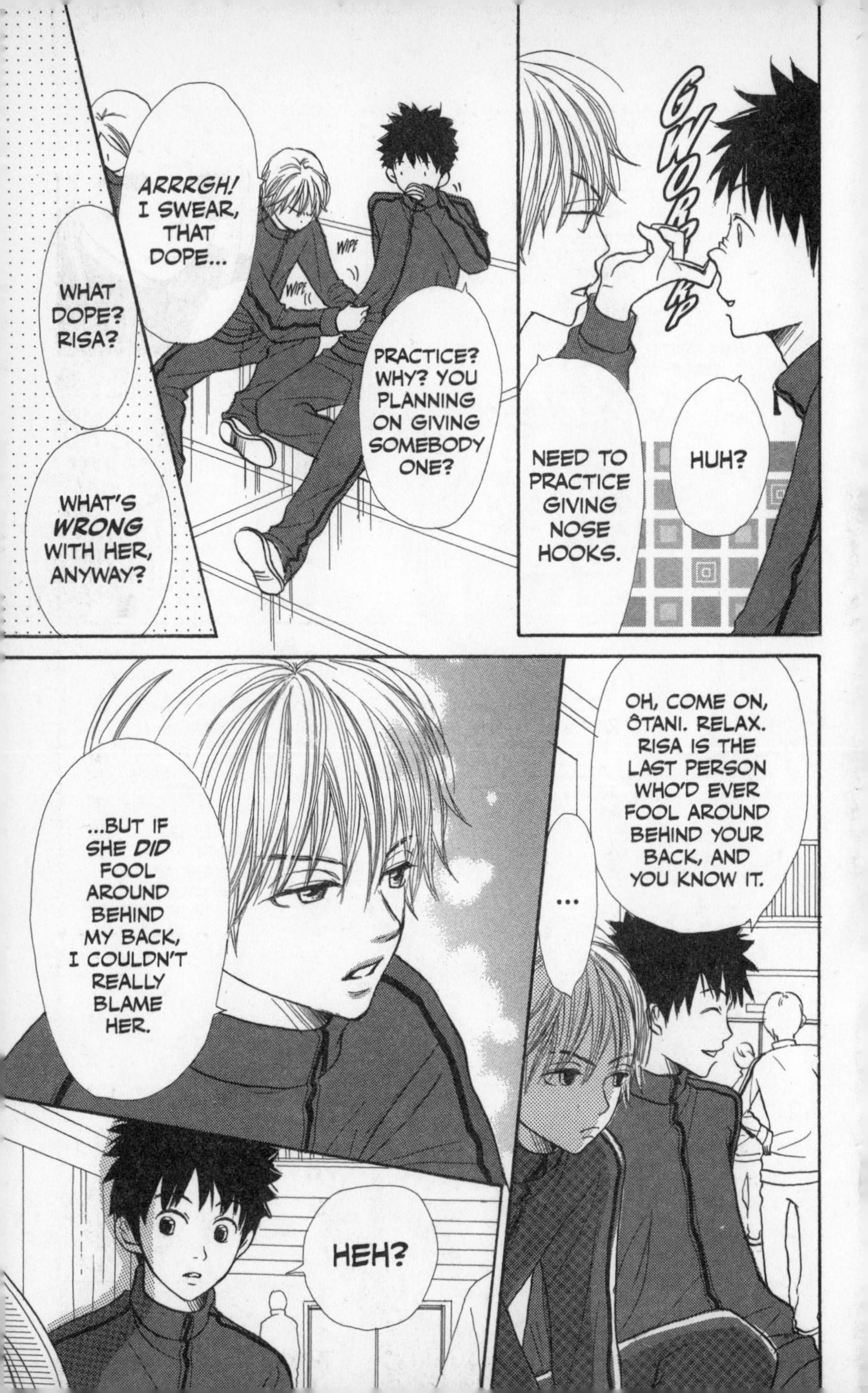
HUH?
NEED TO PRACTICE GIVING NOSE HOOKS.
PRACTICE? WHY? YOU PLANNING ON GIVING SOMEBODY ONE?
WIPE
WIPE
ARRRGH! I SWEAR, THAT DOPE...
WHAT DOPE? RISA?
WHAT'S WRONG WITH HER, ANYWAY?
OH, COME ON, ŌTANI. RELAX. RISA IS THE LAST PERSON WHO'D EVER FOOL AROUND BEHIND YOUR BACK, AND YOU KNOW IT.
...
...BUT IF SHE DID FOOL AROUND BEHIND MY BACK, I COULDN'T REALLY BLAME HER.
HEH?

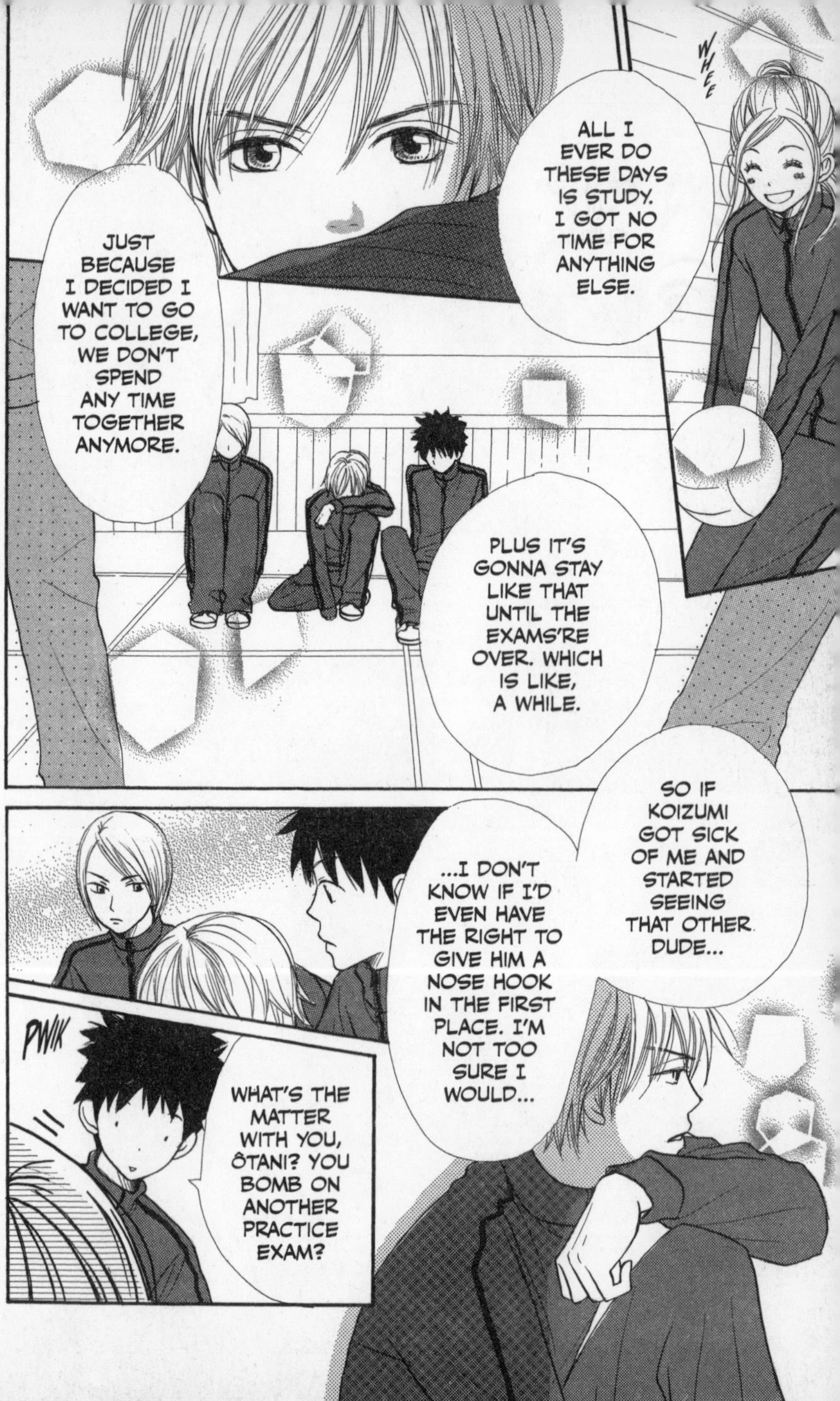
WHEE
ALL I EVER DO THESE DAYS IS STUDY. I GOT NO TIME FOR ANYTHING ELSE.
JUST BECAUSE I DECIDED I WANT TO GO TO COLLEGE, WE DON'T SPEND ANY TIME TOGETHER ANYMORE.
PLUS IT'S GONNA STAY LIKE THAT UNTIL THE EXAMS'RE OVER. WHICH IS LIKE, A WHILE.
SO IF KOIZUMI GOT SICK OF ME AND STARTED SEEING THAT OTHER DUDE...
...I DON'T KNOW IF I'D EVEN HAVE THE RIGHT TO GIVE HIM A NOSE HOOK IN THE FIRST PLACE. I'M NOT TOO SURE I WOULD...
PWIK
WHAT'S THE MATTER WITH YOU, ŌTANI? YOU BOMB ON ANOTHER PRACTICE EXAM?

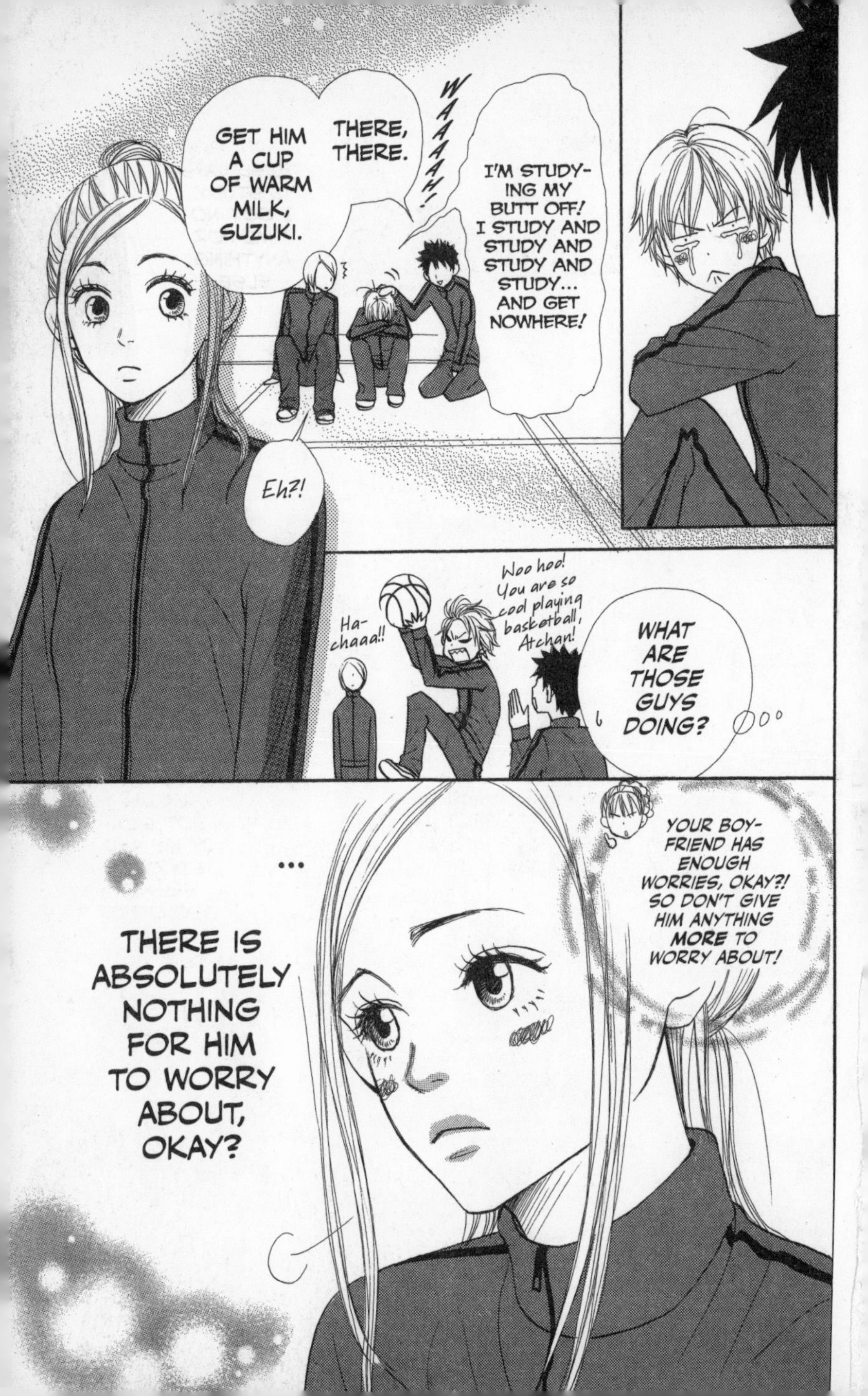
WHAT ARE THOSE GUYS DOING?
Woo hoo! You are so cool playing basketball, Atchan!
Ha-chaaa!!
I'M STUDYING MY BUTT OFF! I STUDY AND STUDY AND STUDY AND STUDY... AND GET NOWHERE!
WAAAAAH!
THERE, THERE.
GET HIM A CUP OF WARM MILK, SUZUKI.
Eh?!
YOUR BOYFRIEND HAS ENOUGH WORRIES, OKAY?! SO DON'T GIVE HIM ANYTHING MORE TO WORRY ABOUT!
...
THERE IS ABSOLUTELY NOTHING FOR HIM TO WORRY ABOUT, OKAY?

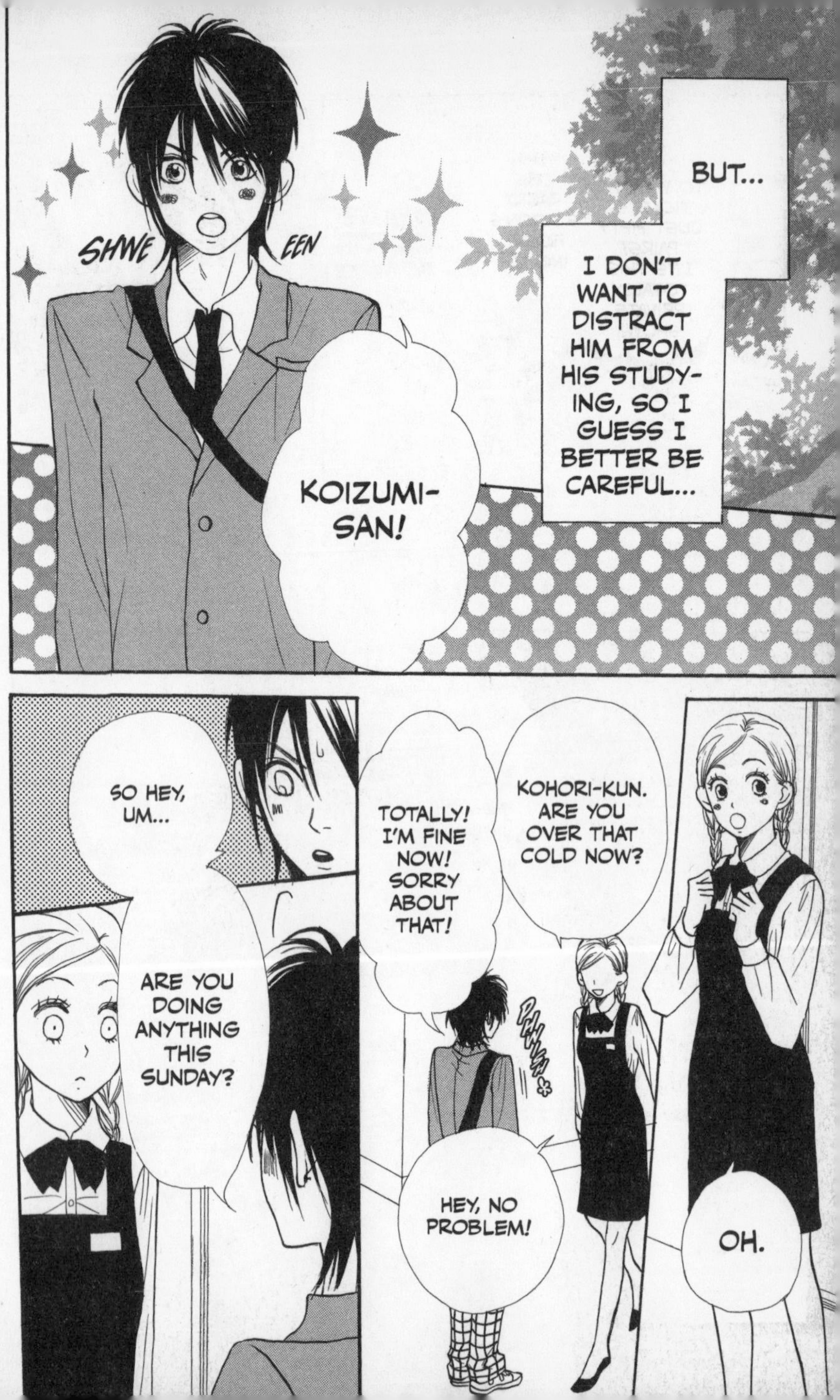
BUT...
I DON'T WANT TO DISTRACT HIM FROM HIS STUDYING, SO I GUESS I BETTER BE CAREFUL...
SHWE EEN
KOIZUMI-SAN!
KOHORI-KUN. ARE YOU OVER THAT COLD NOW?
TOTALLY! I'M FINE NOW! SORRY ABOUT THAT!
OH.
HEY, NO PROBLEM!
SO HEY, UM...
ARE YOU DOING ANYTHING THIS SUNDAY?

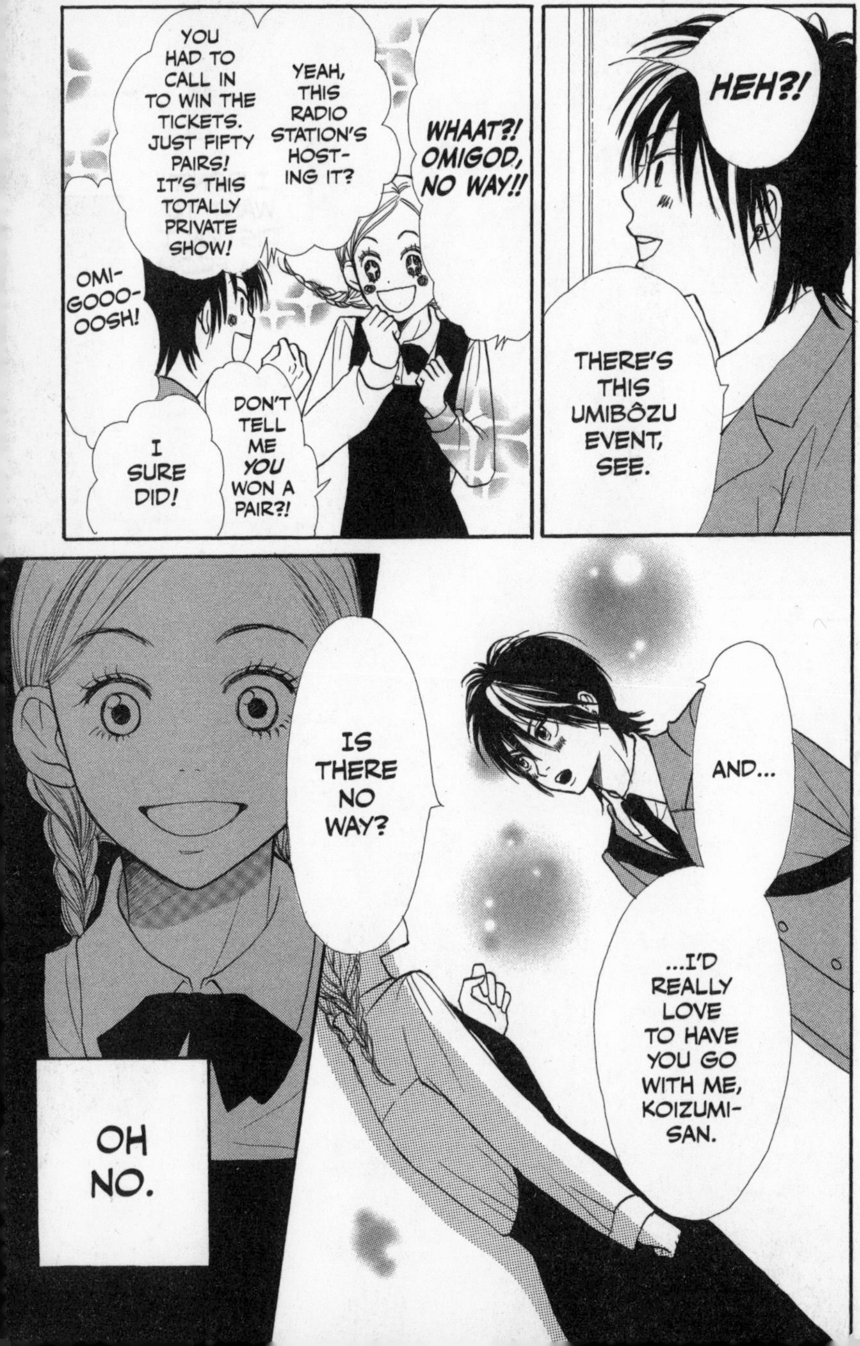
HEH?!
THERE'S THIS UMIBÔZU EVENT, SEE.
WHAAT?! OMIGOD, NO WAY!!
YEAH, THIS RADIO STATION'S HOST-ING IT?
YOU HAD TO CALL IN TO WIN THE TICKETS. JUST FIFTY PAIRS! IT'S THIS TOTALLY PRIVATE SHOW!
OMI-GOOOO-OOSH!
DON'T TELL ME YOU WON A PAIR?!
I SURE DID!
AND...
...I'D REALLY LOVE TO HAVE YOU GO WITH ME, KOIZUMI-SAN.
IS THERE NO WAY?
OH NO.

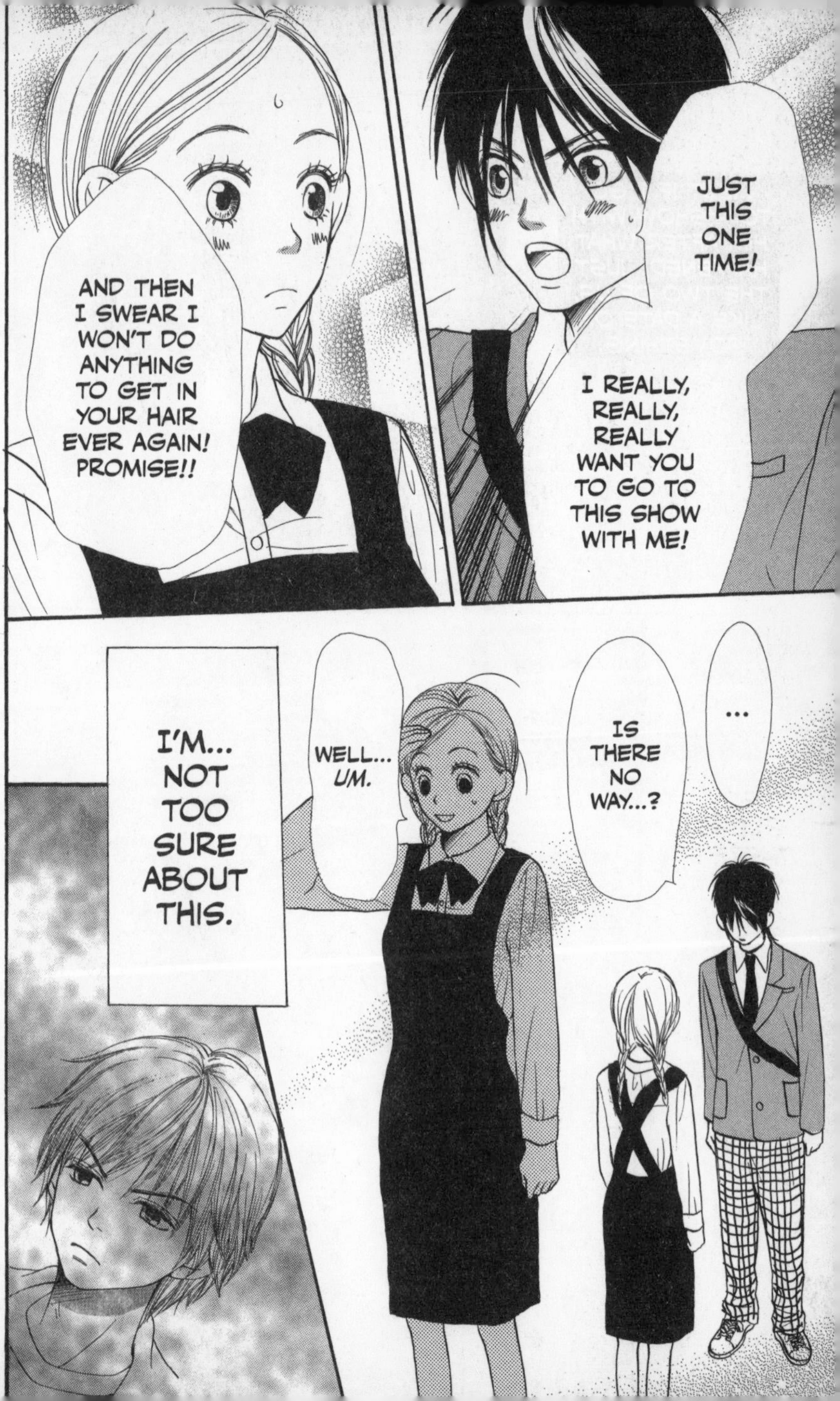
JUST THIS ONE TIME!
I REALLY, REALLY, REALLY WANT YOU TO GO TO THIS SHOW WITH ME!
AND THEN I SWEAR I WON'T DO ANYTHING TO GET IN YOUR HAIR EVER AGAIN! PROMISE!!
...
IS THERE NO WAY...?
WELL... *UM.*
I'M... NOT TOO SURE ABOUT THIS.

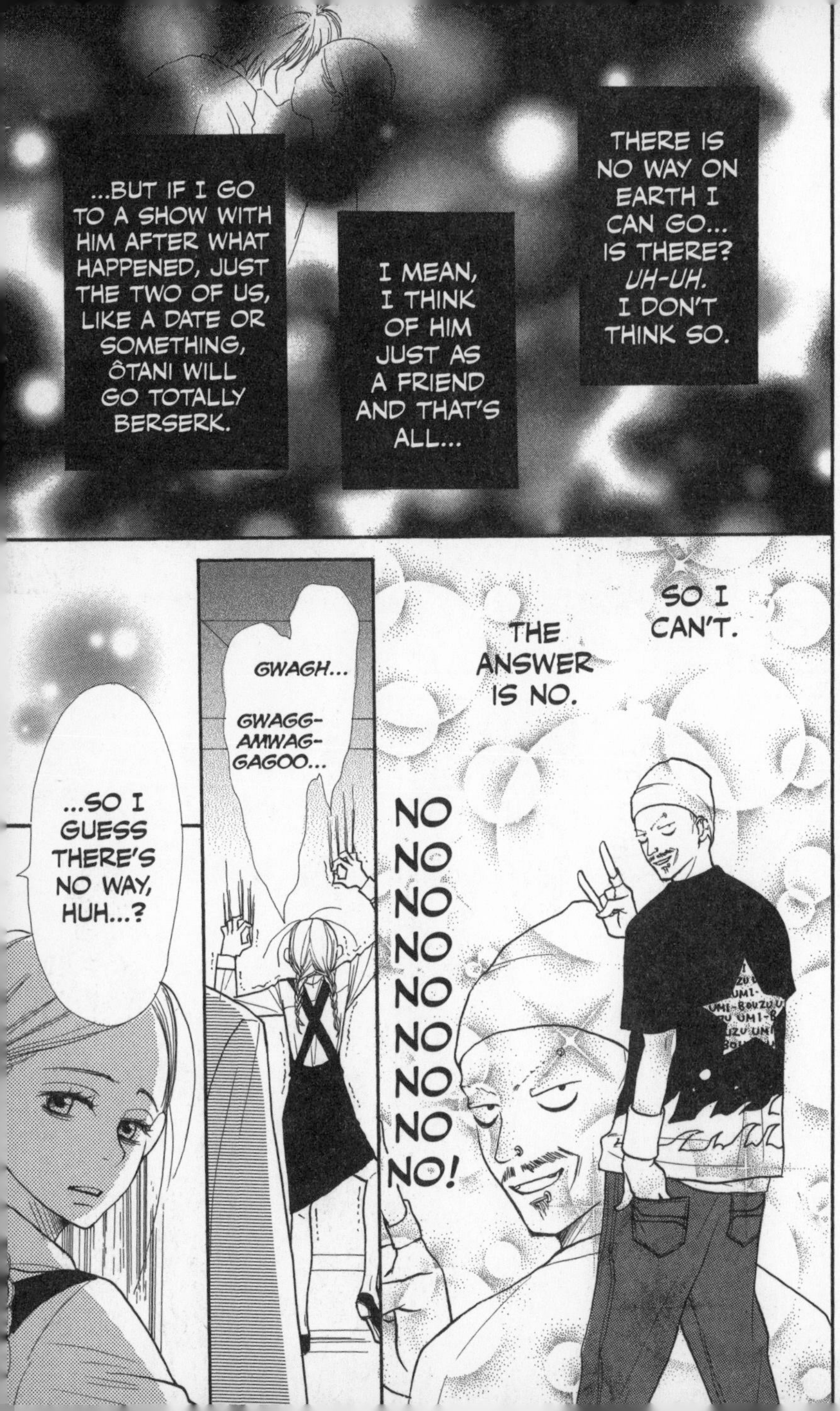
THERE IS NO WAY ON EARTH I CAN GO... IS THERE? *UH-UH.* I DON'T THINK SO.
I MEAN, I THINK OF HIM JUST AS A FRIEND AND THAT'S ALL...
...BUT IF I GO TO A SHOW WITH HIM AFTER WHAT HAPPENED, JUST THE TWO OF US, LIKE A DATE OR SOMETHING, ÔTANI WILL GO TOTALLY BERSERK.
SO I CAN'T.
THE ANSWER IS NO.
NO NO NO NO NO NO NO NO NO!
GWAGH...
GWAGG-AMWAG-GAGOO...
...SO I GUESS THERE'S NO WAY, HUH...?

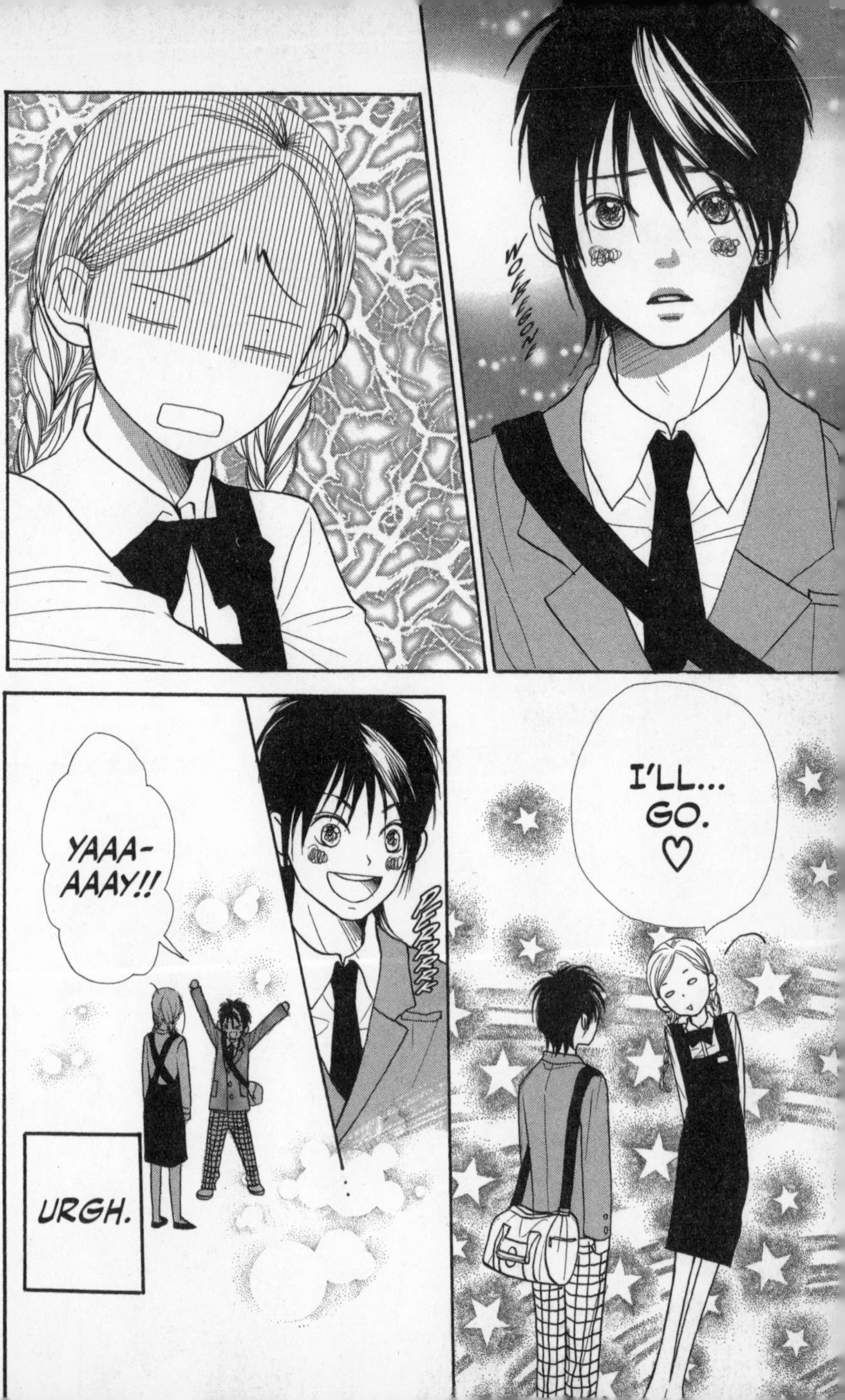
I'LL... GO. ♡
YAAA-AAAY!!
URGH.

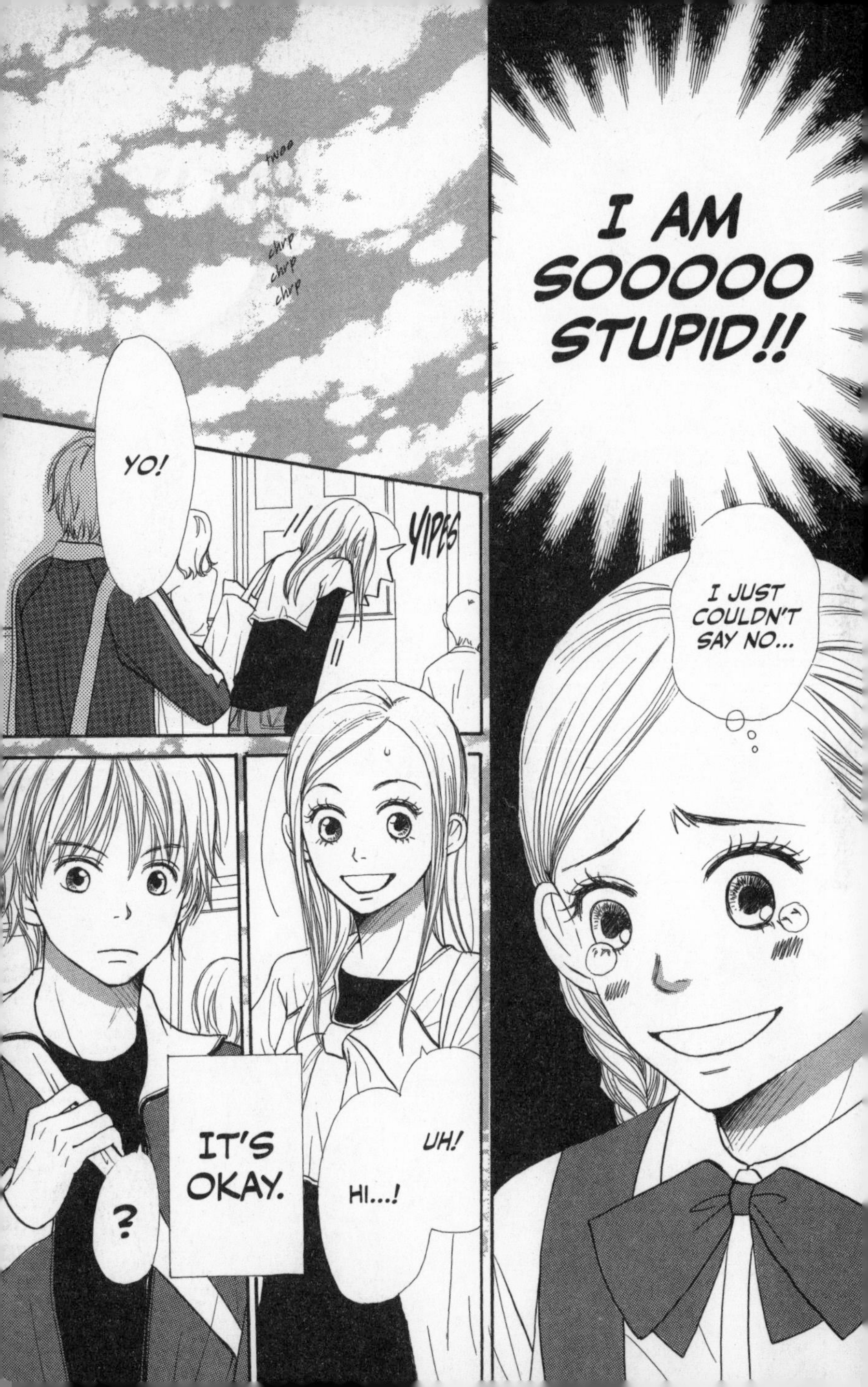
I AM SOOOOO STUPID!!
I JUST COULDN'T SAY NO...
twee
chrp chrp chrp
YO!
YIPES
UH!
HI...!
IT'S OKAY.
?

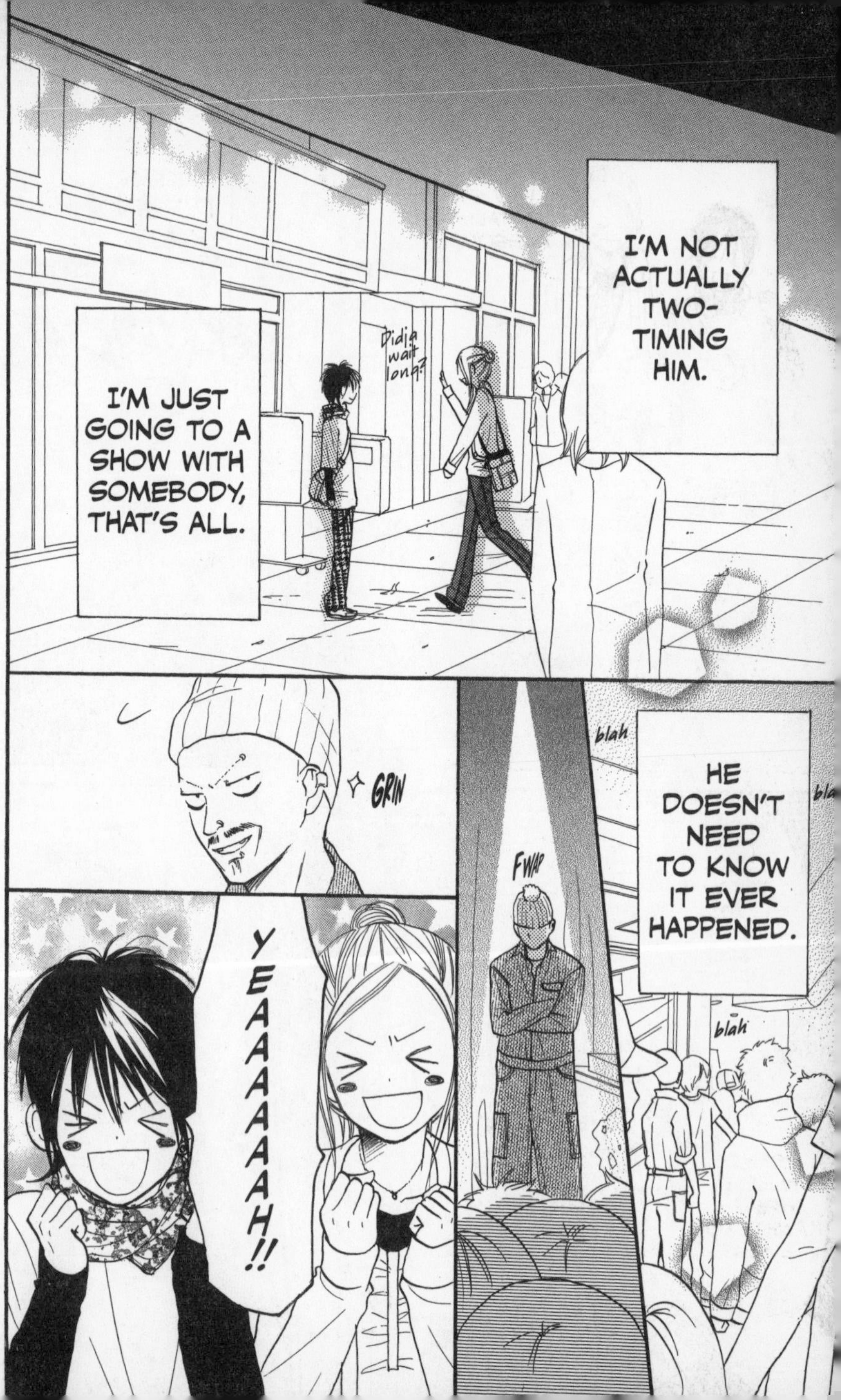

I'M NOT ACTUALLY TWO-TIMING HIM.
Didja wait long?
I'M JUST GOING TO A SHOW WITH SOMEBODY, THAT'S ALL.
blah
HE DOESN'T NEED TO KNOW IT EVER HAPPENED.
FWAP
blah
GRIN
YEAAAAAAAH!!

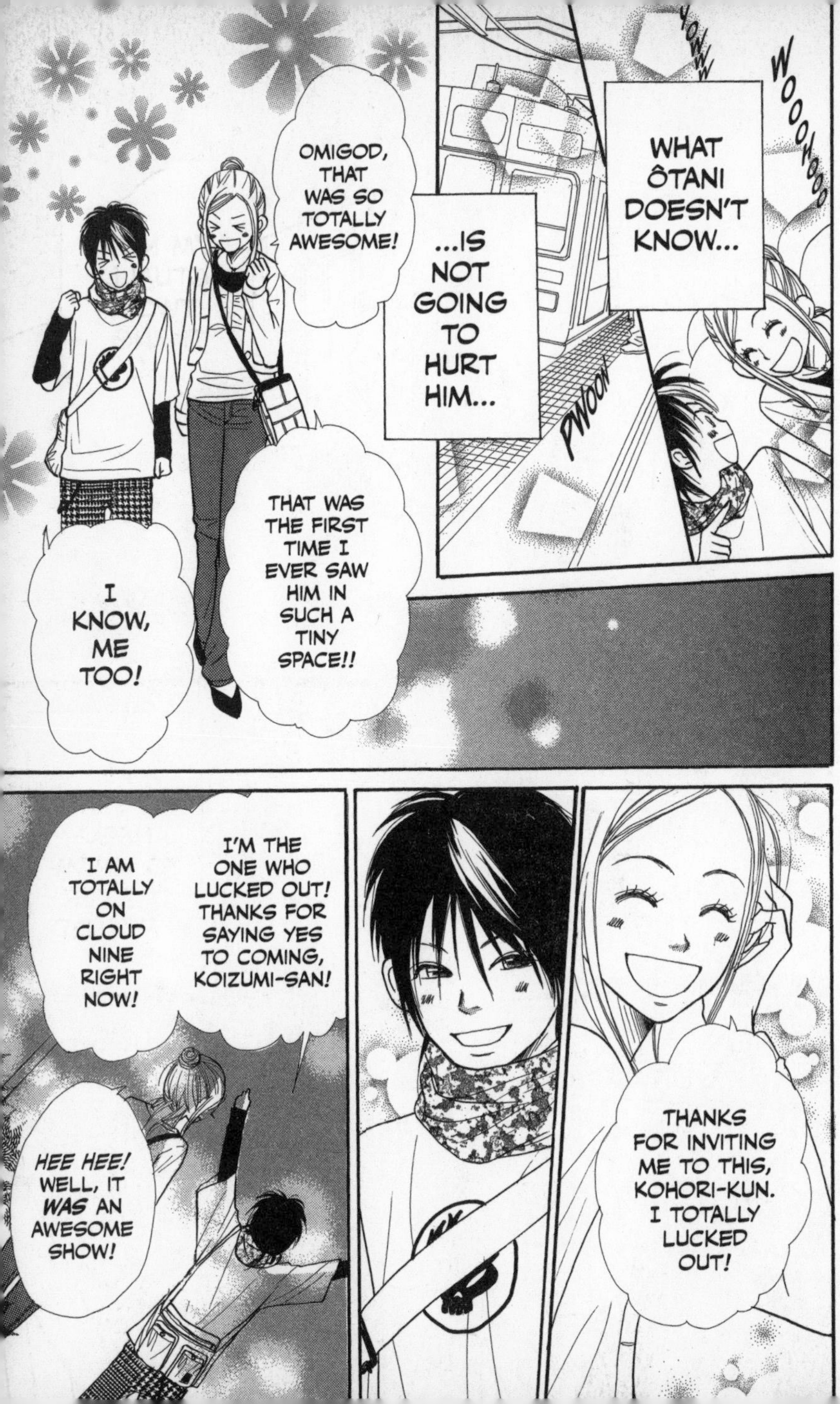
WOOOHOOO
YOWWW
WHAT ÔTANI DOESN'T KNOW...
...IS NOT GOING TO HURT HIM...
PWOON
OMIGOD, THAT WAS SO TOTALLY AWESOME!
THAT WAS THE FIRST TIME I EVER SAW HIM IN SUCH A TINY SPACE!!
I KNOW, ME TOO!
THANKS FOR INVITING ME TO THIS, KOHORI-KUN. I TOTALLY LUCKED OUT!
I'M THE ONE WHO LUCKED OUT! THANKS FOR SAYING YES TO COMING, KOIZUMI-SAN!
I AM TOTALLY ON CLOUD NINE RIGHT NOW!
HEE HEE! WELL, IT *WAS* AN AWESOME SHOW!

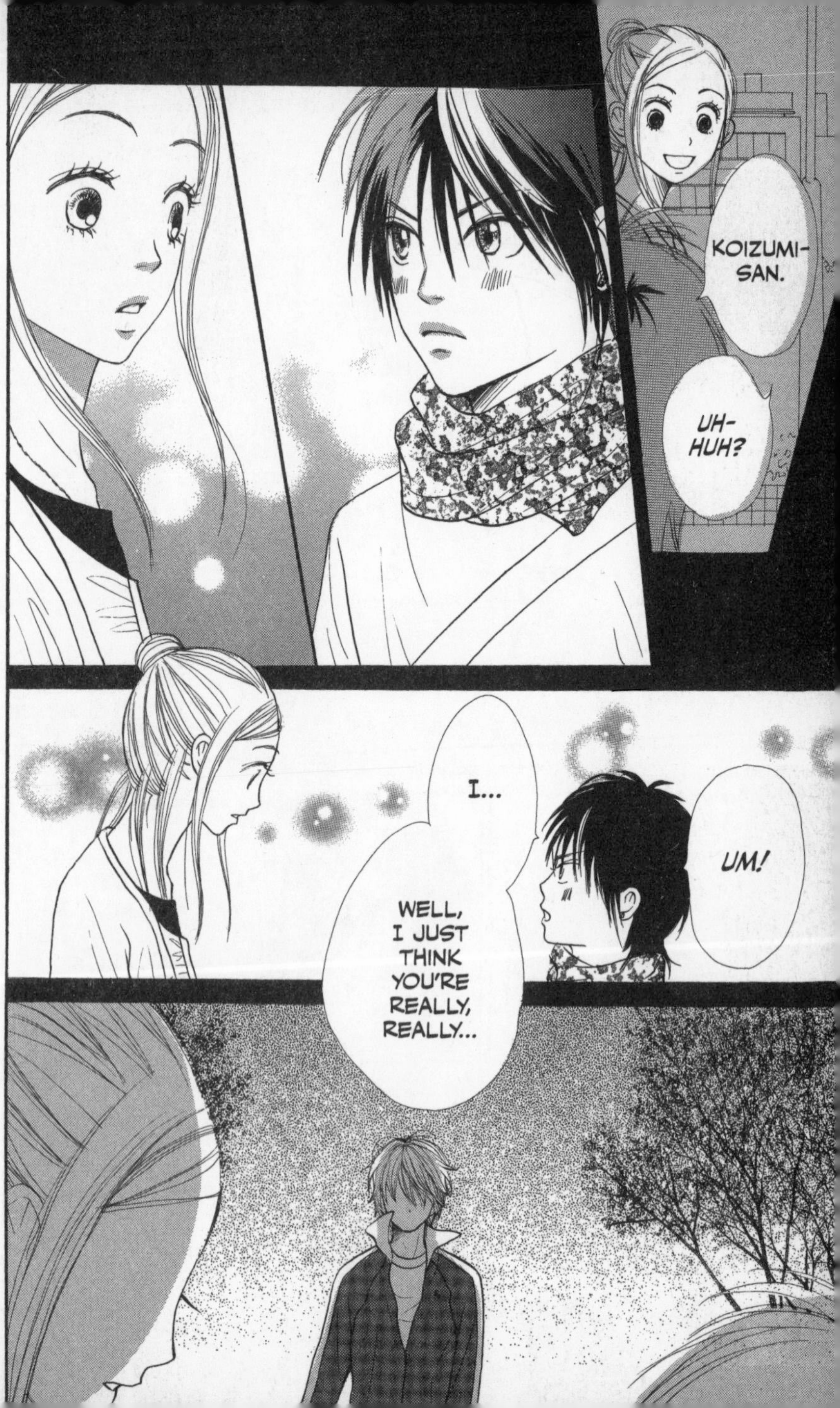
KOIZUMI-SAN.
UH-HUH?
UM!
I...
WELL, I JUST THINK YOU'RE REALLY, REALLY...

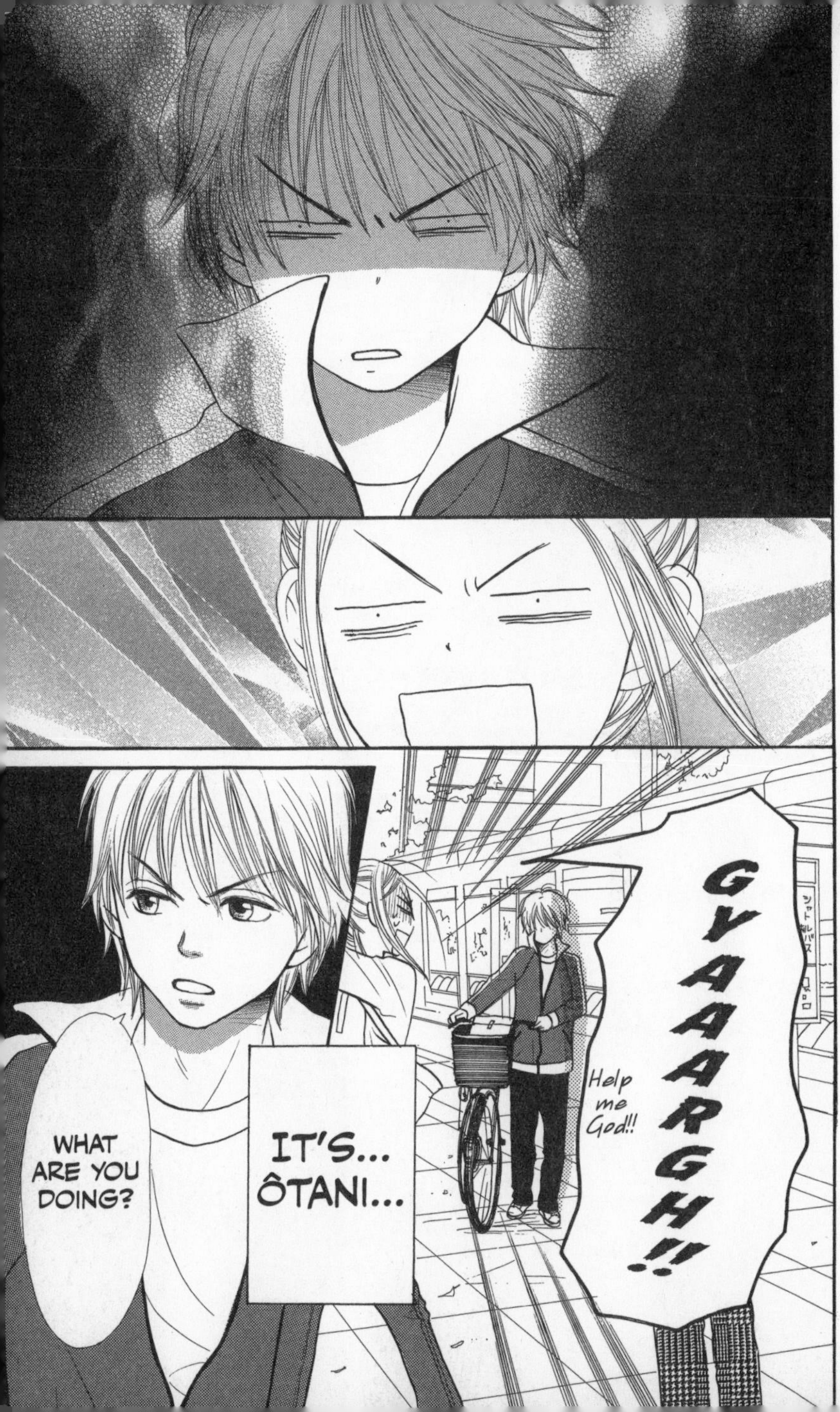
GYAAARGH!!
Help me God!!
IT'S... ÔTANI...
WHAT ARE YOU DOING?

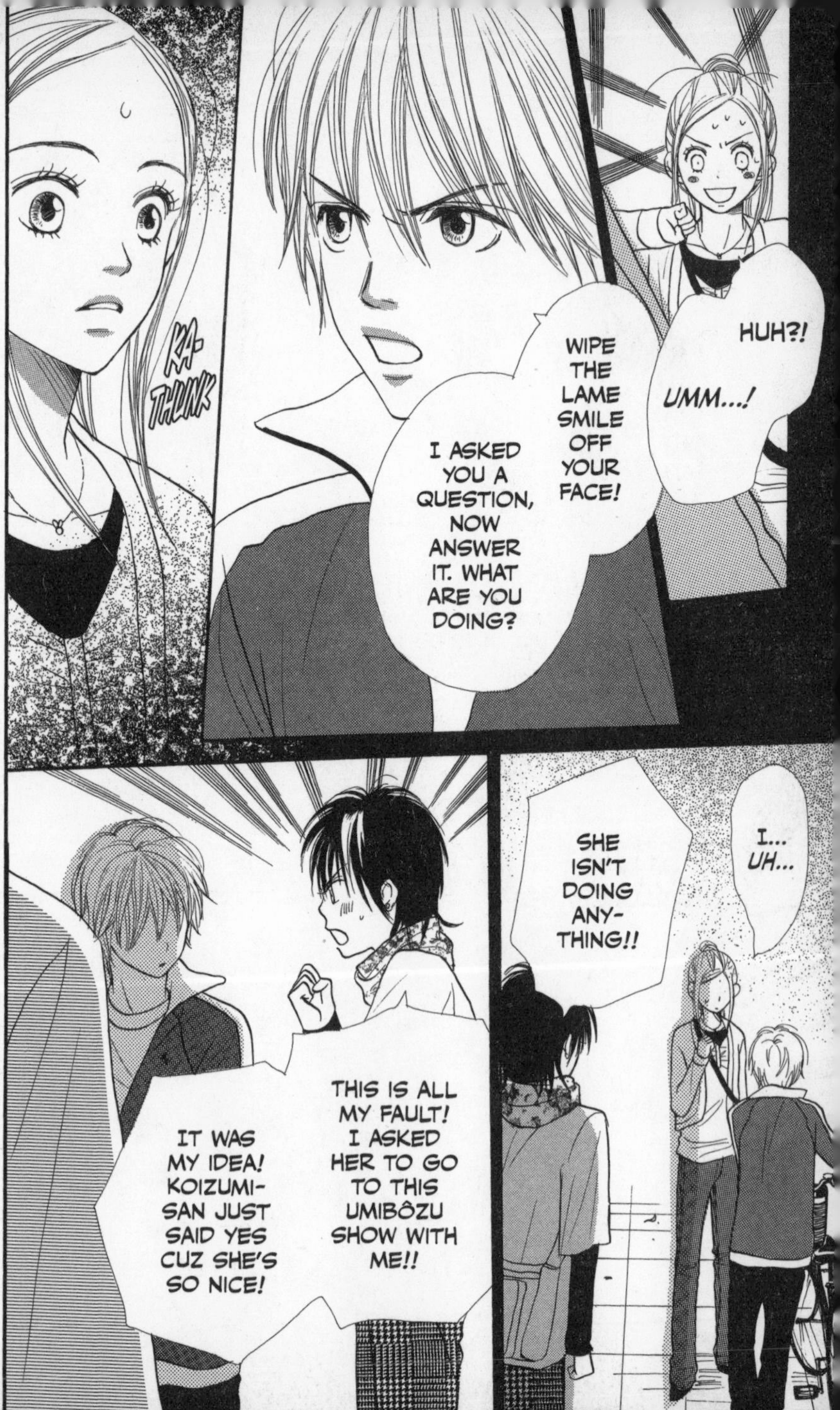
HUH?!
UMM...!
WIPE THE LAME SMILE OFF YOUR FACE!
I ASKED YOU A QUESTION, NOW ANSWER IT. WHAT ARE YOU DOING?
KA-THUNK
I... UH...
SHE ISN'T DOING ANY-THING!!
THIS IS ALL MY FAULT! I ASKED HER TO GO TO THIS UMIBÔZU SHOW WITH ME!!
IT WAS MY IDEA! KOIZUMI-SAN JUST SAID YES CUZ SHE'S SO NICE!

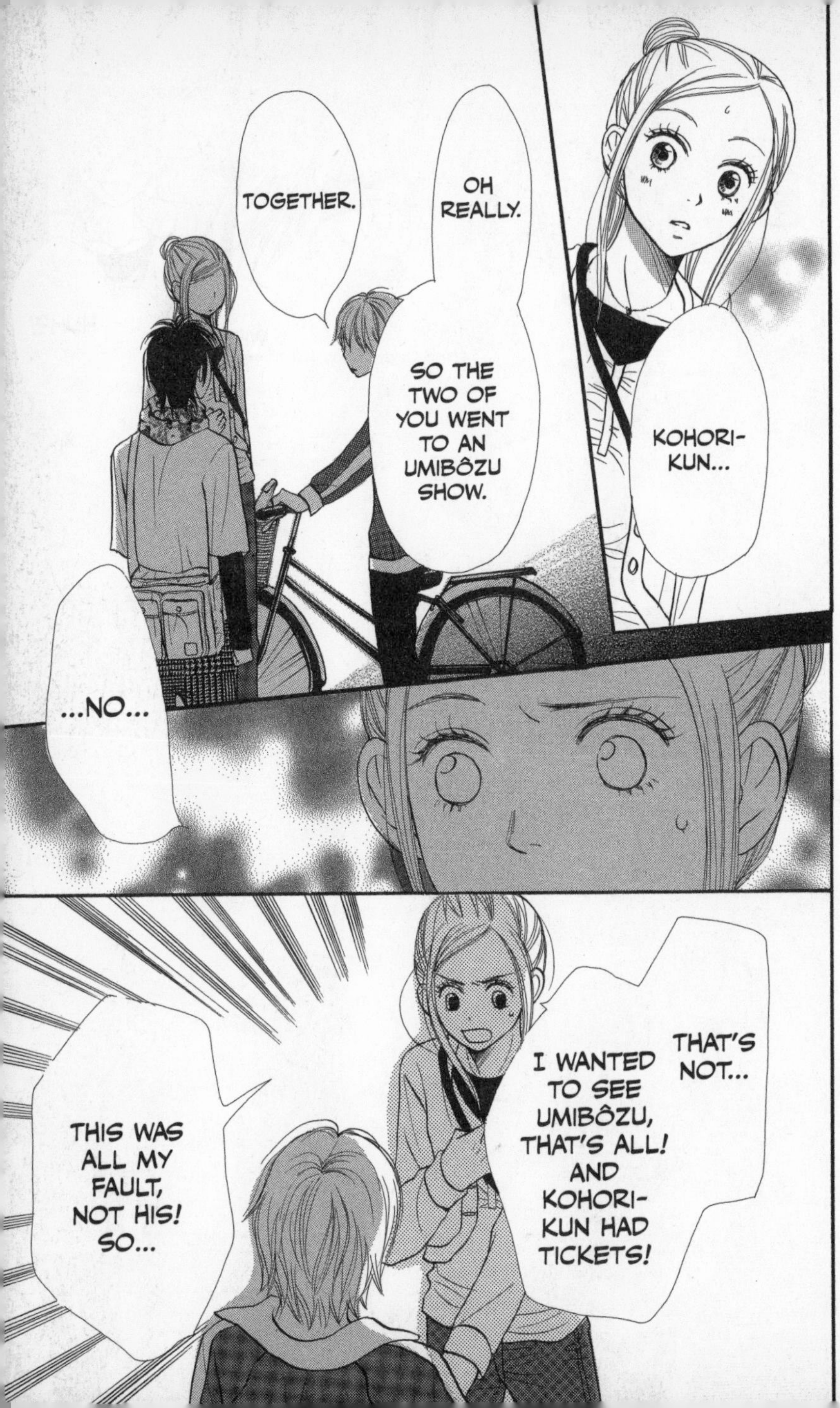
KOHORI-KUN...
OH REALLY.
TOGETHER.
SO THE TWO OF YOU WENT TO AN UMIBÔZU SHOW.
...NO...
THAT'S NOT...
I WANTED TO SEE UMIBÔZU, THAT'S ALL! AND KOHORI-KUN HAD TICKETS!
THIS WAS ALL MY FAULT, NOT HIS! SO...

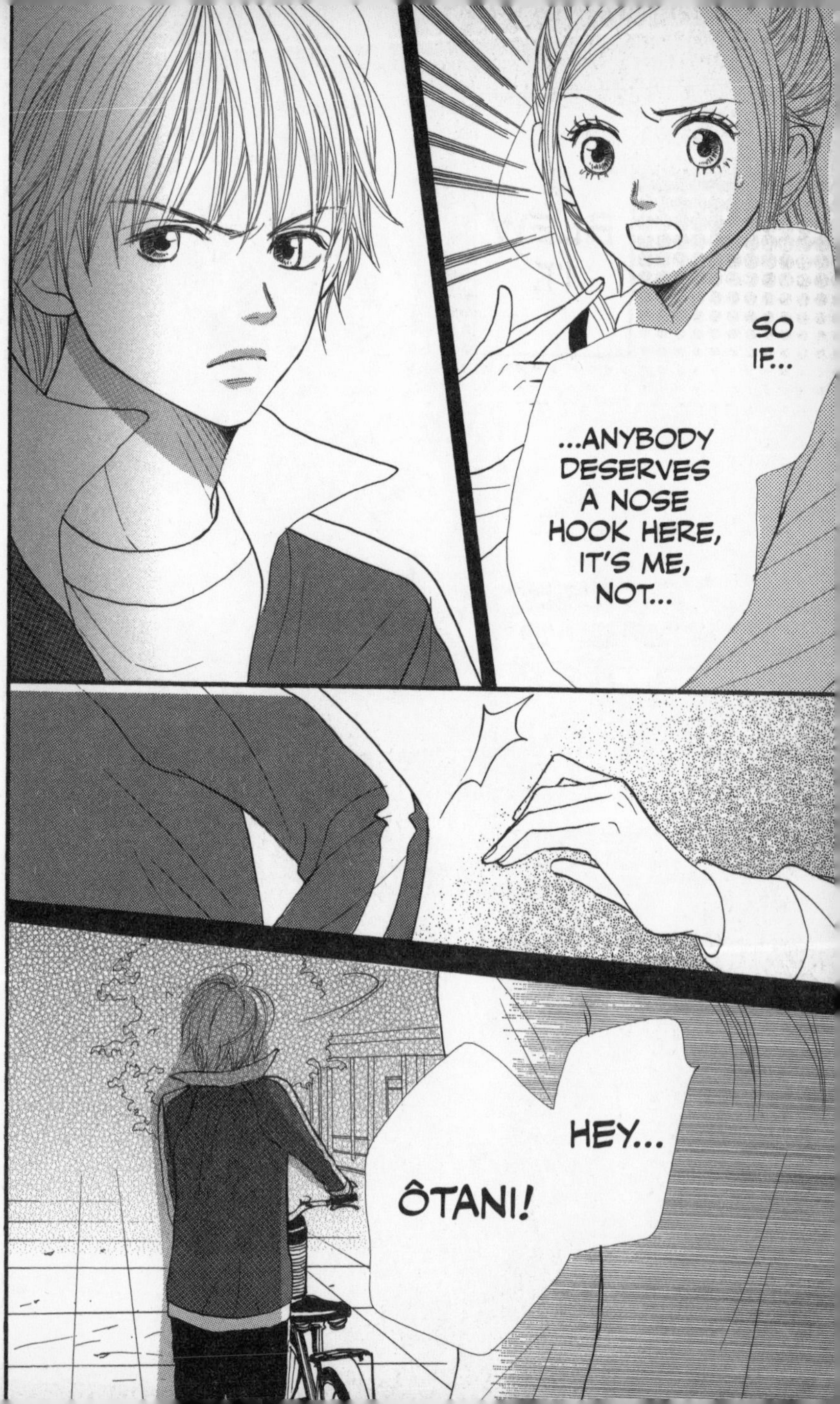
SO IF...
...ANYBODY DESERVES A NOSE HOOK HERE, IT'S ME, NOT...
HEY...
ÔTANI!

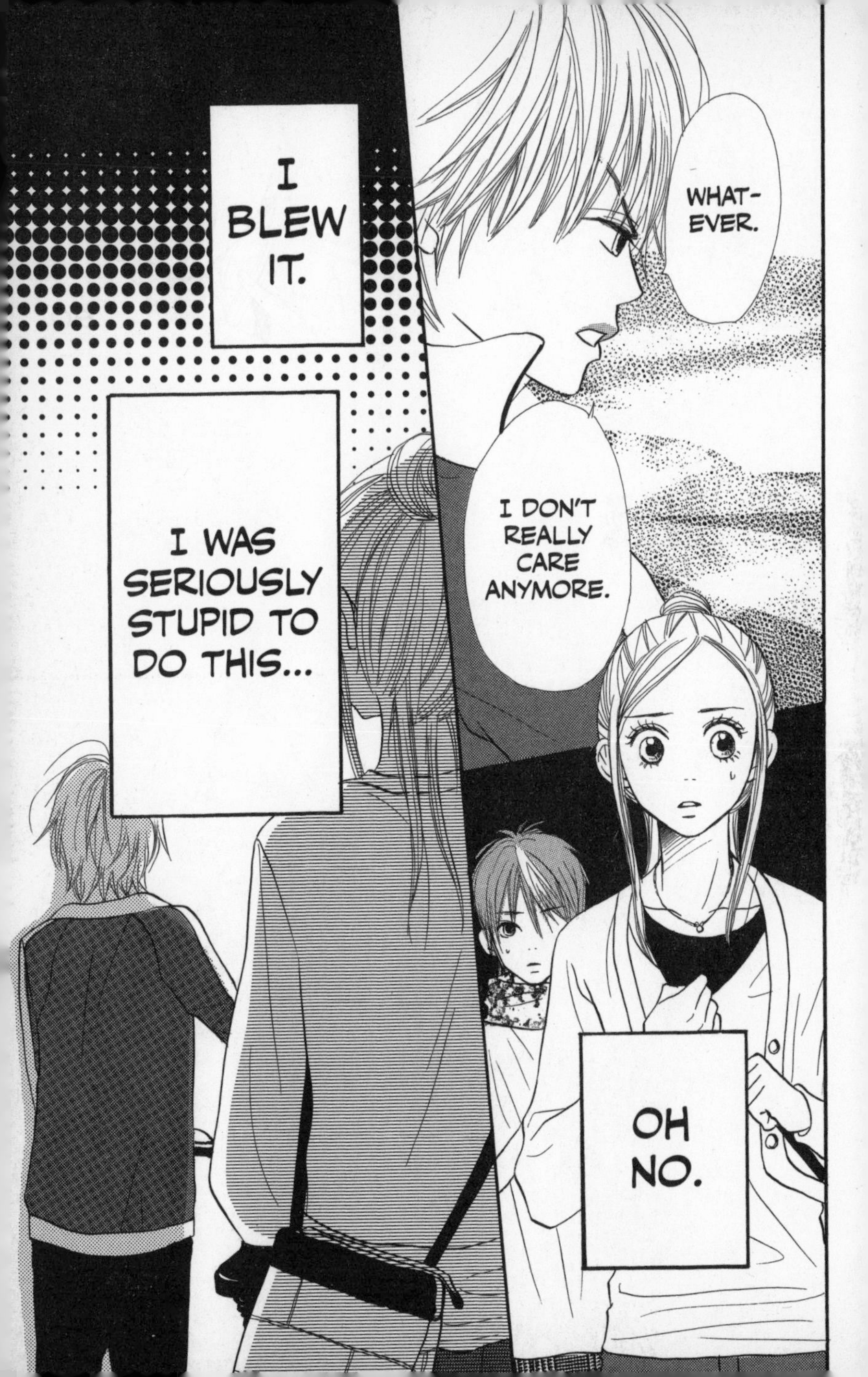
WHAT-EVER.
I BLEW IT.
I DON'T REALLY CARE ANYMORE.
I WAS SERIOUSLY STUPID TO DO THIS...
OH NO.

LOVELY ★ COMPLEX

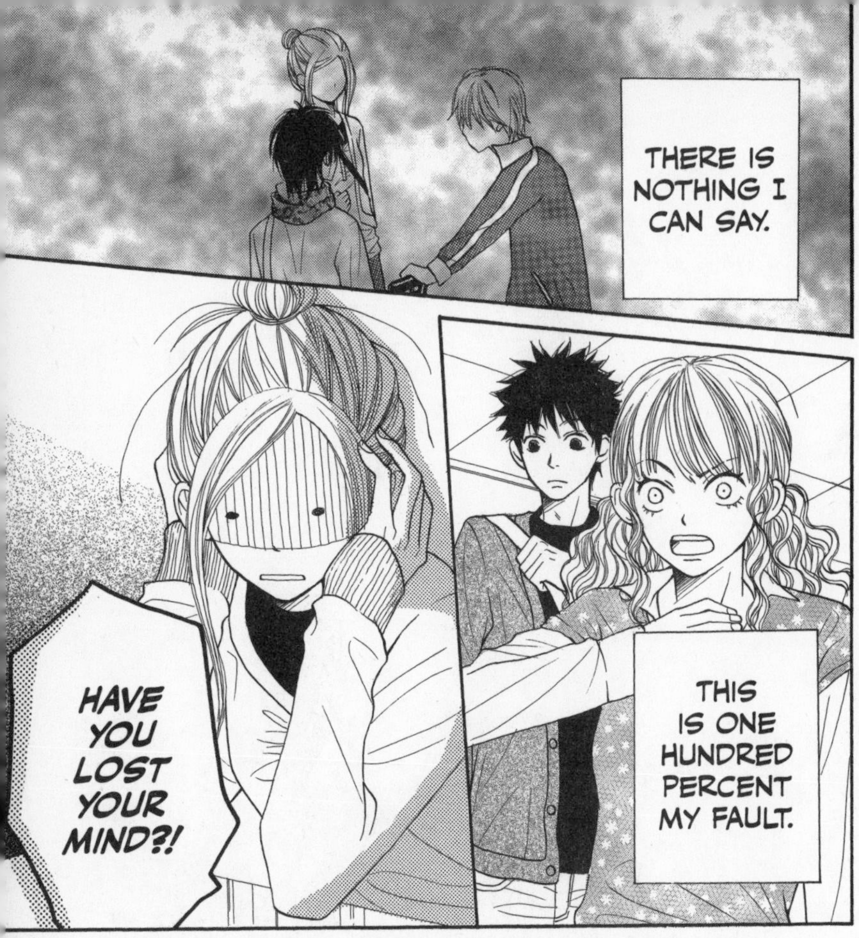
THERE IS NOTHING I CAN SAY.
THIS IS ONE HUNDRED PERCENT MY FAULT.
HAVE YOU LOST YOUR MIND?!

CHAPTER 39

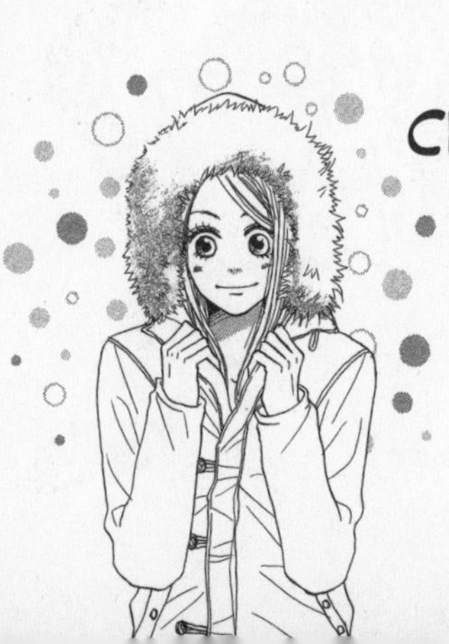

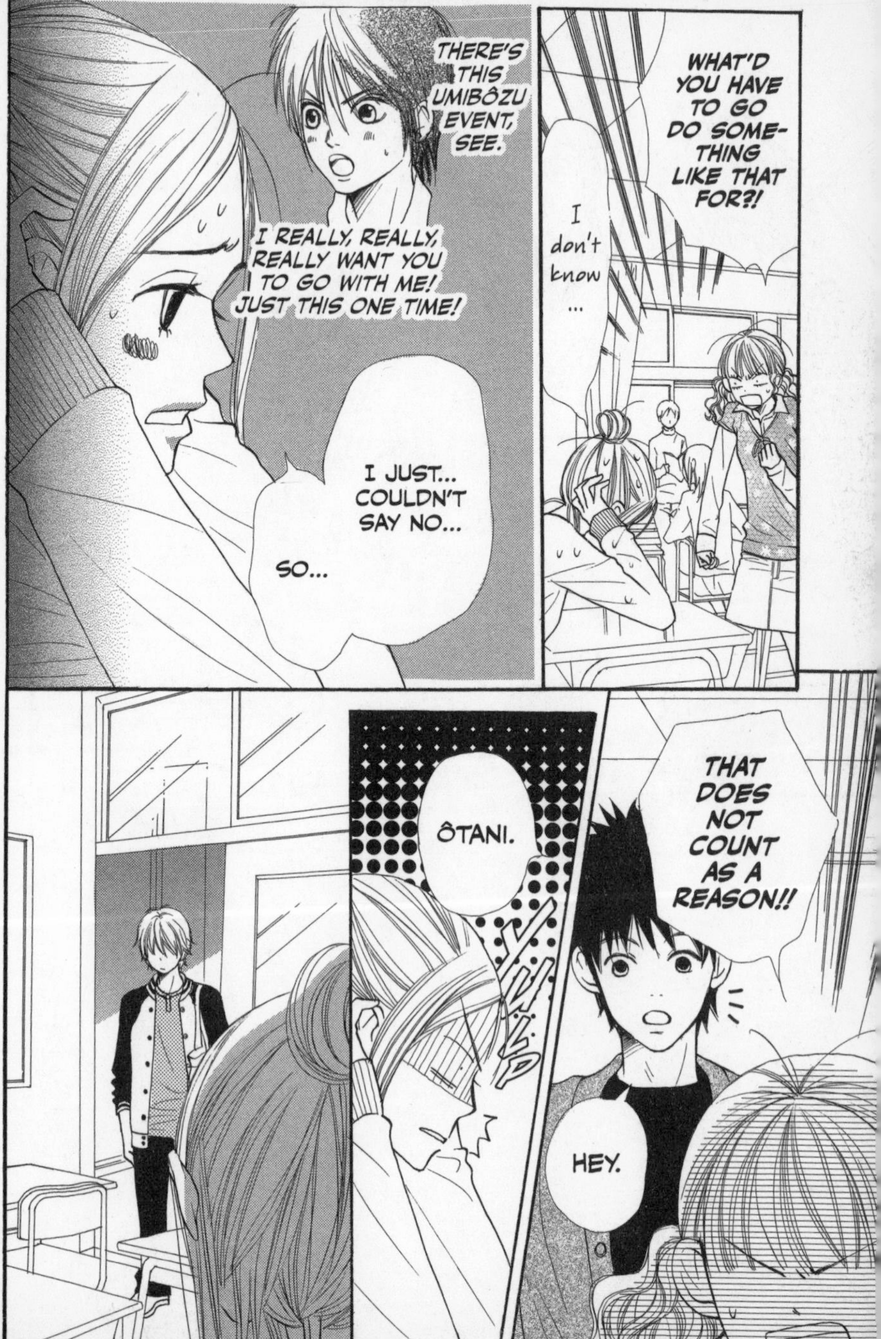
WHAT'D YOU HAVE TO GO DO SOME-THING LIKE THAT FOR?!
I don't know...
THERE'S THIS UMIBÔZU EVENT, SEE.
I REALLY, REALLY, REALLY WANT YOU TO GO WITH ME! JUST THIS ONE TIME!
I JUST... COULDN'T SAY NO...
SO...
THAT DOES NOT COUNT AS A REASON!!
HEY.
ÔTANI.

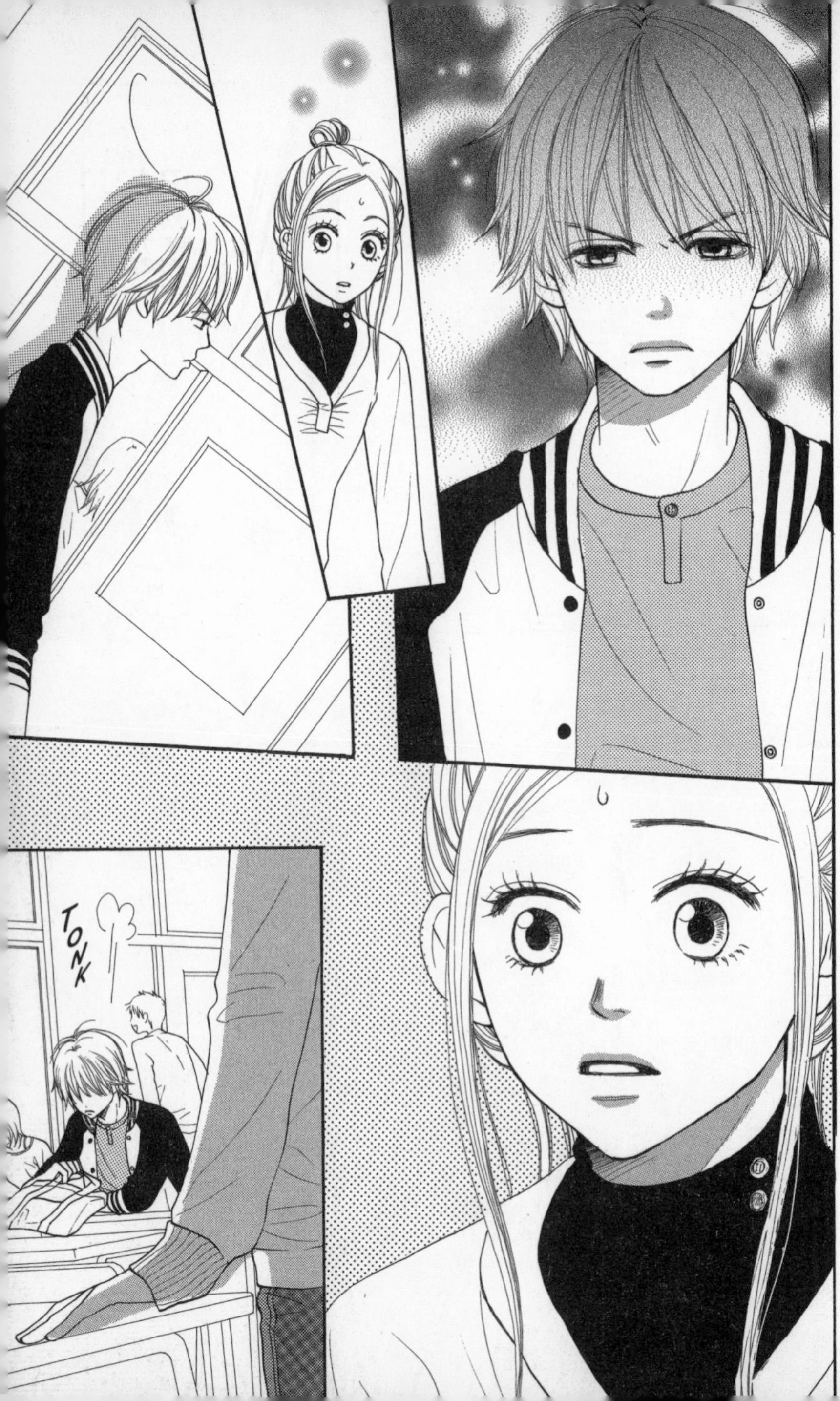
TONK

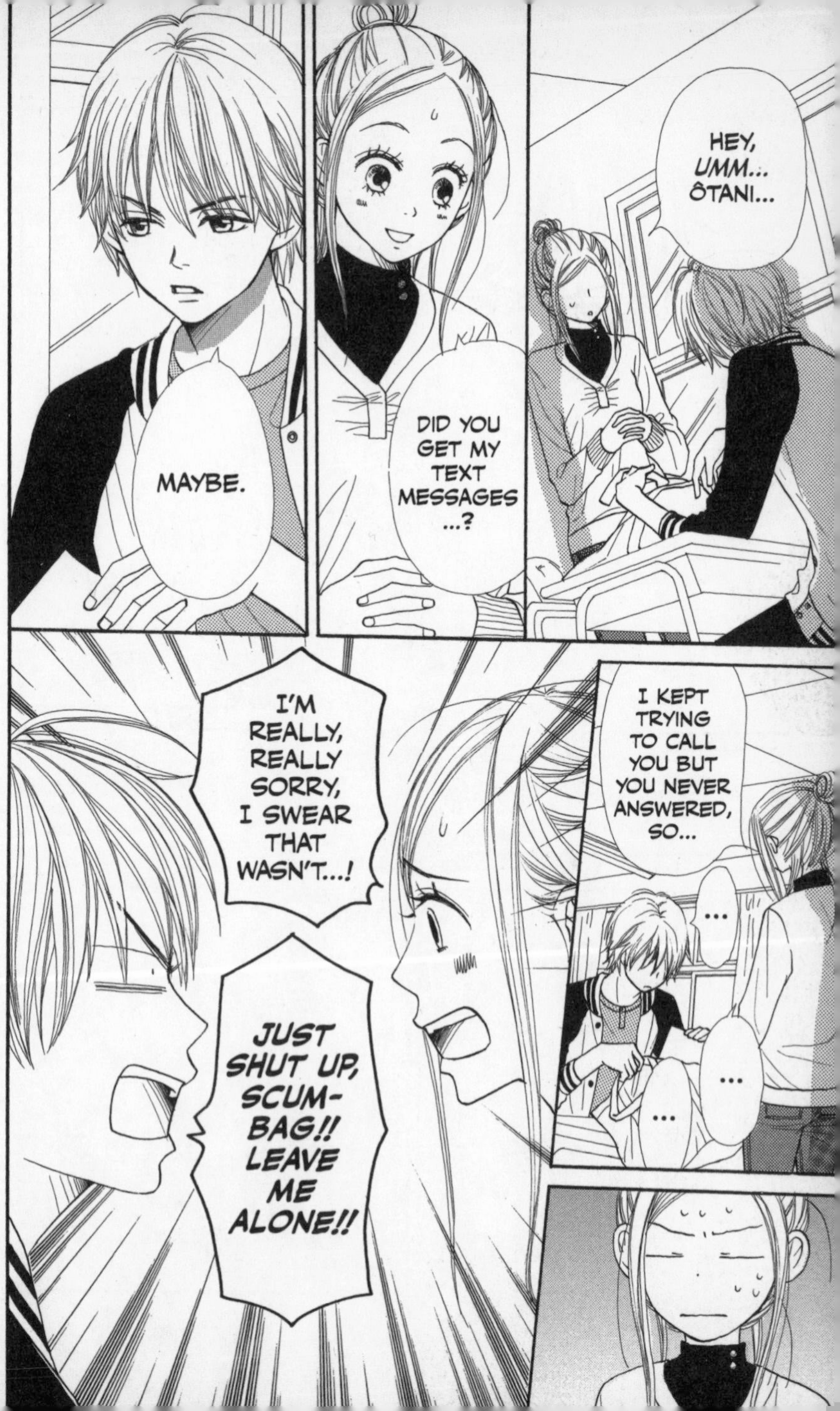
HEY, *UMM...* ÔTANI...
DID YOU GET MY TEXT MESSAGES ...?
MAYBE.
I KEPT TRYING TO CALL YOU BUT YOU NEVER ANSWERED, SO...
...
...
...
I'M REALLY, REALLY SORRY, I SWEAR THAT WASN'T...!
JUST SHUT UP, SCUM-BAG!! LEAVE ME ALONE!!

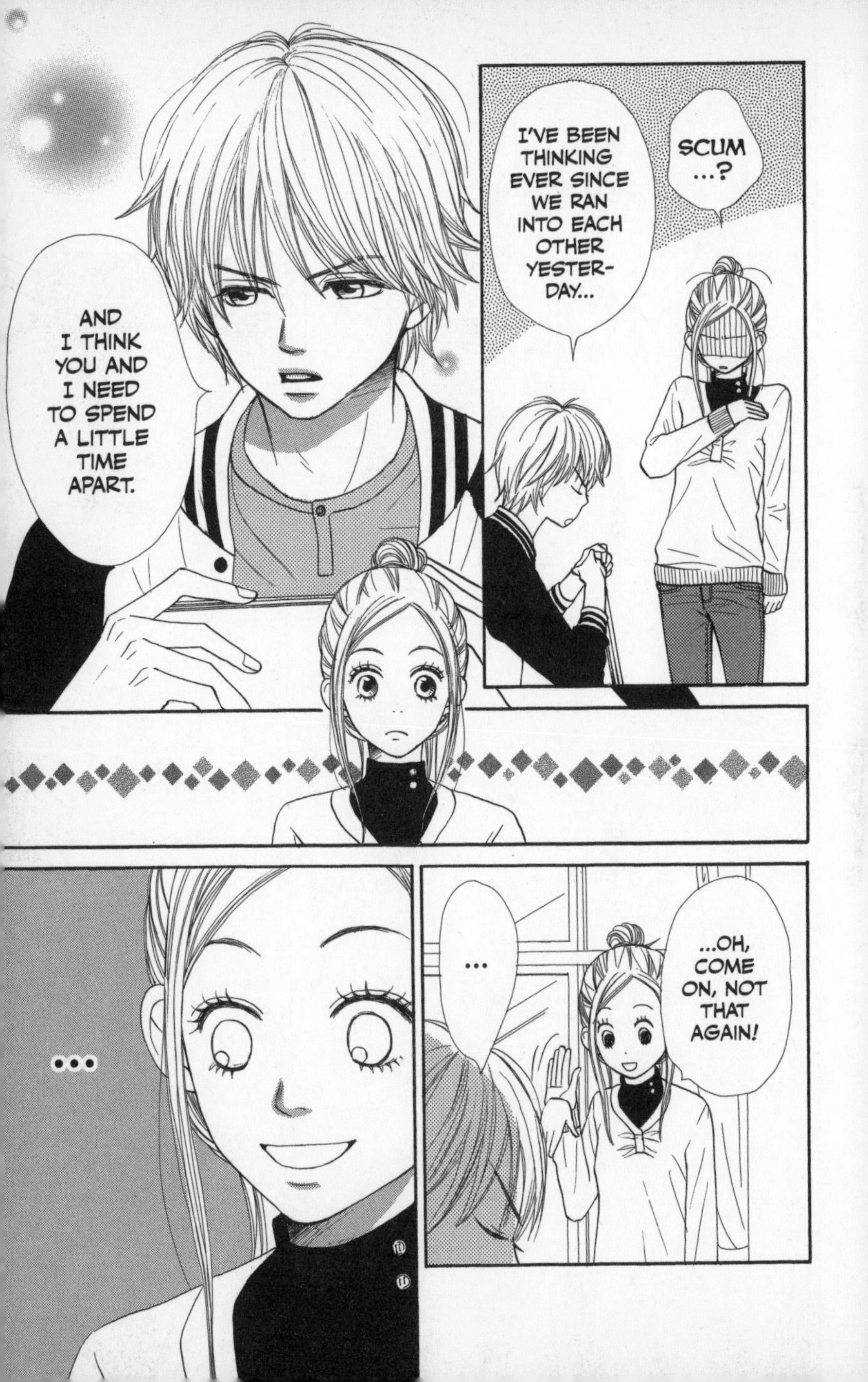
SCUM ...?
I'VE BEEN THINKING EVER SINCE WE RAN INTO EACH OTHER YESTER-DAY...
AND I THINK YOU AND I NEED TO SPEND A LITTLE TIME APART.
...OH, COME ON, NOT THAT AGAIN!
...
•••

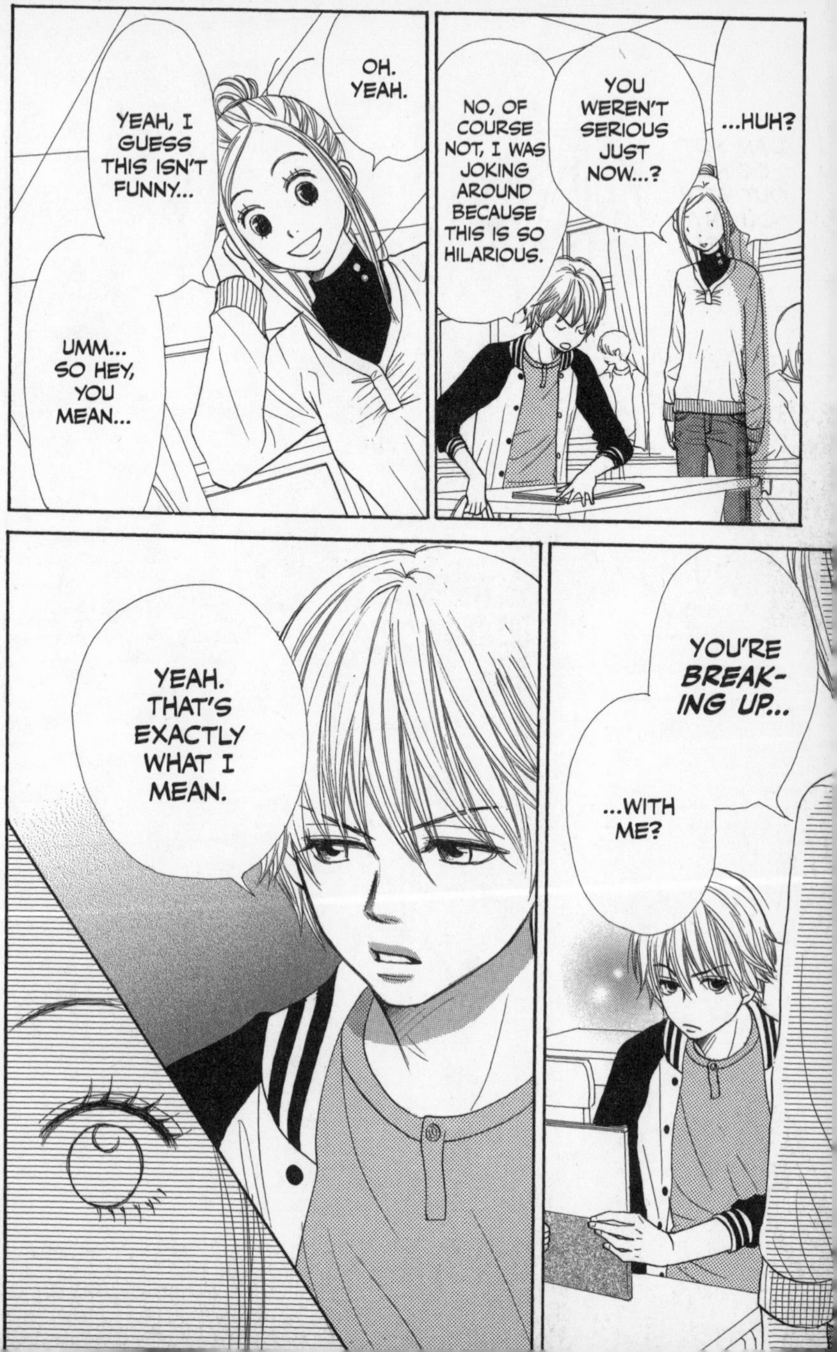
...HUH?
YOU WEREN'T SERIOUS JUST NOW...?
NO, OF COURSE NOT, I WAS JOKING AROUND BECAUSE THIS IS SO HILARIOUS.
OH. YEAH.
YEAH, I GUESS THIS ISN'T FUNNY...
UMM... SO HEY, YOU MEAN...
YOU'RE *BREAKING UP*...
...WITH ME?
YEAH. THAT'S EXACTLY WHAT I MEAN.

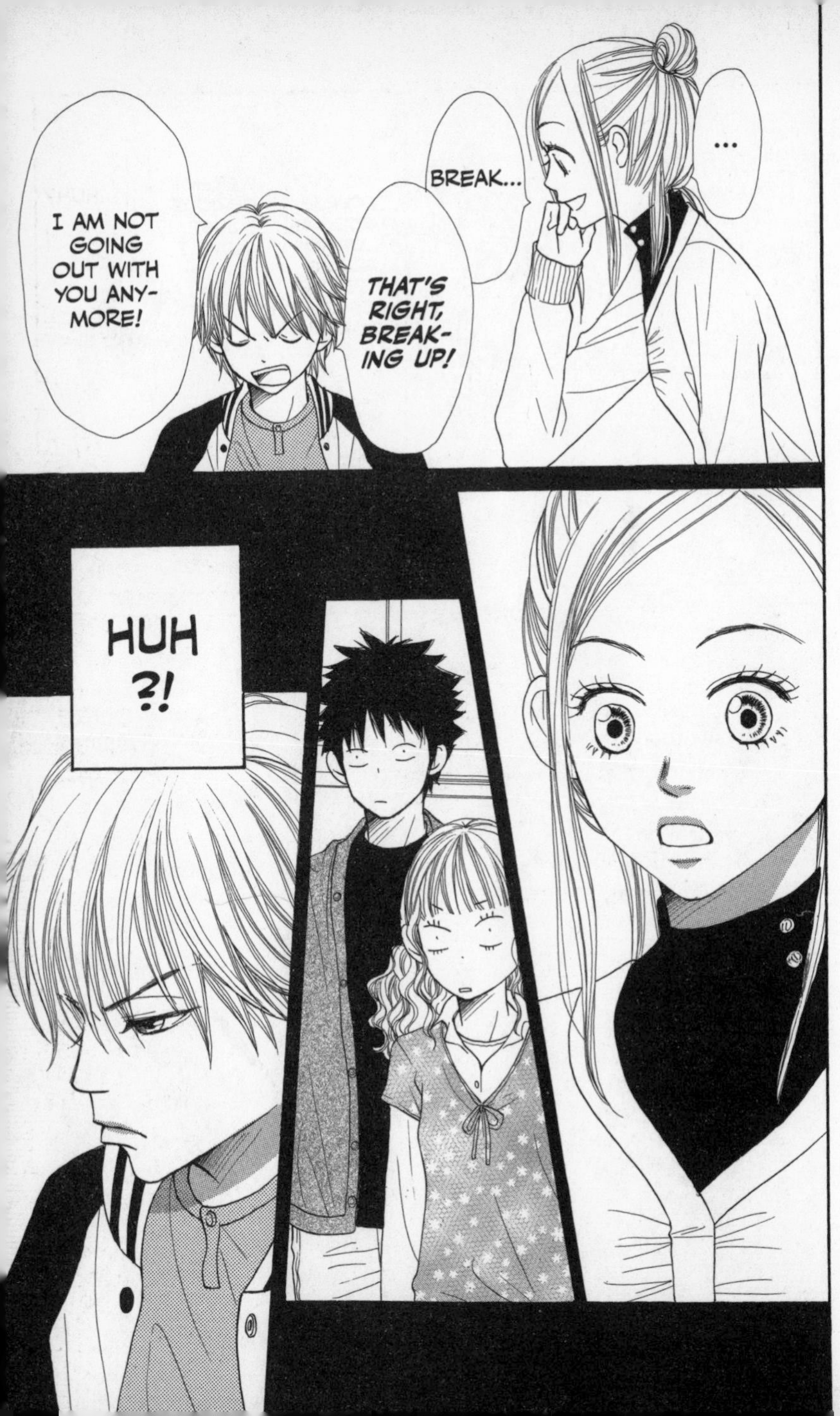
...
BREAK...
THAT'S RIGHT, BREAKING UP!
I AM NOT GOING OUT WITH YOU ANYMORE!
HUH ?!

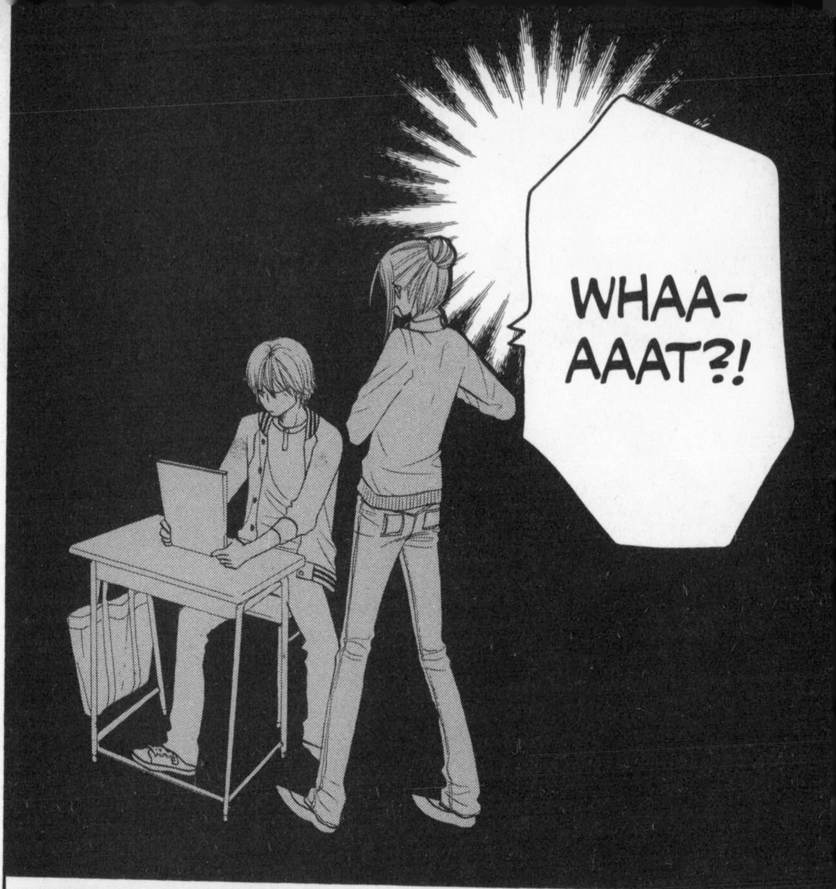
WHAA-
AAAT?!

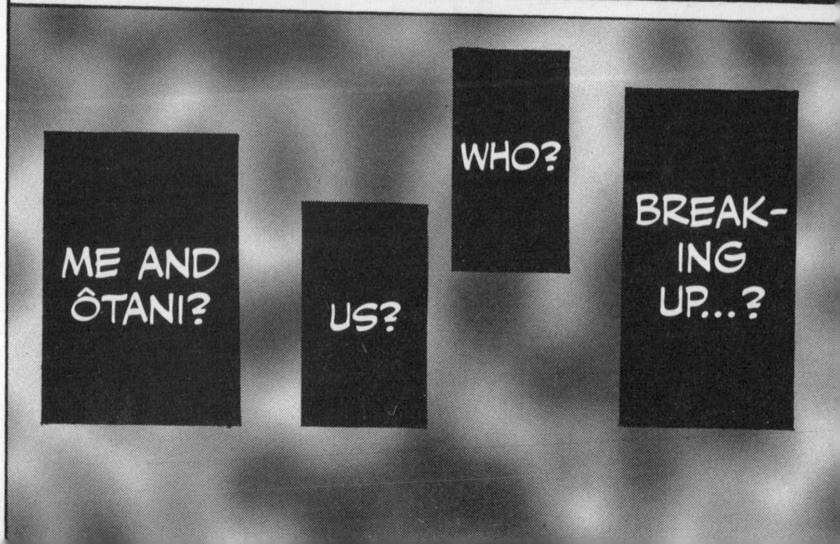
BREAK-
ING
UP...?
WHO?
US?
ME AND
ÔTANI?

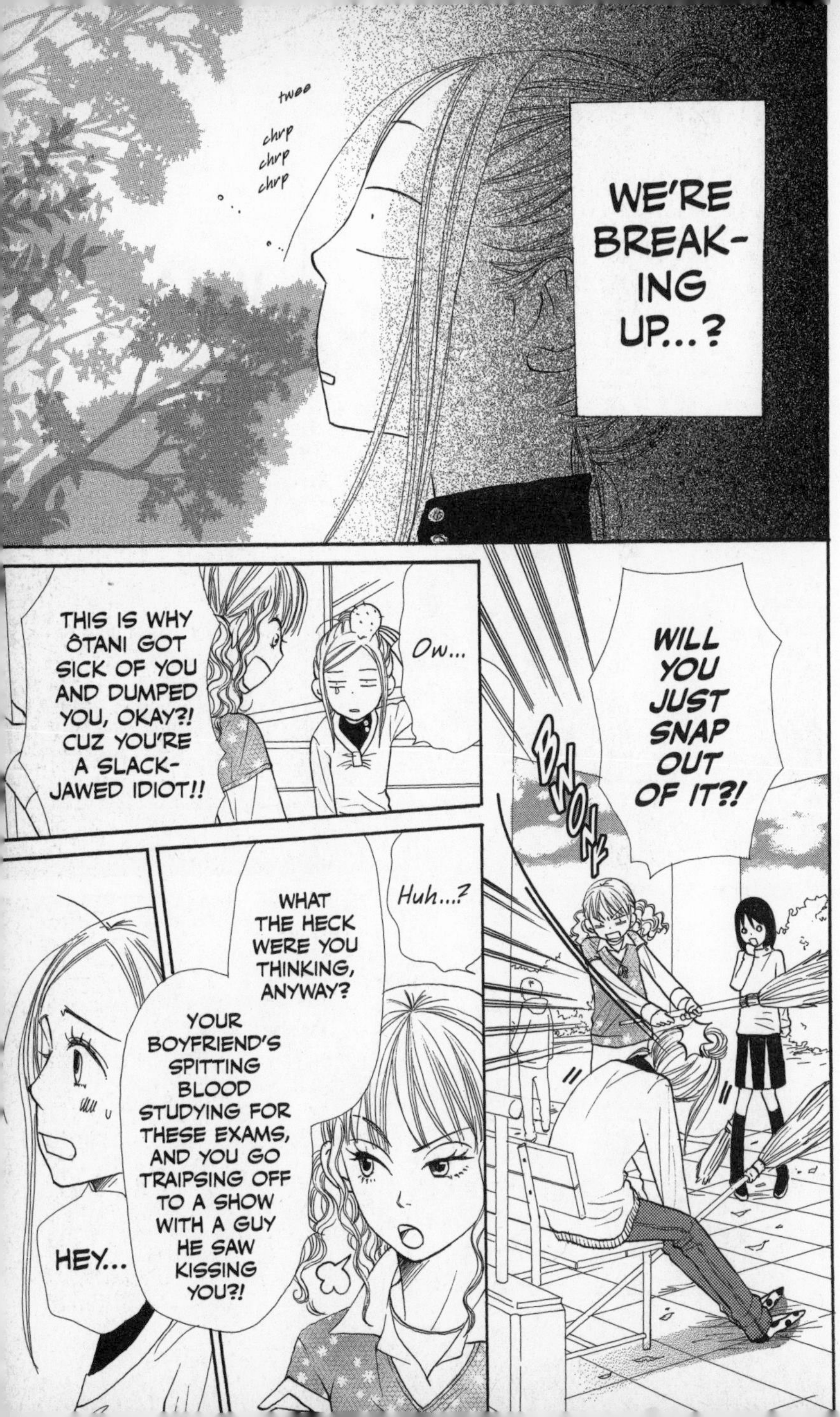
WE'RE BREAKING-ING UP...?
twee
chrp chrp chrp
WILL YOU JUST SNAP OUT OF IT?!
BWONK
Ow...
THIS IS WHY ÔTANI GOT SICK OF YOU AND DUMPED YOU, OKAY?! CUZ YOU'RE A SLACK-JAWED IDIOT!!
Huh...?
WHAT THE HECK WERE YOU THINKING, ANYWAY?
YOUR BOYFRIEND'S SPITTING BLOOD STUDYING FOR THESE EXAMS, AND YOU GO TRAIPSING OFF TO A SHOW WITH A GUY HE SAW KISSING YOU?!
HEY...

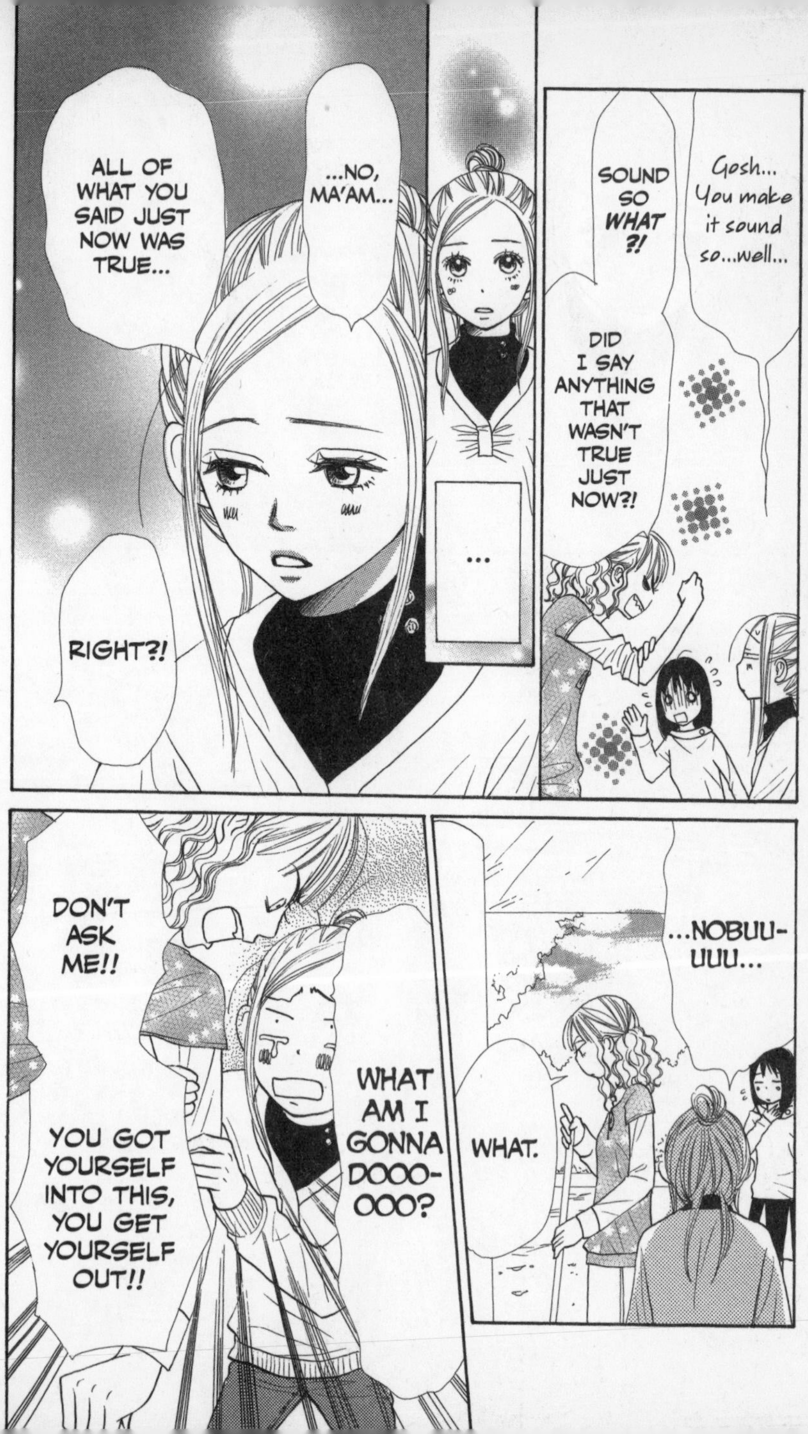
Gosh... You make it sound so...well...
SOUND SO WHAT?!
DID I SAY ANYTHING THAT WASN'T TRUE JUST NOW?!
...NO, MA'AM...
ALL OF WHAT YOU SAID JUST NOW WAS TRUE...
...
RIGHT?!
...NOBUU-UUU...
WHAT.
WHAT AM I GONNA DOOOO-OOO?
DON'T ASK ME!!
YOU GOT YOURSELF INTO THIS, YOU GET YOURSELF OUT!!

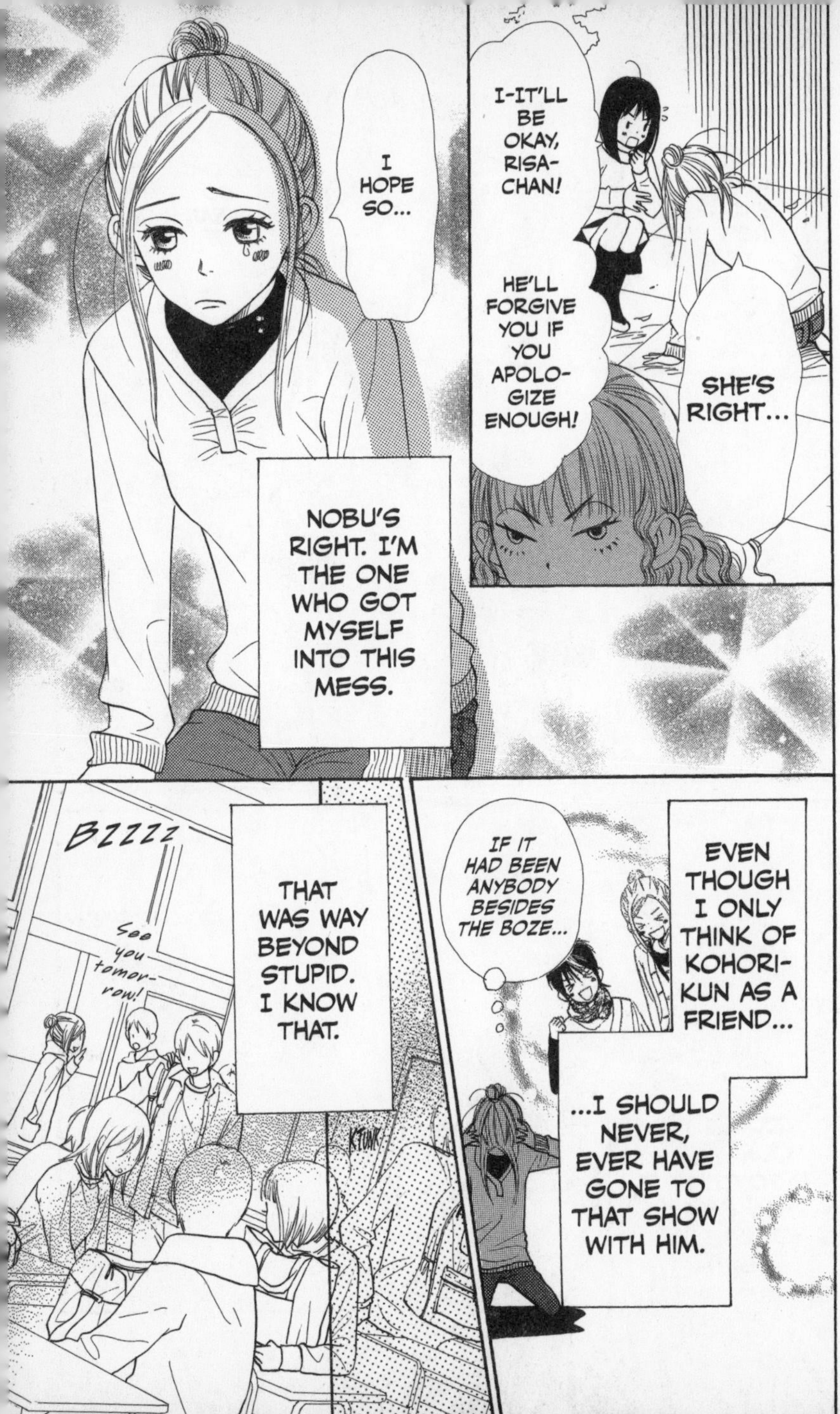
I-IT'LL BE OKAY, RISA-CHAN!
HE'LL FORGIVE YOU IF YOU APOLOGIZE ENOUGH!
SHE'S RIGHT...
I HOPE SO...
NOBU'S RIGHT. I'M THE ONE WHO GOT MYSELF INTO THIS MESS.
EVEN THOUGH I ONLY THINK OF KOHORI-KUN AS A FRIEND...
IF IT HAD BEEN ANYBODY BESIDES THE BOZE...
...I SHOULD NEVER, EVER HAVE GONE TO THAT SHOW WITH HIM.
KTUNK
THAT WAS WAY BEYOND STUPID. I KNOW THAT.
BZZZZ
See you tomorrow!

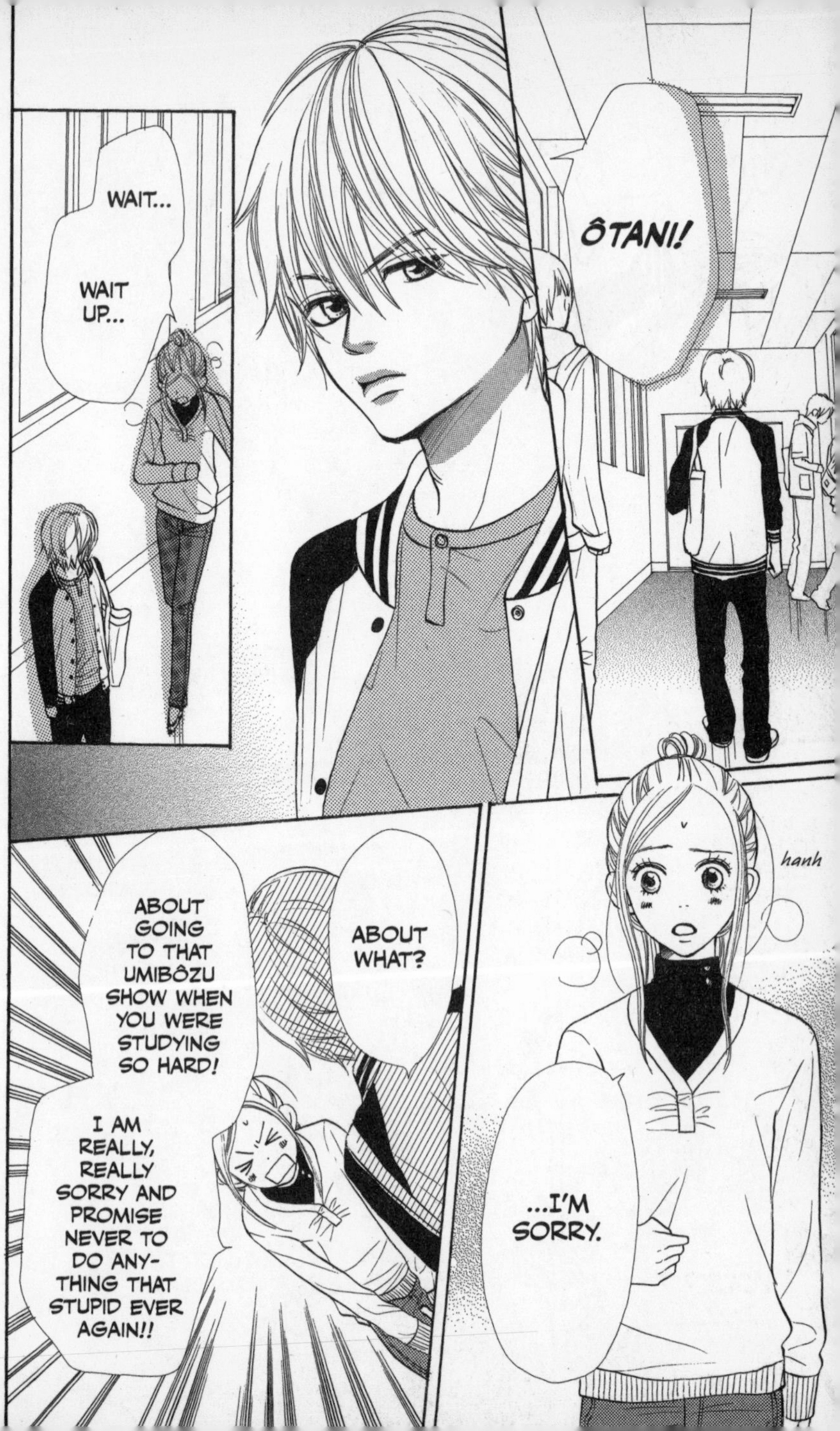
ÔTANI!
WAIT...
WAIT UP...
hanh
...I'M SORRY.
ABOUT WHAT?
ABOUT GOING TO THAT UMIBÔZU SHOW WHEN YOU WERE STUDYING SO HARD!
I AM REALLY, REALLY SORRY AND PROMISE NEVER TO DO ANY-THING THAT STUPID EVER AGAIN!!

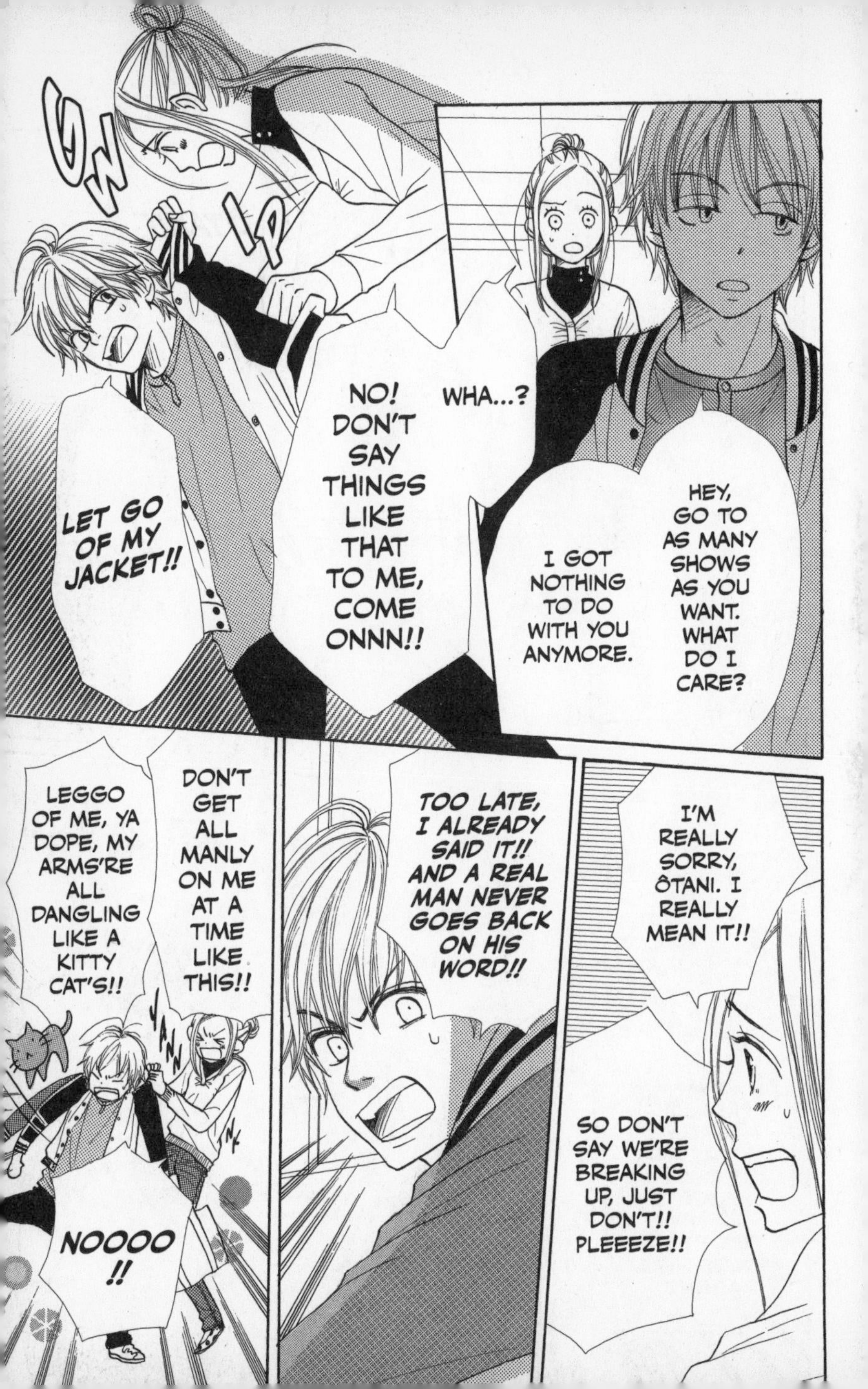
HEY, GO TO AS MANY SHOWS AS YOU WANT. WHAT DO I CARE?
I GOT NOTHING TO DO WITH YOU ANYMORE.
WHA...?
NO! DON'T SAY THINGS LIKE THAT TO ME, COME ONNN!!
GWIP
LET GO OF MY JACKET!!
I'M REALLY SORRY, ÔTANI. I REALLY MEAN IT!!
SO DON'T SAY WE'RE BREAKING UP, JUST DON'T!! PLEEEZE!!
TOO LATE, I ALREADY SAID IT!! AND A REAL MAN NEVER GOES BACK ON HIS WORD!!
DON'T GET ALL MANLY ON ME AT A TIME LIKE THIS!!
LEGGO OF ME, YA DOPE, MY ARMS'RE ALL DANGLING LIKE A KITTY CAT'S!!
NOOOO!!

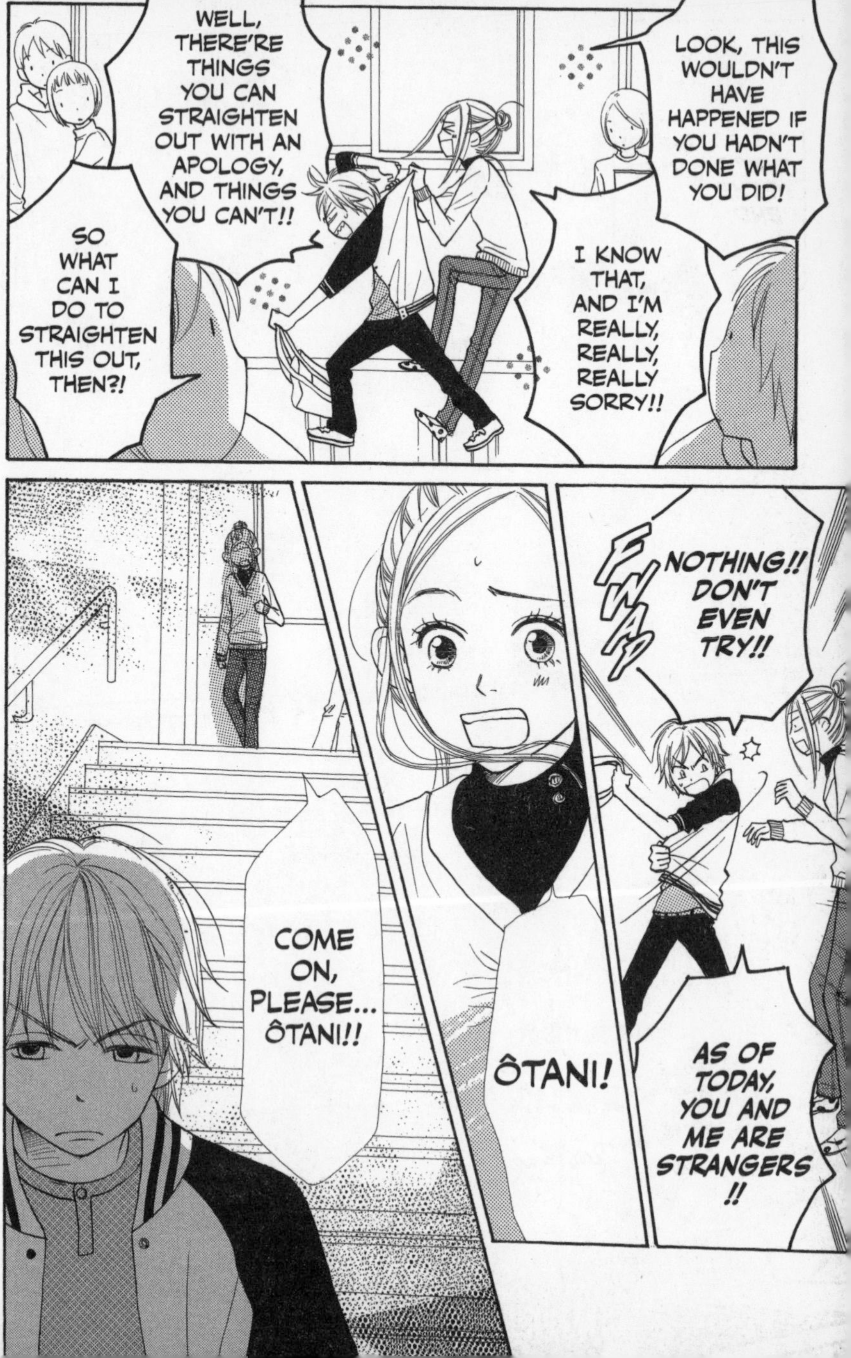

LOOK, THIS WOULDN'T HAVE HAPPENED IF YOU HADN'T DONE WHAT YOU DID!
I KNOW THAT, AND I'M REALLY, REALLY, REALLY SORRY!!
WELL, THERE'RE THINGS YOU CAN STRAIGHTEN OUT WITH AN APOLOGY, AND THINGS YOU CAN'T!!
SO WHAT CAN I DO TO STRAIGHTEN THIS OUT, THEN?!
FWAP
NOTHING!! DON'T EVEN TRY!!
AS OF TODAY, YOU AND ME ARE STRANGERS!!
ÔTANI!
COME ON, PLEASE... ÔTANI!!

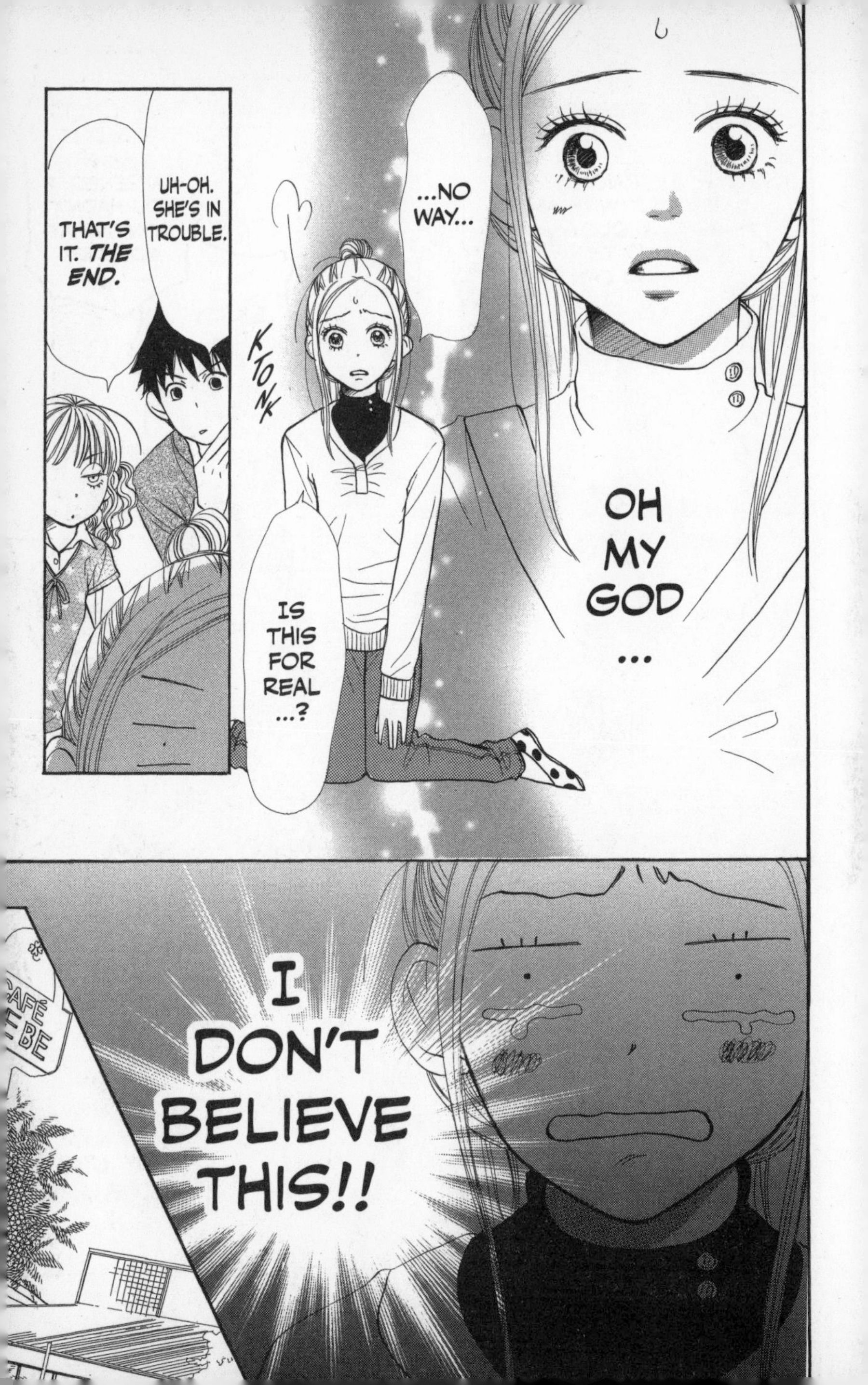
OH MY GOD ...
...NO WAY...
KTONK
IS THIS FOR REAL ...?
UH-OH. SHE'S IN TROUBLE.
THAT'S IT. ***THE END.***
I DON'T BELIEVE THIS!!

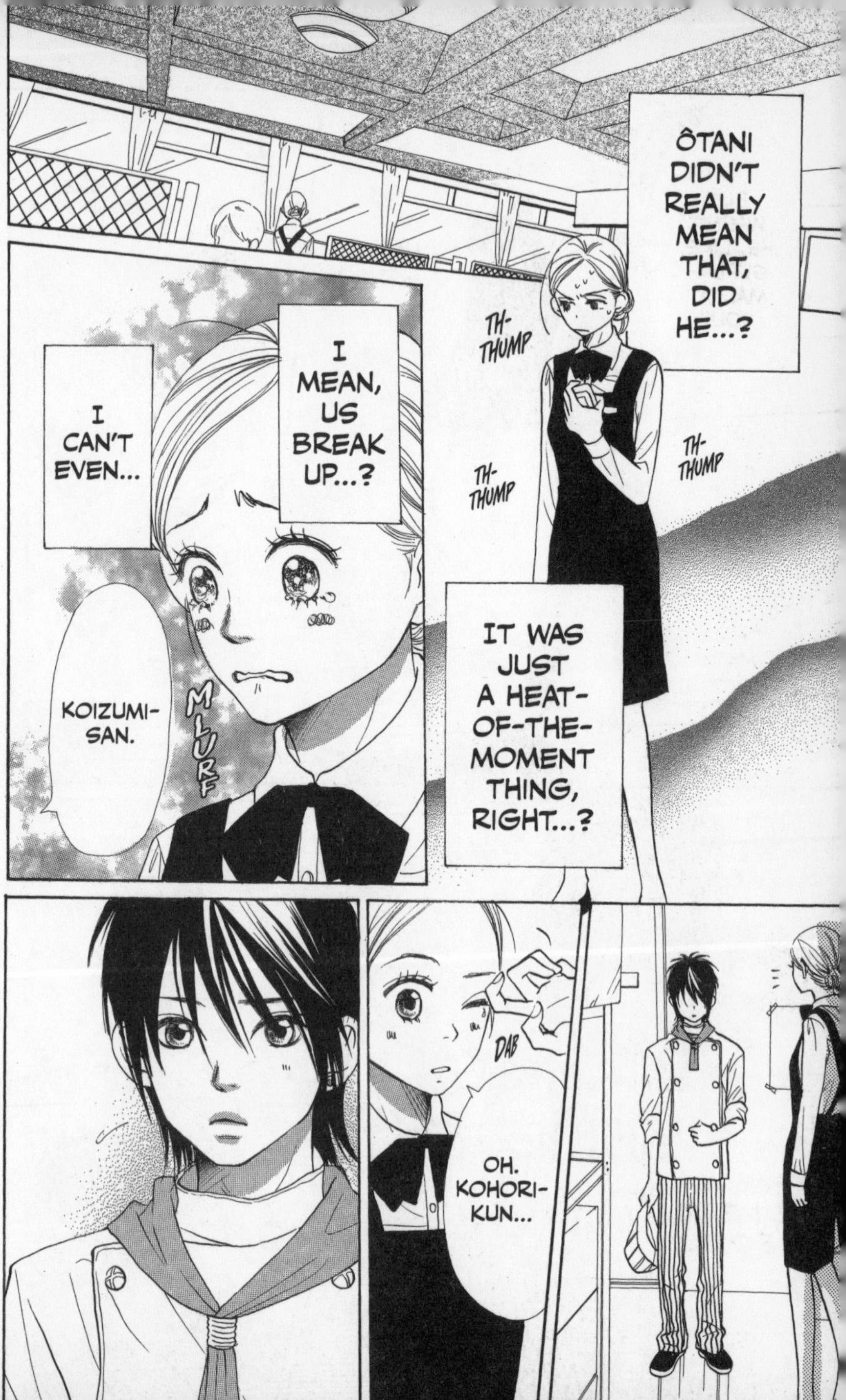
ÔTANI DIDN'T REALLY MEAN THAT, DID HE...?
TH-THUMP
TH-THUMP
TH-THUMP
IT WAS JUST A HEAT-OF-THE-MOMENT THING, RIGHT...?
I MEAN, US BREAK UP...?
I CAN'T EVEN...
MLURF
KOIZUMI-SAN.
DAB
OH. KOHORI-KUN...

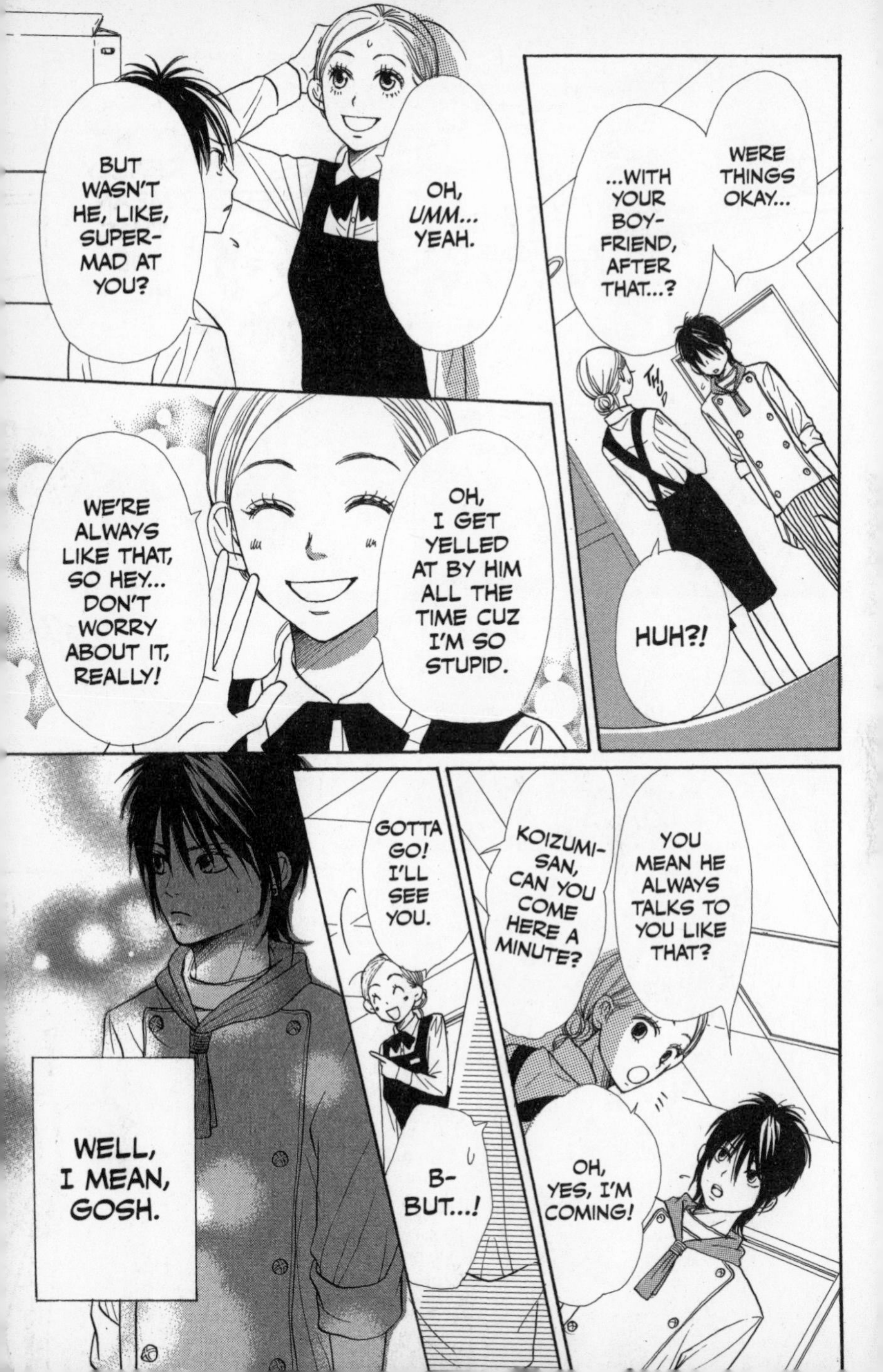
WERE THINGS OKAY...
...WITH YOUR BOY-FRIEND, AFTER THAT...?
HUH?!
OH, UMM... YEAH.
BUT WASN'T HE, LIKE, SUPER-MAD AT YOU?
OH, I GET YELLED AT BY HIM ALL THE TIME CUZ I'M SO STUPID.
WE'RE ALWAYS LIKE THAT, SO HEY... DON'T WORRY ABOUT IT, REALLY!
YOU MEAN HE ALWAYS TALKS TO YOU LIKE THAT?
KOIZUMI-SAN, CAN YOU COME HERE A MINUTE?
OH, YES, I'M COMING!
GOTTA GO! I'LL SEE YOU.
B-BUT...!
WELL, I MEAN, GOSH.

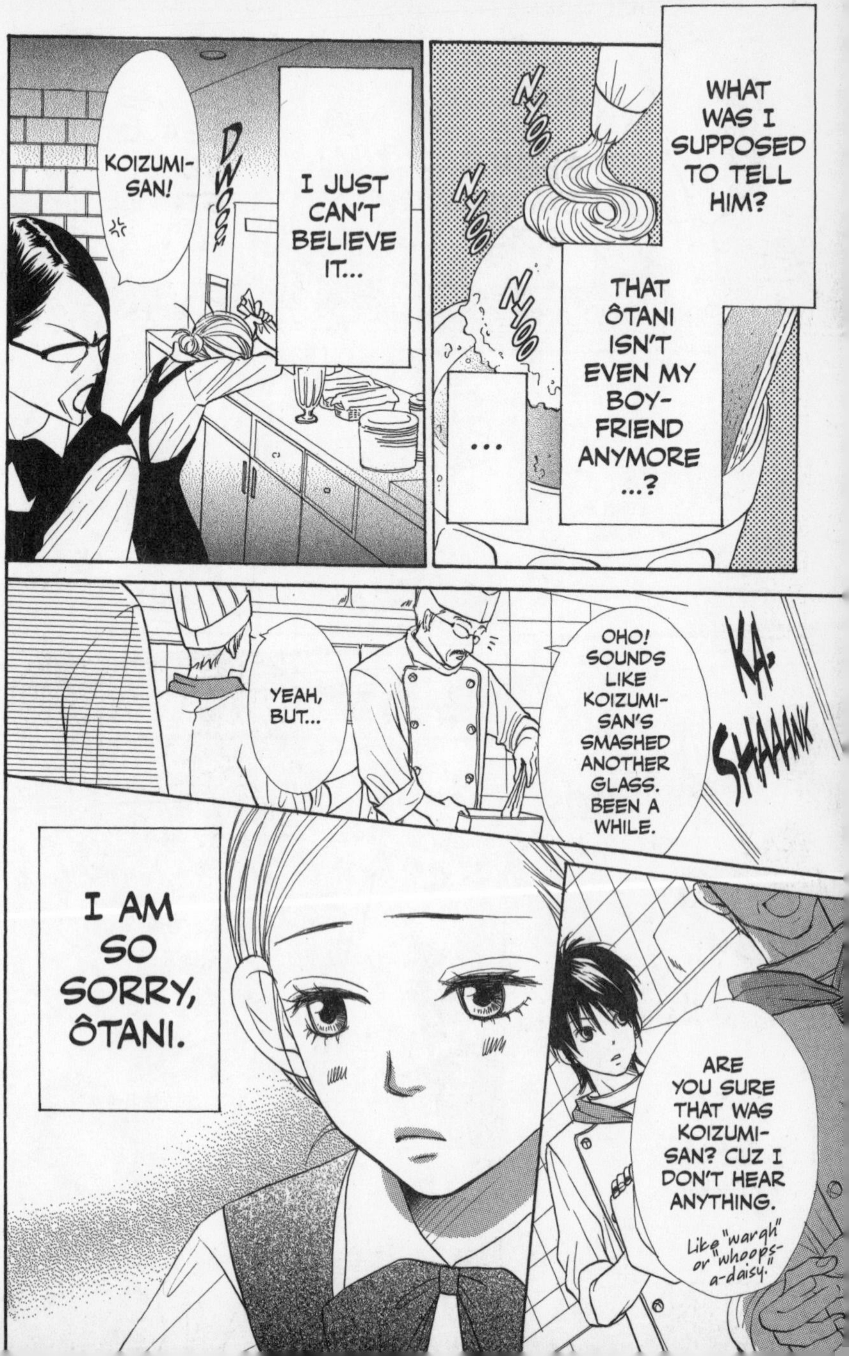
WHAT WAS I SUPPOSED TO TELL HIM?
NYOO
NYOO
NYOO
NYOO
THAT ÔTANI ISN'T EVEN MY BOY-FRIEND ANYMORE ...?
...
I JUST CAN'T BELIEVE IT...
KOIZUMI-SAN!
KA-SHAAANK
OHO! SOUNDS LIKE KOIZUMI-SAN'S SMASHED ANOTHER GLASS. BEEN A WHILE.
YEAH, BUT...
ARE YOU SURE THAT WAS KOIZUMI-SAN? CUZ I DON'T HEAR ANYTHING.
Like "wargh" or "whoops-a-daisy."
I AM SO SORRY, ÔTANI.

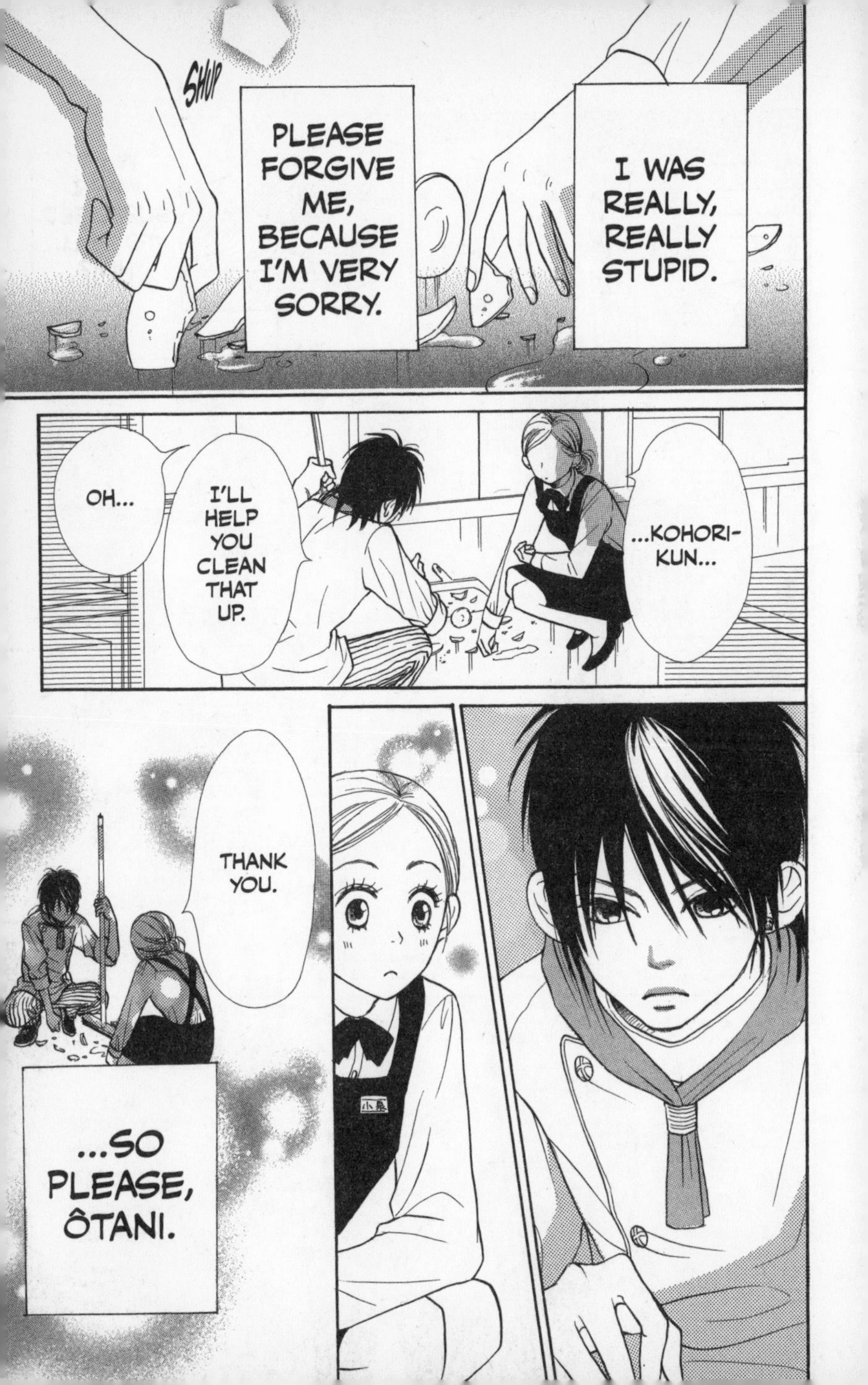
I WAS REALLY, REALLY STUPID.
SHUP
PLEASE FORGIVE ME, BECAUSE I'M VERY SORRY.
...KOHORI-KUN...
I'LL HELP YOU CLEAN THAT UP.
OH...
THANK YOU.
...SO PLEASE, ÔTANI.

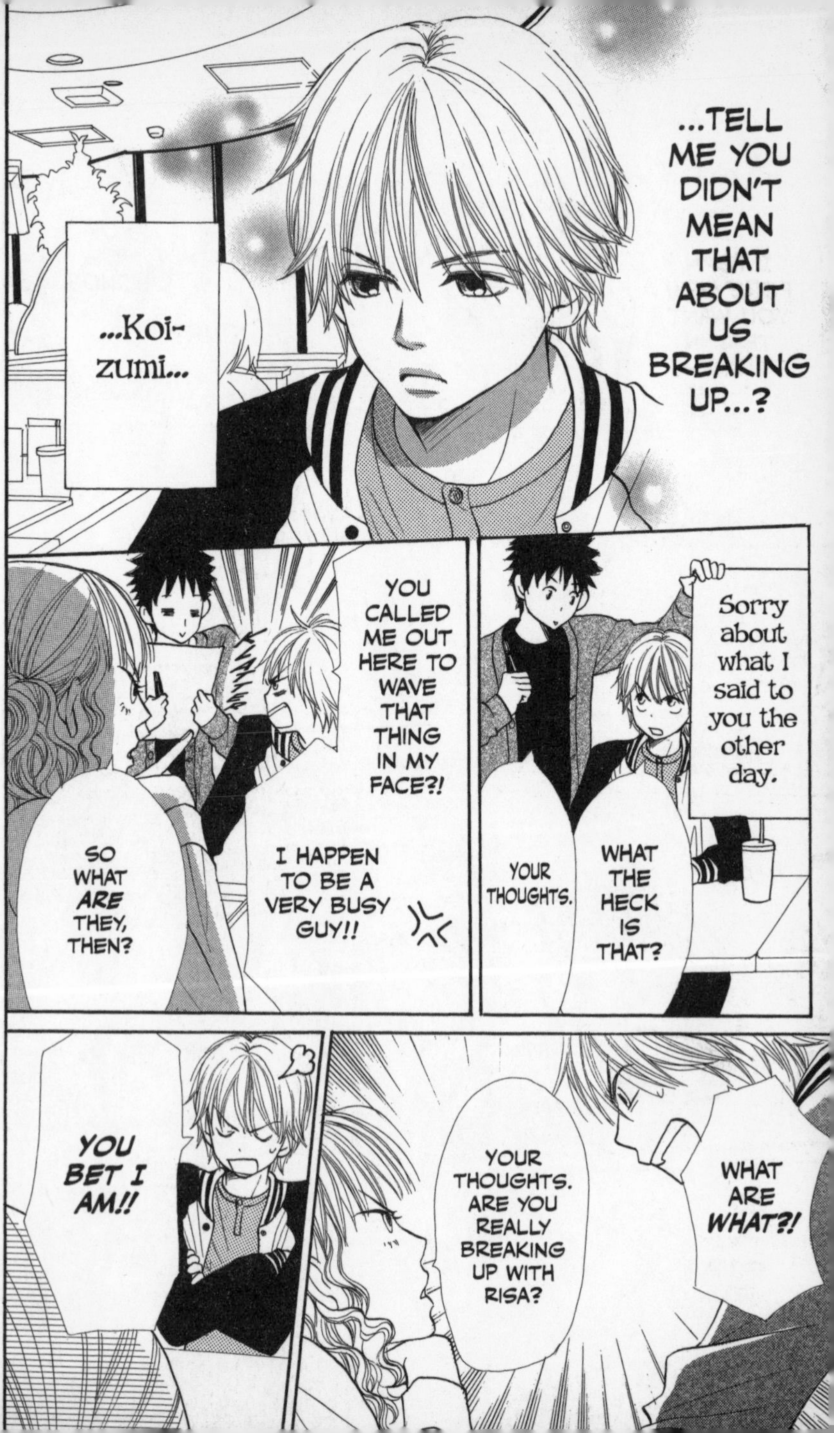

...TELL ME YOU DIDN'T MEAN THAT ABOUT US BREAKING UP...?
...Koi-zumi...
Sorry about what I said to you the other day.
WHAT THE HECK IS THAT?
YOUR THOUGHTS.
YOU CALLED ME OUT HERE TO WAVE THAT THING IN MY FACE?!
I HAPPEN TO BE A VERY BUSY GUY!!
SO WHAT *ARE* THEY, THEN?
WHAT ARE *WHAT?!*
YOUR THOUGHTS. ARE YOU REALLY BREAKING UP WITH RISA?
YOU BET I AM!!

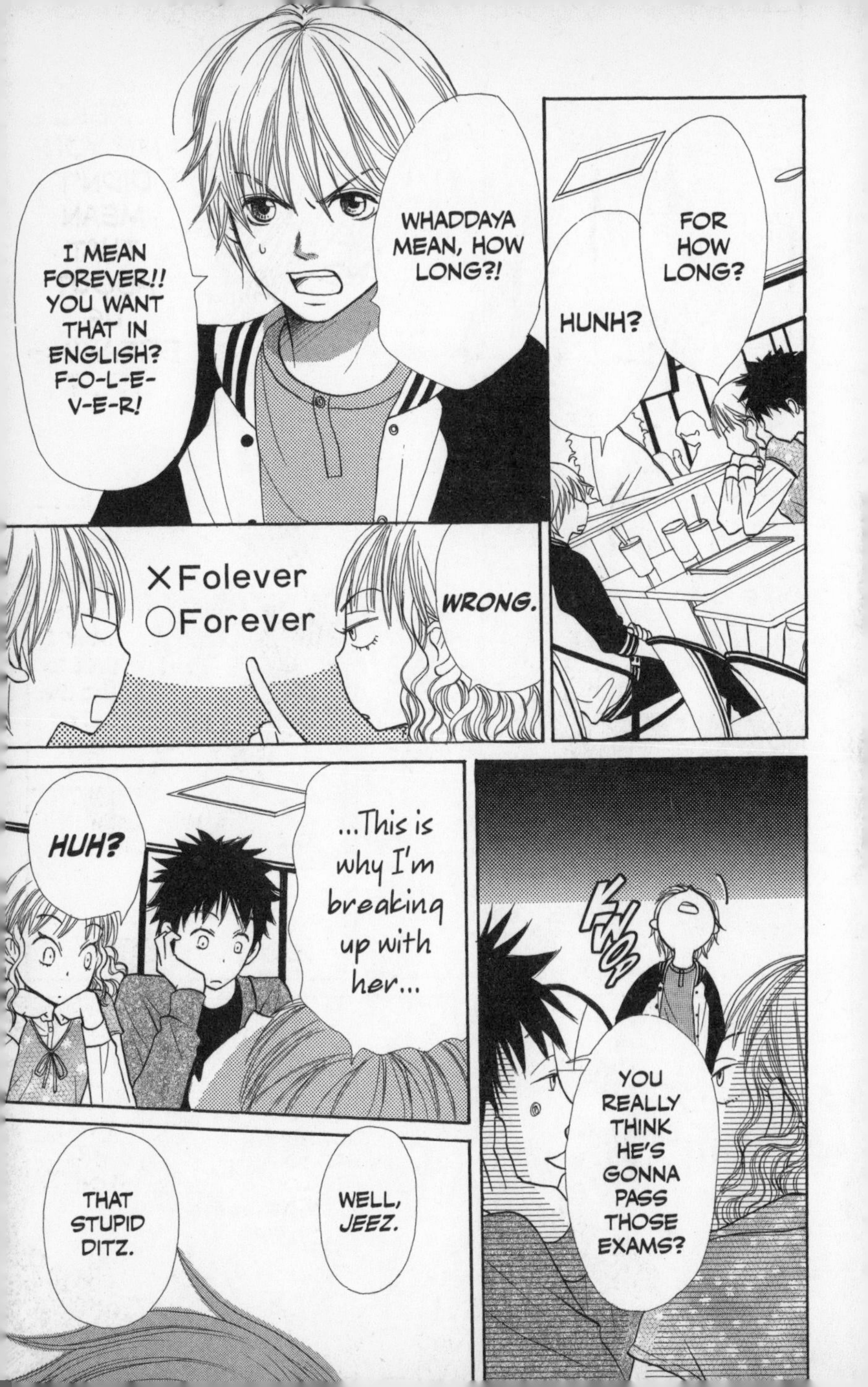
FOR HOW LONG?
HUNH?
WHADDAYA MEAN, HOW LONG?!
I MEAN FOREVER!! YOU WANT THAT IN ENGLISH? F-O-L-E-V-E-R!
WRONG.
×Folever
○Forever
KNOK
YOU REALLY THINK HE'S GONNA PASS THOSE EXAMS?
...This is why I'm breaking up with her...
HUH?
WELL, JEEZ.
THAT STUPID DITZ.

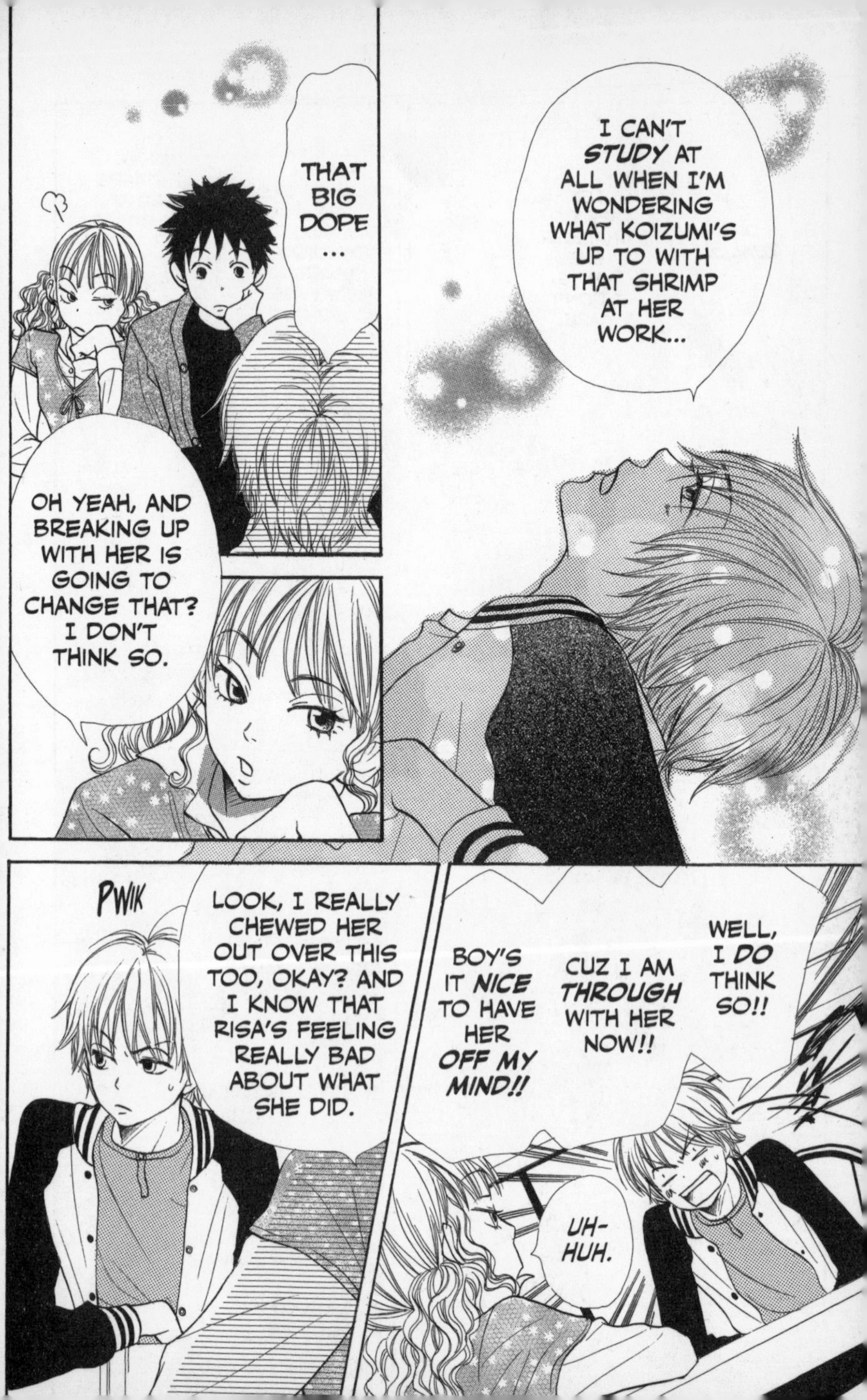
I CAN'T STUDY AT ALL WHEN I'M WONDERING WHAT KOIZUMI'S UP TO WITH THAT SHRIMP AT HER WORK...
THAT BIG DOPE ...
OH YEAH, AND BREAKING UP WITH HER IS GOING TO CHANGE THAT? I DON'T THINK SO.
WELL, I DO THINK SO!!
CUZ I AM THROUGH WITH HER NOW!!
BOY'S IT NICE TO HAVE HER OFF MY MIND!!
UH-HUH.
PWIK
LOOK, I REALLY CHEWED HER OUT OVER THIS TOO, OKAY? AND I KNOW THAT RISA'S FEELING REALLY BAD ABOUT WHAT SHE DID.

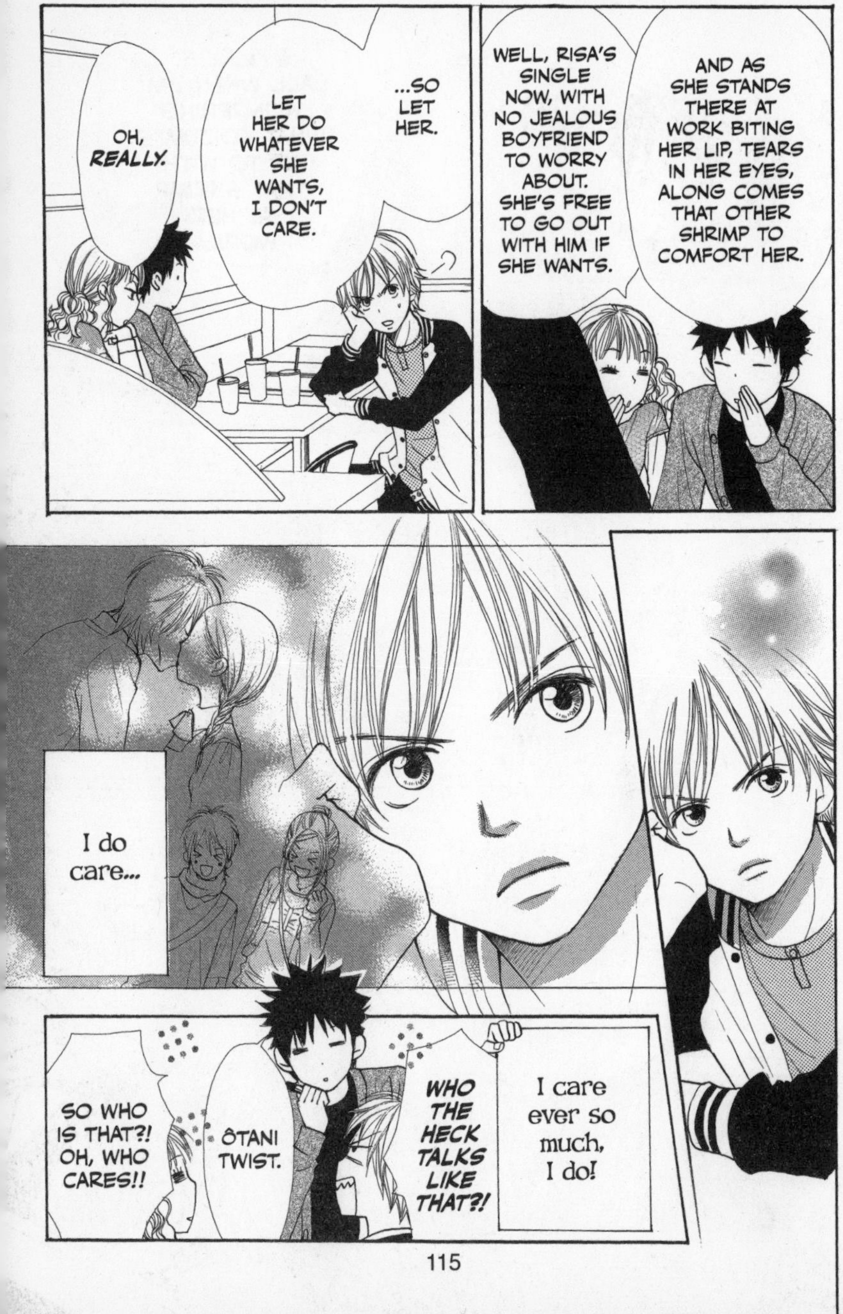
AND AS SHE STANDS THERE AT WORK BITING HER LIP, TEARS IN HER EYES, ALONG COMES THAT OTHER SHRIMP TO COMFORT HER.
WELL, RISA'S SINGLE NOW, WITH NO JEALOUS BOYFRIEND TO WORRY ABOUT. SHE'S FREE TO GO OUT WITH HIM IF SHE WANTS.
...SO LET HER.
LET HER DO WHATEVER SHE WANTS, I DON'T CARE.
OH, *REALLY.*
I do care...
I care ever so much, I do!
WHO THE HECK TALKS LIKE THAT?!
ÔTANI TWIST.
SO WHO IS THAT?! OH, WHO CARES!!

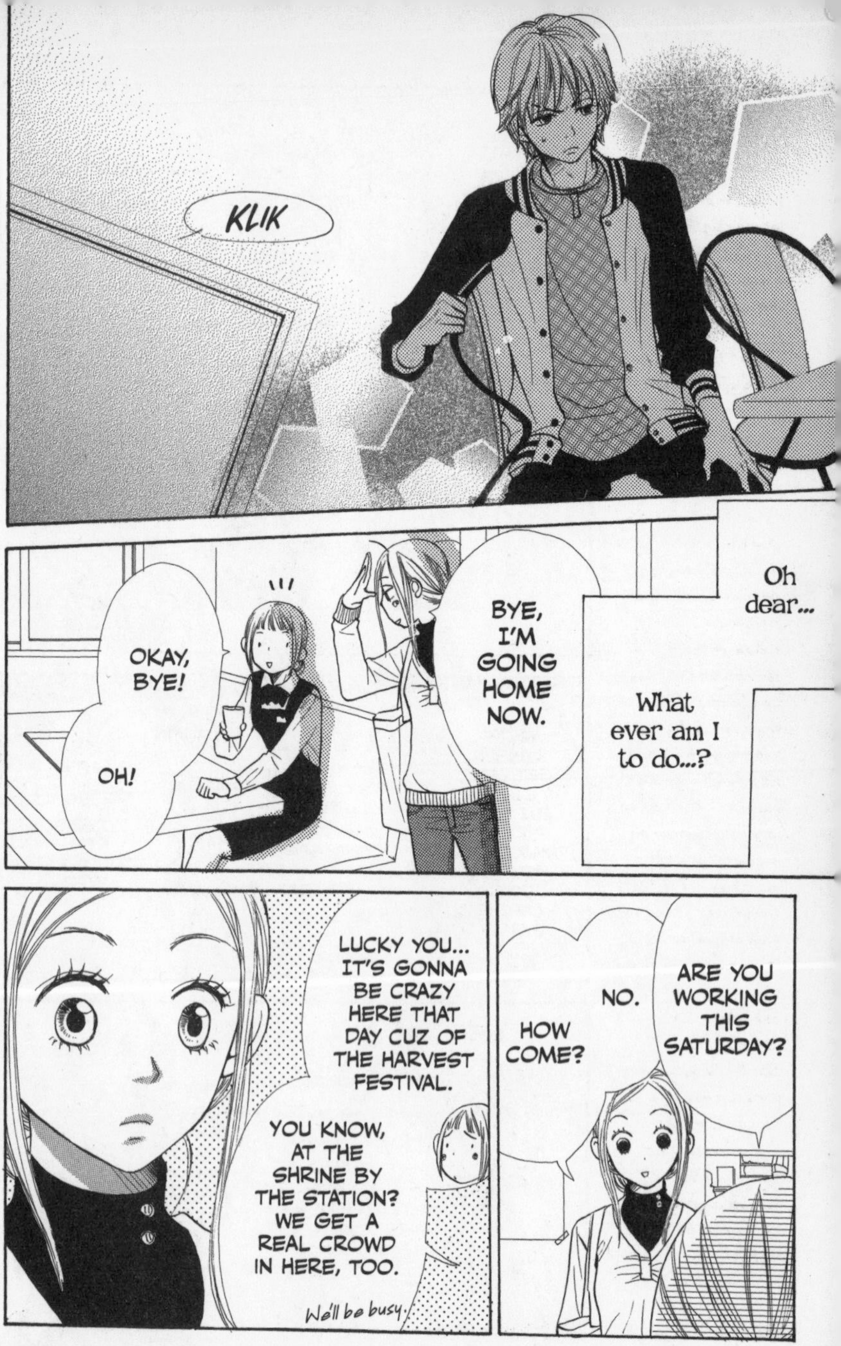
KLIK
Oh dear...
What ever am I to do...?
BYE, I'M GOING HOME NOW.
OKAY, BYE!
OH!
ARE YOU WORKING THIS SATURDAY?
NO.
HOW COME?
LUCKY YOU... IT'S GONNA BE CRAZY HERE THAT DAY CUZ OF THE HARVEST FESTIVAL.
YOU KNOW, AT THE SHRINE BY THE STATION? WE GET A REAL CROWD IN HERE, TOO.
We'll be busy.

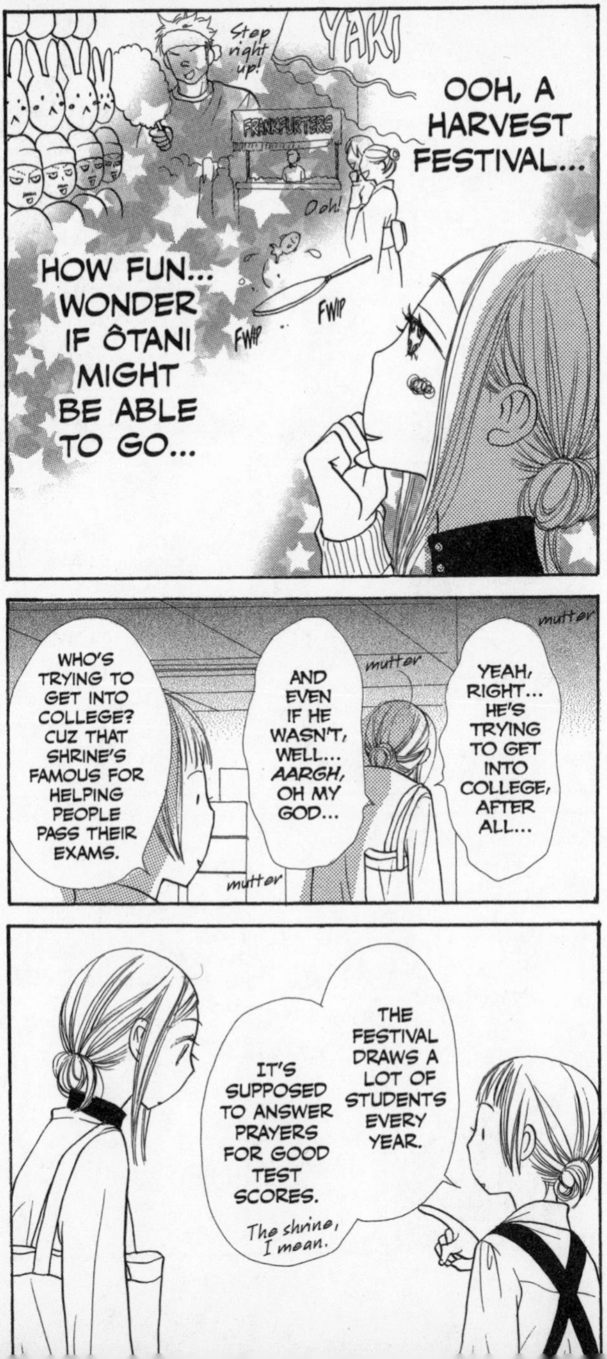
YAKI
OOH, A HARVEST FESTIVAL...
Step right up!
FRANKFURTERS
Ooh!
FWIP
FWIP
HOW FUN... WONDER IF ÔTANI MIGHT BE ABLE TO GO...
mutter
YEAH, RIGHT... HE'S TRYING TO GET INTO COLLEGE, AFTER ALL...
mutter
AND EVEN IF HE WASN'T, WELL... *AARGH,* OH MY GOD...
WHO'S TRYING TO GET INTO COLLEGE? CUZ THAT SHRINE'S FAMOUS FOR HELPING PEOPLE PASS THEIR EXAMS.
mutter
THE FESTIVAL DRAWS A LOT OF STUDENTS EVERY YEAR.
IT'S SUPPOSED TO ANSWER PRAYERS FOR GOOD TEST SCORES.
The shrine, I mean.

3

While I'm at it, let me plug Himitsu Kichi (Secret Base), a collection of short manga stories that came out last year (2004). bow It includes stories I wrote while Love☆Com was being serialized. Like one about my boring dad. My dad is not funny. At all. But that doesn't stop him from bothering people with lame puns and one-liners, oh no. He's what Kansai folks call an ichibiri. He'll go to the store and say the dumbest things to the clerk and crack himself up. He'll pinch his daughter-in-law's butt when she's riding in front of him on an escalator and get a giant kick out of that. Sometimes I get really mad at him for real... But once every three years or so, he'll do something that's actually funny. Like his Kanbi Fujiyama imitation when we went to a rather fancy Italian restaurant. That was hilarious. He's always asking me to write about him, so I did.

pff

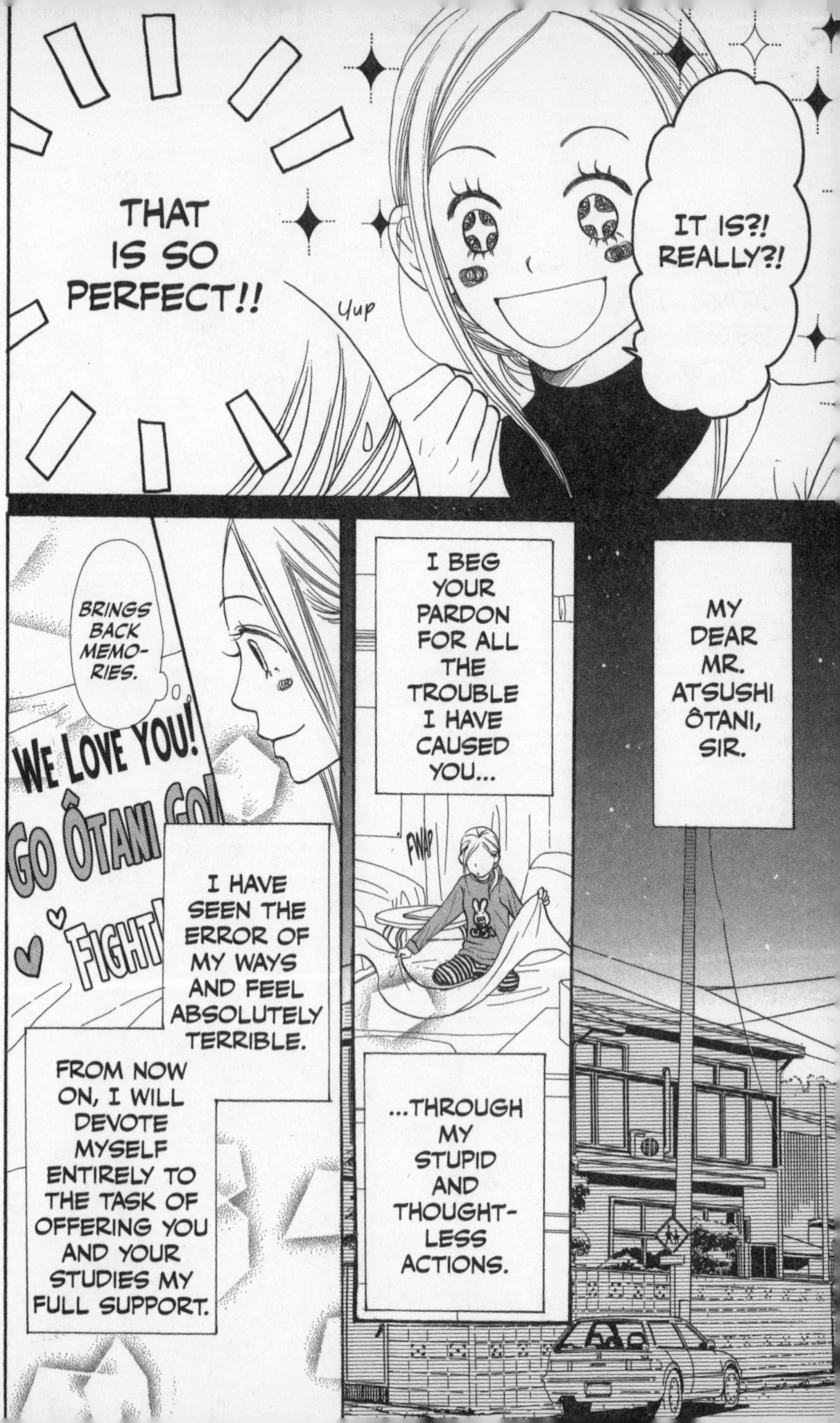
IT IS?! REALLY?!
THAT IS SO PERFECT!!
Yup
MY DEAR MR. ATSUSHI ÔTANI, SIR.
I BEG YOUR PARDON FOR ALL THE TROUBLE I HAVE CAUSED YOU...
FWAP
...THROUGH MY STUPID AND THOUGHT-LESS ACTIONS.
BRINGS BACK MEMO-RIES.
WE LOVE YOU!
GO ÔTANI
FIGHT
I HAVE SEEN THE ERROR OF MY WAYS AND FEEL ABSOLUTELY TERRIBLE.
FROM NOW ON, I WILL DEVOTE MYSELF ENTIRELY TO THE TASK OF OFFERING YOU AND YOUR STUDIES MY FULL SUPPORT.

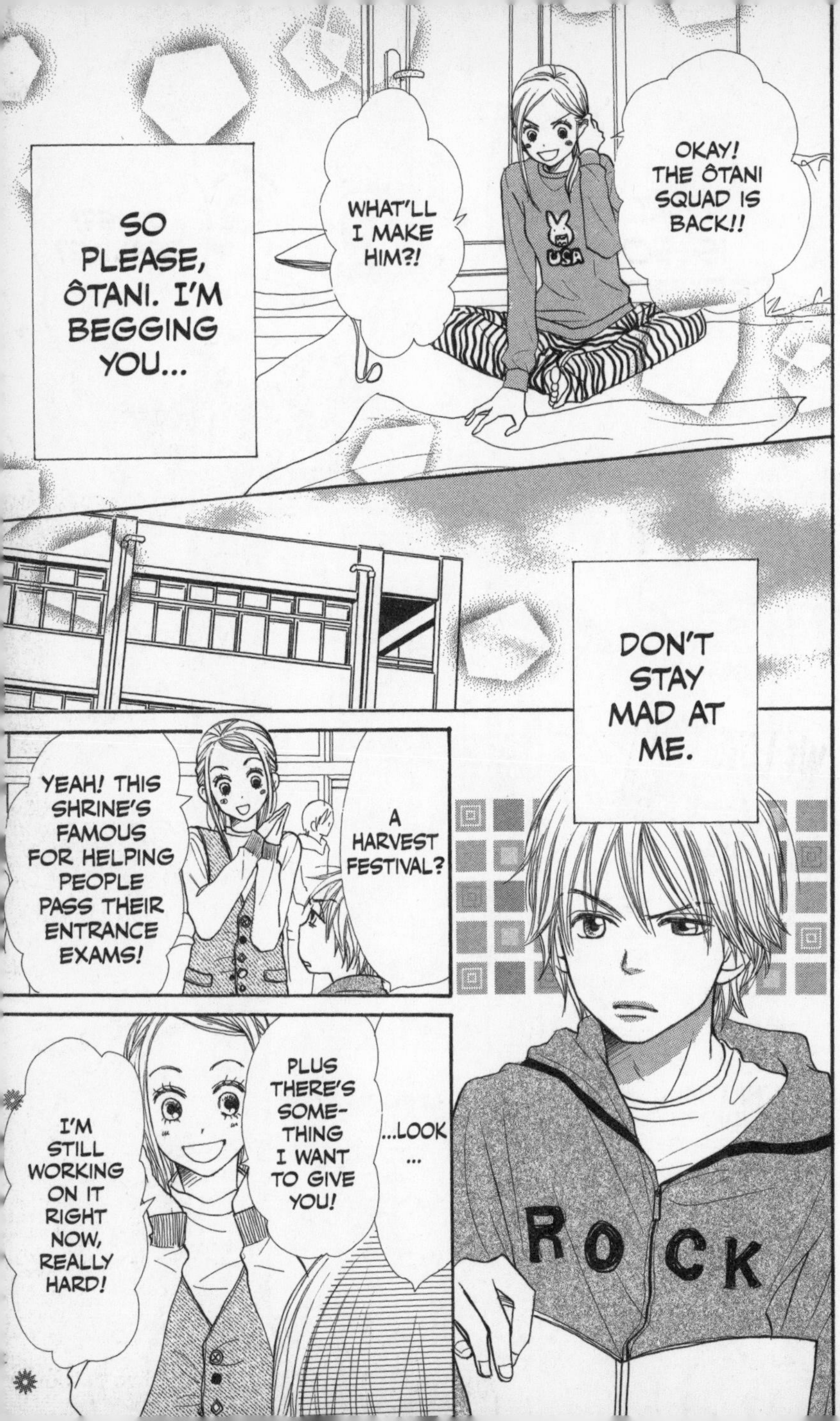
OKAY! THE ÔTANI SQUAD IS BACK!!
USA
WHAT'LL I MAKE HIM?!
SO PLEASE, ÔTANI. I'M BEGGING YOU...
DON'T STAY MAD AT ME.
ROCK
A HARVEST FESTIVAL?
YEAH! THIS SHRINE'S FAMOUS FOR HELPING PEOPLE PASS THEIR ENTRANCE EXAMS!
...LOOK ...
PLUS THERE'S SOME-THING I WANT TO GIVE YOU!
I'M STILL WORKING ON IT RIGHT NOW, REALLY HARD!

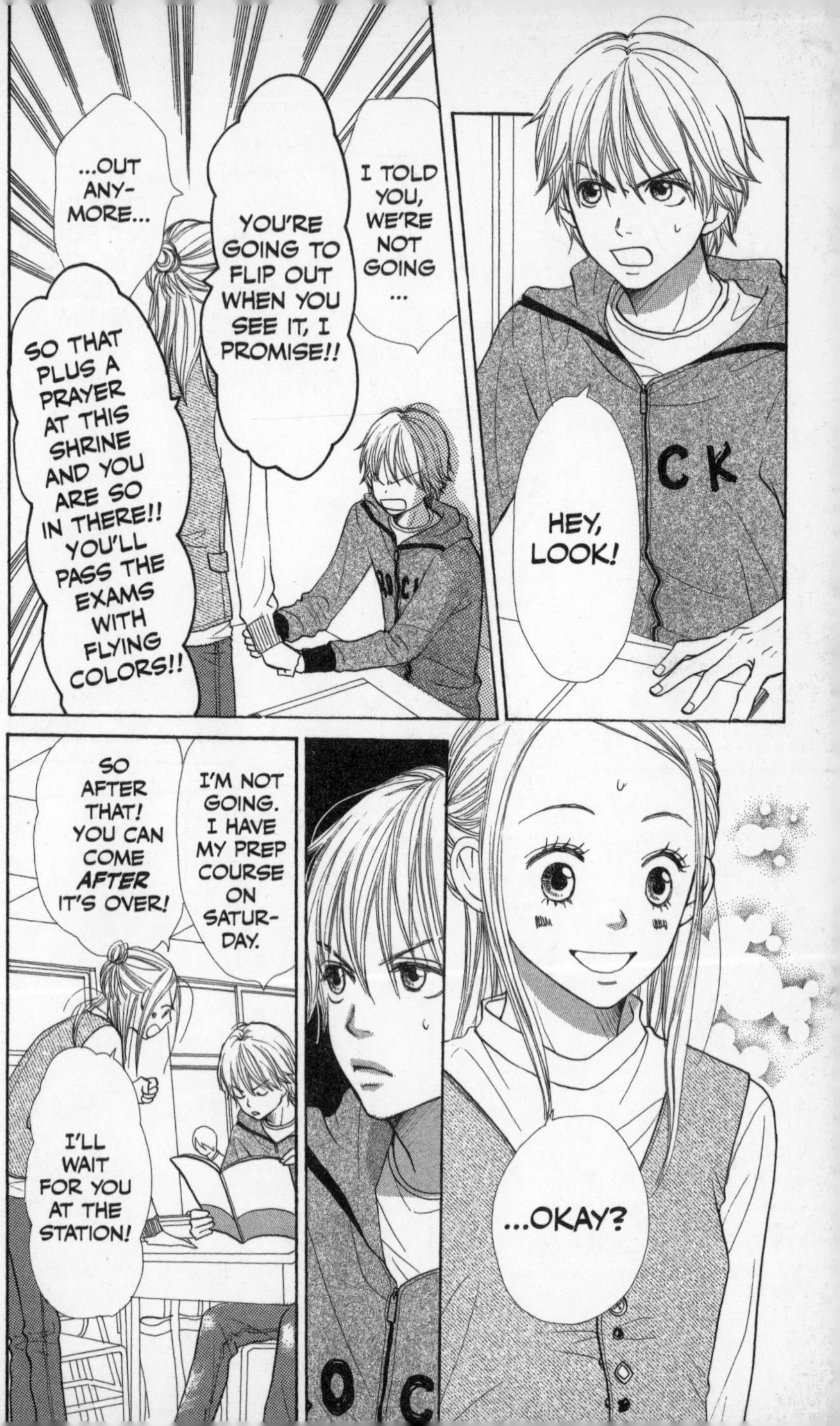
HEY, LOOK!
I TOLD YOU, WE'RE NOT GOING ...
YOU'RE GOING TO FLIP OUT WHEN YOU SEE IT, I PROMISE!!
...OUT ANYMORE...
SO THAT PLUS A PRAYER AT THIS SHRINE AND YOU ARE SO IN THERE!! YOU'LL PASS THE EXAMS WITH FLYING COLORS!!
...OKAY?
I'M NOT GOING. I HAVE MY PREP COURSE ON SATUR-DAY.
SO AFTER THAT! YOU CAN COME *AFTER* IT'S OVER!
I'LL WAIT FOR YOU AT THE STATION!

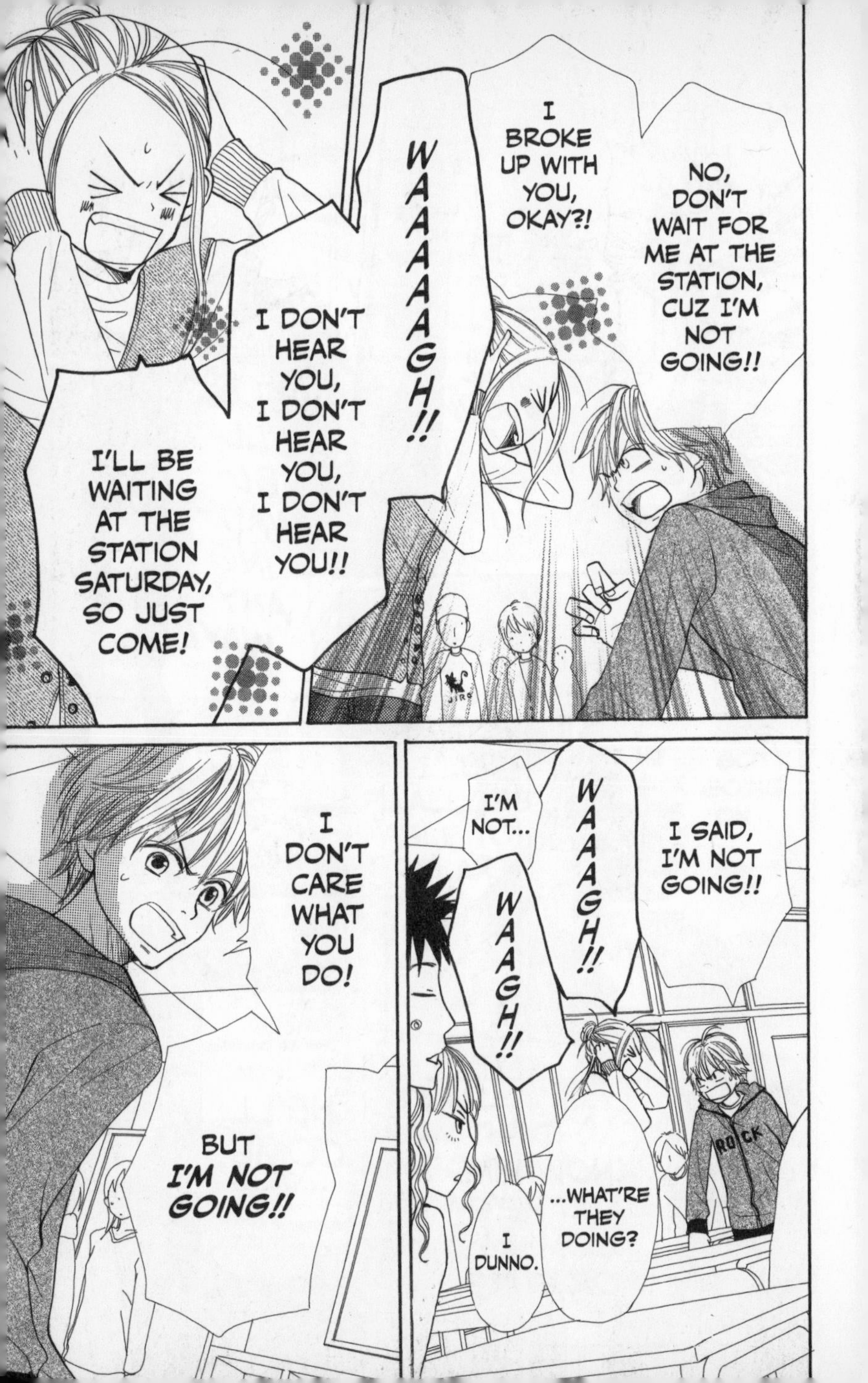
NO, DON'T WAIT FOR ME AT THE STATION, CUZ I'M NOT GOING!!
I BROKE UP WITH YOU, OKAY?!
WAAAAAAGH!!
I DON'T HEAR YOU, I DON'T HEAR YOU, I DON'T HEAR YOU!!
I'LL BE WAITING AT THE STATION SATURDAY, SO JUST COME!
I SAID, I'M NOT GOING!!
WAAAAGH!!
I'M NOT...
WAAGH!!
...WHAT'RE THEY DOING?
I DUNNO.
I DON'T CARE WHAT YOU DO!
BUT *I'M NOT GOING!!*

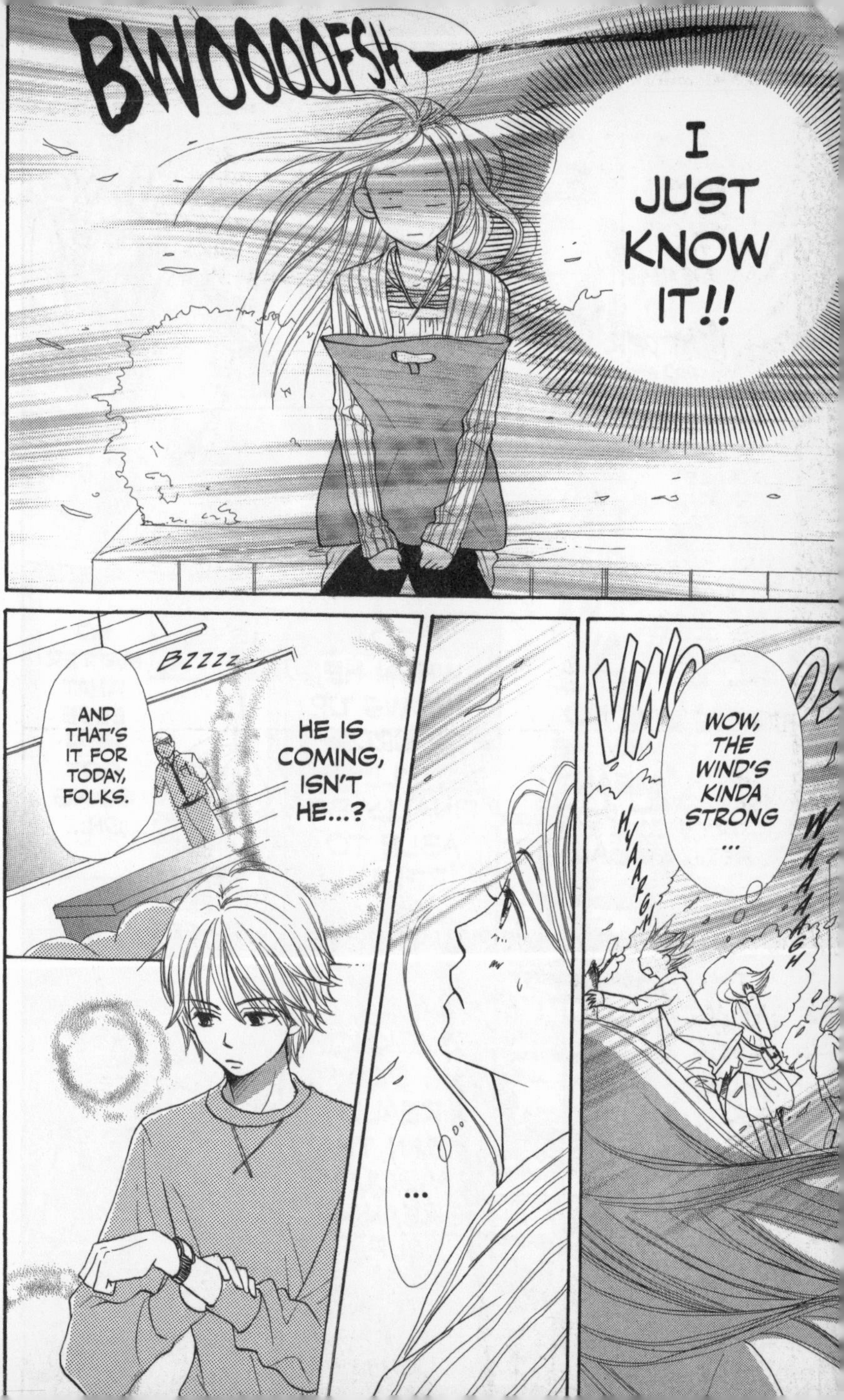
BWOOOOFSH
I JUST KNOW IT!!
WOW, THE WIND'S KINDA STRONG ...
HYAAARGH
WAAAAAGH
...
BZZZZ...
AND THAT'S IT FOR TODAY, FOLKS.
HE IS COMING, ISN'T HE...?

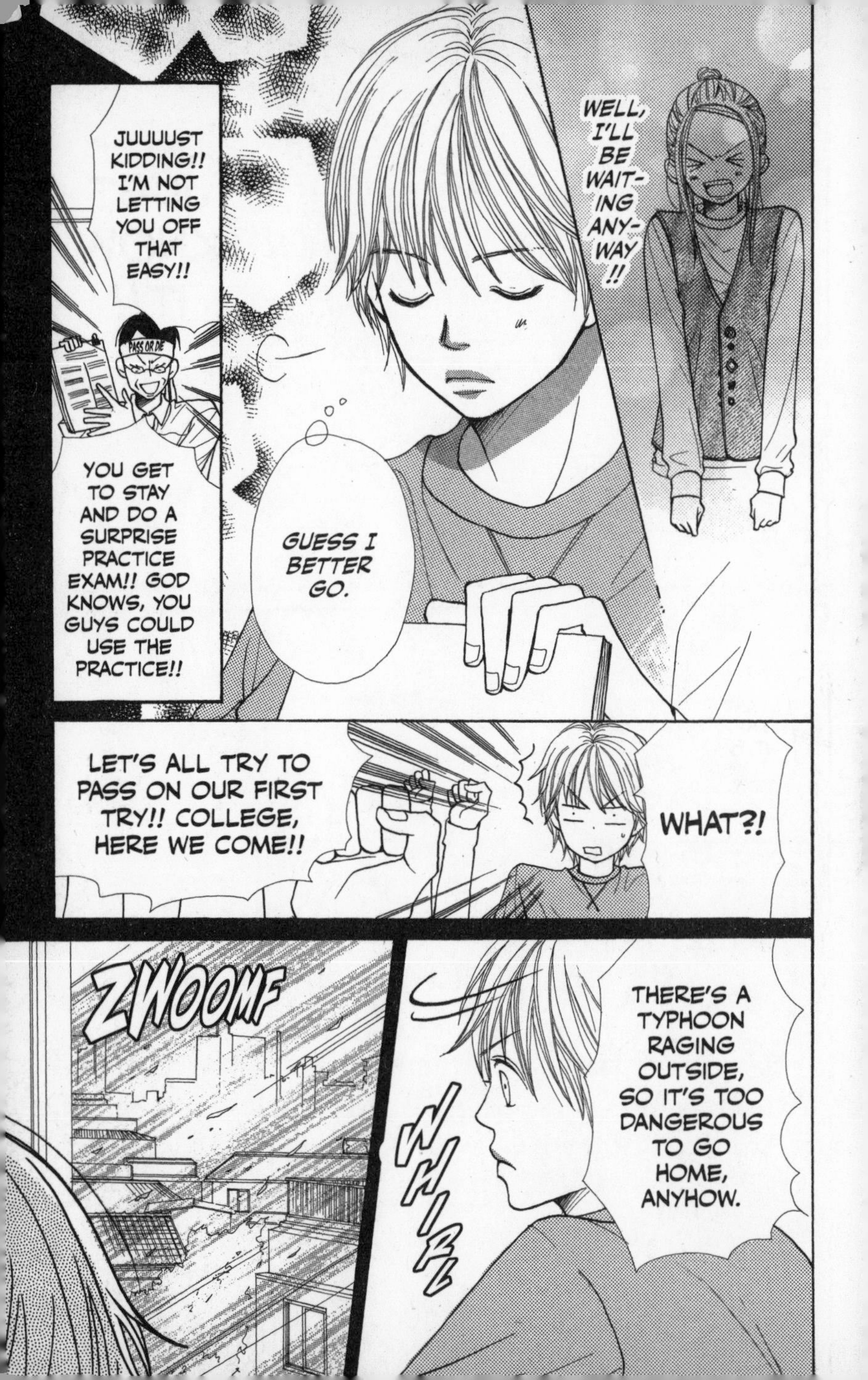
WELL, I'LL BE WAITING ANYWAY!!
GUESS I BETTER GO.
JUUUUST KIDDING!! I'M NOT LETTING YOU OFF THAT EASY!!
PASS OR DIE
YOU GET TO STAY AND DO A SURPRISE PRACTICE EXAM!! GOD KNOWS, YOU GUYS COULD USE THE PRACTICE!!
WHAT?!
LET'S ALL TRY TO PASS ON OUR FIRST TRY!! COLLEGE, HERE WE COME!!
THERE'S A TYPHOON RAGING OUTSIDE, SO IT'S TOO DANGEROUS TO GO HOME, ANYHOW.
ZWOOMF

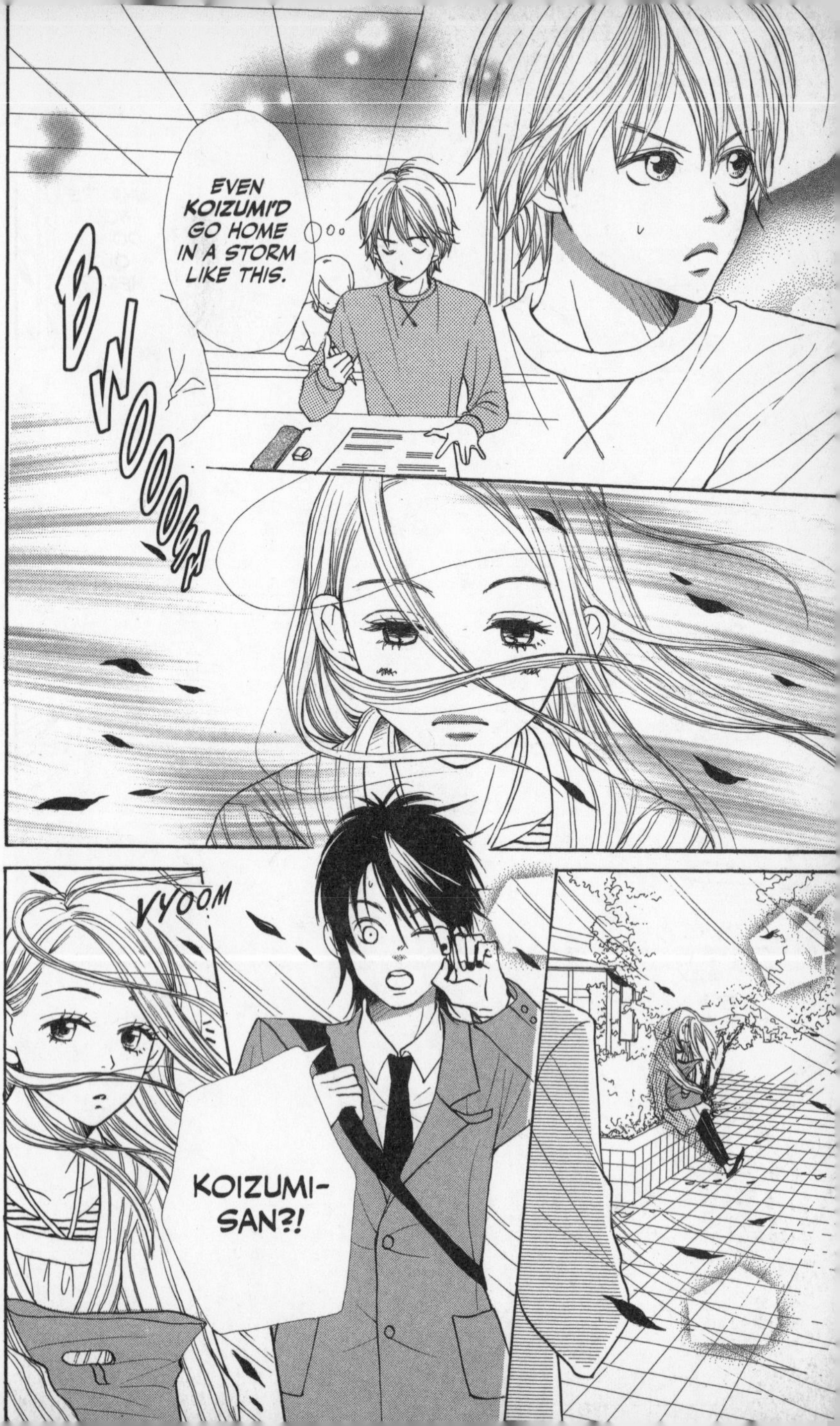
EVEN KOIZUMI'D GO HOME IN A STORM LIKE THIS.
BWOOOSH
VYOOM
KOIZUMI-SAN?!

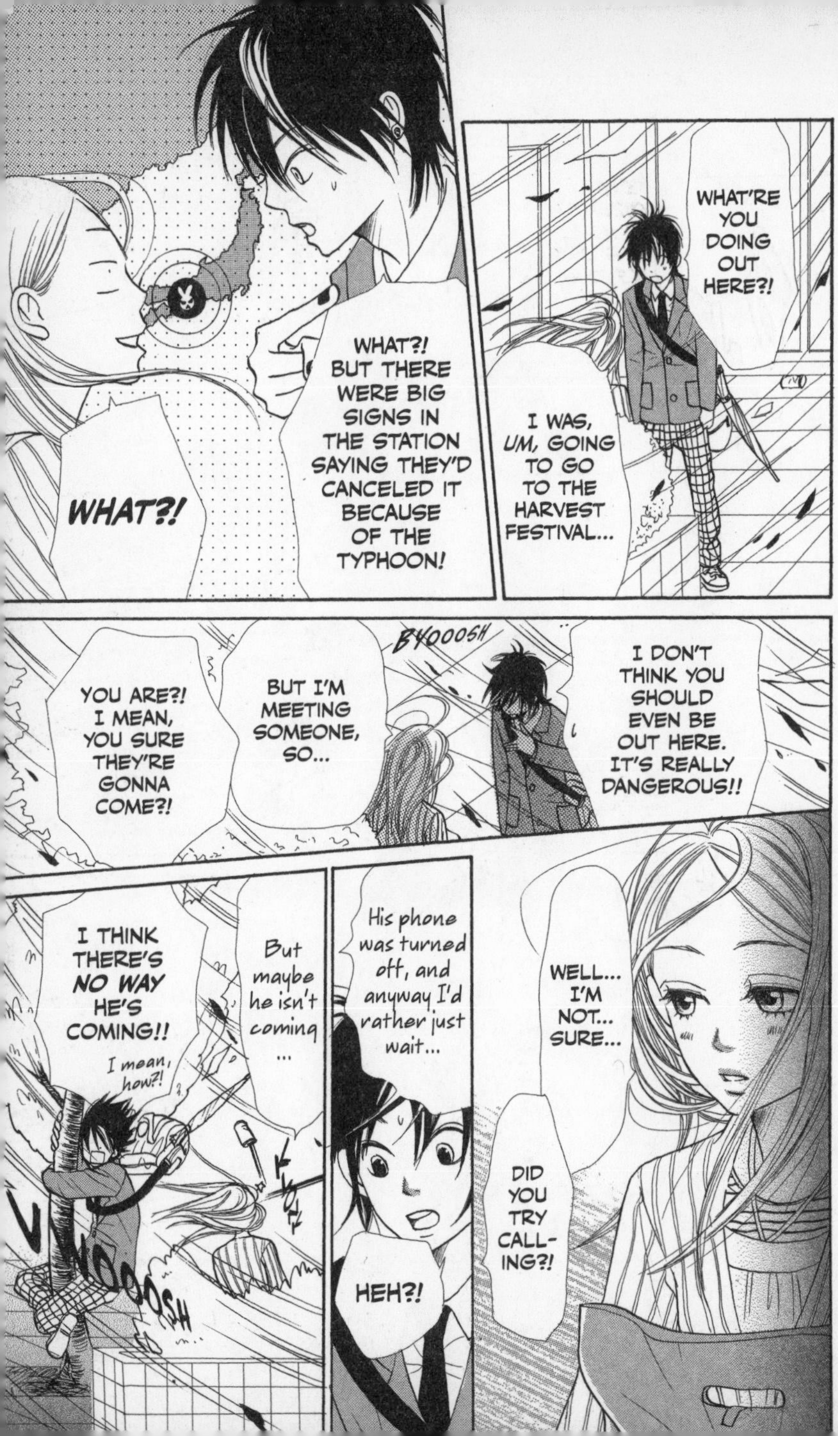
WHAT'RE YOU DOING OUT HERE?!
I WAS, UM, GOING TO GO TO THE HARVEST FESTIVAL...
WHAT?! BUT THERE WERE BIG SIGNS IN THE STATION SAYING THEY'D CANCELED IT BECAUSE OF THE TYPHOON!
WHAT?!
I DON'T THINK YOU SHOULD EVEN BE OUT HERE. IT'S REALLY DANGEROUS!!
BYOOOSH
BUT I'M MEETING SOMEONE, SO...
YOU ARE?! I MEAN, YOU SURE THEY'RE GONNA COME?!
WELL... I'M NOT... SURE...
DID YOU TRY CALLING?!
His phone was turned off, and anyway I'd rather just wait...
HEH?!
But maybe he isn't coming ...
I THINK THERE'S NO WAY HE'S COMING!!
I mean, how?!

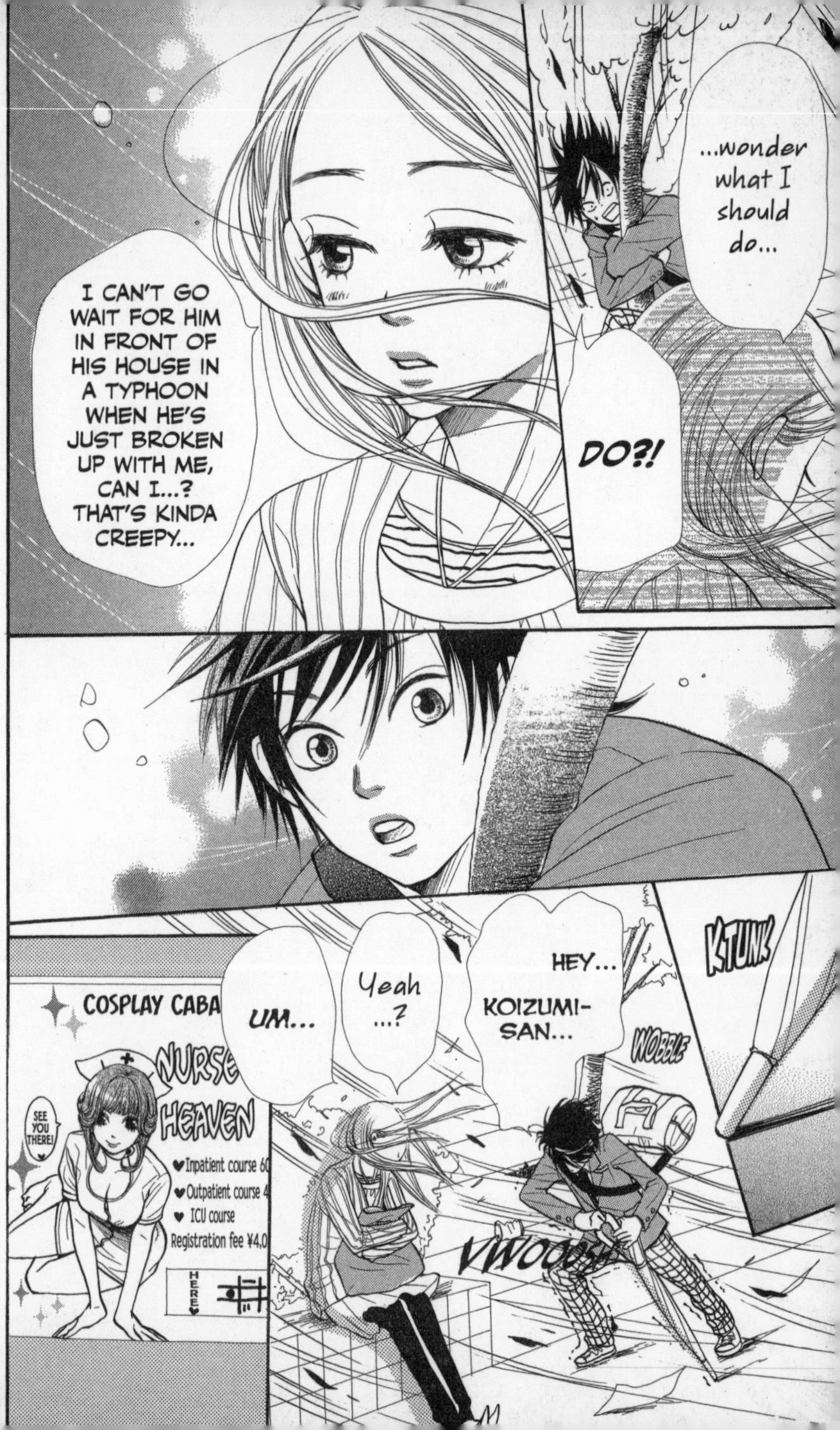
...wonder what I should do...
DO?!
I CAN'T GO WAIT FOR HIM IN FRONT OF HIS HOUSE IN A TYPHOON WHEN HE'S JUST BROKEN UP WITH ME, CAN I...? THAT'S KINDA CREEPY...
KTUNK
HEY... KOIZUMI-SAN...
Yeah ...?
UM...
WOBBLE
VWOOSH
COSPLAY CABA
NURSE HEAVEN
SEE YOU THERE!
Inpatient course 60
Outpatient course 4
ICU course
Registration fee ¥4,0
HERE

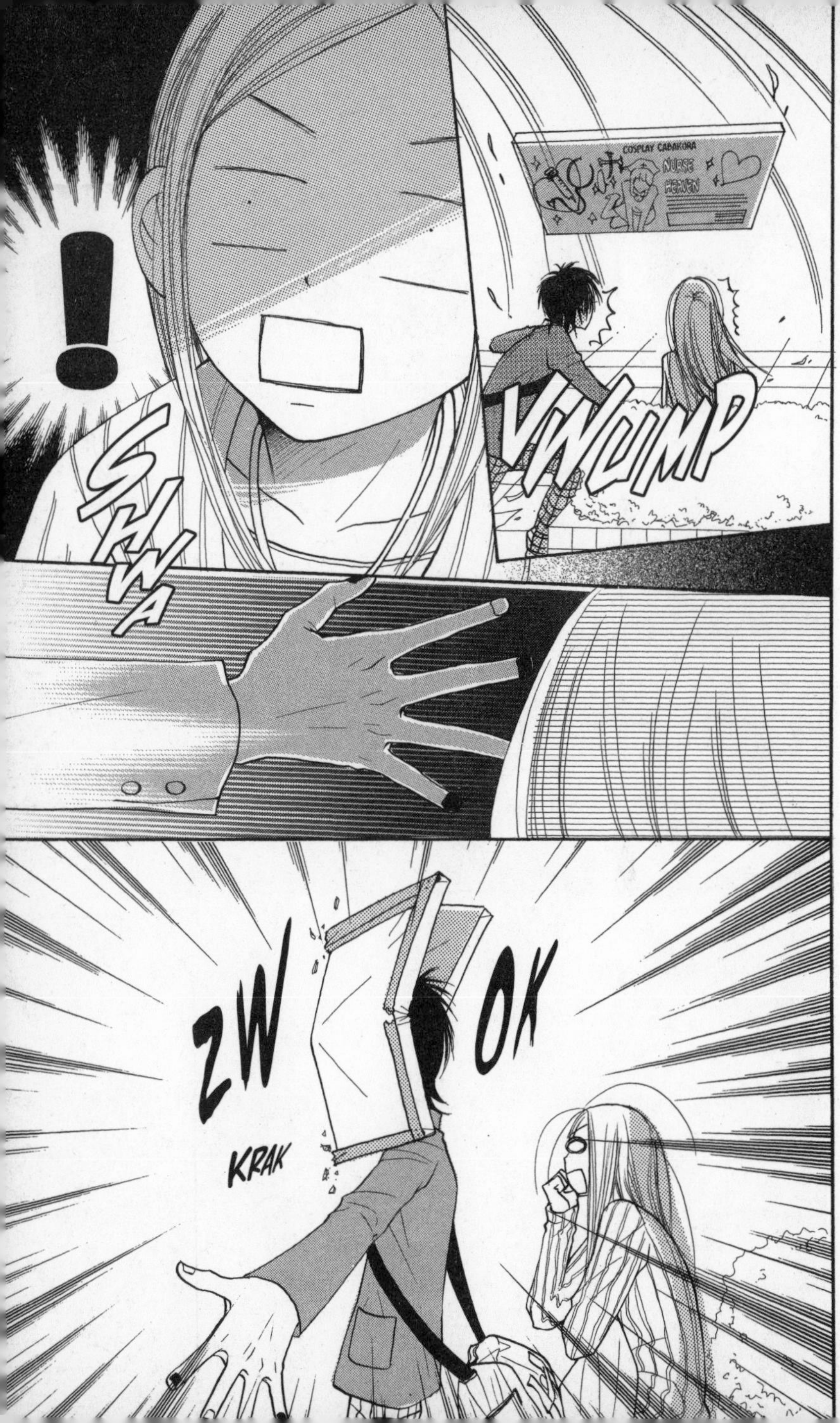
COSPLAY CABAKURA
NURSE HEAVEN
VWUMP
!
SHWA
ZWOK
KRAK

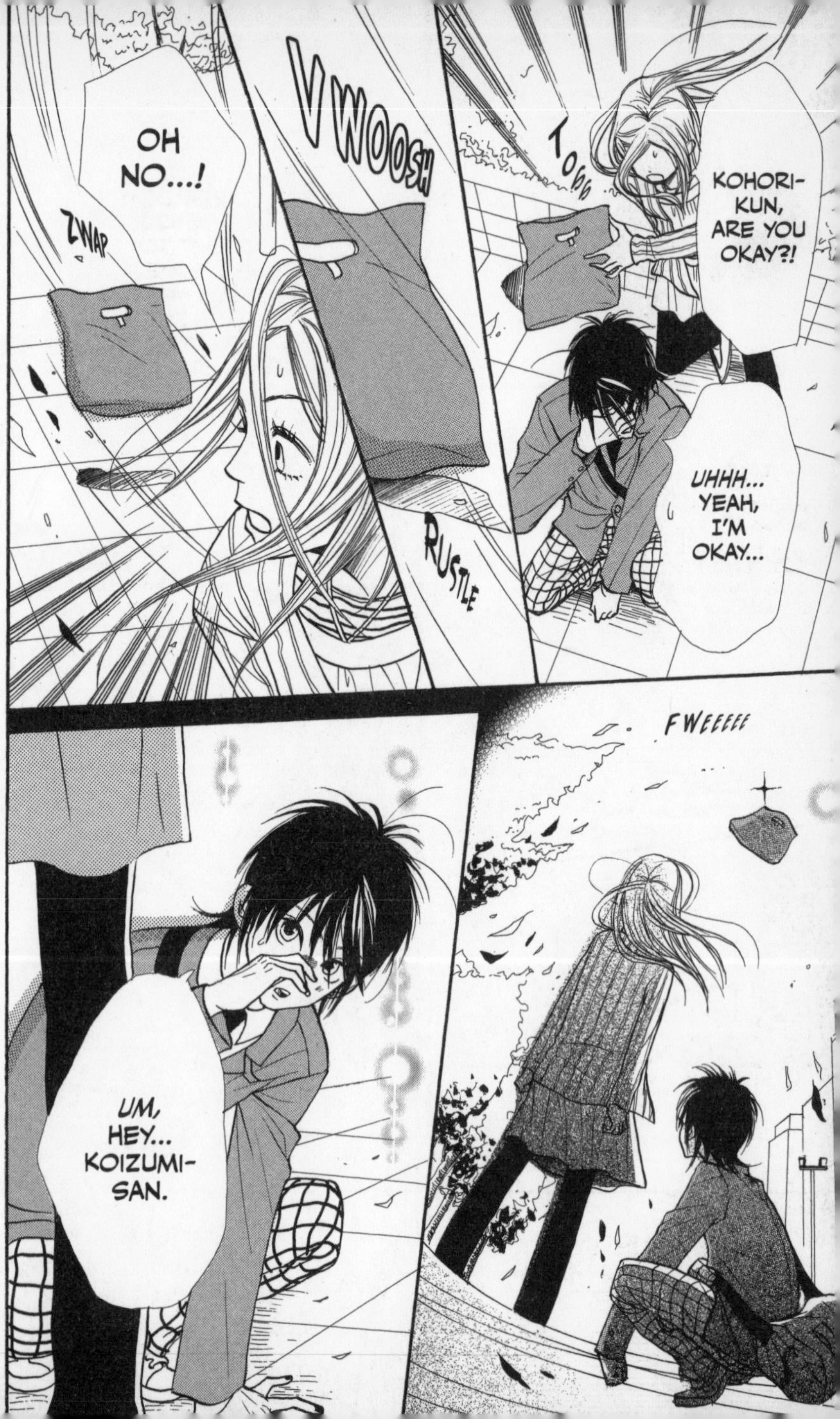
KOHORI-KUN, ARE YOU OKAY?!
TOSS
UHHH... YEAH, I'M OKAY...
VWOOSH
RUSTLE
OH NO...!
ZWAP
FWEEEEE
UM, HEY... KOIZUMI-SAN.

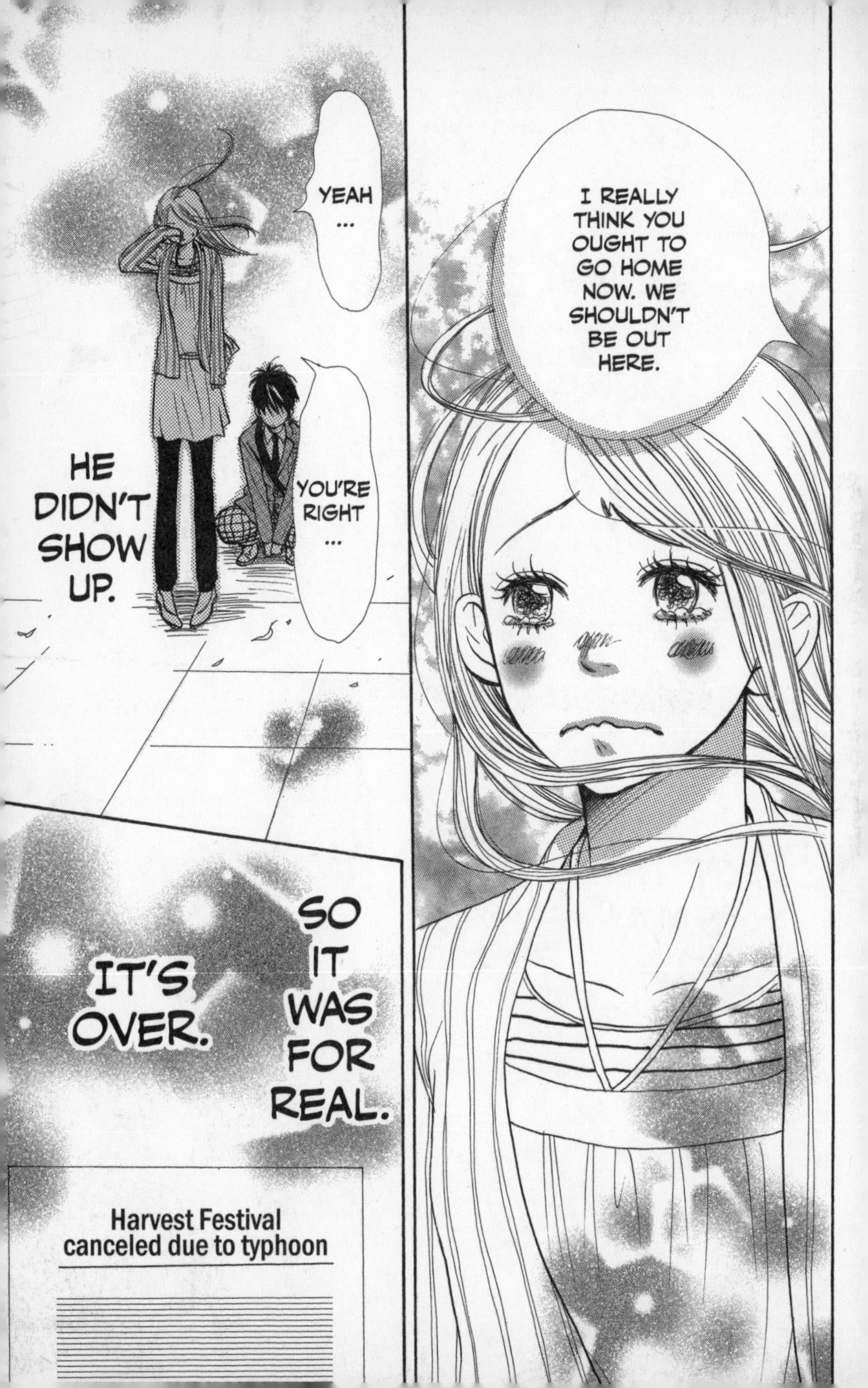
I REALLY THINK YOU OUGHT TO GO HOME NOW. WE SHOULDN'T BE OUT HERE.
YEAH ...
YOU'RE RIGHT ...
HE DIDN'T SHOW UP.
SO IT WAS FOR REAL.
IT'S OVER.
Harvest Festival canceled due to typhoon

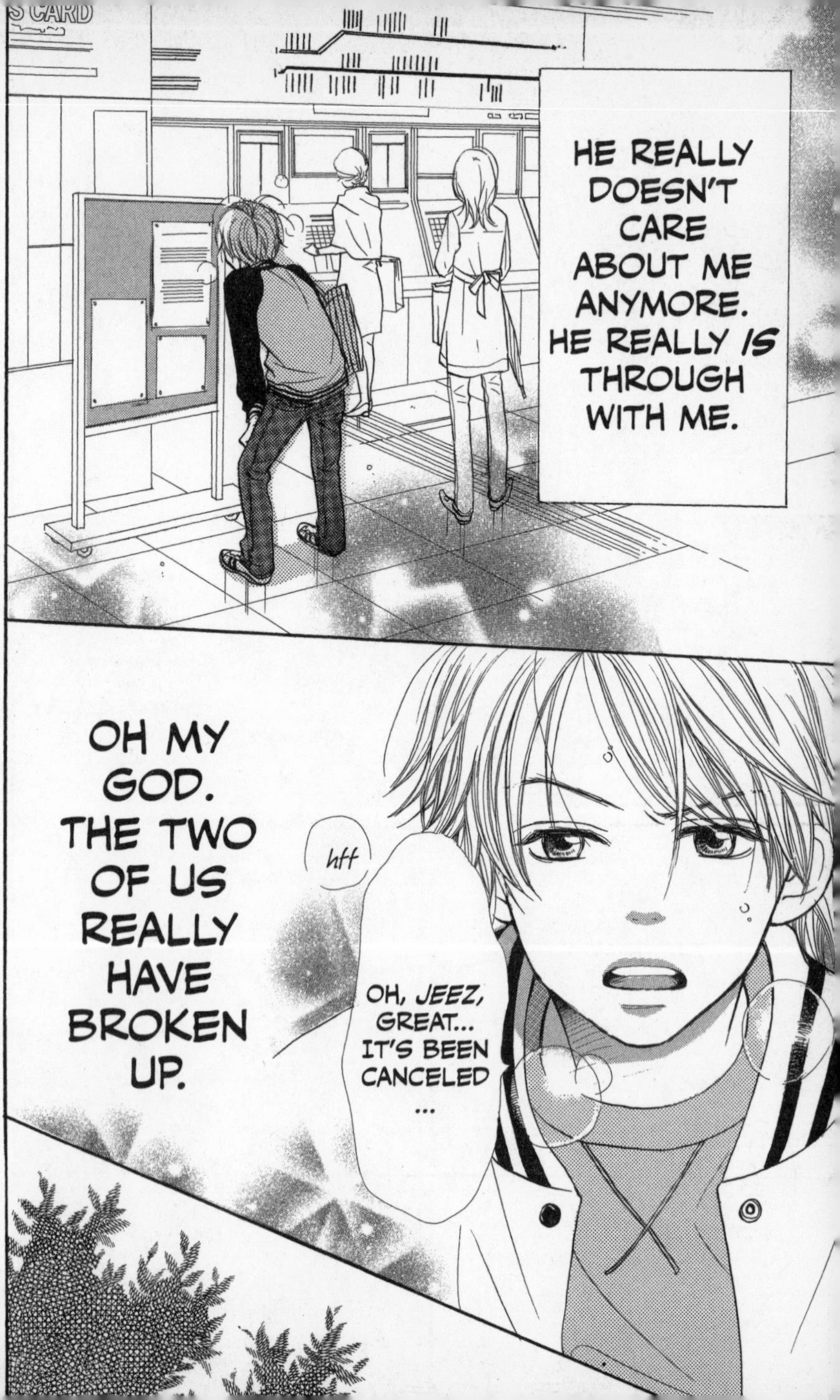
S CARD
HE REALLY DOESN'T CARE ABOUT ME ANYMORE. HE REALLY *IS* THROUGH WITH ME.
hff
OH, JEEZ, GREAT... IT'S BEEN CANCELED ...
OH MY GOD. THE TWO OF US REALLY HAVE BROKEN UP.

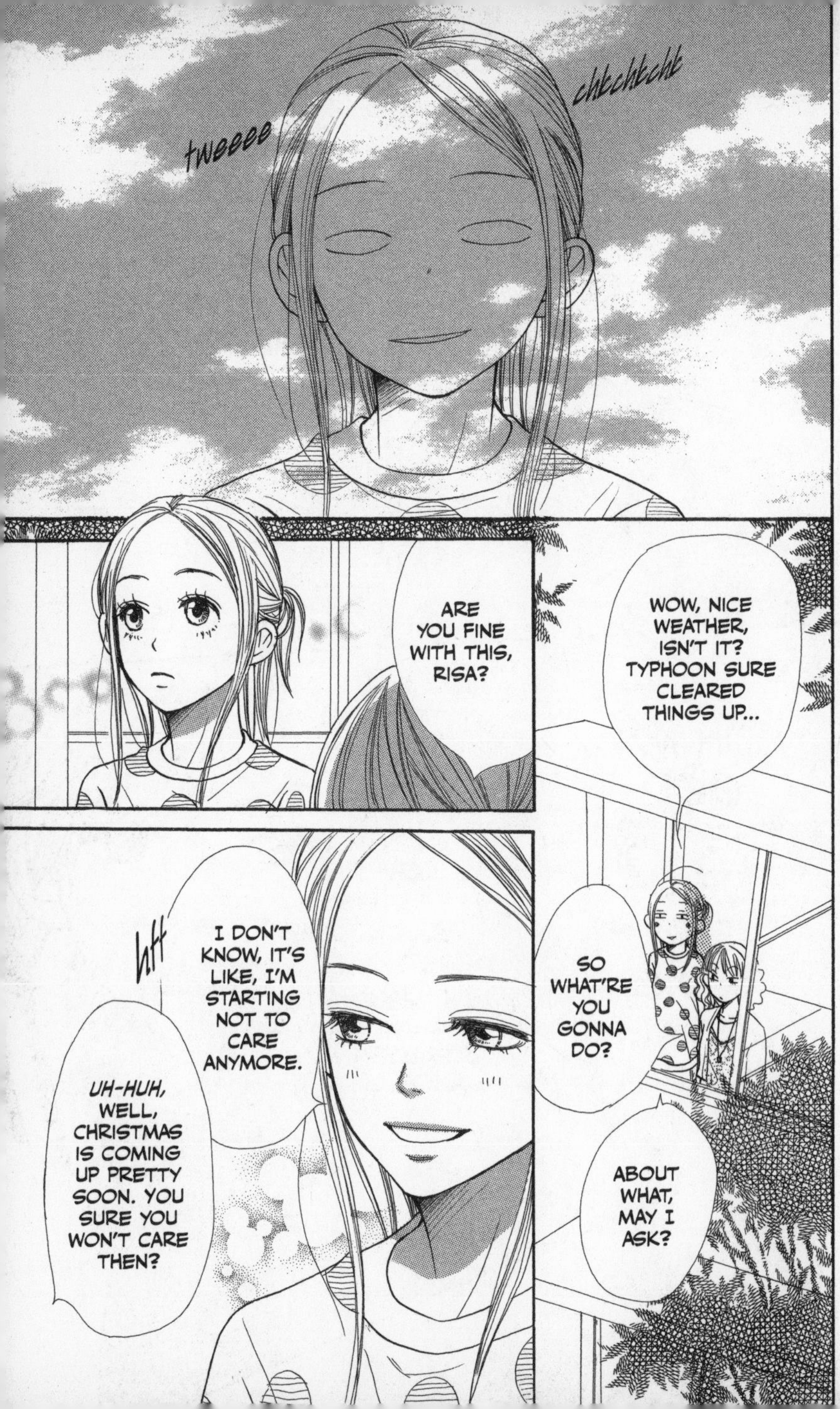
chkchkchk
tweeee
WOW, NICE WEATHER, ISN'T IT? TYPHOON SURE CLEARED THINGS UP...
SO WHAT'RE YOU GONNA DO?
ABOUT WHAT, MAY I ASK?
ARE YOU FINE WITH THIS, RISA?
I DON'T KNOW, IT'S LIKE, I'M STARTING NOT TO CARE ANYMORE.
hff
UH-HUH, WELL, CHRISTMAS IS COMING UP PRETTY SOON. YOU SURE YOU WON'T CARE THEN?

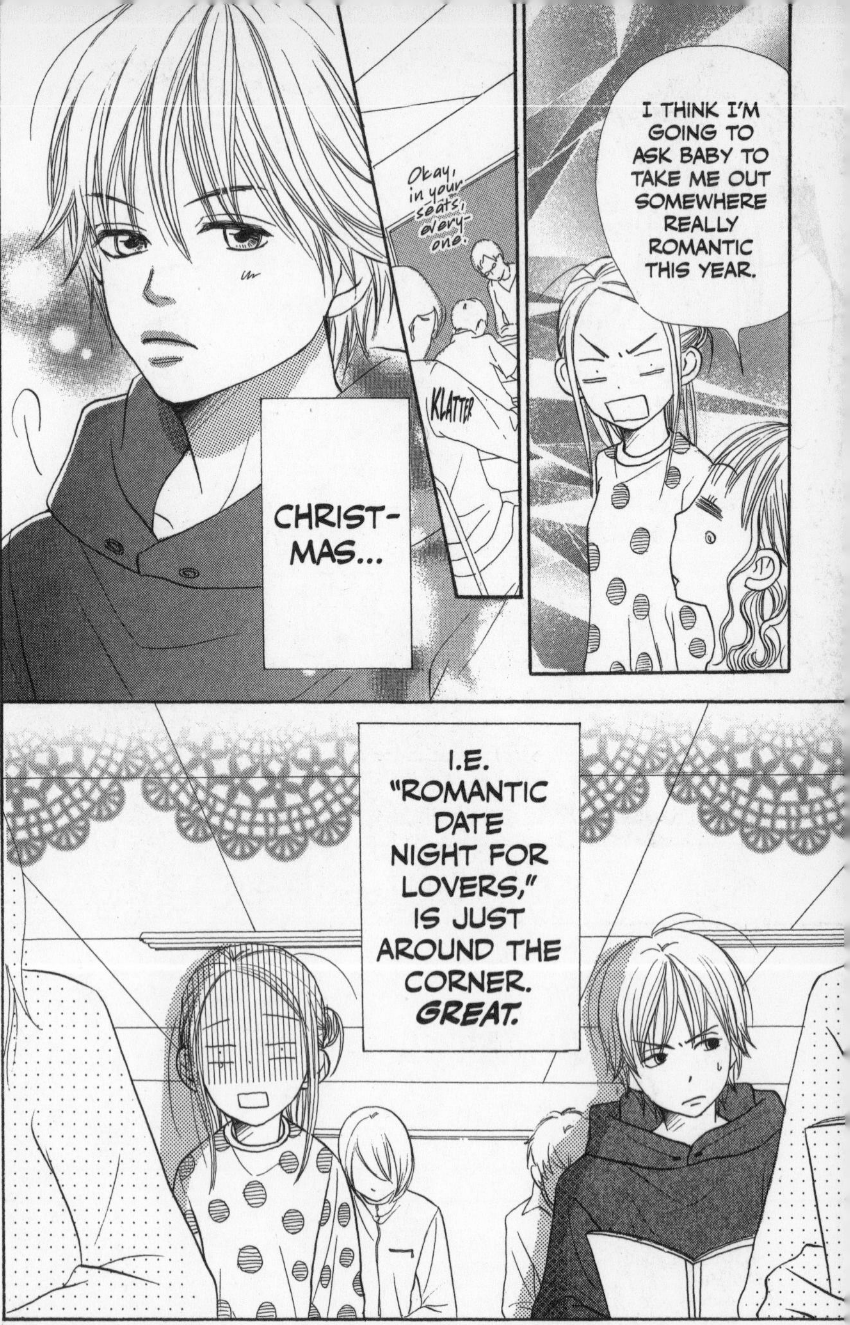
I THINK I'M GOING TO ASK BABY TO TAKE ME OUT SOMEWHERE REALLY ROMANTIC THIS YEAR.
Okay, in your seats, every-one.
KLATTER
CHRIST-MAS...
I.E. "ROMANTIC DATE NIGHT FOR LOVERS," IS JUST AROUND THE CORNER. *GREAT.*

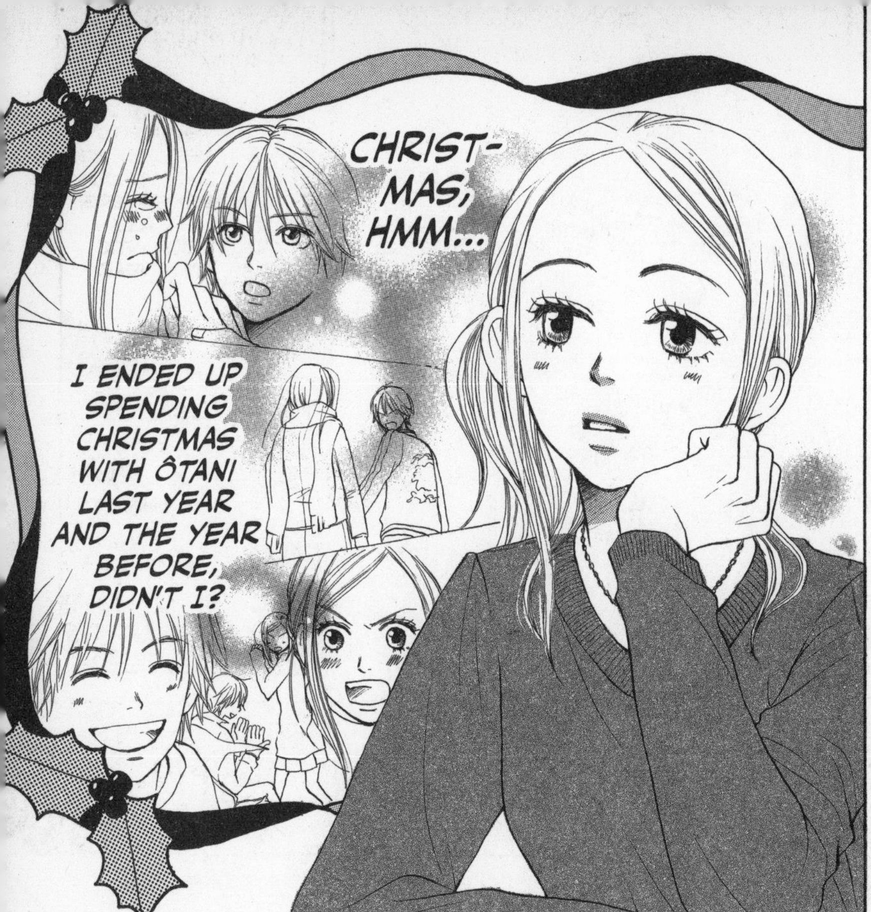
CHRIST-MAS, HMM...
I ENDED UP SPENDING CHRISTMAS WITH ÔTANI LAST YEAR AND THE YEAR BEFORE, DIDN'T I?

CHAPTER 40

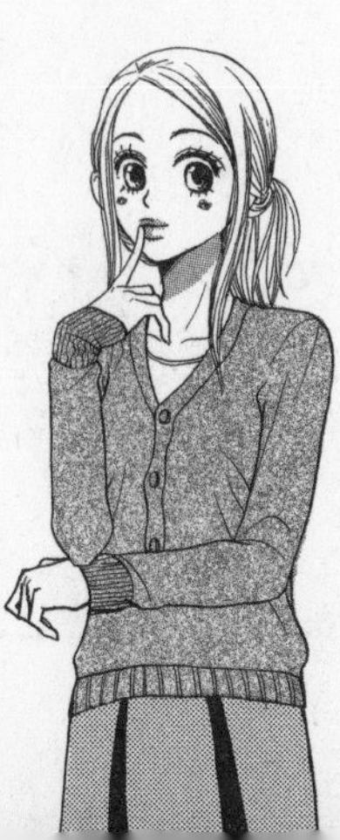

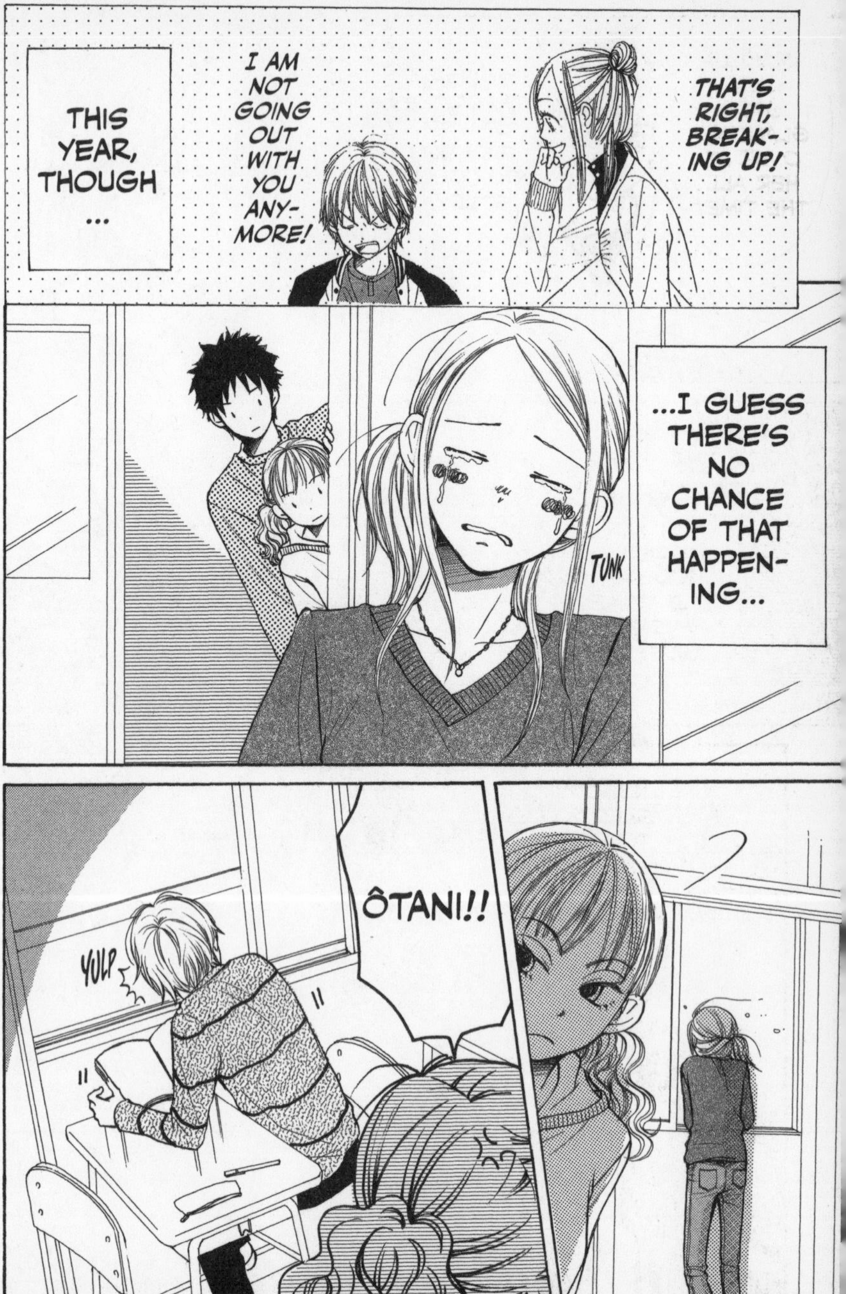
THAT'S RIGHT, BREAK-ING UP!
I AM NOT GOING OUT WITH YOU ANY-MORE!
THIS YEAR, THOUGH ...
...I GUESS THERE'S NO CHANCE OF THAT HAPPEN-ING...
TUNK
ÔTANI!!
YULP

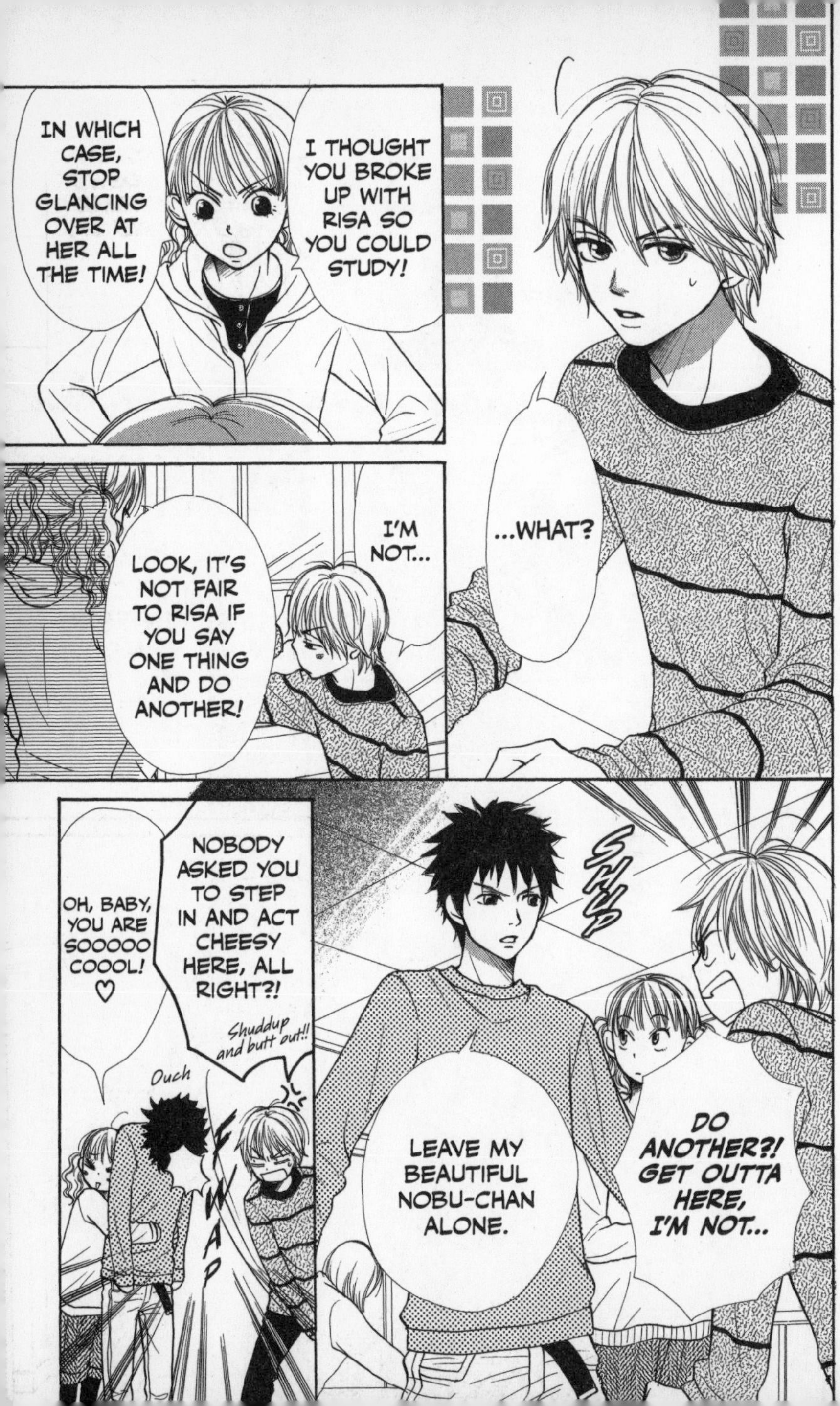
...WHAT?
I THOUGHT YOU BROKE UP WITH RISA SO YOU COULD STUDY!
IN WHICH CASE, STOP GLANCING OVER AT HER ALL THE TIME!
I'M NOT...
LOOK, IT'S NOT FAIR TO RISA IF YOU SAY ONE THING AND DO ANOTHER!
SHUP
DO ANOTHER?! GET OUTTA HERE, I'M NOT...
LEAVE MY BEAUTIFUL NOBU-CHAN ALONE.
NOBODY ASKED YOU TO STEP IN AND ACT CHEESY HERE, ALL RIGHT?!
OH, BABY, YOU ARE SOOOOO COOOL! ♡
Shuddup and butt out!!
Ouch
FWAP

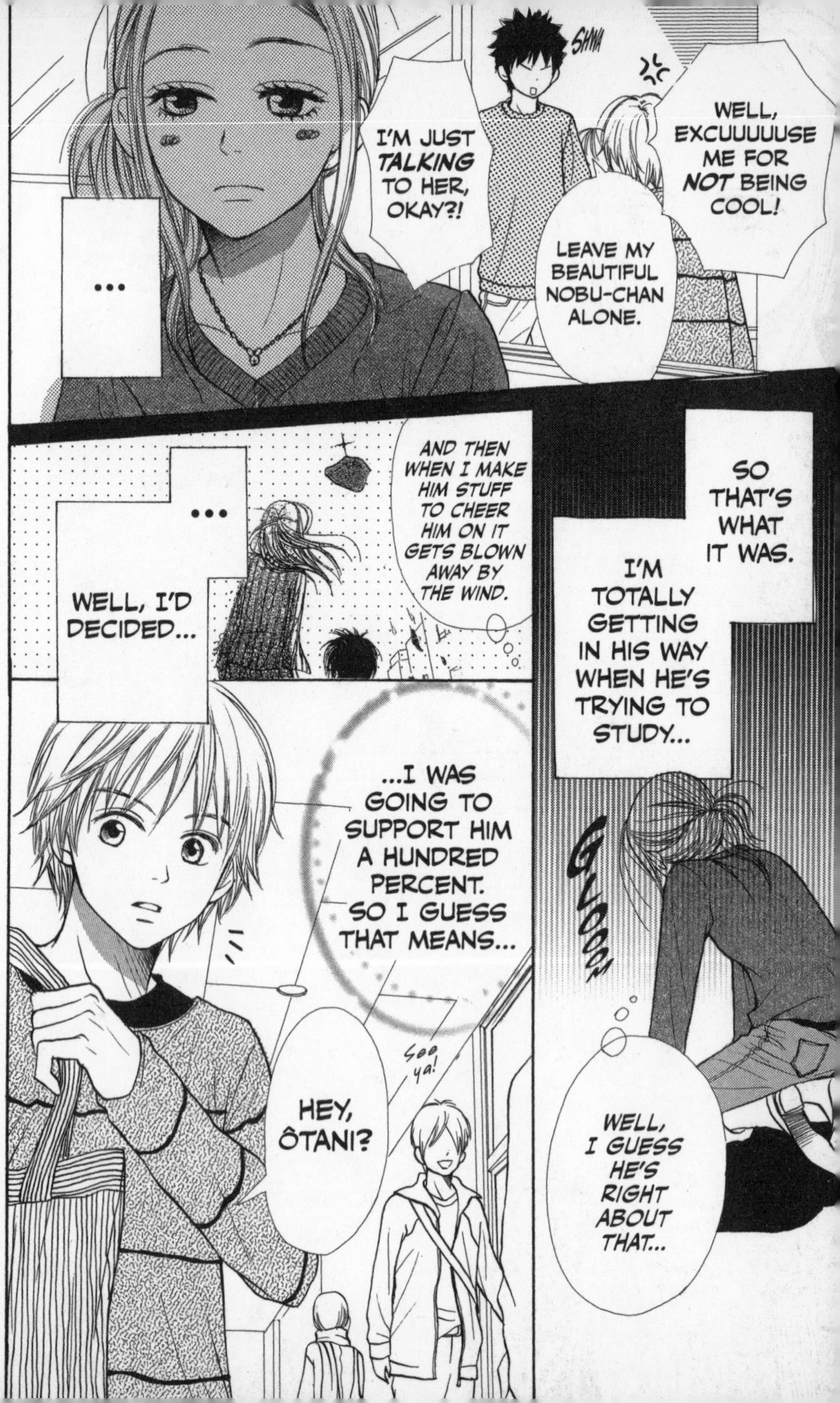
SHWA
WELL, EXCUUUUUSE ME FOR *NOT* BEING COOL!
LEAVE MY BEAUTIFUL NOBU-CHAN ALONE.
I'M JUST *TALKING* TO HER, OKAY?!
...
SO THAT'S WHAT IT WAS.
I'M TOTALLY GETTING IN HIS WAY WHEN HE'S TRYING TO STUDY...
GLOOOM
WELL, I GUESS HE'S RIGHT ABOUT THAT...
AND THEN WHEN I MAKE HIM STUFF TO CHEER HIM ON IT GETS BLOWN AWAY BY THE WIND.
...
WELL, I'D DECIDED...
...I WAS GOING TO SUPPORT HIM A HUNDRED PERCENT. SO I GUESS THAT MEANS...
See ya!
HEY, ÔTANI?

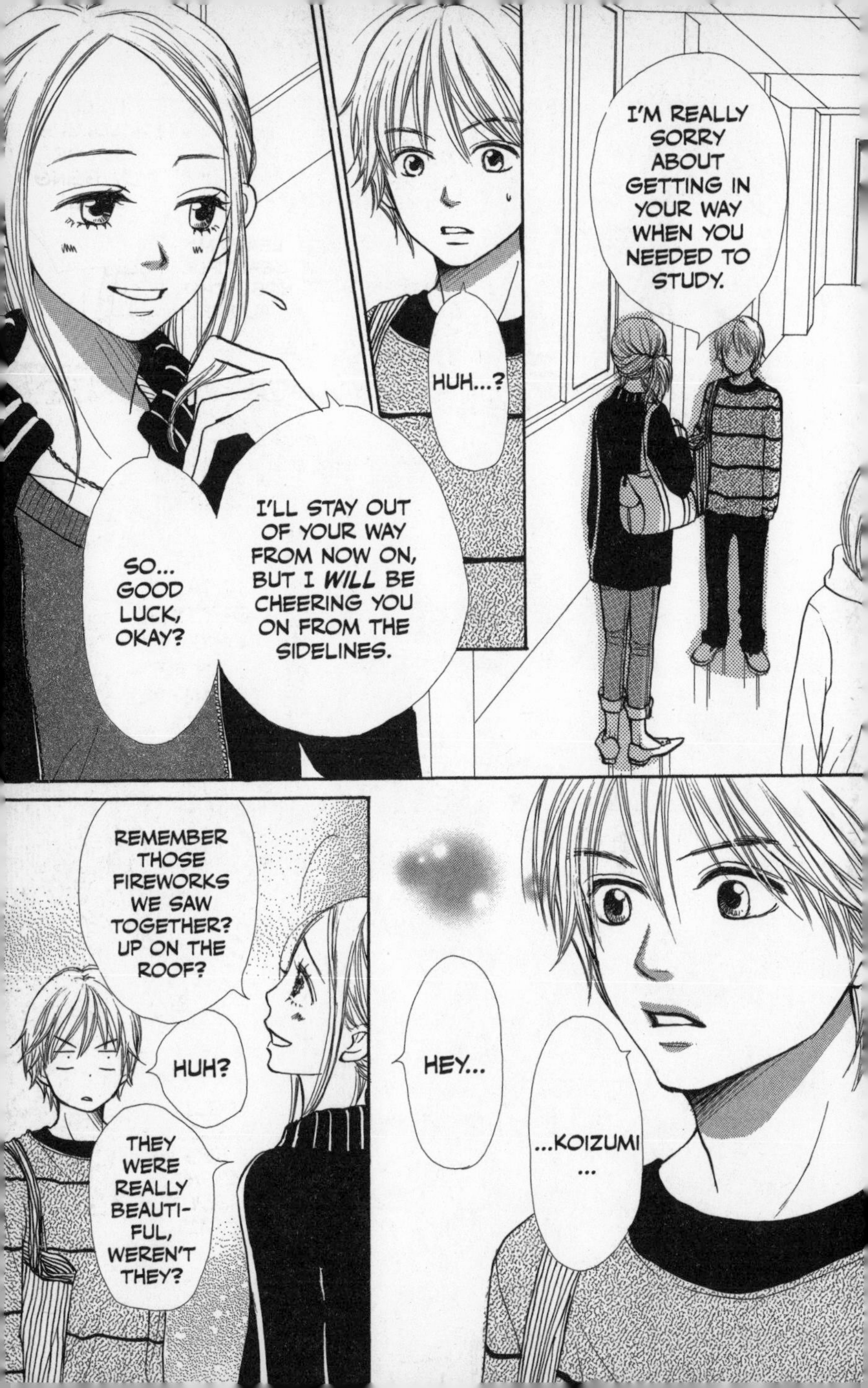
I'M REALLY SORRY ABOUT GETTING IN YOUR WAY WHEN YOU NEEDED TO STUDY.
HUH...?
I'LL STAY OUT OF YOUR WAY FROM NOW ON, BUT I *WILL* BE CHEERING YOU ON FROM THE SIDELINES.
SO... GOOD LUCK, OKAY?
HEY...
...KOIZUMI ...
REMEMBER THOSE FIREWORKS WE SAW TOGETHER? UP ON THE ROOF?
HUH?
THEY WERE REALLY BEAUTI- FUL, WEREN'T THEY?

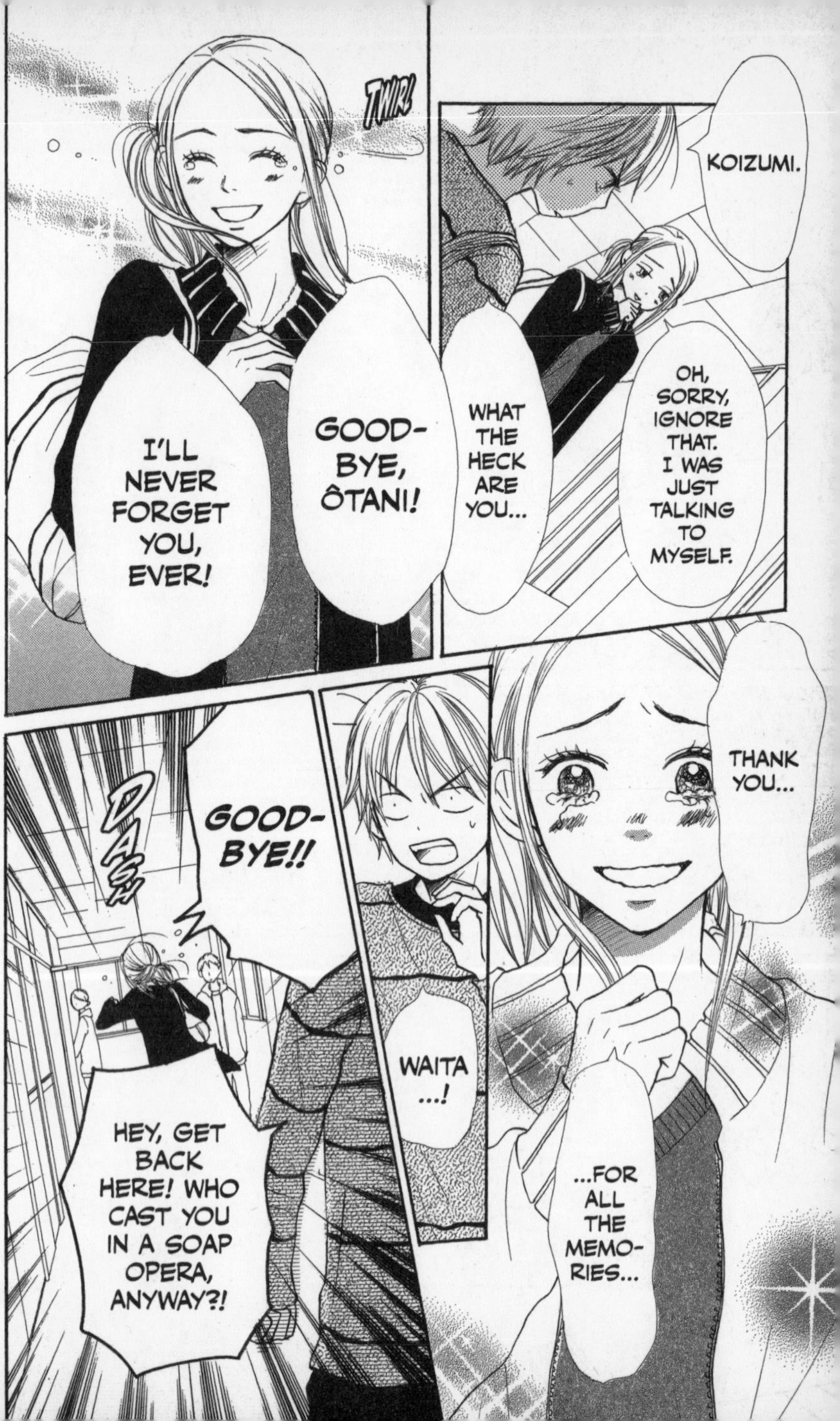
KOIZUMI.
OH, SORRY, IGNORE THAT. I WAS JUST TALKING TO MYSELF.
WHAT THE HECK ARE YOU...
TWIRL
GOOD-BYE, ÔTANI!
I'LL NEVER FORGET YOU, EVER!
THANK YOU...
...FOR ALL THE MEMORIES...
WAITA ...!
GOOD-BYE!!
DASH
HEY, GET BACK HERE! WHO CAST YOU IN A SOAP OPERA, ANYWAY?!

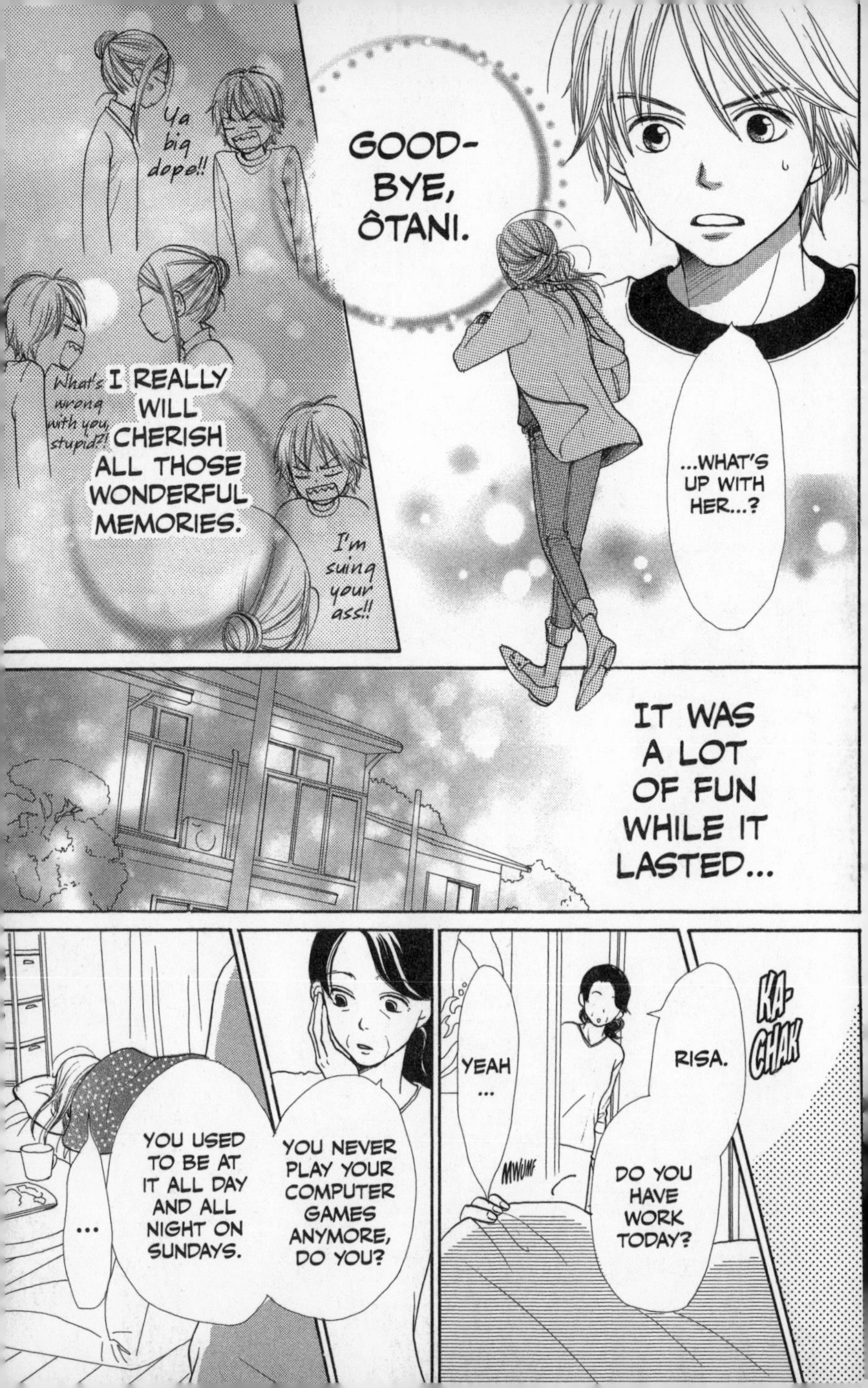
GOOD-BYE, ÔTANI.
...WHAT'S UP WITH HER...?
Ya big dope!!
I REALLY WILL CHERISH ALL THOSE WONDERFUL MEMORIES.
What's wrong with you, stupid?!
I'm suing your ass!!
IT WAS A LOT OF FUN WHILE IT LASTED...
KA-CHAK
RISA.
DO YOU HAVE WORK TODAY?
YEAH...
MWUMF
YOU NEVER PLAY YOUR COMPUTER GAMES ANYMORE, DO YOU?
YOU USED TO BE AT IT ALL DAY AND ALL NIGHT ON SUNDAYS.
...

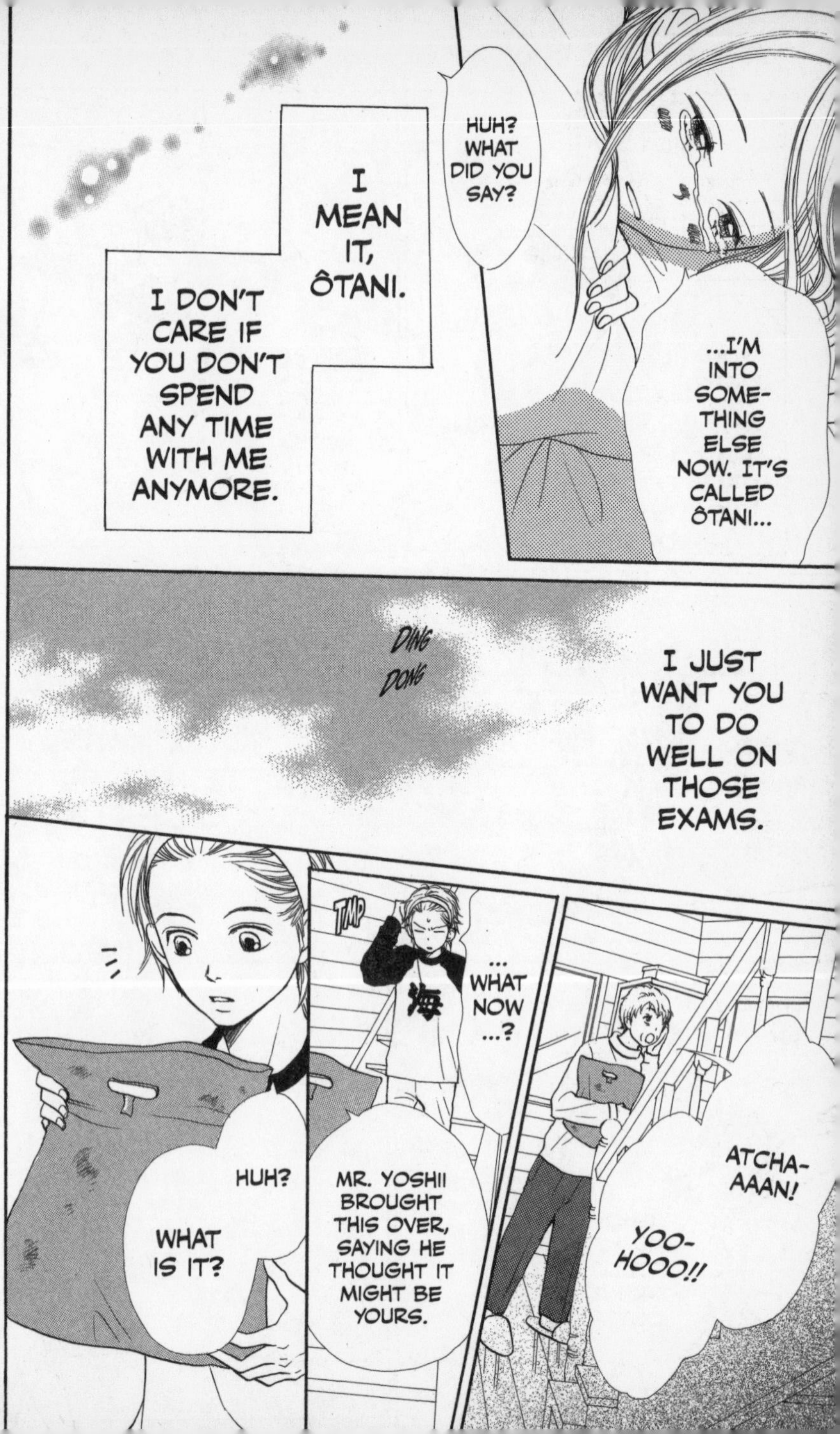
HUH? WHAT DID YOU SAY?
...I'M INTO SOME-THING ELSE NOW. IT'S CALLED ÔTANI...
I MEAN IT, ÔTANI.
I DON'T CARE IF YOU DON'T SPEND ANY TIME WITH ME ANYMORE.
I JUST WANT YOU TO DO WELL ON THOSE EXAMS.
DING DONG
ATCHA-AAAN!
YOO-HOOO!!
TMP
...WHAT NOW...?
MR. YOSHII BROUGHT THIS OVER, SAYING HE THOUGHT IT MIGHT BE YOURS.
HUH?
WHAT IS IT?

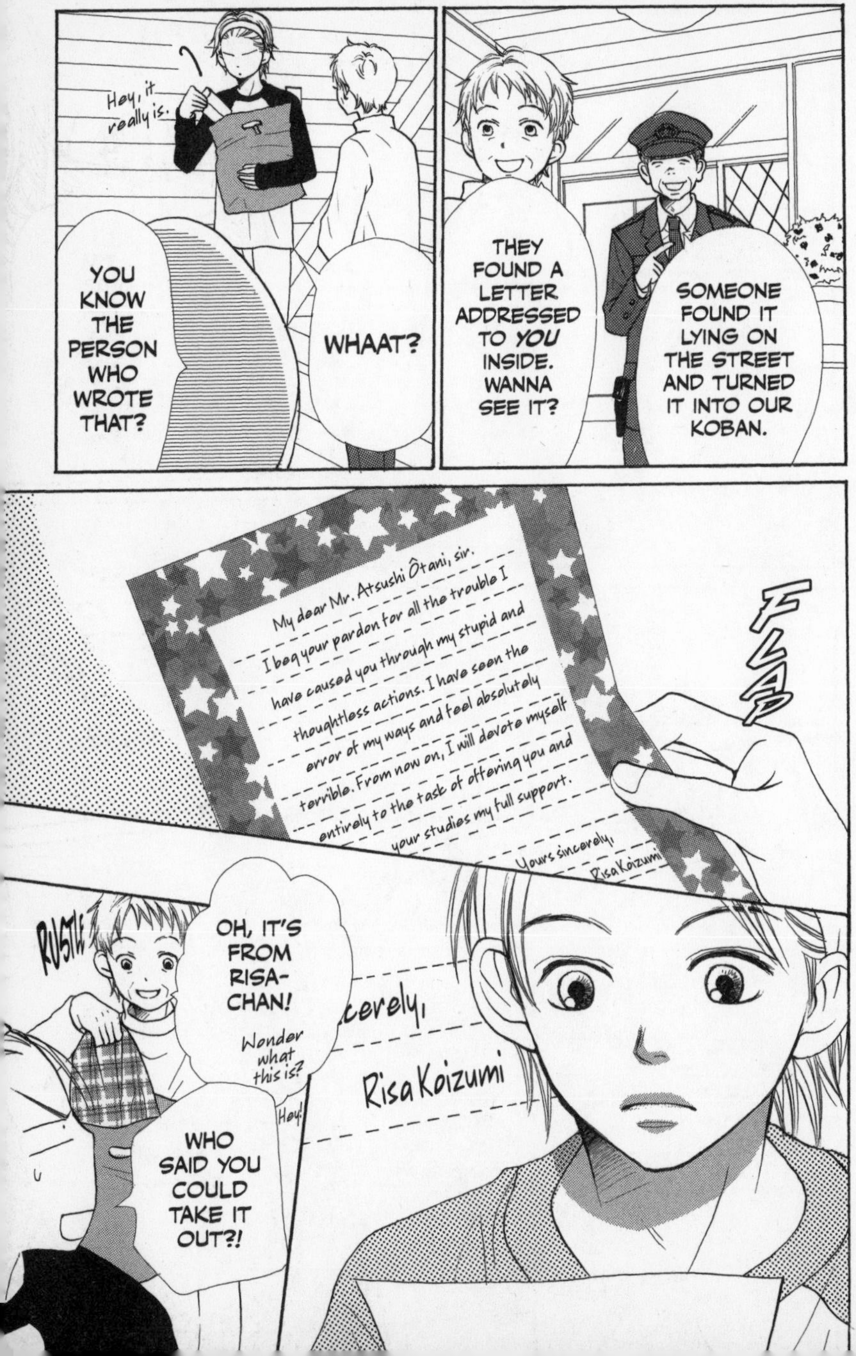
SOMEONE FOUND IT LYING ON THE STREET AND TURNED IT INTO OUR KOBAN.
THEY FOUND A LETTER ADDRESSED TO *YOU* INSIDE. WANNA SEE IT?
WHAAT?
Hey, it really is.
YOU KNOW THE PERSON WHO WROTE THAT?
FLAP
My dear Mr. Atsushi Ôtani, sir.
I beg your pardon for all the trouble I have caused you through my stupid and thoughtless actions. I have seen the error of my ways and feel absolutely terrible. From now on, I will devote myself entirely to the task of offering you and your studies my full support.
Yours sincerely,
Risa Koizumi
cerely,
Risa Koizumi
RUSTLE
OH, IT'S FROM RISA-CHAN!
Wonder what this is?
Hey!
WHO SAID YOU COULD TAKE IT OUT?!

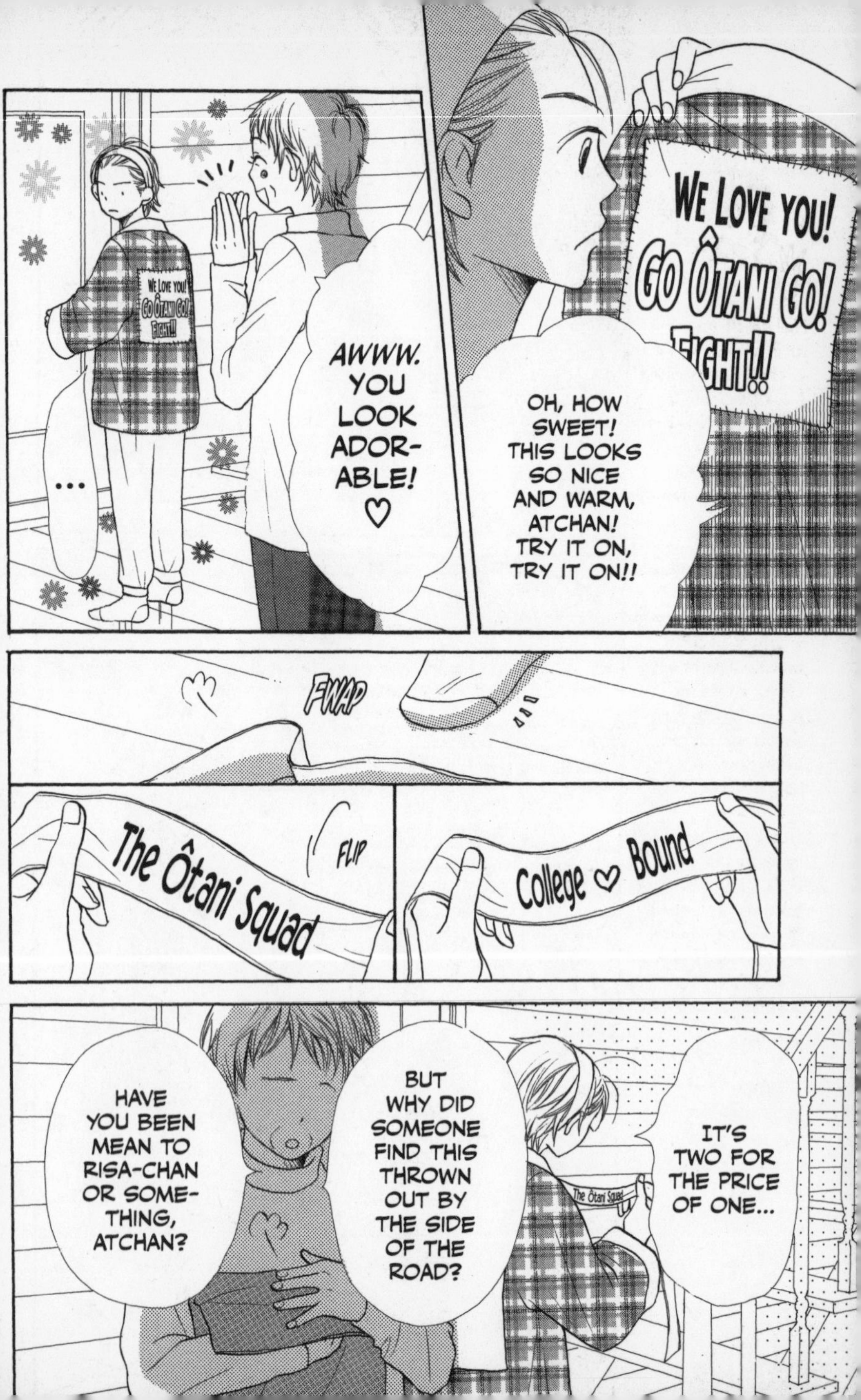
WE LOVE YOU! GO ÔTANI GO! FIGHT!!
OH, HOW SWEET! THIS LOOKS SO NICE AND WARM, ATCHAN! TRY IT ON, TRY IT ON!!
AWWW. YOU LOOK ADORABLE! ♡
WE LOVE YOU! GO ÔTANI GO! FIGHT!!
...
FWAP
College ♡ Bound
FLIP
The Ôtani Squad
IT'S TWO FOR THE PRICE OF ONE...
The Ôtani Squad
BUT WHY DID SOMEONE FIND THIS THROWN OUT BY THE SIDE OF THE ROAD?
HAVE YOU BEEN MEAN TO RISA-CHAN OR SOMETHING, ATCHAN?

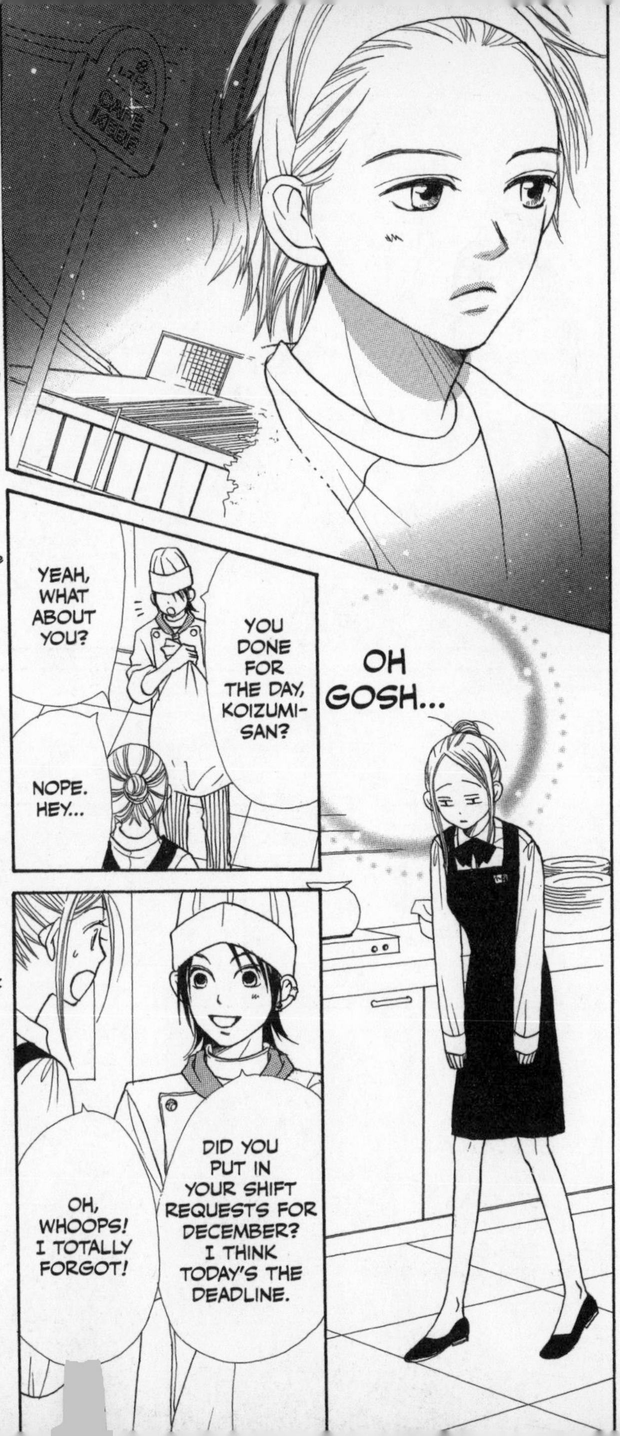
OH GOSH...
YOU DONE FOR THE DAY, KOIZUMI-SAN?
YEAH, WHAT ABOUT YOU?
NOPE. HEY...
DID YOU PUT IN YOUR SHIFT REQUESTS FOR DECEMBER? I THINK TODAY'S THE DEADLINE.
OH, WHOOPS! I TOTALLY FORGOT!

4

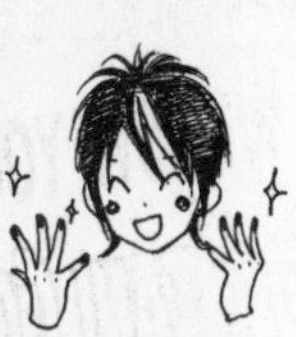

Nail polish is a no-no if you work in a restaurant kitchen! I used to have a job in a restaurant kitchen myself, so I know about these things, see, and I actually drew a scene where Kohori-kun gets in trouble for it. It didn't fit, though, so I had to cut it and never got a chance to work it in anywhere else. So let me get on his case now: Hey, you! No polish! So. Anyway. Thank you for even reading these little sidebars. Next up, Volume 11! If you can, please stick around with us a little longer. Well, then, see you! pa-twoo pa-twoo!

Aya
Feb. 2005

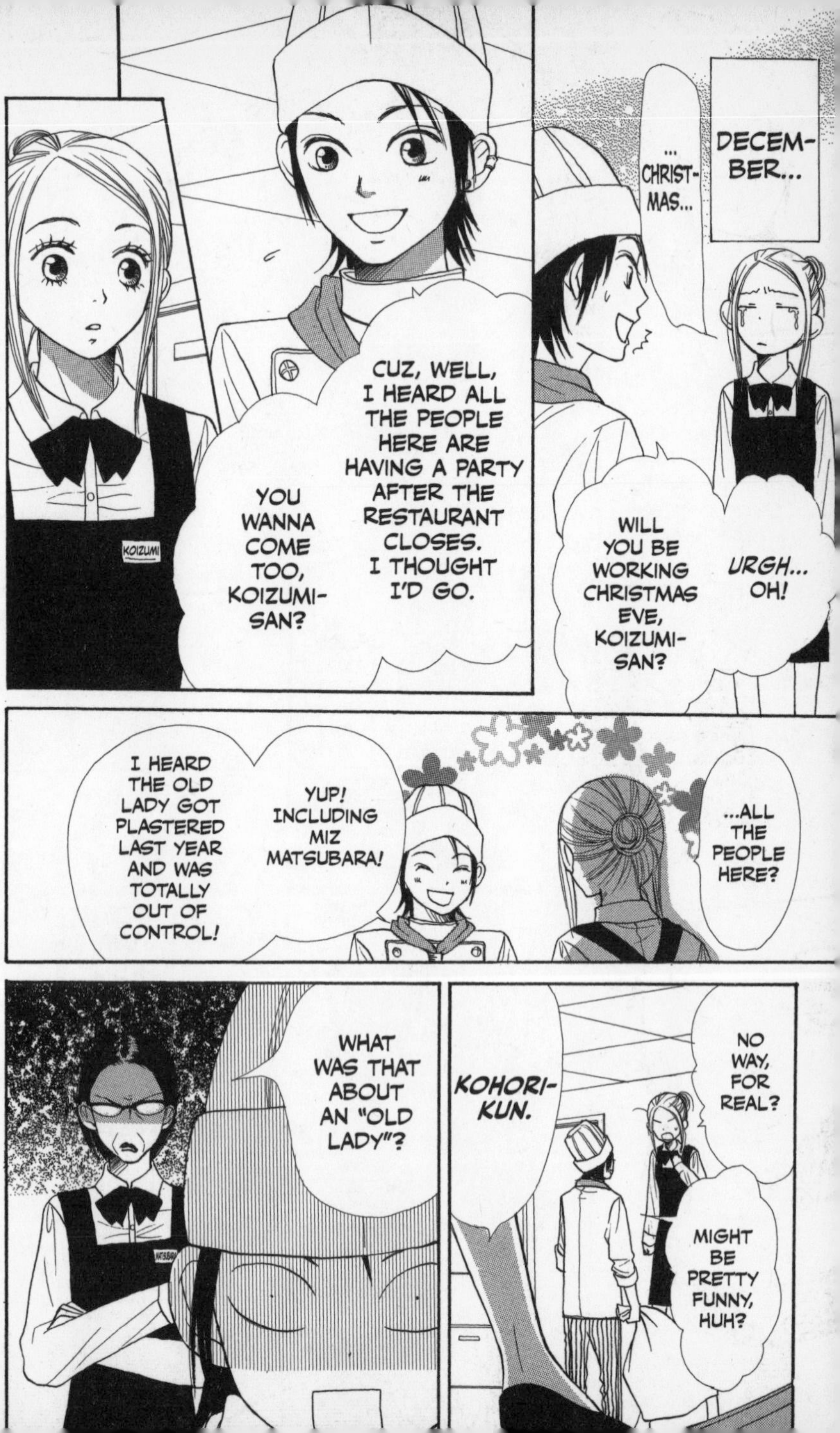
DECEMBER...
...CHRISTMAS...
WILL YOU BE WORKING CHRISTMAS EVE, KOIZUMI-SAN?
URGH... OH!
CUZ, WELL, I HEARD ALL THE PEOPLE HERE ARE HAVING A PARTY AFTER THE RESTAURANT CLOSES. I THOUGHT I'D GO.
YOU WANNA COME TOO, KOIZUMI-SAN?
KOIZUMI
...ALL THE PEOPLE HERE?
YUP! INCLUDING MIZ MATSUBARA!
I HEARD THE OLD LADY GOT PLASTERED LAST YEAR AND WAS TOTALLY OUT OF CONTROL!
NO WAY, FOR REAL?
MIGHT BE PRETTY FUNNY, HUH?
KOHORI-KUN.
WHAT WAS THAT ABOUT AN "OLD LADY"?

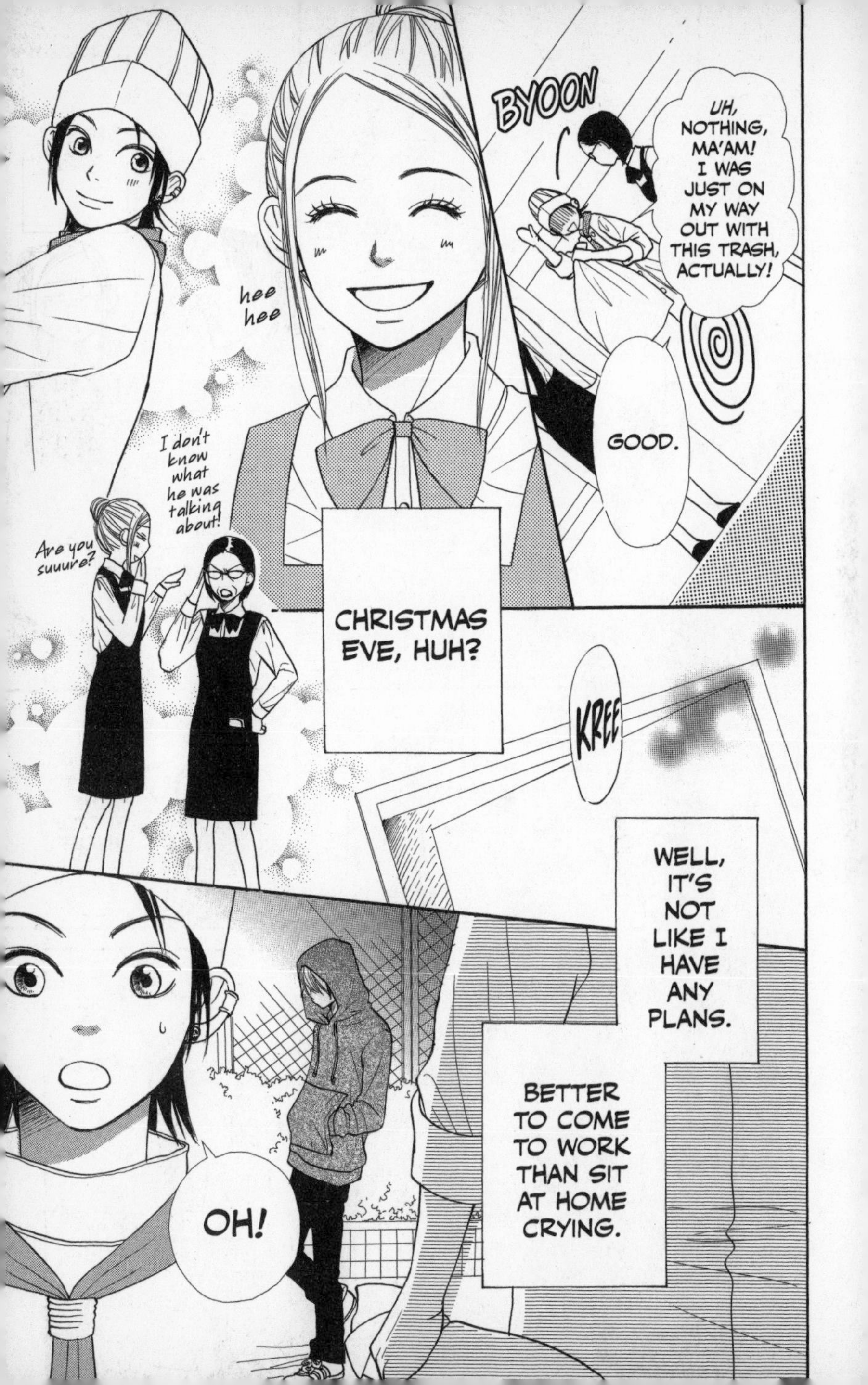
BYOON
UH, NOTHING, MA'AM! I WAS JUST ON MY WAY OUT WITH THIS TRASH, ACTUALLY!
GOOD.
hee hee
I don't know what he was talking about!
Are you suuure?
CHRISTMAS EVE, HUH?
KREE
WELL, IT'S NOT LIKE I HAVE ANY PLANS.
BETTER TO COME TO WORK THAN SIT AT HOME CRYING.
OH!

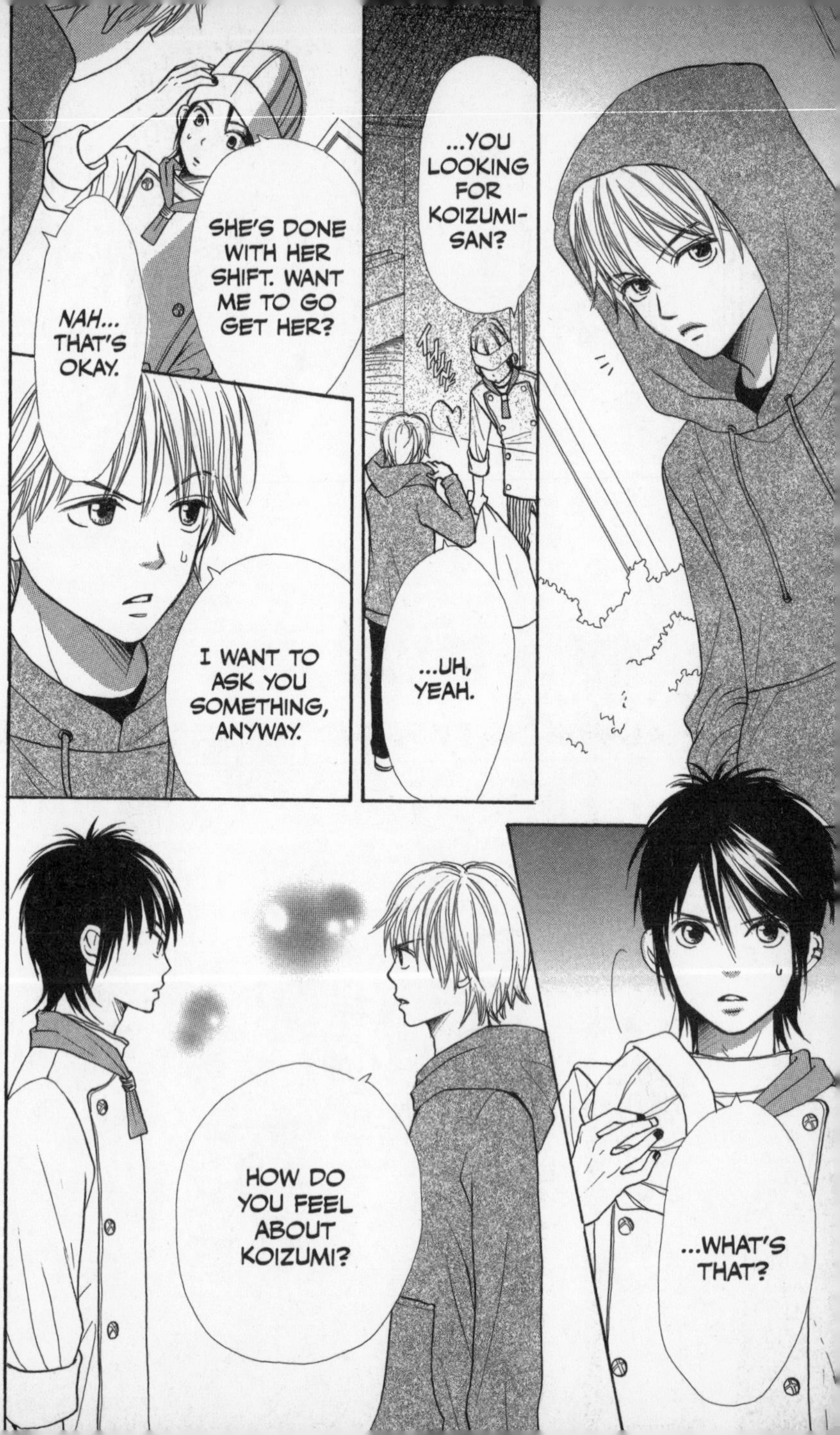
...YOU LOOKING FOR KOIZUMI-SAN?
...UH, YEAH.
SHE'S DONE WITH HER SHIFT. WANT ME TO GO GET HER?
NAH... THAT'S OKAY.
I WANT TO ASK YOU SOMETHING, ANYWAY.
...WHAT'S THAT?
HOW DO YOU FEEL ABOUT KOIZUMI?

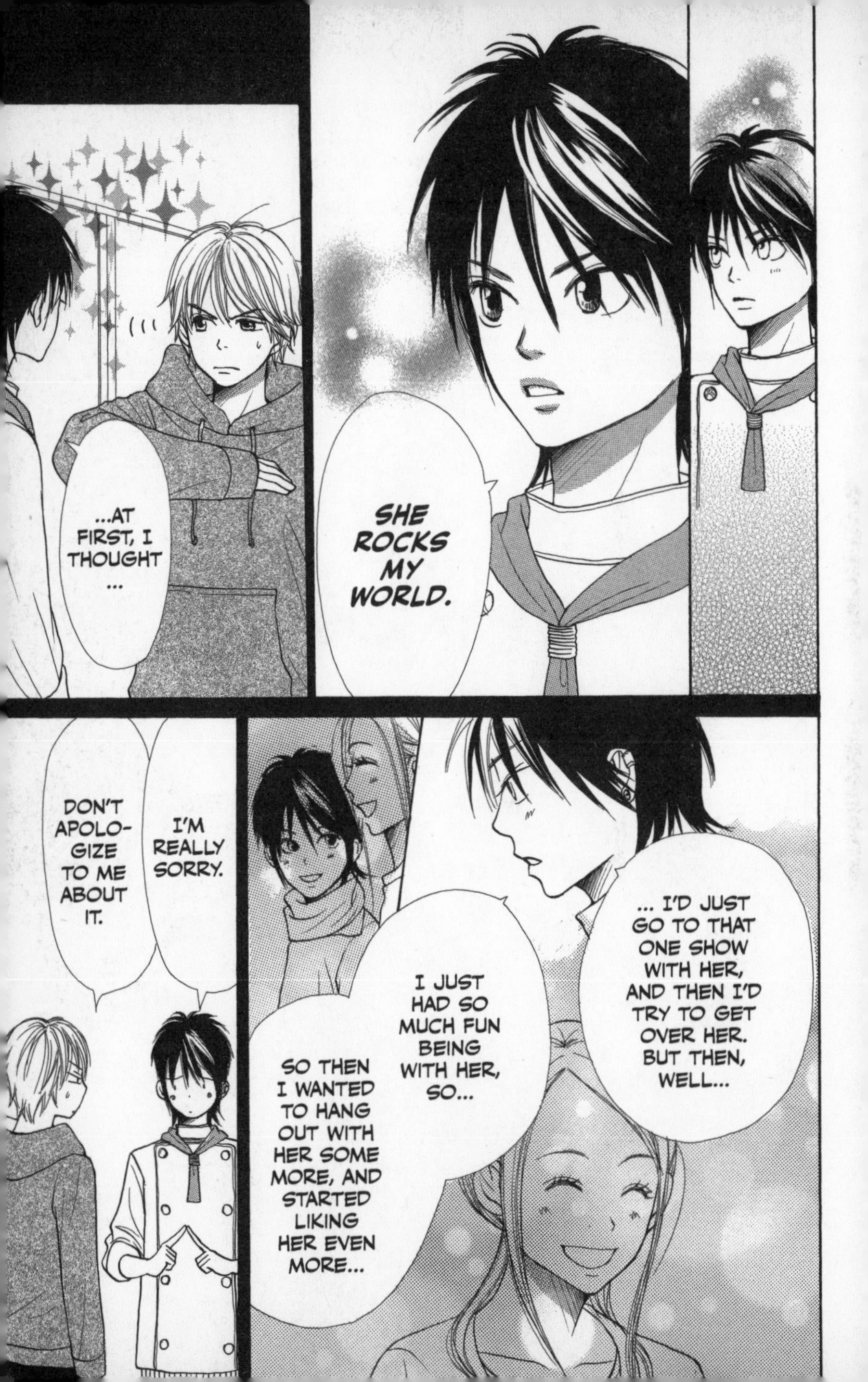
SHE ROCKS MY WORLD.
...AT FIRST, I THOUGHT ...
... I'D JUST GO TO THAT ONE SHOW WITH HER, AND THEN I'D TRY TO GET OVER HER. BUT THEN, WELL...
I JUST HAD SO MUCH FUN BEING WITH HER, SO...
SO THEN I WANTED TO HANG OUT WITH HER SOME MORE, AND STARTED LIKING HER EVEN MORE...
I'M REALLY SORRY.
DON'T APOLO-GIZE TO ME ABOUT IT.

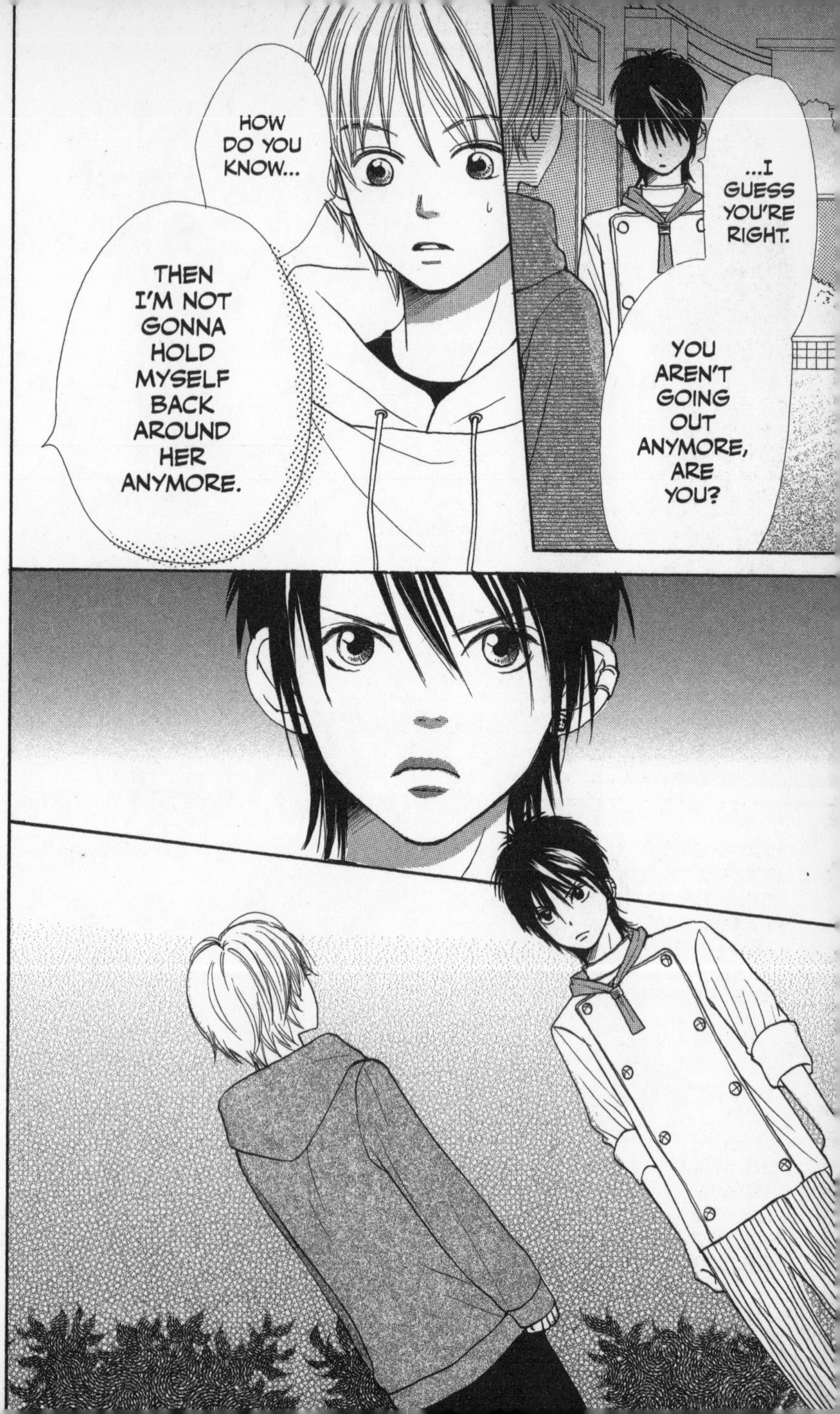
...I GUESS YOU'RE RIGHT.
YOU AREN'T GOING OUT ANYMORE, ARE YOU?
HOW DO YOU KNOW...
THEN I'M NOT GONNA HOLD MYSELF BACK AROUND HER ANYMORE.

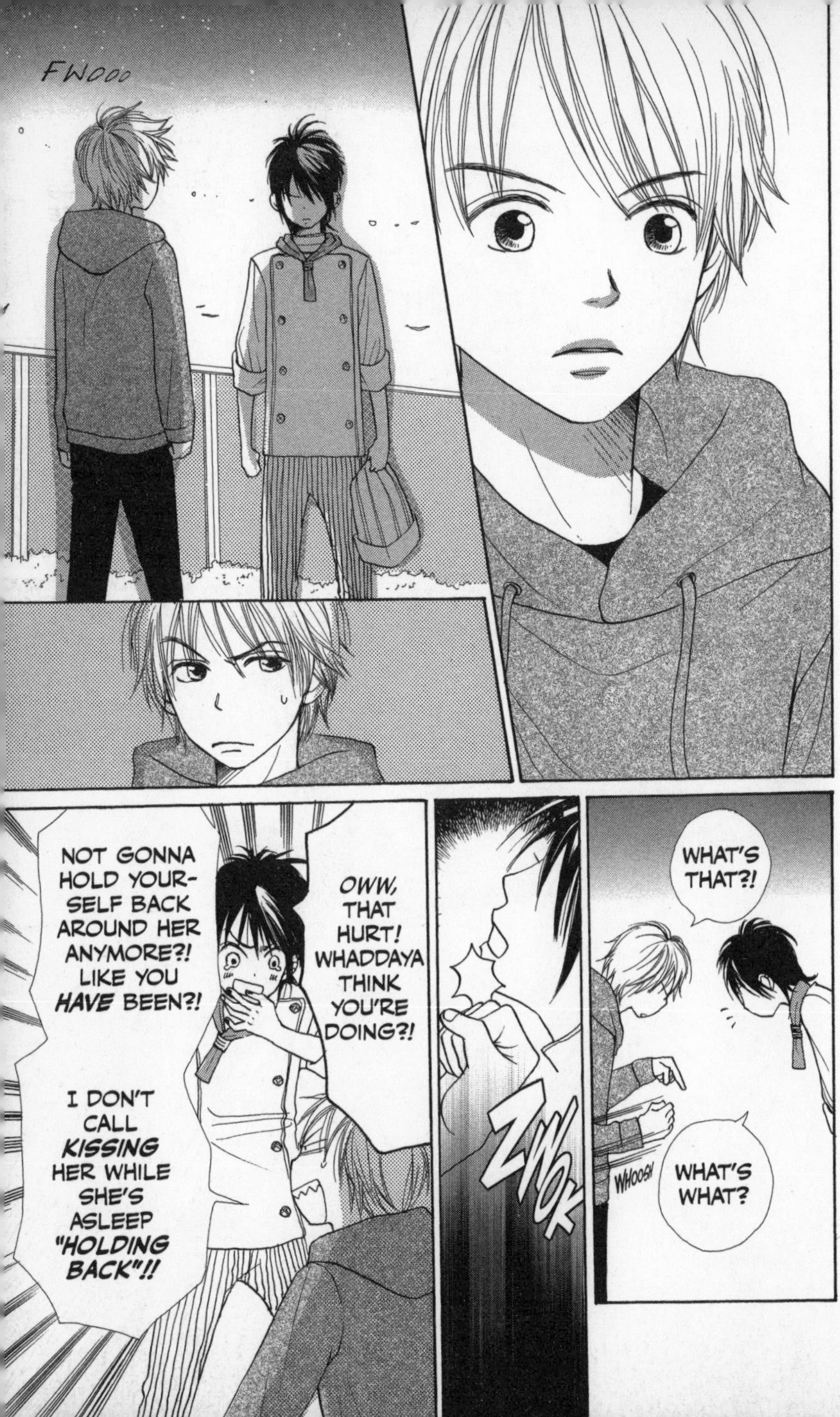
FWOOO
WHAT'S THAT?!
WHAT'S WHAT?
WHOOSH
ZWOK
OWW, THAT HURT! WHADDAYA THINK YOU'RE DOING?!
NOT GONNA HOLD YOURSELF BACK AROUND HER ANYMORE?! LIKE YOU HAVE BEEN?!
I DON'T CALL KISSING HER WHILE SHE'S ASLEEP "HOLDING BACK"!!

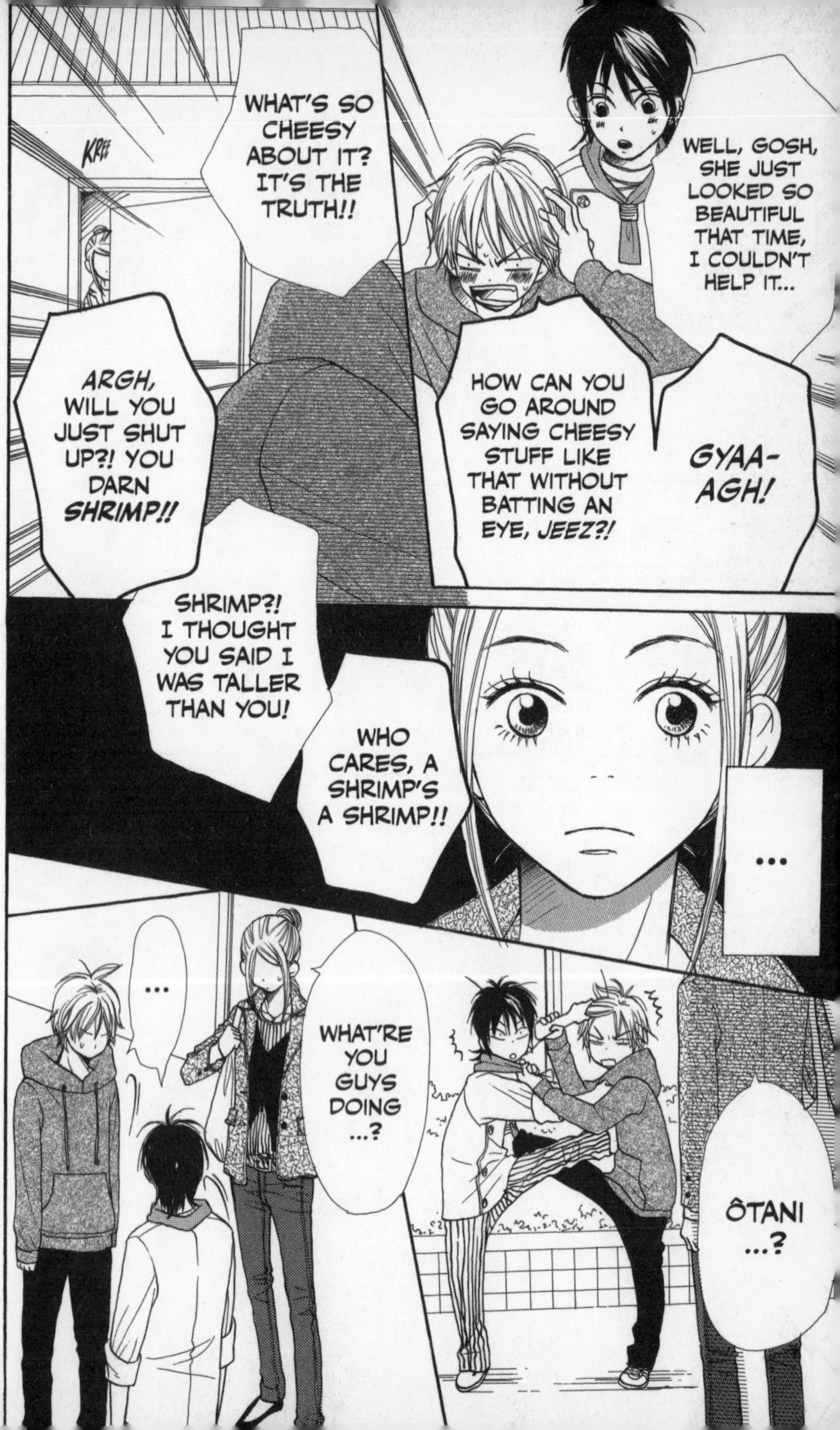

WELL, GOSH, SHE JUST LOOKED SO BEAUTIFUL THAT TIME, I COULDN'T HELP IT...
WHAT'S SO CHEESY ABOUT IT? IT'S THE TRUTH!!
GYAA-AGH!
HOW CAN YOU GO AROUND SAYING CHEESY STUFF LIKE THAT WITHOUT BATTING AN EYE, JEEZ?!
KREE
ARGH, WILL YOU JUST SHUT UP?! YOU DARN SHRIMP!!
SHRIMP?! I THOUGHT YOU SAID I WAS TALLER THAN YOU!
WHO CARES, A SHRIMP'S A SHRIMP!!
...
ÔTANI ...?
WHAT'RE YOU GUYS DOING ...?
...

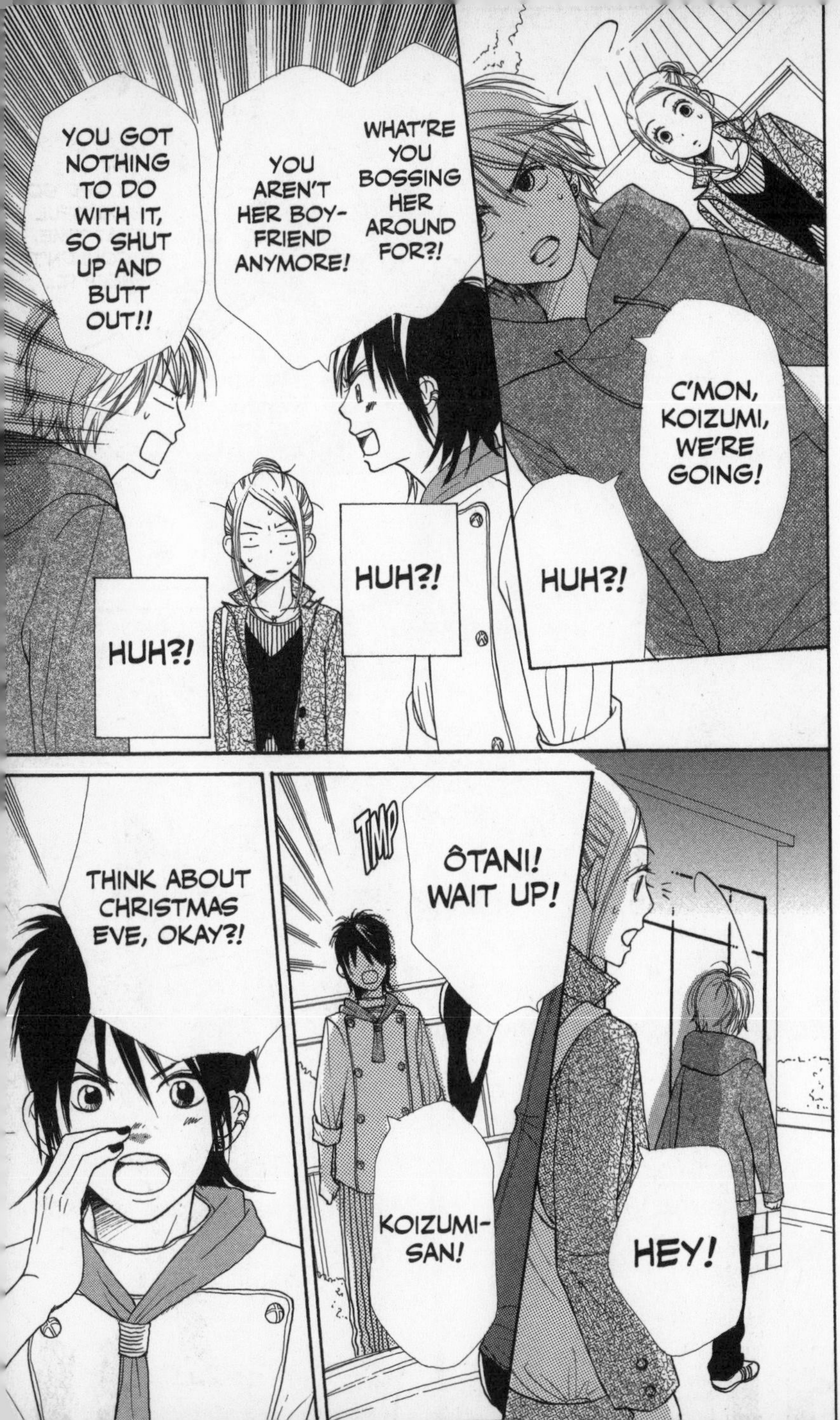
C'MON, KOIZUMI, WE'RE GOING!
HUH?!
WHAT'RE YOU BOSSING HER AROUND FOR?!
YOU AREN'T HER BOY-FRIEND ANYMORE!
YOU GOT NOTHING TO DO WITH IT, SO SHUT UP AND BUTT OUT!!
HUH?!
HUH?!
ÔTANI! WAIT UP!
HEY!
TMP
KOIZUMI-SAN!
THINK ABOUT CHRISTMAS EVE, OKAY?!

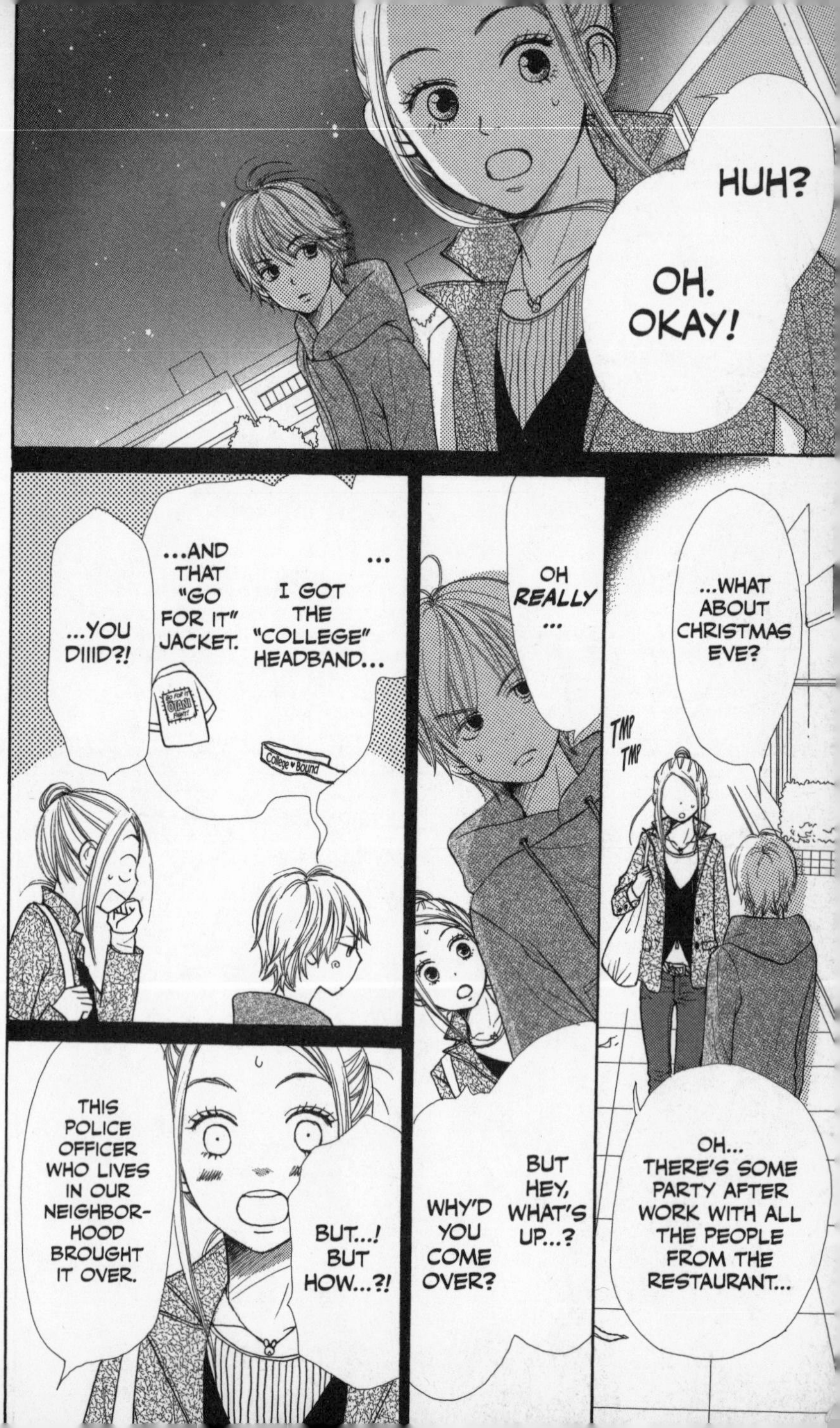
HUH?
OH. OKAY!
...WHAT ABOUT CHRISTMAS EVE?
TMP TMP
OH... THERE'S SOME PARTY AFTER WORK WITH ALL THE PEOPLE FROM THE RESTAURANT...
OH *REALLY* ...
BUT HEY, WHAT'S UP...?
WHY'D YOU COME OVER?
... I GOT THE "COLLEGE" HEADBAND...
...AND THAT "GO FOR IT" JACKET.
...YOU DIIID?!
College Bound
BUT...! BUT HOW...?!
THIS POLICE OFFICER WHO LIVES IN OUR NEIGHBOR-HOOD BROUGHT IT OVER.

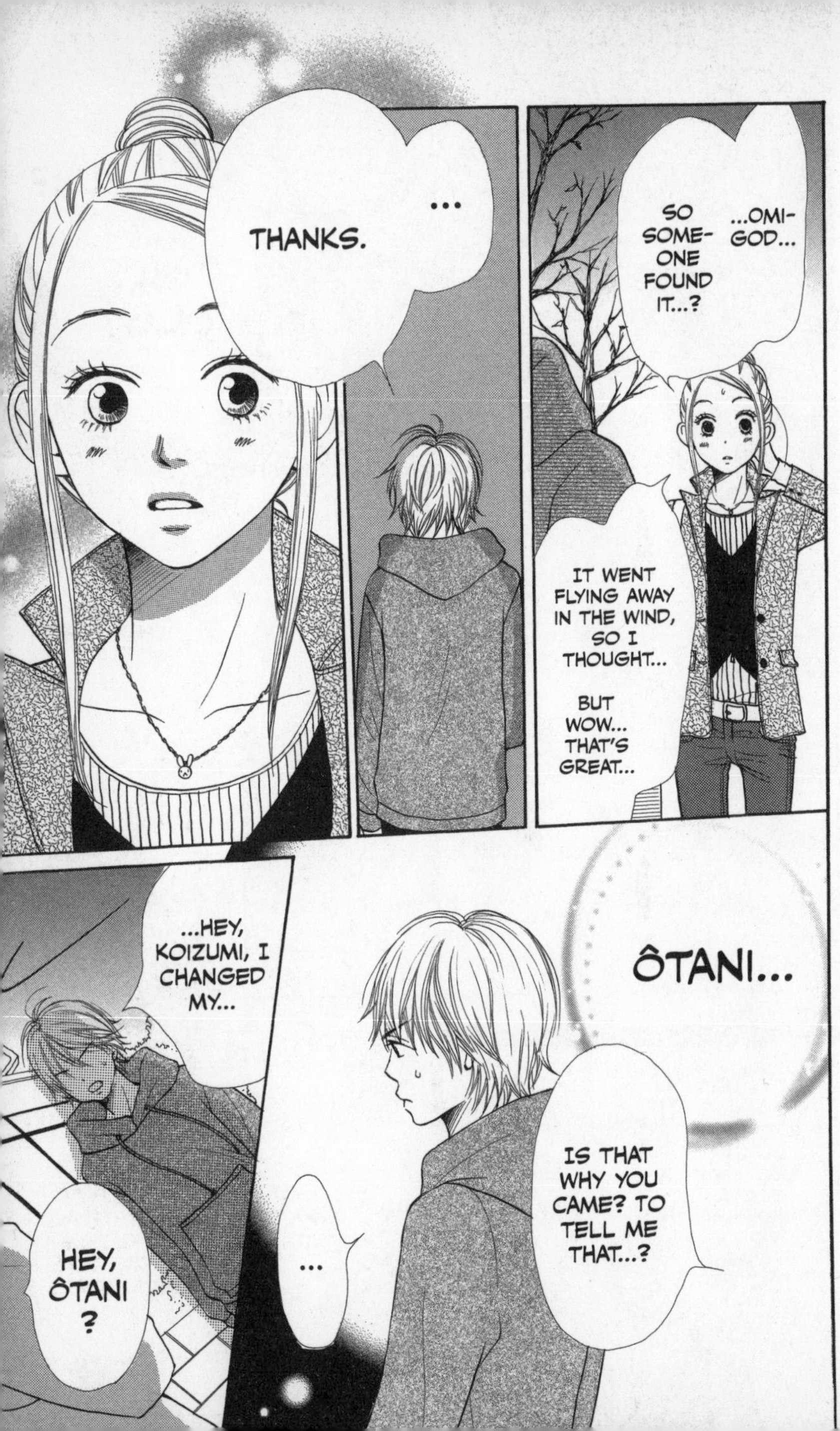
...OMIGOD...
SO SOMEONE FOUND IT...?
IT WENT FLYING AWAY IN THE WIND, SO I THOUGHT...
BUT WOW... THAT'S GREAT...
... THANKS.
ÔTANI...
IS THAT WHY YOU CAME? TO TELL ME THAT...?
...
...HEY, KOIZUMI, I CHANGED MY...
HEY, ÔTANI?

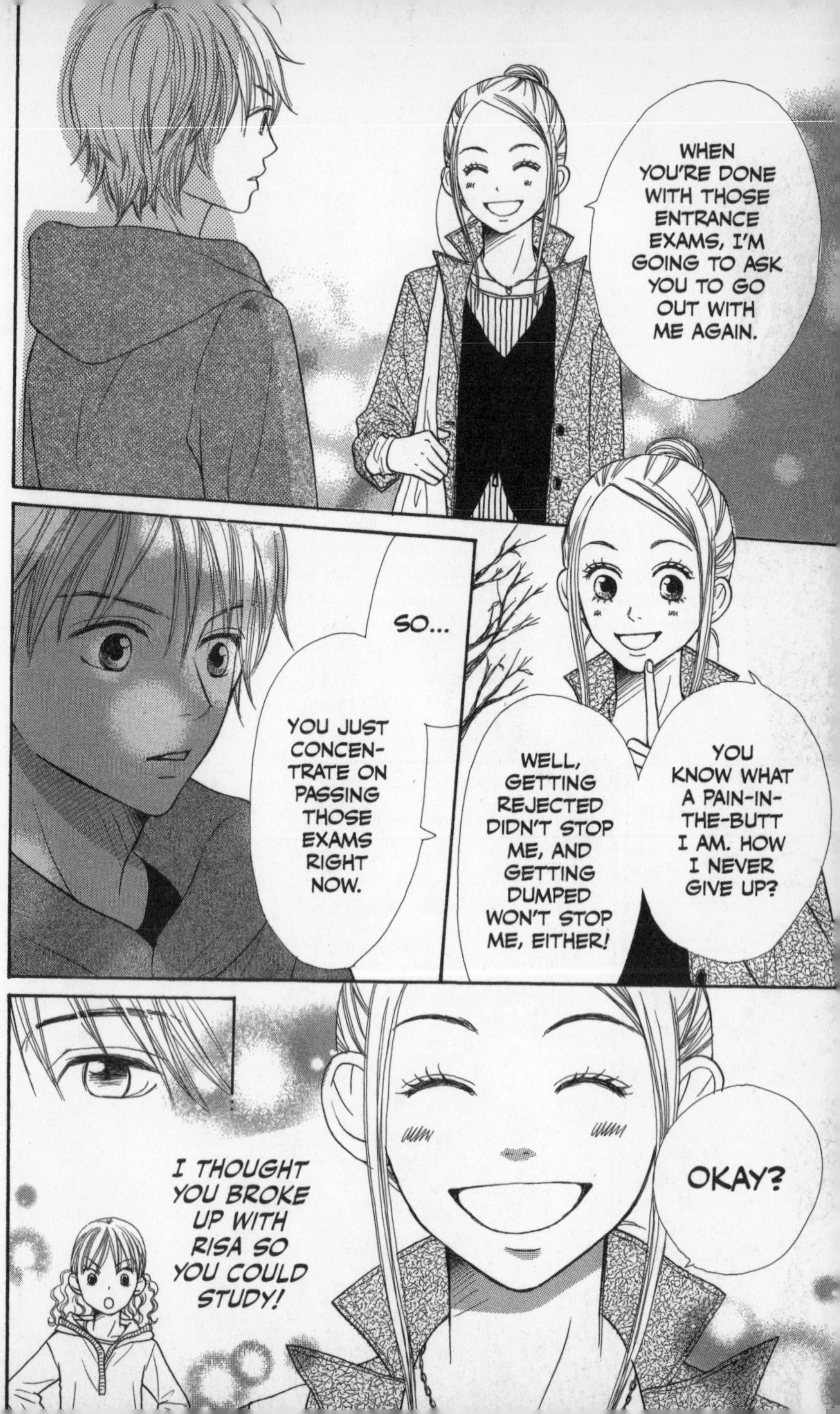
WHEN YOU'RE DONE WITH THOSE ENTRANCE EXAMS, I'M GOING TO ASK YOU TO GO OUT WITH ME AGAIN.
YOU KNOW WHAT A PAIN-IN-THE-BUTT I AM. HOW I NEVER GIVE UP?
WELL, GETTING REJECTED DIDN'T STOP ME, AND GETTING DUMPED WON'T STOP ME, EITHER!
SO...
YOU JUST CONCENTRATE ON PASSING THOSE EXAMS RIGHT NOW.
OKAY?
I THOUGHT YOU BROKE UP WITH RISA SO YOU COULD STUDY!

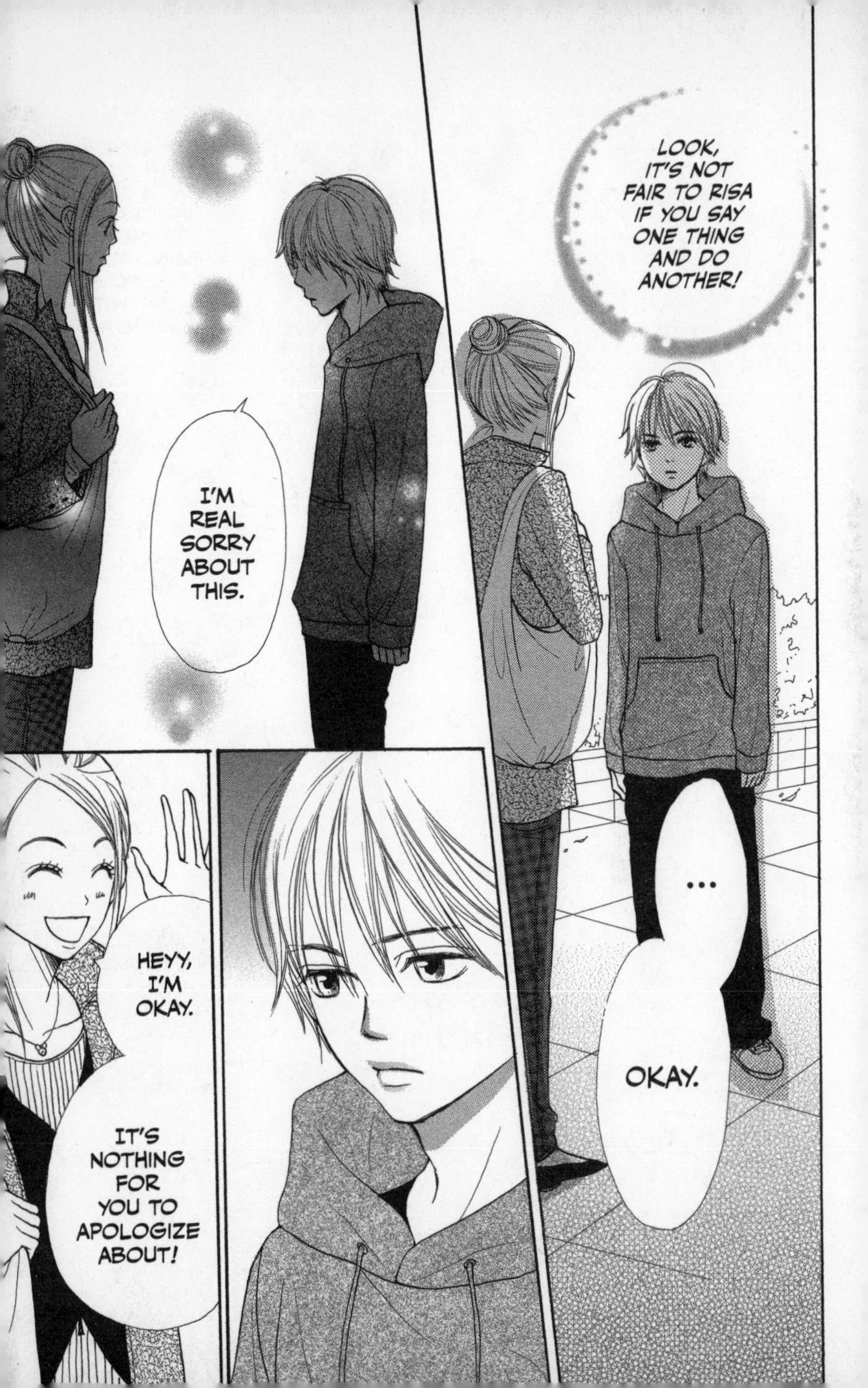
LOOK, IT'S NOT FAIR TO RISA IF YOU SAY ONE THING AND DO ANOTHER!
...
OKAY.
I'M REAL SORRY ABOUT THIS.
HEYY, I'M OKAY.
IT'S NOTHING FOR YOU TO APOLOGIZE ABOUT!

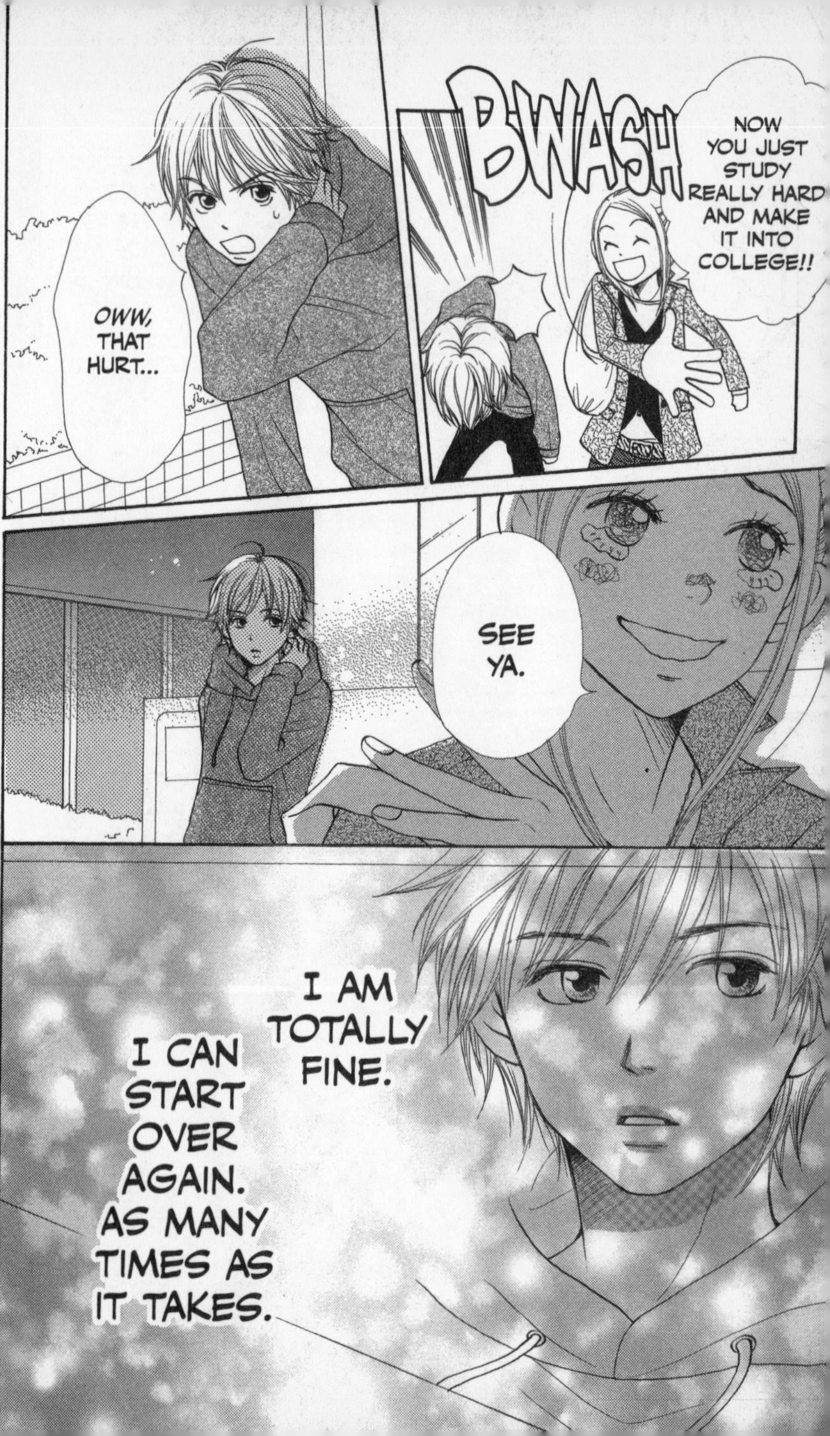
NOW YOU JUST STUDY REALLY HARD AND MAKE IT INTO COLLEGE!!
BWASH
OWW, THAT HURT...
SEE YA.
I AM TOTALLY FINE.
I CAN START OVER AGAIN. AS MANY TIMES AS IT TAKES.

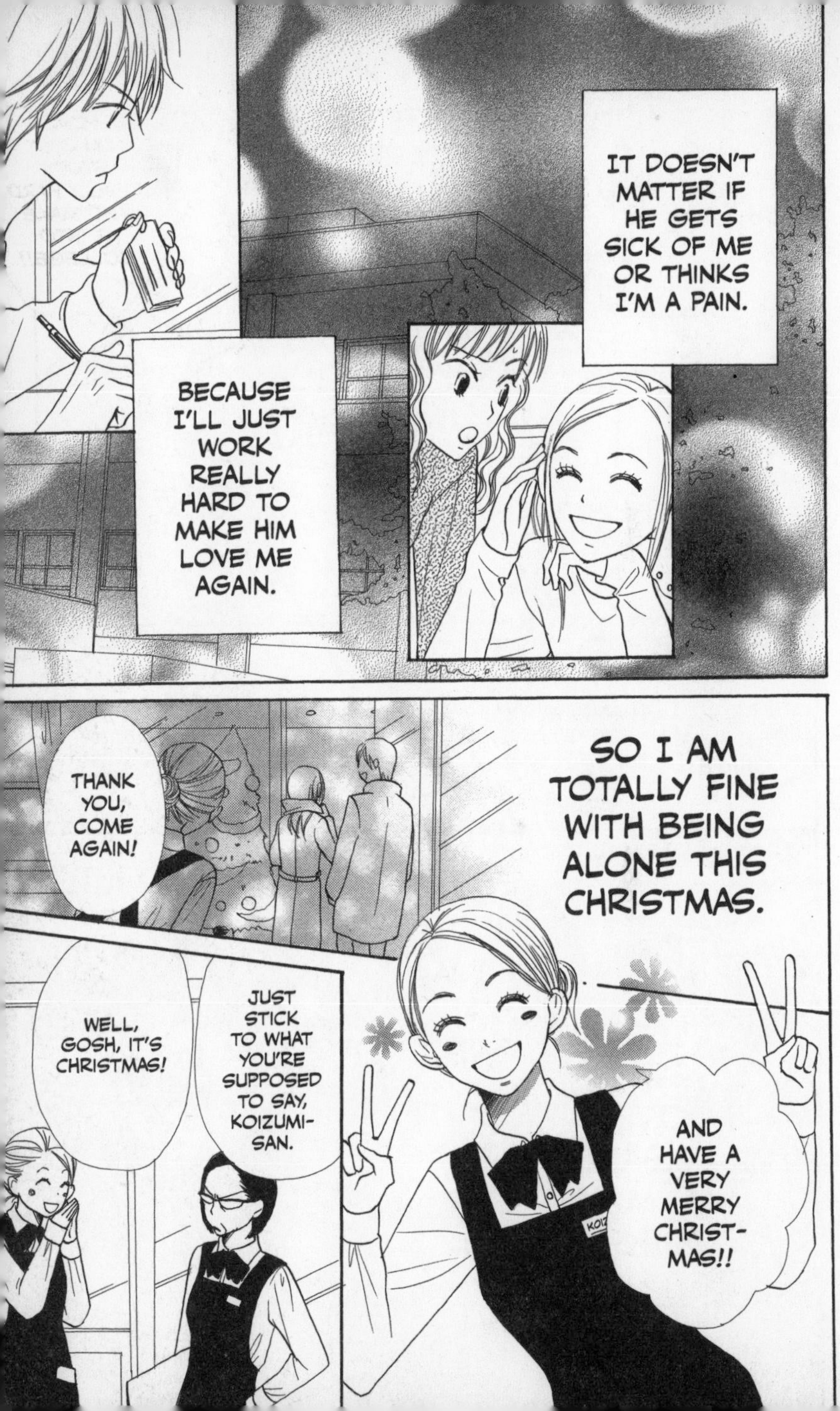
IT DOESN'T MATTER IF HE GETS SICK OF ME OR THINKS I'M A PAIN.
BECAUSE I'LL JUST WORK REALLY HARD TO MAKE HIM LOVE ME AGAIN.
SO I AM TOTALLY FINE WITH BEING ALONE THIS CHRISTMAS.
THANK YOU, COME AGAIN!
AND HAVE A VERY MERRY CHRIST-MAS!!
JUST STICK TO WHAT YOU'RE SUPPOSED TO SAY, KOIZUMI-SAN.
WELL, GOSH, IT'S CHRISTMAS!

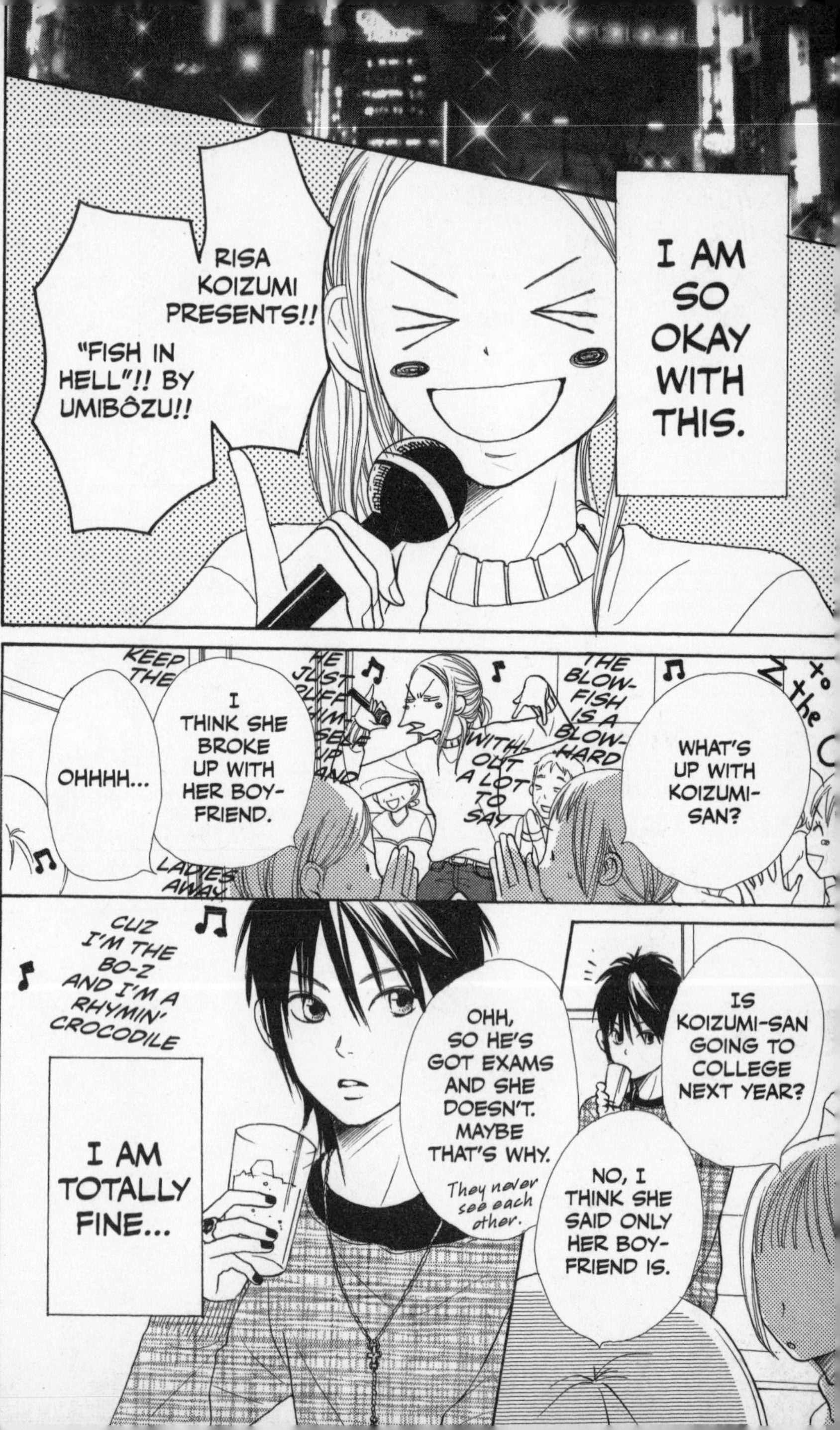
I AM SO OKAY WITH THIS.
RISA KOIZUMI PRESENTS!!
"FISH IN HELL"!! BY UMIBÔZU!!
WHAT'S UP WITH KOIZUMI-SAN?
THE BLOW-FISH IS A BLOW-HARD
WITH-OUT A LOT TO SAY
HE JUST PUFF HIMSELF UP AND
KEEP THE LADIES AWAY
I THINK SHE BROKE UP WITH HER BOY-FRIEND.
OHHHH...
IS KOIZUMI-SAN GOING TO COLLEGE NEXT YEAR?
NO, I THINK SHE SAID ONLY HER BOY-FRIEND IS.
OHH, SO HE'S GOT EXAMS AND SHE DOESN'T. MAYBE THAT'S WHY.
They never see each other.
CUZ I'M THE BO-Z AND I'M A RHYMIN' CROCODILE
I AM TOTALLY FINE...

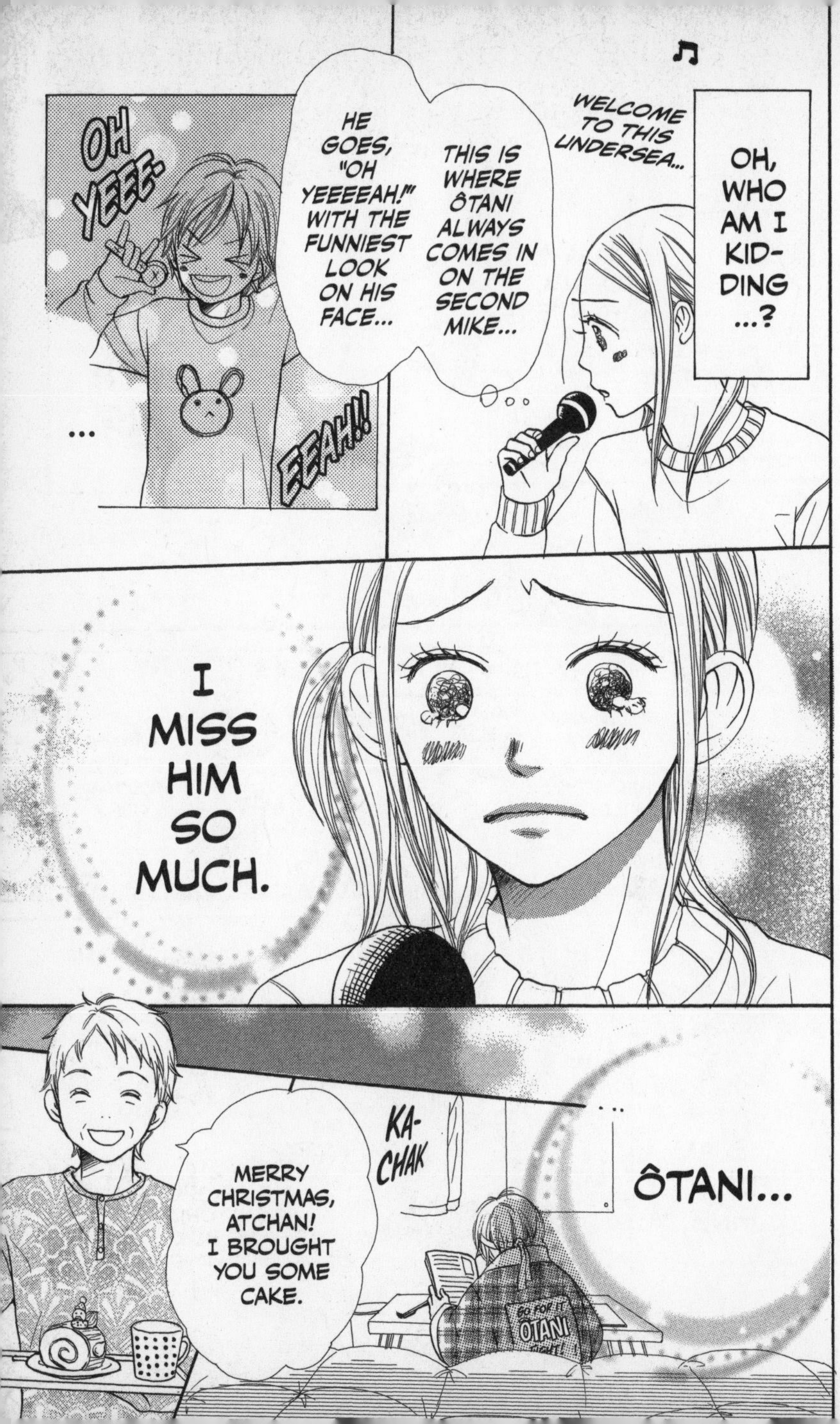
♪
WELCOME TO THIS UNDERSEA...
THIS IS WHERE ÔTANI ALWAYS COMES IN ON THE SECOND MIKE...
HE GOES, "OH YEEEEAH!" WITH THE FUNNIEST LOOK ON HIS FACE...
OH, WHO AM I KID-DING ...?
OH YEEE-
EEAH!!
...
I MISS HIM SO MUCH.
ÔTANI...
...
KA-CHAK
GO FOR IT ÔTANI
MERRY CHRISTMAS, ATCHAN! I BROUGHT YOU SOME CAKE.

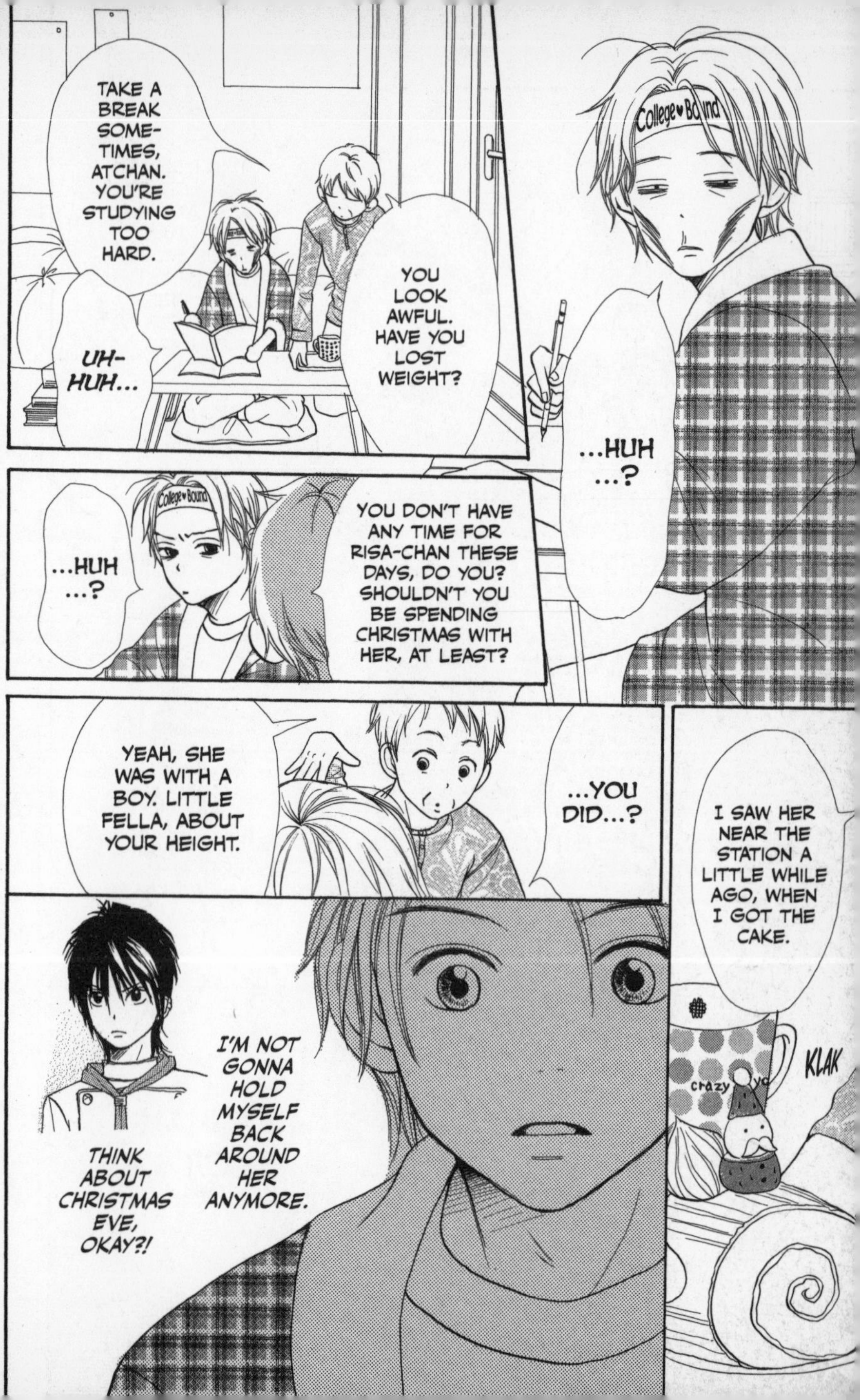
College♥Bound
...HUH ...?
YOU LOOK AWFUL. HAVE YOU LOST WEIGHT?
TAKE A BREAK SOME-TIMES, ATCHAN. YOU'RE STUDYING TOO HARD.
UH-HUH...
YOU DON'T HAVE ANY TIME FOR RISA-CHAN THESE DAYS, DO YOU? SHOULDN'T YOU BE SPENDING CHRISTMAS WITH HER, AT LEAST?
College♥Bound
...HUH ...?
I SAW HER NEAR THE STATION A LITTLE WHILE AGO, WHEN I GOT THE CAKE.
KLAK
...YOU DID...?
YEAH, SHE WAS WITH A BOY. LITTLE FELLA, ABOUT YOUR HEIGHT.
I'M NOT GONNA HOLD MYSELF BACK AROUND HER ANYMORE.
THINK ABOUT CHRISTMAS EVE, OKAY?!

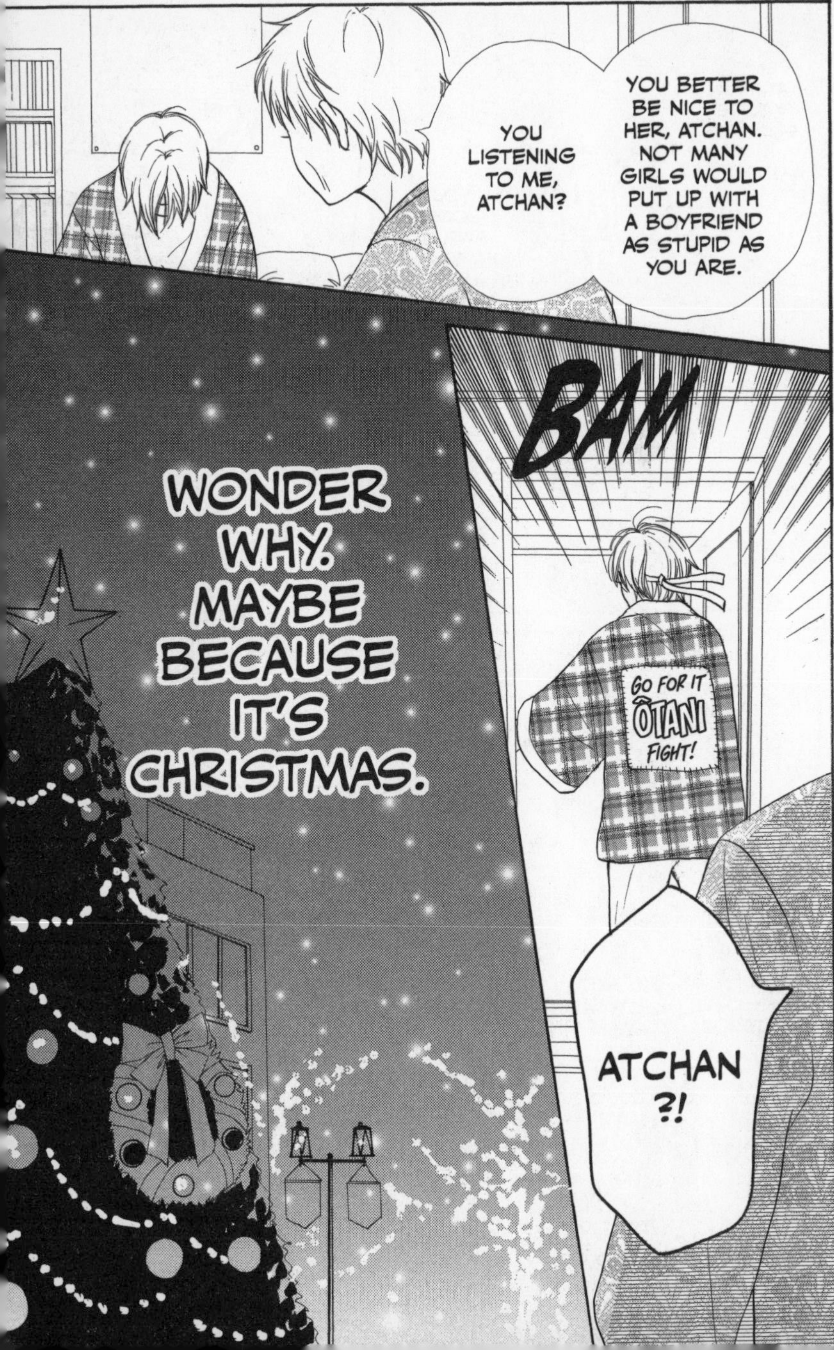
YOU BETTER BE NICE TO HER, ATCHAN. NOT MANY GIRLS WOULD PUT UP WITH A BOYFRIEND AS STUPID AS YOU ARE.
YOU LISTENING TO ME, ATCHAN?
BAM
GO FOR IT ŌTANI FIGHT!
ATCHAN ?!
WONDER WHY. MAYBE BECAUSE IT'S CHRISTMAS.

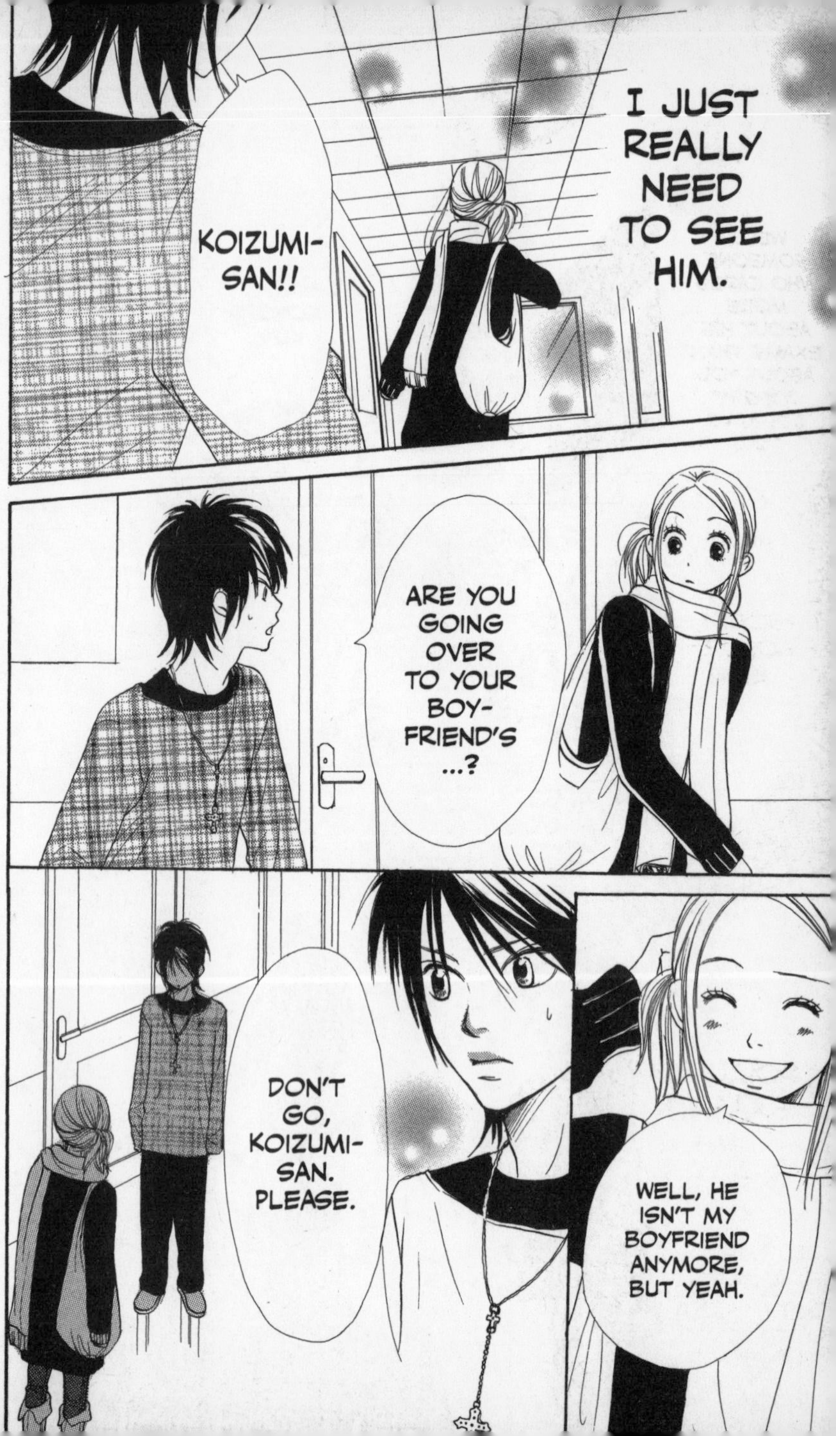
I JUST REALLY NEED TO SEE HIM.
KOIZUMI-SAN!!
ARE YOU GOING OVER TO YOUR BOY-FRIEND'S ...?
WELL, HE ISN'T MY BOYFRIEND ANYMORE, BUT YEAH.
DON'T GO, KOIZUMI-SAN. PLEASE.

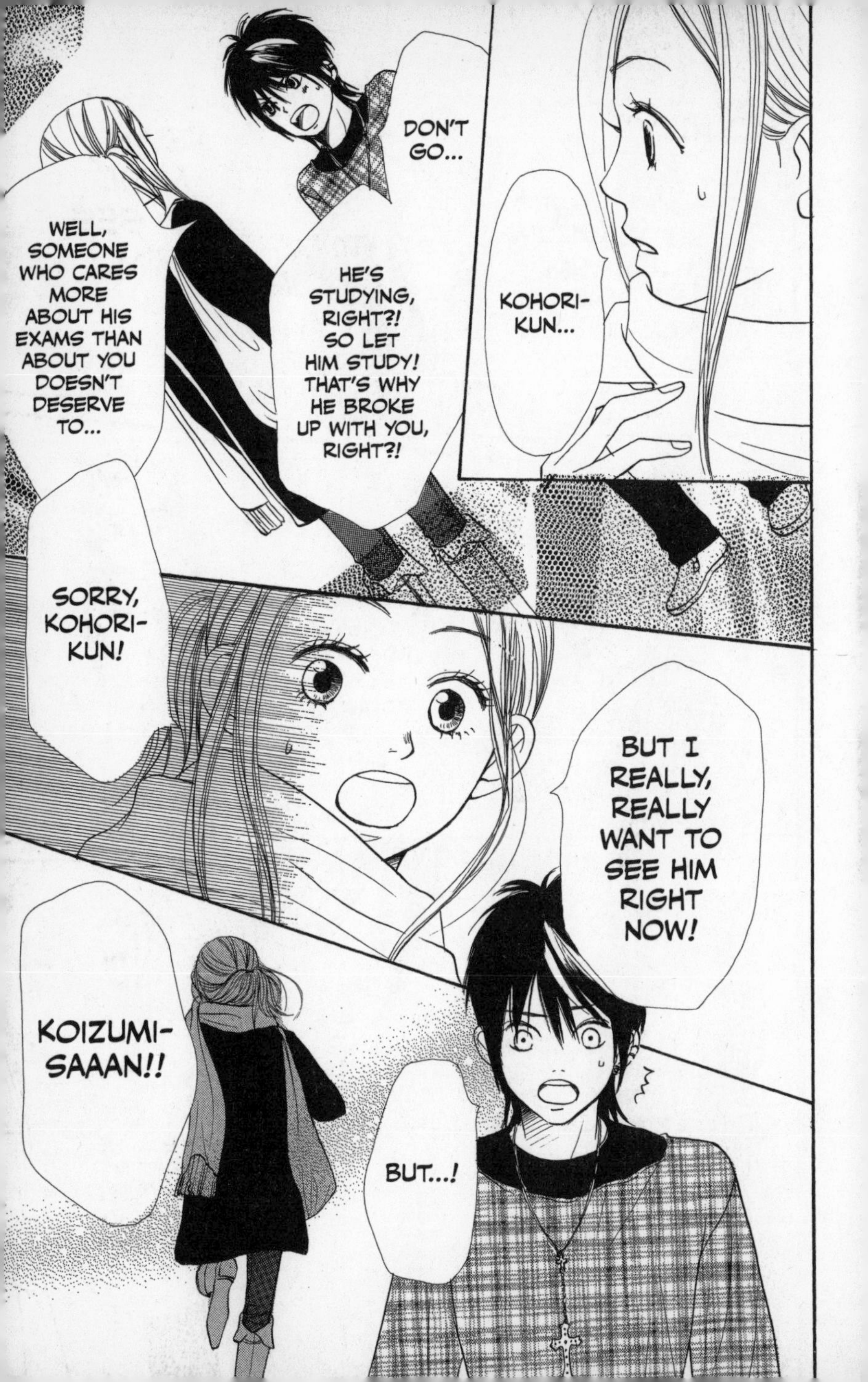
KOHORI-KUN...
DON'T GO...
HE'S STUDYING, RIGHT?! SO LET HIM STUDY! THAT'S WHY HE BROKE UP WITH YOU, RIGHT?!
WELL, SOMEONE WHO CARES MORE ABOUT HIS EXAMS THAN ABOUT YOU DOESN'T DESERVE TO...
SORRY, KOHORI-KUN!
BUT I REALLY, REALLY WANT TO SEE HIM RIGHT NOW!
BUT...!
KOIZUMI-SAAAN!!

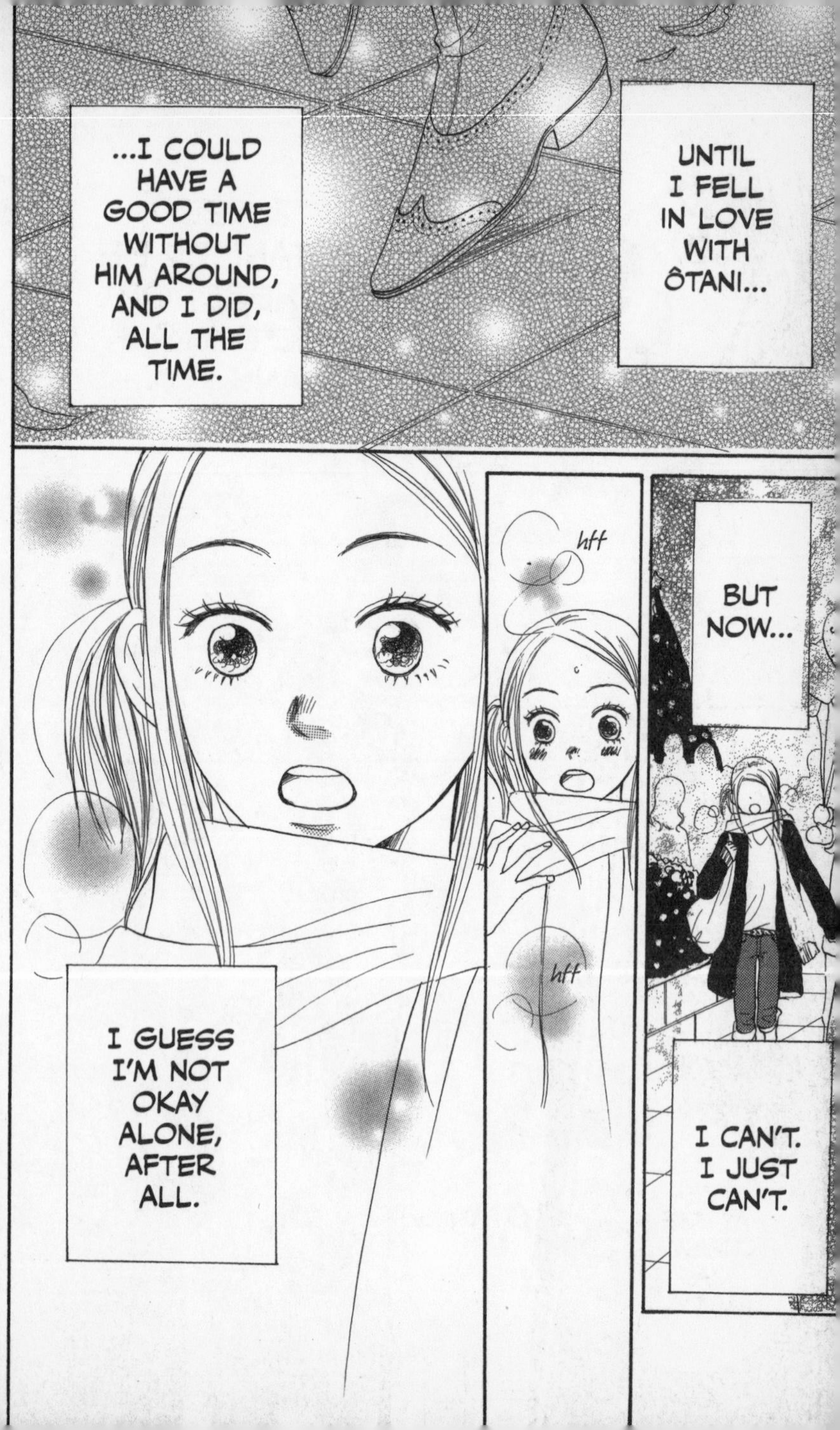
UNTIL I FELL IN LOVE WITH ÔTANI...
...I COULD HAVE A GOOD TIME WITHOUT HIM AROUND, AND I DID, ALL THE TIME.
BUT NOW...
I CAN'T. I JUST CAN'T.
hff
hff
I GUESS I'M NOT OKAY ALONE, AFTER ALL.

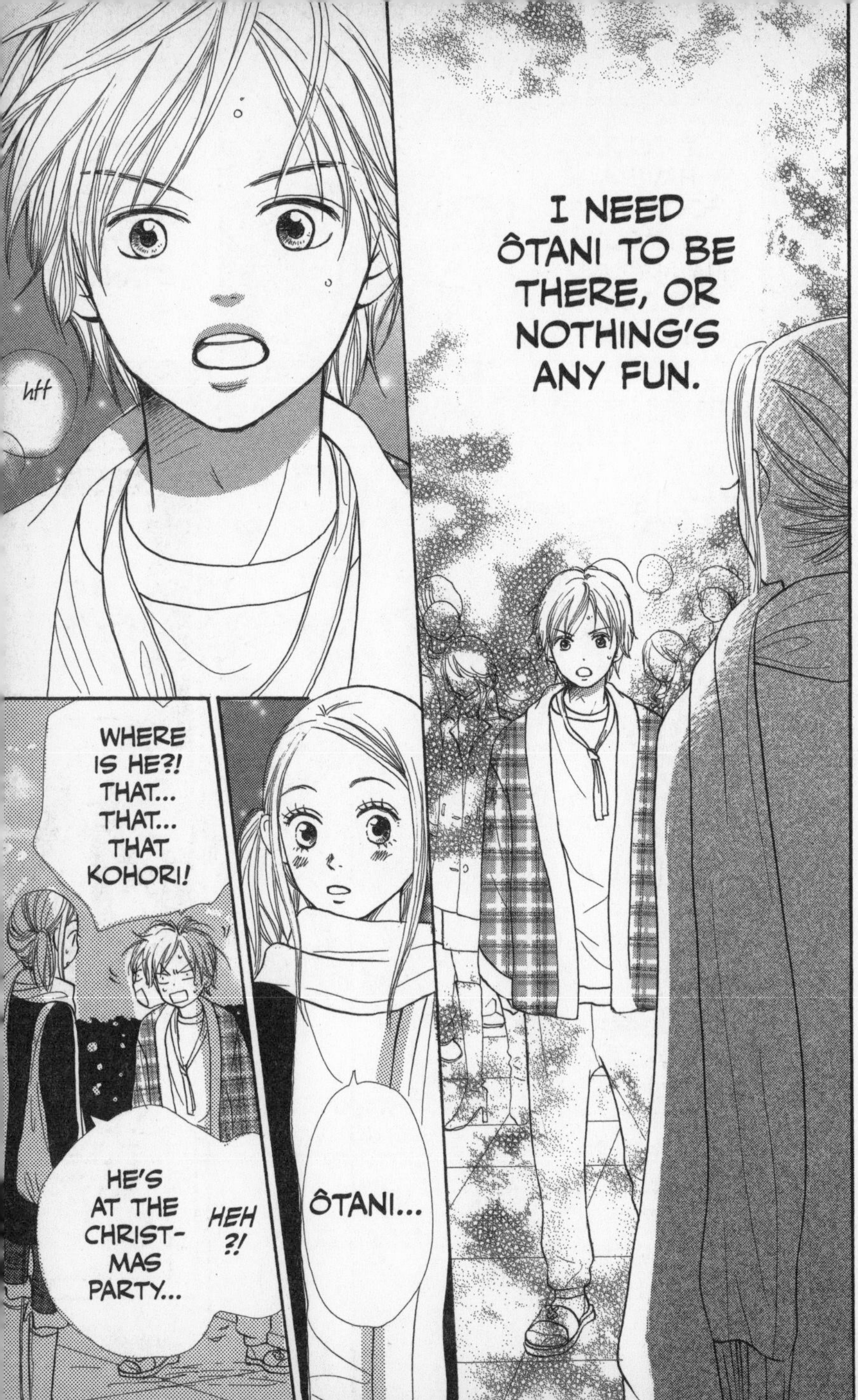
I NEED ÔTANI TO BE THERE, OR NOTHING'S ANY FUN.
hff
ÔTANI...
WHERE IS HE?! THAT... THAT... THAT KOHORI!
HE'S AT THE CHRIST-MAS PARTY...
HEH ?!

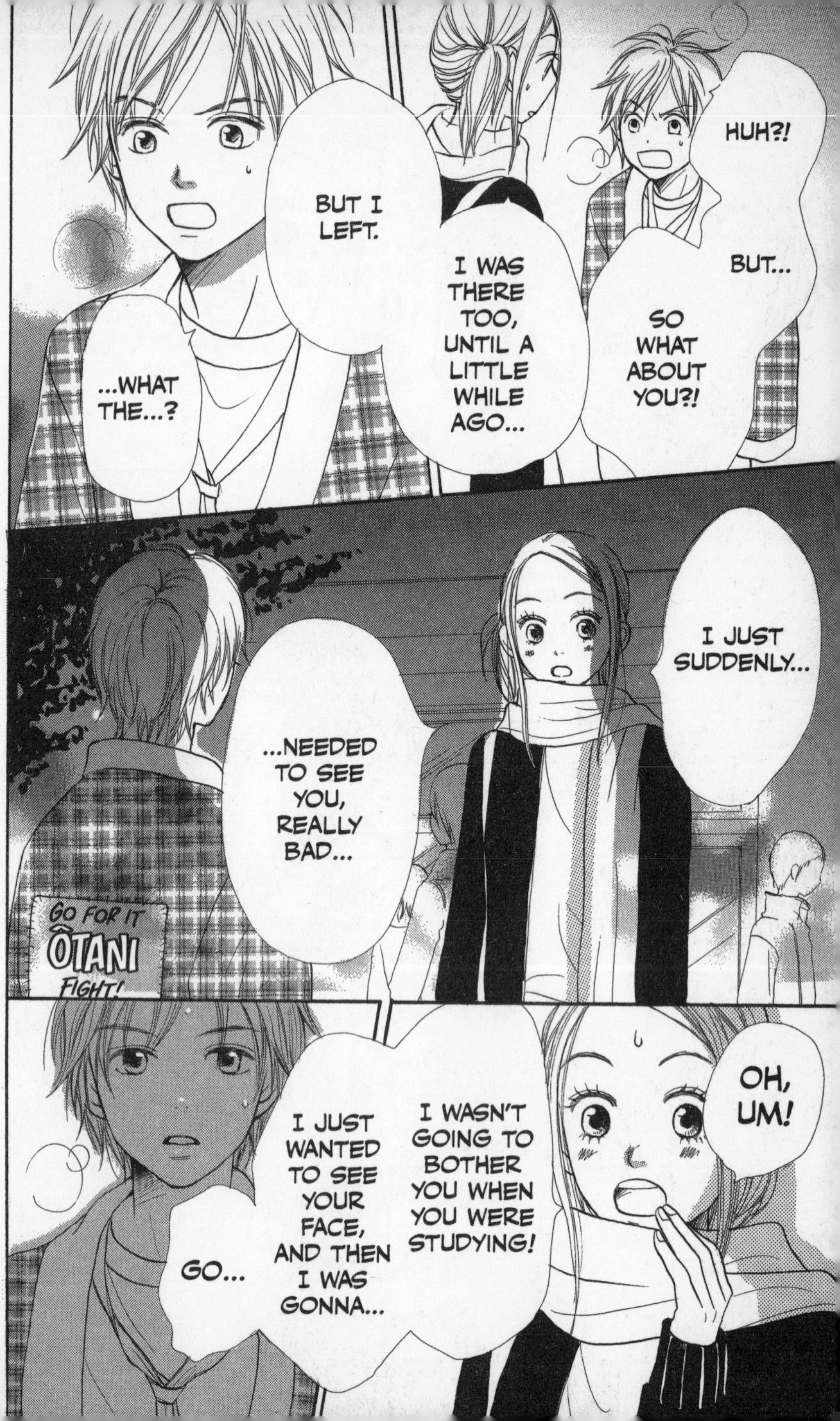
HUH?!
BUT...
SO WHAT ABOUT YOU?!
I WAS THERE TOO, UNTIL A LITTLE WHILE AGO...
BUT I LEFT.
...WHAT THE...?
I JUST SUDDENLY...
...NEEDED TO SEE YOU, REALLY BAD...
GO FOR IT ŌTANI FIGHT!
OH, UM!
I WASN'T GOING TO BOTHER YOU WHEN YOU WERE STUDYING!
I JUST WANTED TO SEE YOUR FACE, AND THEN I WAS GONNA...
GO...

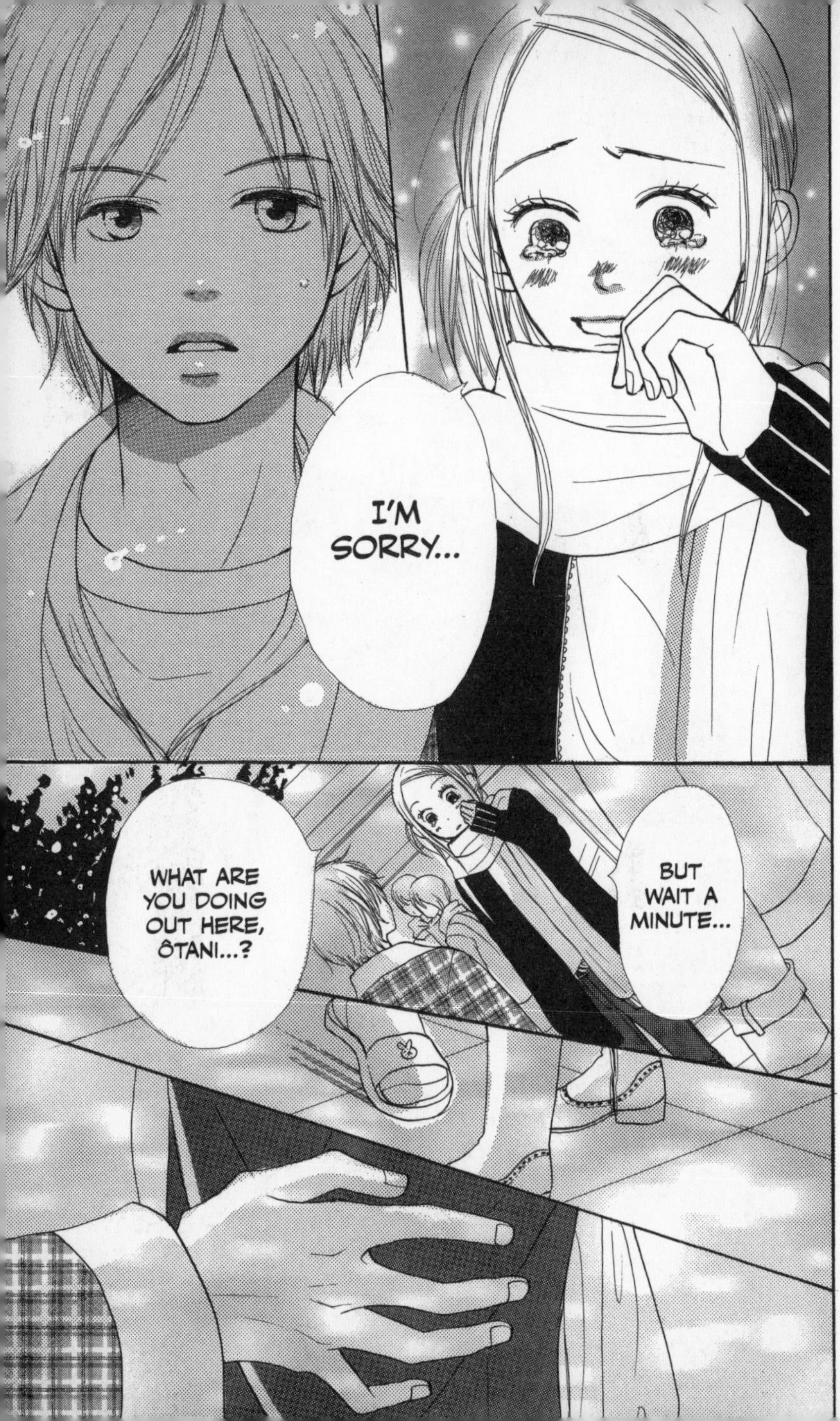
I'M SORRY...
BUT WAIT A MINUTE...
WHAT ARE YOU DOING OUT HERE, ŌTANI...?

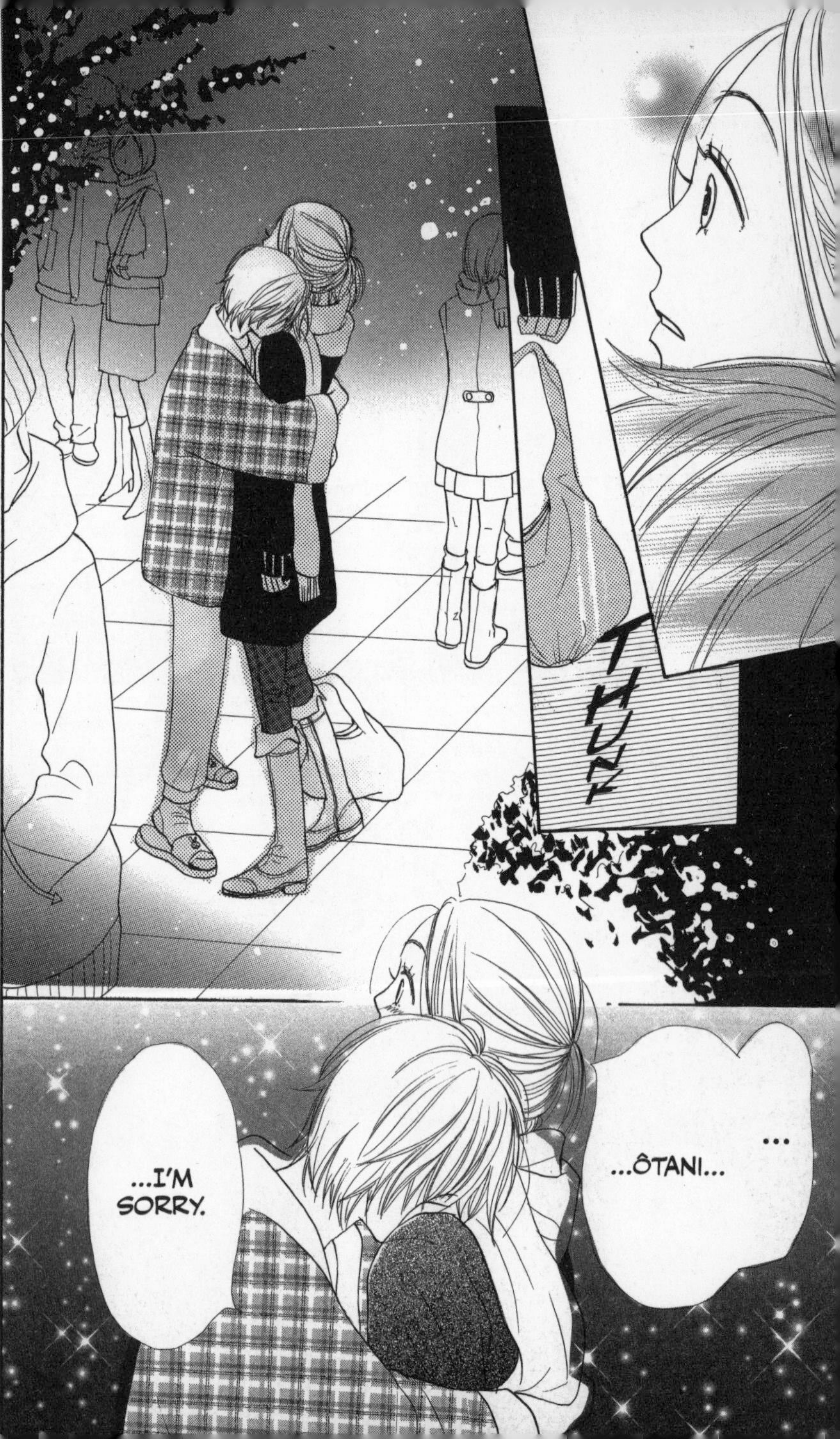
THUNK
...
...ÔTANI...
...I'M SORRY.

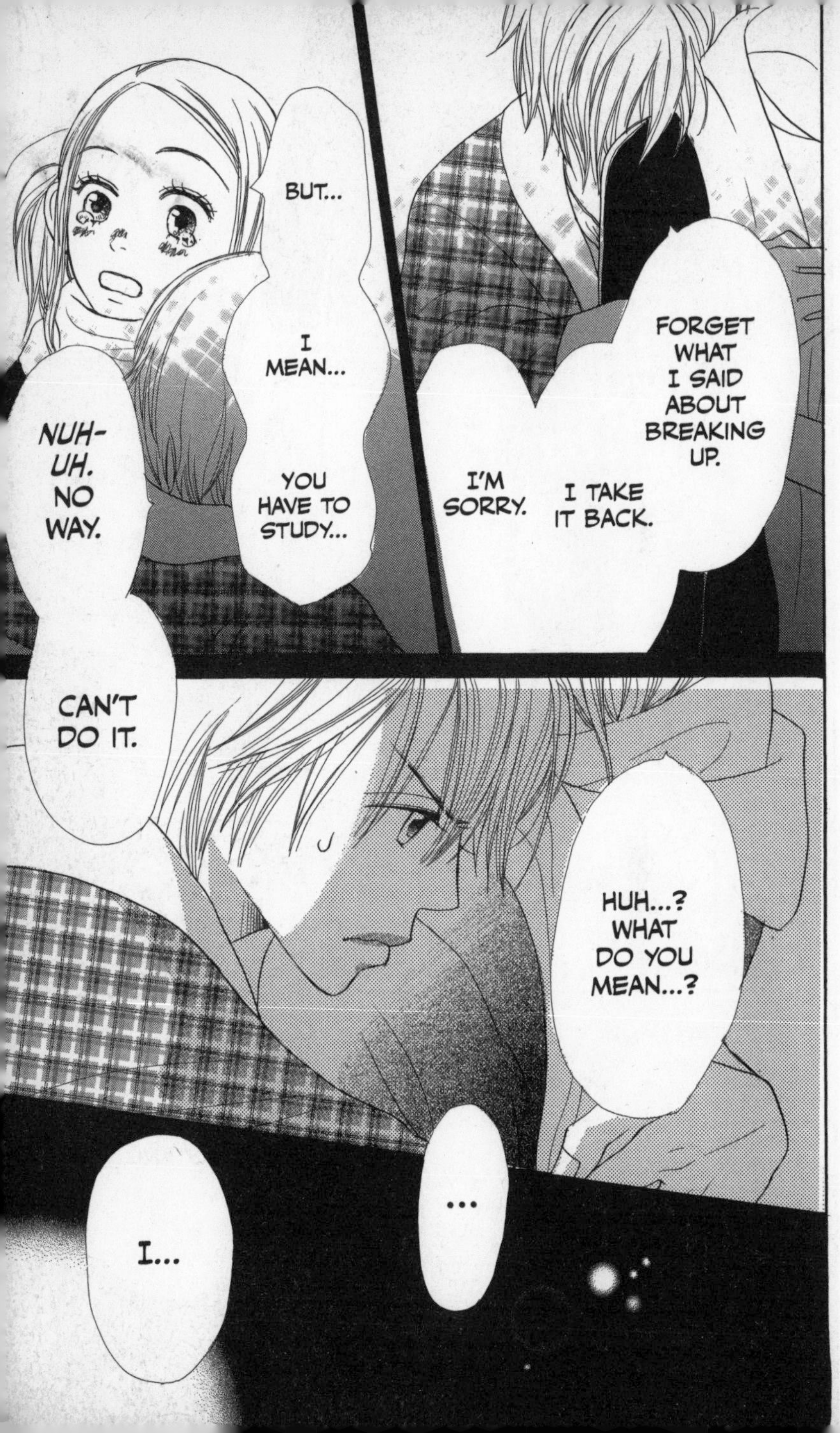
FORGET WHAT I SAID ABOUT BREAKING UP.
I TAKE IT BACK.
I'M SORRY.
BUT...
I MEAN...
YOU HAVE TO STUDY...
NUH-UH. NO WAY.
CAN'T DO IT.
HUH...? WHAT DO YOU MEAN...?
...
I...

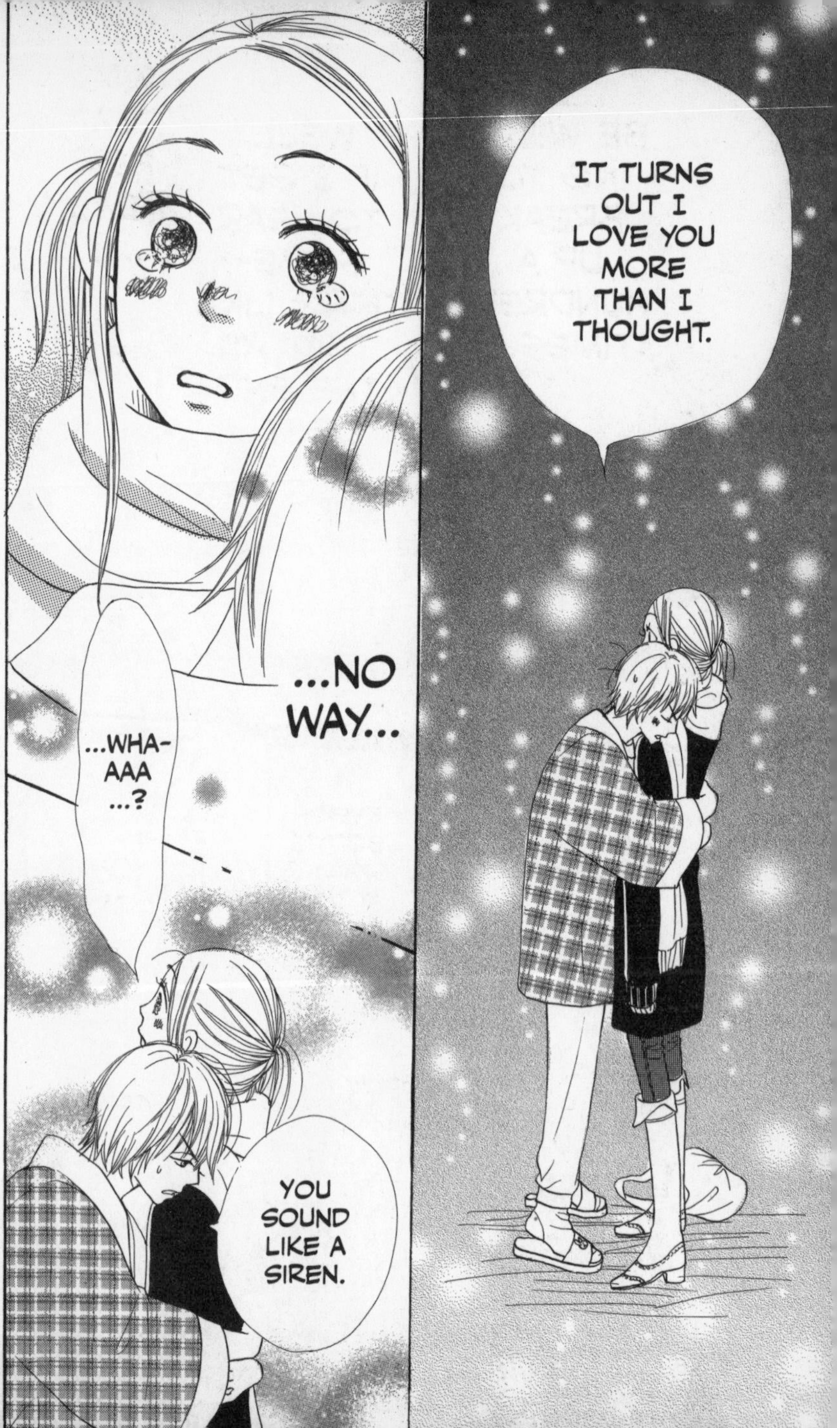
IT TURNS OUT I LOVE YOU MORE THAN I THOUGHT.
...NO WAY...
...WHA-AAA ...?
YOU SOUND LIKE A SIREN.

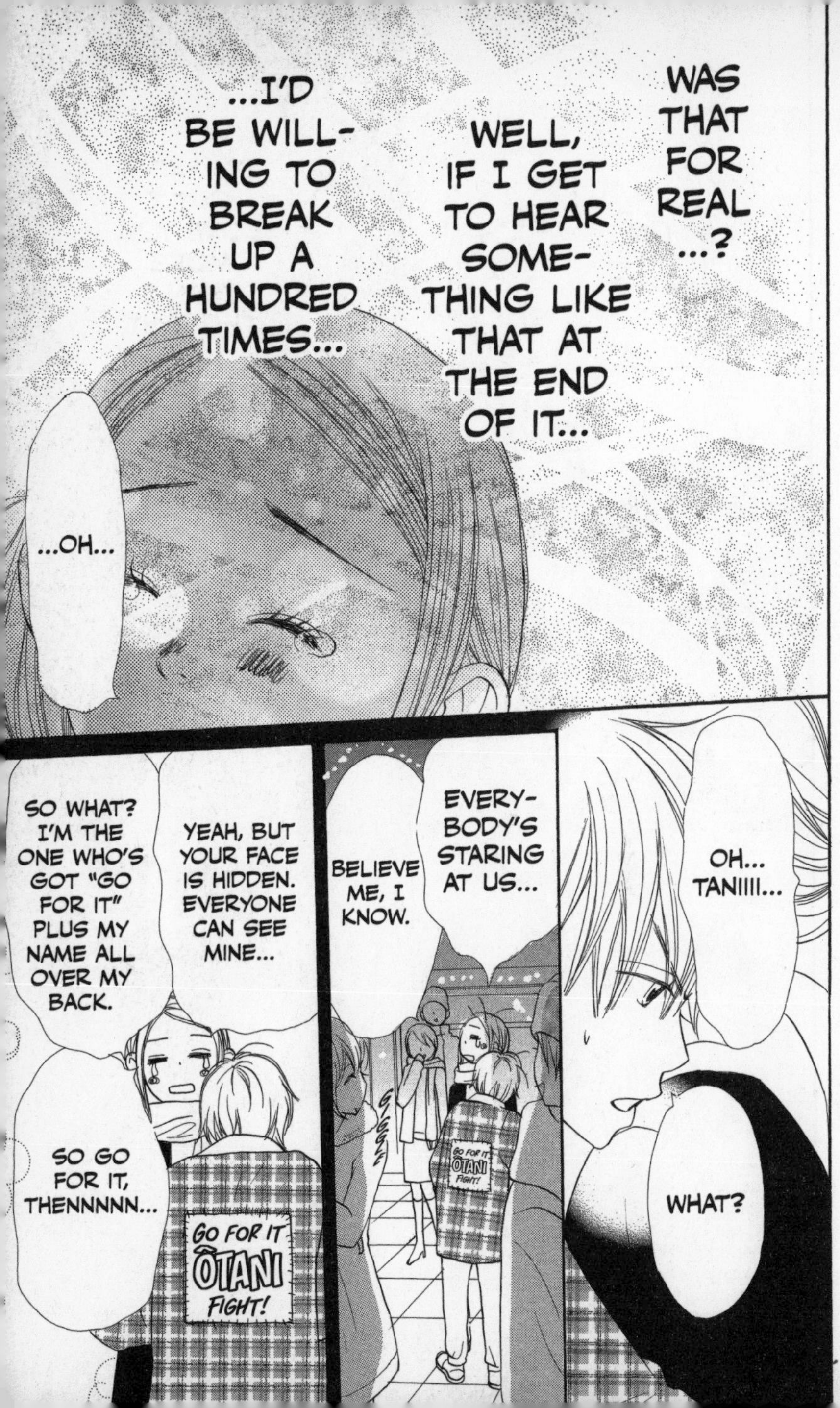
WAS THAT FOR REAL...?
WELL, IF I GET TO HEAR SOMETHING LIKE THAT AT THE END OF IT...
...I'D BE WILLING TO BREAK UP A HUNDRED TIMES...
...OH...
OH... TANIIII...
WHAT?
EVERYBODY'S STARING AT US...
BELIEVE ME, I KNOW.
GIGGLE
GO FOR IT ŌTANI FIGHT!
YEAH, BUT YOUR FACE IS HIDDEN. EVERYONE CAN SEE MINE...
SO WHAT? I'M THE ONE WHO'S GOT "GO FOR IT" PLUS MY NAME ALL OVER MY BACK.
SO GO FOR IT, THENNNNN...
GO FOR IT ŌTANI FIGHT!

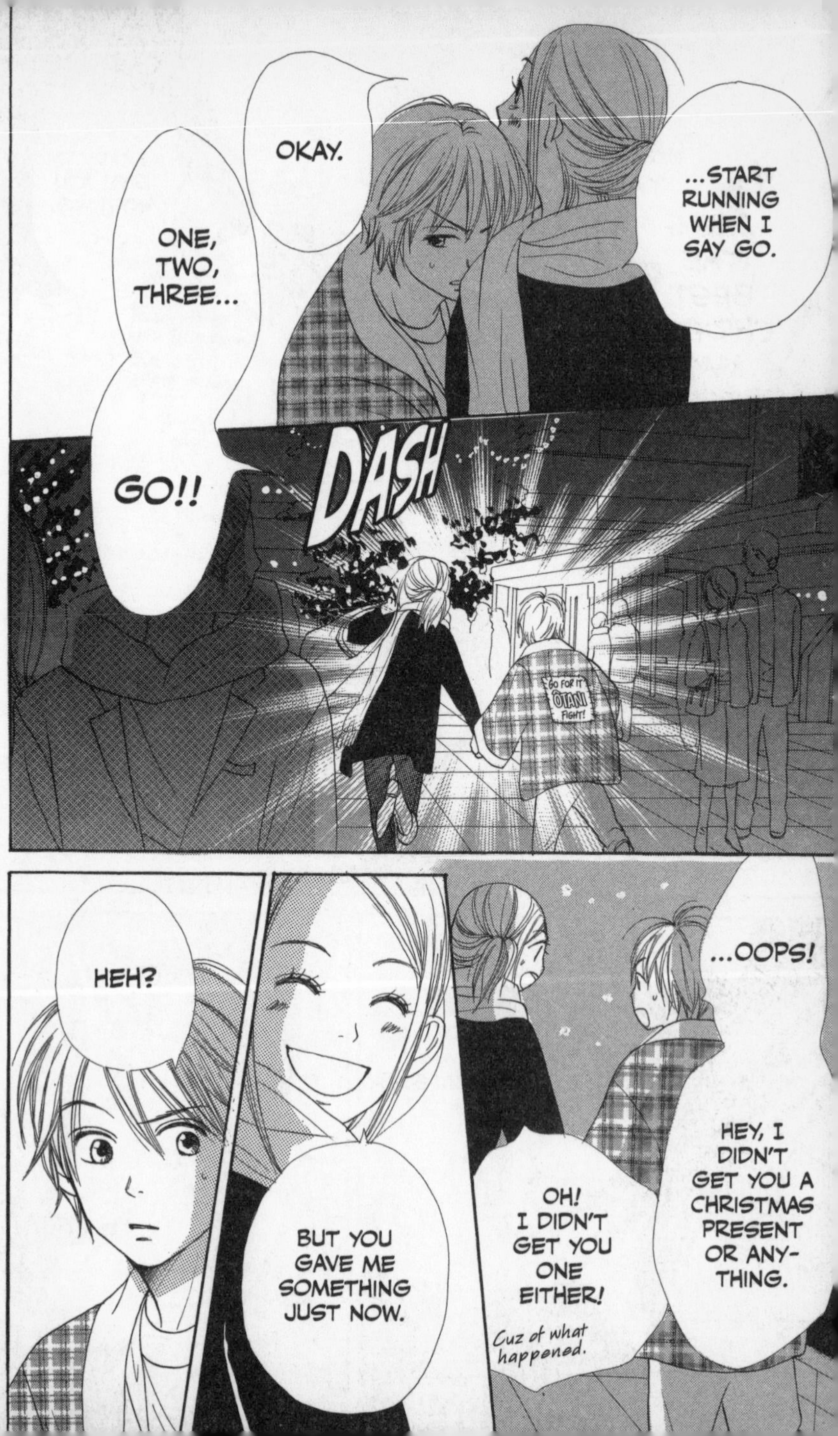
...START RUNNING WHEN I SAY GO.
OKAY.
ONE, TWO, THREE...
GO!!
DASH
GO FOR IT ŌTANI FIGHT!
...OOPS!
HEY, I DIDN'T GET YOU A CHRISTMAS PRESENT OR ANY-THING.
OH! I DIDN'T GET YOU ONE EITHER!
Cuz of what happened.
BUT YOU GAVE ME SOMETHING JUST NOW.
HEH?

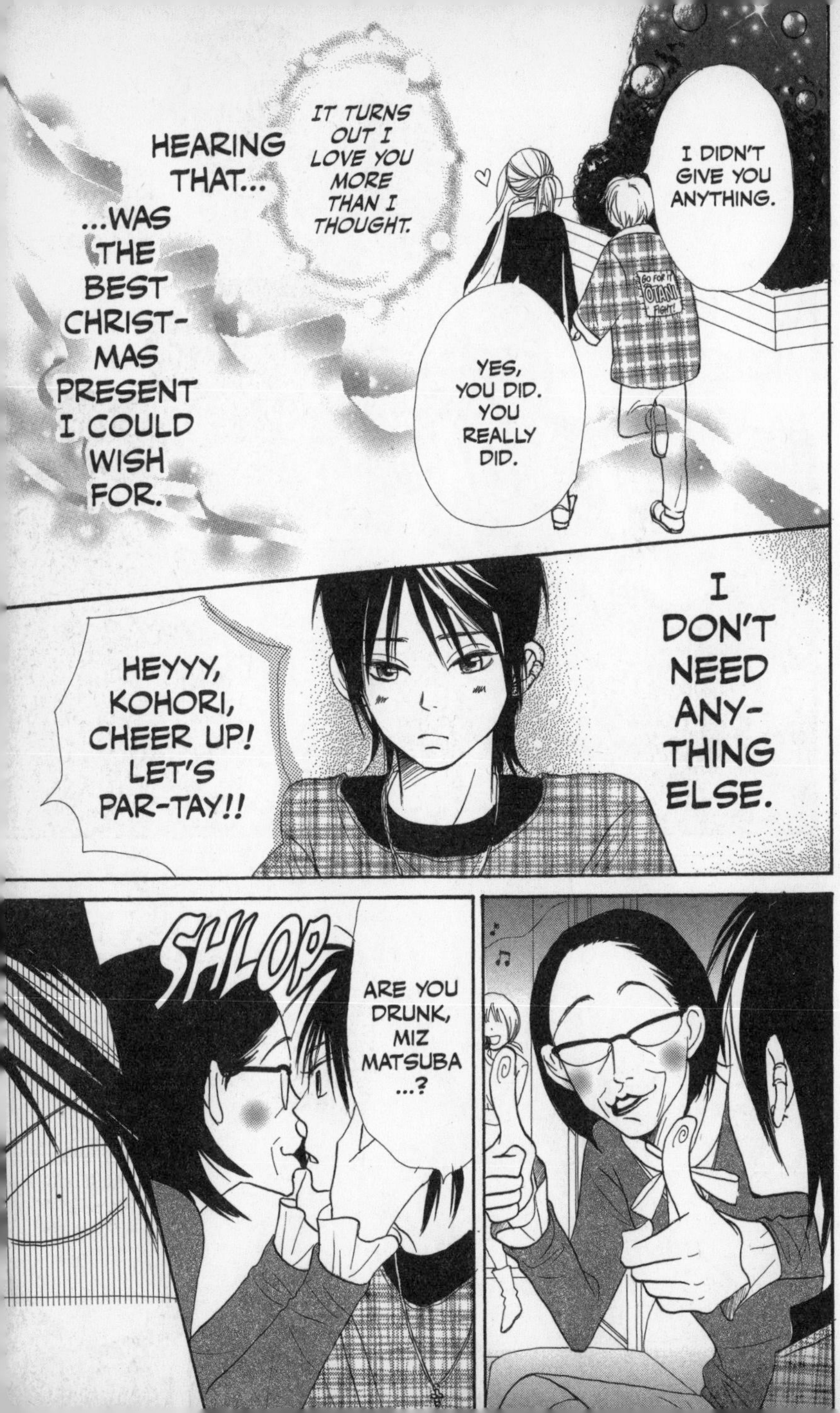
I DIDN'T GIVE YOU ANYTHING.
GO FOR IT OTANI FIGHT!
YES, YOU DID. YOU REALLY DID.
IT TURNS OUT I LOVE YOU MORE THAN I THOUGHT.
HEARING THAT...
...WAS THE BEST CHRISTMAS PRESENT I COULD WISH FOR.
I DON'T NEED ANYTHING ELSE.
HEYYY, KOHORI, CHEER UP! LET'S PAR-TAY!!
SHLOP
ARE YOU DRUNK, MIZ MATSUBA ...?

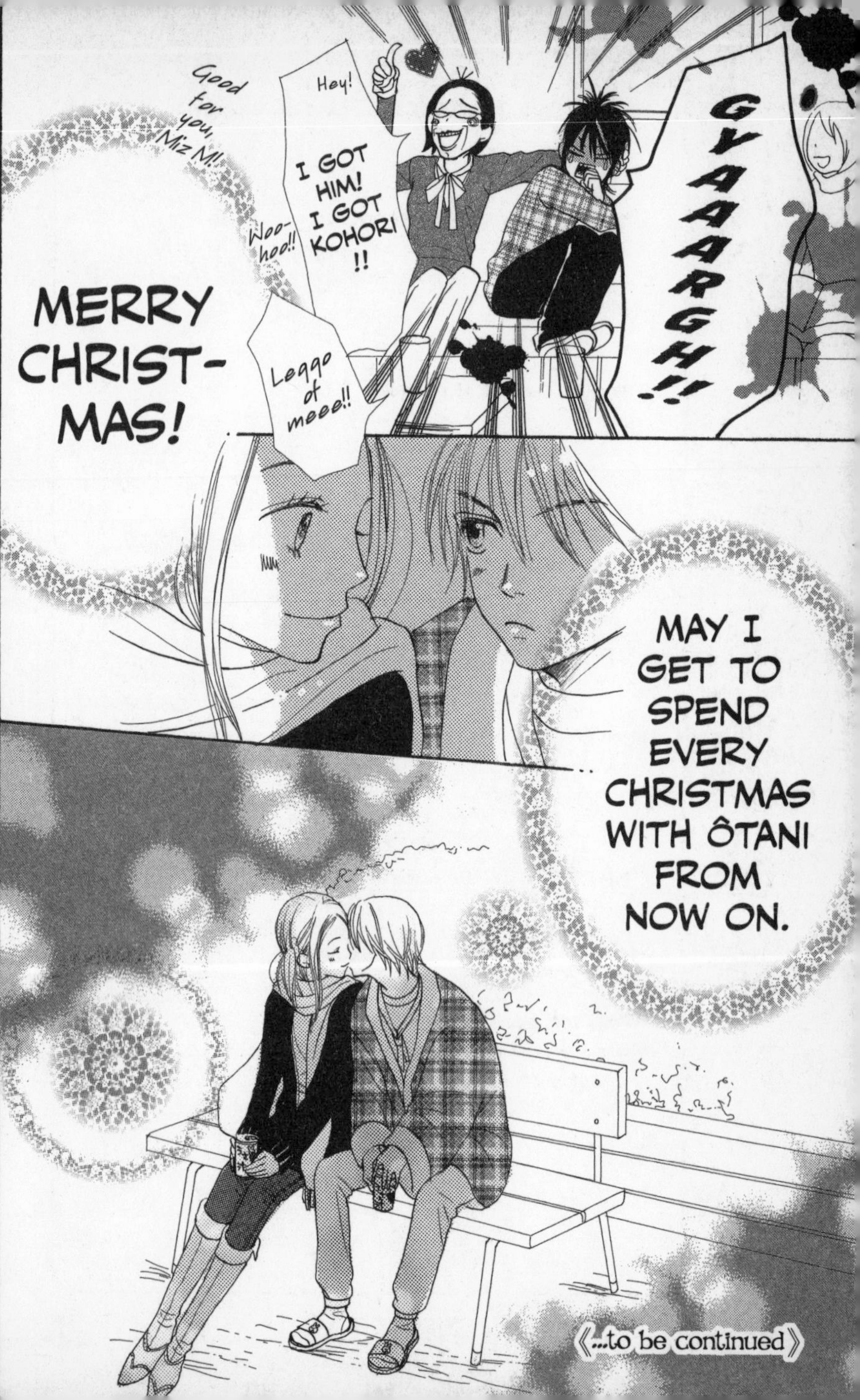
GYAAAARGH!!
Hey!
I GOT HIM! I GOT KOHORI!!
Good for you, Miz M!!
Woo-hoo!!
Leggo of meee!!
MERRY CHRIST-MAS!
MAY I GET TO SPEND EVERY CHRISTMAS WITH ÔTANI FROM NOW ON.
《...to be continued》

glossary

Page 23, sidebar: Dynamite Shikoku

Dynamite Shikoku is the name of a masked pro wrestler played by comedian Shôzô Endô on Downtown's TV show, *Gaki no Tsukai ya Arahende!!*

Page 58, panel 3: Nose hook

Used in nose bondage, where a hook on a leather strap pulls the nostrils up and open to give a pig-like appearance. Check out *Love★Com* volume 3 for another nose hook appearance.

Page 74, panel 4: Floor cushions

This saying comes from a comedy show on TV featuring traditional *rakugo* storytellers wearing kimono who are seated on floor cushions (*zabuton*), given topics by an elderly MC and asked to come up with snappy puns and jokes on the spur of the moment. If they're good, the MC says "Give him another zabuton," and if they bomb, their zabuton gets taken away. A really good joke will give the teller two or three zabuton, and so on. This has caught on in Osaka so that when someone tells a good one, people will say "Three zabuton!"

Page 117, sidebar: Fujiyama Kanbi

An older comedian and actor from Osaka. He appeared in the 1965 *Zatoichi and the Doomed Man*.

Page 143, panel 1: Koban

Koban, also called police boxes, are small buildings in busy areas manned by a few police officers, and work as an official Neighborhood Watch. The officers at a koban can offer directions, provide lost and found services, take crime reports, and offer emergency assistance.

I always wear contact lenses so you might not know this, but I have really bad eyesight. Boy, I wish they could do something about those vision tests. It's depressing to keep repeating, "I can't tell" in front of total strangers. In fact, I hate admitting I can't see the darn symbols so much that even when I'm not sure, I try guessing. The "hmmm" I get in reply isn't very reassuring... The whole thing is a huge pain. Why can't they develop a machine that measures your eyesight for you?!

Aya Nakahara won the 2003 Shogakukan manga award for her breakthrough hit *Love★Com*, which was made into a major motion picture and a PS2 game in 2006. She debuted with *Haru to Kuuki Nichiyou-bi* in 1995, and her other works include *HANADA* and *Himitsu Kichi*.

LOVE★COM VOL 10

The Shojo Beat Manga Edition

STORY AND ART BY
AYA NAKAHARA

Translation & English Adaptation/Pookie Rolf
Touch-up Art & Lettering/Gia Cam Luc
Design/Yuki Ameda
Editor/Pancha Diaz

Editor in Chief, Books/Alvin Lu
Editor in Chief, Magazines/Marc Weidenbaum
VP, Publishing Licensing /Rika Inouye
VP, Sales & Product Marketing/Gonzalo Ferreyra
VP, Creative/Linda Espinosa
Publisher/Hyoe Narita

Printed in Canada

Published by VIZ Media, LLC
P.O. Box 77010
San Francisco, CA 94107

Shojo Beat Manga Edition
10 9 8 7 6 5 4 3 2 1
First printing, January 2009

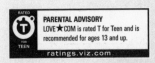

store.viz.com

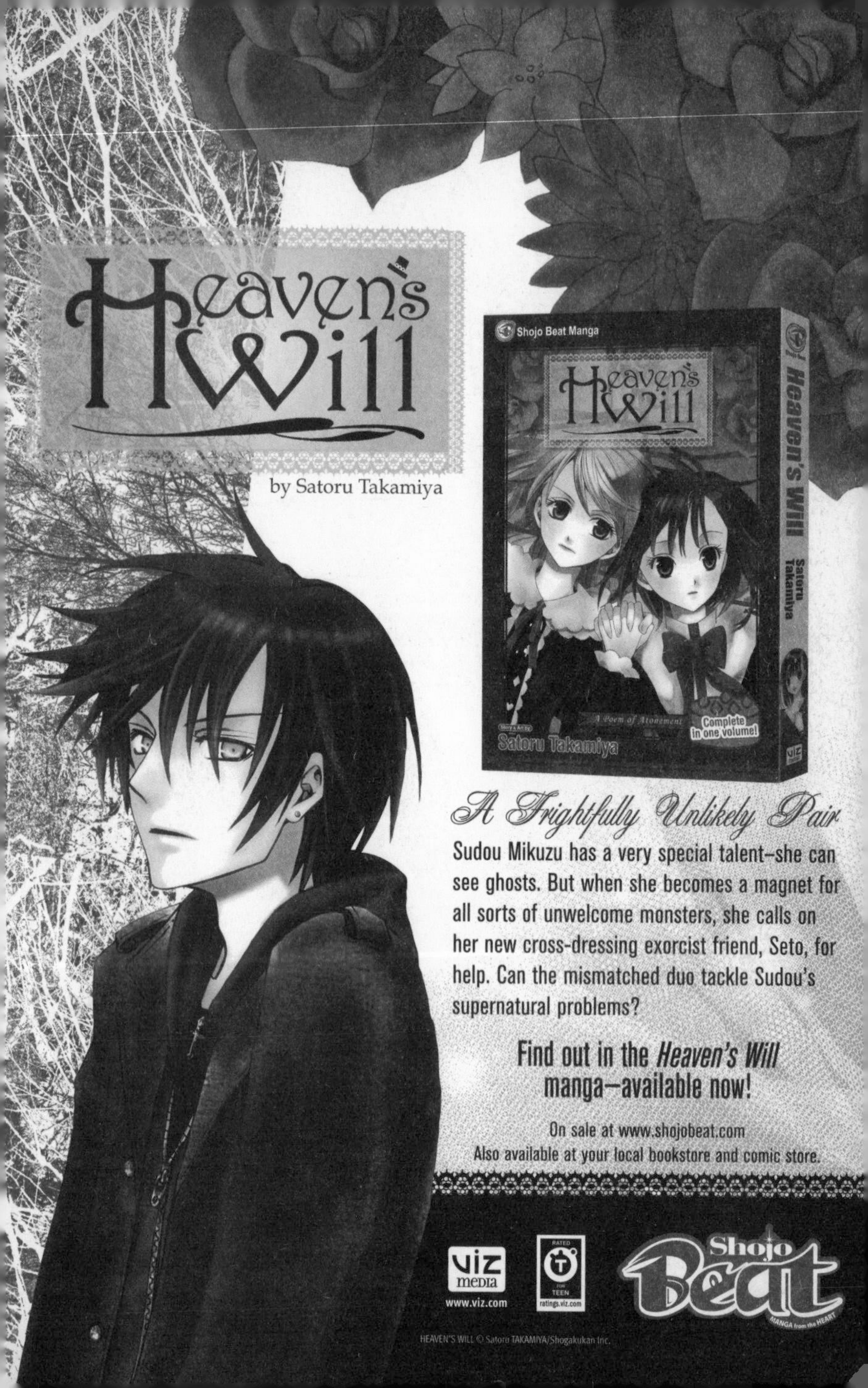
Heaven's Will
by Satoru Takamiya
Shojo Beat Manga
Heaven's Will
A Poem of Atonement
Complete in one volume!
Story & Art by Satoru Takamiya
A Frightfully Unlikely Pair
Sudou Mikuzu has a very special talent–she can see ghosts. But when she becomes a magnet for all sorts of unwelcome monsters, she calls on her new cross-dressing exorcist friend, Seto, for help. Can the mismatched duo tackle Sudou's supernatural problems?
Find out in the Heaven's Will manga–available now!
On sale at www.shojobeat.com
Also available at your local bookstore and comic store.
viz media
www.viz.com
RATED T FOR TEEN
ratings.viz.com
Shojo Beat
MANGA from the HEART
HEAVEN'S WILL © Satoru TAKAMIYA/Shogakukan Inc.